DAW Titles by C.J. CHERRYH

THE ALLIANCE-UNION UNIVERSE

The Company Wars
DOWNBELOW STATION

The Era of Rapprochement
SERPENT'S REACH
FORTY THOUSAND IN GEHENNA
MERCHANTER'S LUCK

The Chanur Novels
THE PRIDE OF CHANUR
CHANUR'S VENTURE
THE KIF STRIKE BACK
CHANUR'S HOMECOMING
CHANUR'S LEGACY

The Mri Wars
THE FADED SUN: KESRITH
THE FADED SUN: SHON'JIR
THE FADED SUN: KUTATH

Merovingen Nights (Mri Wars period)
ANGEL WITH THE SWORD

Merovingen Nights-Anthologies
FESTIVAL MOON (#1)
FEVER SEASON (#2)
TROUBLED WATERS (#3)
SMUGGLER'S GOLD (#4)
DIVINE RIGHT (#5)
FLOOD TIDE (#6)
ENDGAME (#7)

The Age of Exploration
CUCKOO'S EGG
VOYAGER IN NIGHT
PORT ETERNITY

The Hanan Rebellion
BROTHERS OF EARTH
HUNTER OF WORLDS

THE MORGAINE CYCLE

GATE OF IVREL (#1)
WELL OF SHIUAN (#2)
FIRES OF AZEROTH (#3)
EXILE'S GATE (#4)

THE EALDWOOD NOVELS

THE DREAMSTONE
THE TREE OF SWORDS AND JEWELS

OTHER CHERRYH NOVELS

HESTIA
WAVE WITHOUT A SHORE

COLLECTION

VISIBLE LIGHT

Chanur's Legacy

A Novel of Compact Space

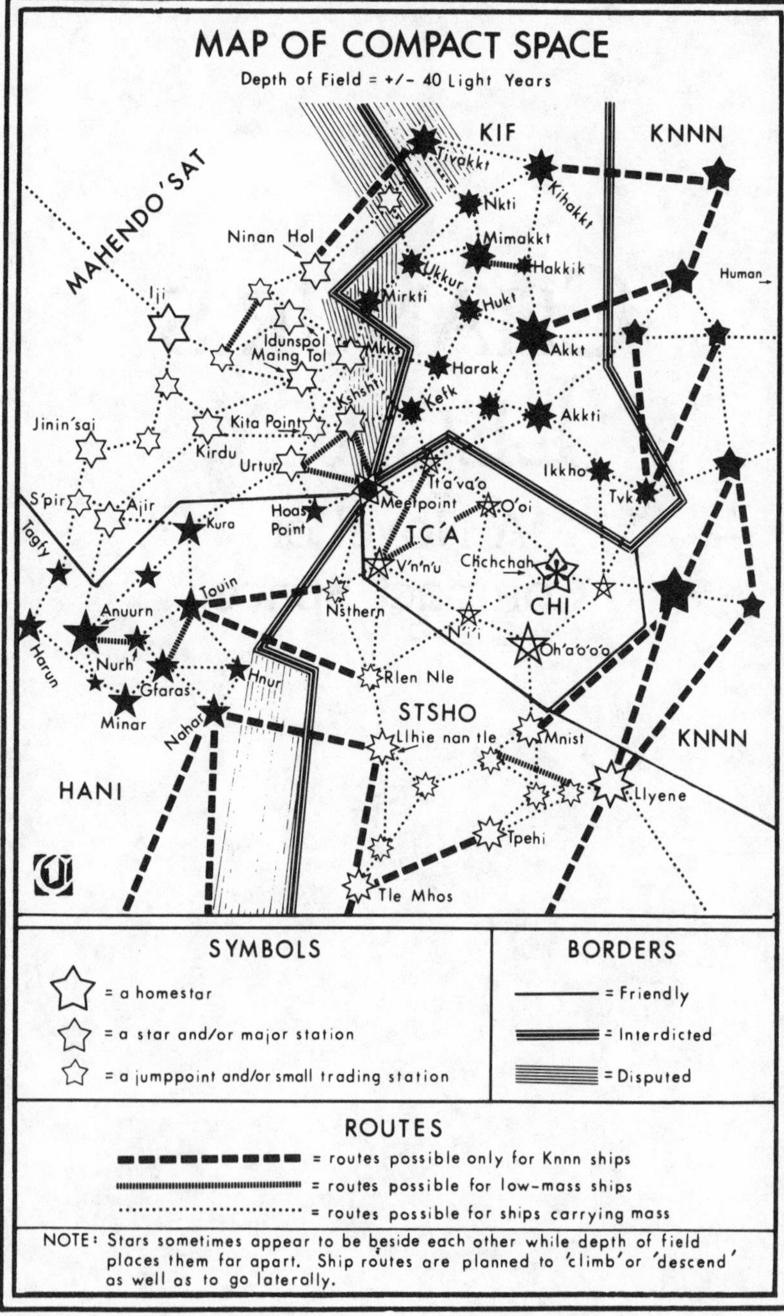
MAP OF COMPACT SPACE
Depth of Field = +/– 40 Light Years
KIF
KNNN
MAHENDO'SAT
Tivakkt
Kihakkt
Nkti
Ninan Hol
Mimakkt
Hakkik
Ukkur
Human
Iji
Mirkti
Hukt
Akkt
Idunspol
Maing Tol
Mkks
Harak
Kshshti
Kefk
Akkti
Jinin'sai
Kita Point
Kirdu
Urtur
Ikkho
It'a'va'o
Tvk
S'pir
Ajir
Hoas Point
Meetpoint
O'oi
Tagfy
Kura
TC'A
V'n'n'u
Chchchah
Touin
CHI
Anuurn
Nsthern
N'i'i
Harun
Nurh
Oh'a'o'o'a
Gfaras
Hnur
Rlen Nle
Minar
STSHO
Nahar
Llhie nan tle
Mnist
KNNN
HANI
Llyene
Tpehi
Tle Mhos
SYMBOLS
= a homestar
= a star and/or major station
= a jumppoint and/or small trading station
BORDERS
= Friendly
= Interdicted
= Disputed
ROUTES
= routes possible only for Knnn ships
= routes possible for low-mass ships
= routes possible for ships carrying mass
NOTE: Stars sometimes appear to be beside each other while depth of field places them far apart. Ship routes are planned to 'climb' or 'descend' as well as to go laterally.

CHANUR'S LEGACY

A Novel of Compact Space

C. J. CHERRYH

DAW BOOKS, INC.
DONALD A. WOLLHEIM, FOUNDER
375 Hudson Street, New York, NY 10014
ELIZABETH R. WOLLHEIM
SHEILA E. GILBERT
PUBLISHERS

Map of Compact Space by David A. Cherry.

Jacket art by Michael Whelan

DAW Book Collectors No. 886.

DAW Books are distributed by Penguin U.S.A.

ISBN 0-88677-519-1

First Printing, August 1992

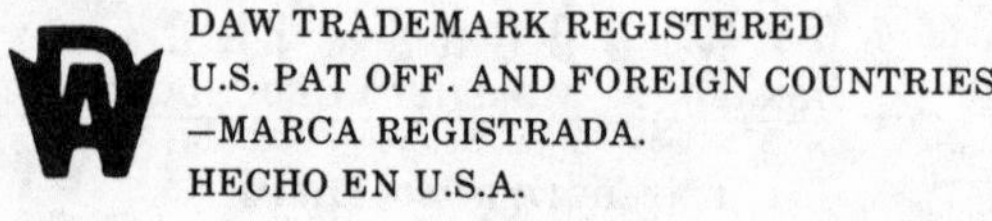

PRINTED IN THE U.S.A.

Chanur's Legacy

A Novel of Compact Space

Chapter One

Meetpoint was in one sense the center of Compact space: in another sense, this place where all the Compact met for trade was the hindside of every species' separate territory, and, along with its cosmopolitan character, it had that chancy watch-your-back kind of feeling on its dockside, even in these days when weapons were discouraged and peace governed the dealings of species. Meetpoint's oxygen docks were redolent of cold and oil and volatiles, its dockside shops and bars echoed of trade and business and offered a selection of vices. Its methane side—the methane folk had to answer for, in their multiple-brained thoughts and stranger songs: but on the oxygen side, the stsho, who were the landlords of Meetpoint, traded in what pleased them. Among those spindly, white-skinned merchants one could find hani, mahendo'sat, kif and (at least when a certain ship was in dock) a stray human from a world named, unenterprisingly, Earth.

That certain ship had been here. That certain ship had departed twenty-odd days ago in pursuit of its own business, a circumstance which completely satisfied Hilfy Chanur, captain of *Chanur's Legacy*, newly in dock at Meetpoint and besieged by her aunt's unreceived mail—beset also by every hanger-on, would-be and might-have-been politician, inventor, and academician with every offer of favor, every piece of influence-peddling, every crackpot idea and complaint for forty light-years about.

Being niece to the President of Compact space, the elected President of the spacefaring amphictiony of Anuurn, the *mekt-hakkikt* of all the kif, the Personage of Personages of the mahendo'sat (gods only knew about the methane folk) . . . in short, entailed a few liabilities.

It remained to be seen, with the *Legacy* past the initial formalities, whether aunt Pyanfar's latest dealing with Meetpoint's governor was about to become another of those liabilities. It remained imminently to be seen, because at the top of the message stack which had landed in the *Legacy*'s files at the instant of their docking, sat a message from *gtst* excellency No'shto-shti-stlen, requesting the presence of "the august niece of the most distinguished (untranslatable) Pyanfar Chanur in the inner most hospitable (?) administrative offices," and so on and so on, "omitting customs formalities which this office will be delighted to obviate," and so on in that vein.

One *didn't* trust that those formalities were going to be ignored, by the gods, one didn't. One set one's second-in-command to handling them, in case the honorable or excellent No'shto-shti-stlen changed *gtst* mind and charged one's ship with smuggling.

So Hilfy put on her administrative-offices best pair of black satin trousers, and (acutely aware of her youth) combed the mane until it crackled with static (and looked fuller) and the mustaches so that they somewhat covered the youthful scantness of beard. Hilfy Chanur's ears at least had no scarcity of rings to signify her voyages. Her red-gold coat was brushed to a sheen. Her mood was even cheerful as she took the lift down from topside to the main lowerdeck corridor and put her head in at lowerdeck ops.

"I'm off, cousin. You're in charge. How's it going?"

"Smooth so far. Are you sure you don't want one of us to go along?"

Tiar was harried, hurried—they were a small crew, in a

strange port, dealing with officials they didn't personally know. The crew was eager to go on liberty, which they couldn't do until the forms were filed and the cargo was delivered.

"I'm fine. I know this place. I know exactly where I'm going."

"You've got the pocket com."

She patted the pocket of her trousers. "No problems. Just a walk down the dock to the lift. You get those forms filed, make *sure* we're clear of customs . . . make them sign the forms anyway. Refer them to the governor's office. I'm not taking any chances."

"Aye, captain," Tiar said, and Hilfy walked on and into the lock, cycled it through to Meetpoint's biting air, and walked the frost-rimed yellow tube of the ramp to the wide open docks.

It was a world of gray steel gantries, towering up into an overhead obscured by blinding light, an overhead so tall it made its own weather, had occasional haze about the lights, and rained condensation puddles on the utilitarian decking. Neon glared from storefronts and bars, oxy-breathing species rubbed shoulders in disregard of differences, and nowadays one could trust there were no weapons—

One could at least carefully hope there were no weapons. She carried none. Since the Peace, guns on dockside were strictly for the police: all species were civilized now. Law decided controversies, ships refrained from piracy, as a historic source of provocation, and from cargo-pilfering, a clear violation of treaties every known species but one now respected.

So Hilfy Chanur didn't hurry on her way—or worry about the attention she drew here. She cut a fair figure, red-gold hide and black silk breeches in a world of dreary grays and garish neon light. Hani were fairly scarce at this end of space, but most of all, the Chanur name on the *Legacy* would not have passed unnoticed. She could imagine the whispers: the Personage's relative, the *mekt-hakkikt's* niece, what's she up to?—justified, since Chanur had a habit of being up to things.

But, credit to Meetpoint's new ordinances, there was not a single interception on her way across the docks, only ordinary traffic; and the lift coordinates she punched in with the number *gtst* excellency's request had provided her were a priority destination: no waiting for the car, not even fellow passengers to deal with, just a *g*-shifting express ride into the great body of Meetpoint Station, to a debarcation into that area the stsho landlords reserved unto themselves, white halls draped in shades of nacre and pastel, and ornamented with the writhing alabaster shapes the stsho called art.

She abandoned cautions, abandoned concerns for untoward encounters: this was a safe place; quiet and peaceful, so harmonious that she no more than blinked in dismay when black-robed kifish guards turned up in her path.

So the stsho were back at *that* foolish practice: uncombative themselves, so fragile a single blow could crush them—they engaged species who could defend them against individuals who might do them violence, the most likely to do violence, unfortunately, being the very species that they hired. One thought that they might have learned that most expensive lesson about the kif—but the stsho made the choices the stsho made: the experiment with mahen and hani guards had apparently not satisfied them, although Hilfy herself had not heard about it; and the fact that the hair rose on a hani captain's nape and that her vision hazed about the edges at the mere sight of these tall, black-robed figures, the fact that a hani of otherwise peaceful intent instantly entertained violent thoughts at meeting these creatures, did not matter to the stsho. It was so polite. So civilized. The kif bowed; she bowed; they said follow, and she followed these thin, long-snouted shadows, these creatures that always, no matter what the circumstances, reeked of ammonia, if only in her memory.

"Chanur captain," they called her, with their peculiar clicking accent, the sound of double, deadly jaws, making consonants that no hani could exactly duplicate. They spoke to her respectfully, for her aunt's sake, for their employers' sake: they showed every sign of fearing her displeasure—as kif might, who had reason to think she had power and influence with their employers. So these were no danger. They were not high in kifish rank or they would not be working here, in alien employ. Kick them and they would estimate you the higher for it.

But she was profoundly relieved to meet a stsho at the end of the corridor, beyond the blowing gossamer curtains, and to leave the guards behind. The spindly, fragile stsho, who was the personal aide, *gtst* told her, to *gtst* excellency the governor No'shto-shti-stlen, drifted in draperies of almost pink and almost gold, fluttered agitatedly along a corridor of blowing drapes of almost-white—wherein a gold-coated, red-maned hani, unsubtle intrusion in a realm of faintest distinctions, refused to be rushed. The aide had not deigned to come in person. She was in no imminent need of the governor's approval. So in the game of diplomatic tit for tat, Hilfy Chanur walked at her own pace into the governor's vast gossamer-curtained audience hall, where multiple bowl-chairs, pastel cushioned depressions in the floor, defined the stsho's sense of elegance, decorum, and, thereby, social status.

In one of these bowl-chairs governor No'shto-shti-stlen waited, plucking pale green leaves from some sort of fruit and eating them one by one.

But the governor set down *gtst* lunch as they approached. Manners improved. The aide, bowing, declared the presence of 'the great hani captain, the birth-bond-relative of the estimable *mekt-hakkikt*' and so on and so on, worthy of *gtst* attention, and so on.

"Sit," the entity lisped in the Trade, with a wave of white, long fingers. *Gtst* excellency seemed half-transparent, hardly a touch of color in the body-paint, to hani eyes, white on white. *Gtst*—not precisely he or she, since stsho had three genders, and two indeterminate states if frightened—called for something in *gtst* rippling planetary language. The attendant scurried to comply, while stsho music played softly in the background, the occasional chime of a single, same note.

Hilfy folded down into the bowl opposite *gtst* excellency No'shto-shti-stlen, knowing better than to rush matters with the governor, as she had refused to be hurried. But very quickly a servant showed up with a tray of crystal bowls and a colorless, exquisitely flavored liquid in a crystal pitcher.

Thereafter, five tiny bowls, savored in silence. She knew the protocols—and knew the giddiness that could set in for a hani partaking of too much stsho hospitality. She kept her ears up and her mouth pursed in hani pleasantness, evidencing the right amount of cultured pleasure in each serving, all the while she watched the minute flutter of feathery lashes and feathery brows, the minute shifts in expression as No'shto-shti-stlen made slow estimation of *gtst* guest and tried (it was second nature to the stsho) to guess her current rank, her mood, and her expectations by her selection of jewelry and her composure in the meeting.

"Do you find it pleasant?"

"Delicate," she said, *in* the stsho's own trade-tongue, and feathery eyebrows went up. "Very delicate. Very pleasant."

"We are astounded at your commendable fluency."

"Your excellency flatters me. And this *is* very fine."

"Please accept a case lot in appreciation."

Ye gods. Appreciation. Of what, one wondered. It was no mean gift. But the obligatory response, with precisely the right degree of gratitude: "Your excellency is most kind. Please be understanding when a gift from my own ship arrives: after seeing the grace and discrimination of your establishment, I can only hope my personal token of admiration finds favor."

"I could not possibly."

"Honor it with your ownership. Your discrimination is of wide repute."

"Your graciousness is most extravagant."

"Your excellency's delicacy and sensitivity amply justify our admiration."

It went on like that for two and three more rounds of compliments and deprecations.

That case of tea was worth about 3000 on the market. A good merchant had her figures in her head. The stsho certainly did.

"There is, however," said No'shto-shti-stlen—(there was always the "however") "—a way in which we might favor ourselves with an opportunity to amplify our association. More tea?"

Gods, the convolutions. One suspected a stsho was trying to lose an upstart foreigner in the verbal underbrush. But one did not decline an offer of further negotiation, not if one wished to remain on good terms. One only hoped one's good sense held out and one's tongue did not trip.

"Of course."

Another round of platitudes, another period of quiet assessment, in which, ample time to reflect on one's capacity for *shis* tea and on the extent of a stsho's connivance. No'shto-shti-stlen was a stsho whom aunt Pyanfar called moderately stable.

That meant both reliable for trade . . . and dangerous by reason of *gtst* long-term personal interests.

"I would wonder," she said, setting down the third emptied cup of the second round of *shis-thi-nli*. "I would ask why my illustrious and esteemed aunt was not foremost to help such a deserving person, if your excellency would enlighten me. Surely your trust in my junior self cannot exceed that you would place in her august person."

"I hope that my request does not cause any—" A flutter of the hands, a hiding of the mouth behind a napkin. "—awkwardness."

Kftli. "Awkwardness." Cognate relationship to "foreignness." Perhaps *gtst* excellency was making a joke. Perhaps *gtst* excellency had not studied the evolution of the trade-tongues.

"The august Director left here, perhaps you are aware—deep—into a territory—ahem—of utmost secrecy. Yes, she might oblige us, she is so extravagant in her good offices toward persons in distress. But we are extremely fortunate in your arrival. We were searching records to find a captain of sufficient—mmm—standing and respectability. Your arrival in-system is a most delightful surprise."

One did *not* want another round of tea. And one could now regret one's youthful enthusiasm for dealing in the other's language. Avoiding a request at this point was something only a stsho could finesse—and one suspected, not at this disadvantage of rank. Did you want your ship to leave on time, your goods to stay unpilfered, most of all, did you want your manifest *not* to display some flaw four and five solar systems away that would cost you days and bribes to straighten out?

Gods rot the scoundrel. She wished this one *had* landed in aunt Py's lap. Or possibly it had been about to, and aunt Py had suddenly decided on a course numerous light-years away.

"And how may we merit your good opinion?"

"I have a cargo," said No'shto-shti-stlen, "an object actually, which must get to Urtur, time being of the essence."

"A precious object."

"Most precious."

"The favor of your trust overwhelms me. But may I ask? The nature of this object."

Hands fluttered. Brows wavered. "An artwork."

"Not living. Not animate."

"Oh, no, no, no, nothing of the sort. But—"

Here it comes. They might have an offer. She was by no means certain she wanted it.

"—its delivery is, understand, *liiyei.*"

A guess, based on the Trade. *"Ceremony."*

"Just so. Just so. But it must go immediately to Urtur."

"Immediately."

"Immediately. What will you charge? By no means be modest."

"Its mass?"

"Oh, very small. I could lift it. Of a dimension . . ." Long, white fingers described an object about the size of one's head.

"Fragile?"

"No more nor less than the cup you lately held. You are so modest. And perhaps have other cargo. Let me name a figure. A million in advance."

Her throat stopped working. She extruded a claw and nudged the cup. The attendant hastened to fill it, and No'shto-shti-stlen's.

"Is there some difficulty?" No'shto-shti-stlen asked.

"By no means. If—I hesitate to impose upon your excellency's already considerable generosity, but I have consignments to pick up here for Hoas port. —I might perhaps arrange a transfer of those orders—I've no contractual problems. . . ."

"No difficulty. None at all. I take it these were open market contracts."

"Open market, nothing illegal about an interline, but your excellency must understand, I have bonds requiring that delivery . . ."

"A trifle, a trifle. My personal guarantee. I personally will put a bond on the interline carrier for your entire and unexcepted protection."

Too good to be true. "My ship certainly has the engines to make the jump, at low mass. But a million, while most generous as an offer . . . does the contract enjoin us from carrying other cargo?"

"Absolutely not. Whatever you can carry safely. And certainly—certainly we can assist you with priorities. Even—hm—information on low-mass stsho goods. I have a contract already drawn up." From an alabaster box by the side of the bowl-chair No'shto-shti-stlen whisked a sole spot of blackness, a data-cube. "This has both the contract for transport and the authorization for the disbursement."

"Cash at undocking."

"Cash at undocking. The whole sum to be paid to the bank on signature of the contract, with no restriction on withdrawals once the *oji* is aboard." A waggle of long fingers. And a tightly sewed-up set of conditions. "Of course one so honorable as yourself would need no contract. But for our mutual protection."

"Of course."

"Please accept *three* cases of the tea, to salve the inconvenience of diverting your ship."

"I do not of course guarantee signing the contract. Please make the gift contingent on our agreement!"

"Your honor is impeccable in my eyes. No such stipulation. Please. Take it for your help in an additional difficulty."

A sip of the tea. Definitely. Two sips. "Additional difficulty."

"A matter in which your honor might, if you will, be a solution."

"In what way might I be the solution of a problem so difficult?"

"A matter of delicacy. A member of your species is stranded here at Meetpoint—clearly an oversight on the part of the ship in question. But we are most anxious to see this resolved."

"They left her."

No'shto-shti-stlen took a sip of tea, and fluttered eyelashes. "Him, if I may be so entirely forward."

Him. Gods. Hilfy did a rapid resorting, with a distinct sense of alarm. "A hani ship? Left a crewman?"

"There was—your honor will please be understanding—a slight intoxication, a breakage of insignificant items of extremely bad taste—most of all—an altercation with a foreign national of—em—higher status—which I assure your honor had been harmlessly resolved."

"The nationality offended, excellency?"

"Kif."

Gods.

"A simple misunderstanding, a few hours detention and filling out of forms . . . but through some inadvertency, his ship—simply claimed a cargo priority and left without our office—em—aware of the oversight. We are excruciatingly embarrassed. We believe that perhaps they believed he was already back aboard, as did—em—an individual in traffic management, who cleared the undock."

"Did no one advise them?"

"They were unalarmed. They sent back word that it was unfortunate, but they had a contractual commitment and they urged us to send him along by the first hani ship that might consent. Your esteemed aunt, of course, had already left. *Handur's Rainbow*, which came in afterward and preceded you out . . . did not have a berth available."

A *contractual* commitment?

Read that *Rainbow* had refused to burden itself. Damn their down-the-nose attitude.

But—gods—hit a kif of rank? Did one *want* to take aboard a hani with that kind of grudge?

"Can we prevail upon your extreme generosity? His presence here is an embarrassment. How do we care for him? How do we lodge him?"

"I quite understand." Think fast, Hilfy Chanur. "What was his ship's course?" Fifty-fifty it was . . .

"Hoas, as happens. But everything passes through Urtur."

"In any case—" Gods, how did I get into this? But, damn it to a mahen hell . . . you don't even ask his clan. He's hani. He's lost. He's been *dumped* here, gods rot them—if the kif claim him, the stsho can't resist that pressure. Small wonder they want him out of here before there's an incident.

"We can *pay* his passage," No'shto-shti-stlen said.

"No. No. Forgive my unseemly distress. I could not possibly accept payment. This is a question of . . ." Stsho had no equivalent for species-honor. ". . . Elegance."

"Another case of tea."

"Please." On the other hand. At three thousand the case. "On the other hand—"

A flutter of distress. No'shto-shti-stlen wanted this lad gone very badly. *Very* badly. And feared he would have to pay heavily for it.

Which he might deserve to do . . . except Hilfy Chanur was not dealing in hani hides, under any circumstances.

"Your esteemed and wise influence might clear any legal obstacles, any defect in his documents, that sort of thing. That would expedite matters."

"We are delighted to assist. There will be *no* impediments."

"No entanglements. No pending charges."

"You have my word. I have so enjoyed this meeting. Please give my regards to your esteemed relative. Advise her that No'shto-shti-stlen admires her exceedingly."

"I shall." There was a civilized way and a barbaric one to quit a bowl-chair: the left foot on the unpadded line, the right onto the rim, no trick at all. She made a small bow, the datacube in hand, and No'shto-shti-stlen nodded with a graceful swaying of *gtst* white center-crest and *gtst* feathery, cosmetically augmented brows.

"Most, most pleasant," No'shto-shti-stlen said.

"A memorable hour, most memorable."

Never underestimate a stsho.

So, so, she had a passenger—but he was an inconsequence; the other question, what was in the contract, took momentary second place to the heady thoughts of a million credit haulage fee for some trinket she could juggle one-handed, and with the hold, after discharging their cargo, altogether free for what she could buy outright at Meetpoint for resale in a port whose fairly recent futures and shortages list *Legacy* had in file?

Far too good to be true, was what it was. She had gotten too far into this. Her disclaimer that she might not sign had not been early enough or forceful enough, and it needed no kifish guards to upset her stomach on the way out.

"All went well?" one had the temerity to ask her.

"Ask the one who feeds you," she retorted, and the kif who had presumed, retreated, hissing.

No love lost, no. The kif knew an implacable enemy; but they had to let her pass back to the dockside.

And how did one at this point refuse the governor who sat at the junction of virtually all trans-sector trade—even if one's aunt *was* the *mekt-hakkikt* of the known universe?

Appeal to Pyanfar's influence?

By the gods, no. Not Hilfy Chanur. Not if she wanted to face herself in the mirror. Not if she didn't want the story spread on every ship that dealt with No'shto-shti-stlen.

And the stsho would spread it. Not strike a blow in anger, oh, no, not the stsho. Their daggers were all figurative and theoretical. Or wielded by kifish hire-ons.

But, dear, featherless gods, if the offer was on the up and up . . .

Legacy was spitting up cans—had at least one truck full already, with the bright red stamp that meant warm-hold goods, and the trucks lined up that would take them to their various destinations, some for the station, some for interline to Kshshti, some on for ports no hani nor mahen ship could reach; and some of them were even destined for the methane-side—fifty more cold-hold cans: hani goods—bound for the t'ca. New markets. New prosperity—for ships that would take the risks and go the far and alien distances.

Competitive ships. Ships that carried clan wealth and clan business where hani clans had no on-world referent. Ships that brought back new ideas to Anuurn. Like the Compact itself. Like making the old women on Anuurn look up instead of inward, and making senior captains hide-bound in their ways admit that Chanur was *not* in exile, Chanur that had respect in every gods-be-feathered port of call in the Compact: make the nay-sayers believe that Chanur *had* more than a proxy head-of-clan in her, and that the head-of-clan had a right to replace *The Pride* and replace Pyanfar Chanur *and* survive by honest trade.

This run could be the break-even that would prove it. This contract could put them at a profit for the first time in the *Legacy*'s existence: the *Legacy*'s construction was entirely paid for and they were running free and clear, if they could take this break and go with it—a million for a ridiculously light haul and a 500,000 current clear take off the cargo, here, against a remaining indebtedness of 14,000,000, plus a turn-around with a mil and a half origin-point purchase for low-mass luxury goods and palladium offering a pay-out of 500% at Urtur above running costs; with, moreover, a price break on cargo guaranteed by No'shto-shti-stlen *gtst*self . . . not to mention the flat-rate hauls they could manage: she was already figuring what they *could* haul on that difficult long-distance jump including express mail; and trying over and over to admonish herself to caution as she walked up and took cousin Tiar quietly by the elbow.

"We have an offer. It involves a turn-around for Urtur. I'm inside to read the contract. If some station guards show up with a passenger, take him."

"Passenger," Tiar echoed. Chihin had stopped work, ears

pricked. Veteran spacers, Tiar Chanur, Chihin Anify, both out of Rhean's crew when Rhean retired. And "station guards" and "him" got Fala's ears up.

"Him?" Tiar asked, wiping her hands. There were two other puzzled frowns.

"Why us?" Tiar asked. "Begging the captain's pardon, of course."

Meaning if "he" was mahe, there were mahen ships to take him, and if "he" was kif there were kif enough, not to mention the stsho.

"Because," she said quietly, "he's hani."

"Gods . . ." Chihin's ears went flat.

"I want him out of here. I want the hide of the captain that dumped him. Most of all, I want him away from the kif. If he shows up—when he shows up—check his papers. Make *sure* of those papers, if you have to keep him waiting to do it: get into station comp and make sure there's no proliferating taint of any kind on his record, you understand. Above all, don't take him aboard until they're clear. The governor wants him out of here, and once he's aboard we don't have that leverage—*immigration* does, you understand?"

"No question," Tiar said.

"Ship *left* him?" Fala asked, her young face all seriousness.

"It's a long story. We're taking him out of here, is all we can promise. Catch his ship if we can. Just be nice. Be nice."

She clapped Tiar on the shoulder, Chihin second, and deliberately did not hear Chihin say, "That's what comes of letting men to space . . ." Chihin was conservative, so was Tiar, and you didn't change her overnight.

But things had changed. They had changed so far a hani ship could bring a hani lad forty lights away from home and *leave* him to a station where kif were the guards and stsho were the only justice.

She walked up the ramp and into the yellow-ribbed access tube, trod the chilly distance to the lock and locked through. In the lowerdeck ops station, she found Tarras working comp on the loaders, and she snagged Tarras for the computer work.

One did *not* drop a strange cube into the ship's main computer or any terminal in touch with it. Not that one didn't trust *gtst* excellency. Of course not.

So it was the downside auxiliary, the computer that suicided and resurrected on command.

"I want a printout," she told Tarras. "One original, one through the translator, stsho formal, but first I want you to diagnose the source. I don't want the thing changing, erasing, or cozying up to our navigation. *Ma'sho?*"

"Sho'shi," Tarras said, ears pricked, all enthusiasm.

"Fast. Inside the hour."

Tarras' ears went to half. "Captain, . . ."

"You can do it."

Tarras muttered another word in mahen trade, gave a shiver and took the cube, looked at it on one side and another—for obvious things like inbuilts.

"I need a laser on this."

"Check for more exotic contagions after we get the print. I need the print, Tarras. All of us need this printout."

"What's up?"

"Only our operating budget. Only a major contract I don't know if I want and I don't know if we can get out of, on which the governor's good will happens to be riding."

"I'm on it," Tarras said, and went.

The sounds and smells of the cells were dreadful. Hallan slept when he could, a sleep disturbed by distant sounds of doors, attendants coming and going. It went on constantly, but you could never see anything: just a blank door and blank gray walls, and the sounds to let you know you were not alone. He had long since lost track of the time. He amused himself by adding chains of figures. They had said when they arrested him that his captain would have to get him out. And then, days and days ago, the kifish guard who brought him his breakfast had said his ship had left without him.

That had been the absolute depth of despair. He had asked

the guard what would they do then, and the guard said, oh, probably keep him here for the rest of his life.

The kif had said, When we want rid of someone we kill him. Hani sneak away and leave him. You're half again bigger than your females. They say you're a fighter. Why didn't you kill them and secure your place?

He had been appalled. But the kif as kif went was a talkative one, and more friendly than he had expected of that dangerous kind. He had had trouble understanding it at first. It interrupted everything with clicks. It smelled of ammonia. It complained that he stank. It had naked, black skin that was gray where the light fell on it, and velvety soft and wrinkled, although in kif that didn't seem to be a sign of age. It had long jaws and a small mouth and what he had heard said it had to have live food, which it diced into a fine paste with a second set of jaws, far up toward the gullet—after which it spat out the bones and the fur. If it bit you, those teeth could get a crippling mouthful. It ate its own kind and it did not feel remorse. Such statements were not prejudicial: its psychology was different, utterly self-interested, and one had better believe so and not judge it by hani standards: that was what he had learned about kif in his books.

But that kif was the only one who spoke to him, the only living being he had seen besides the mahen doctor, who had not had much to say to him, except what he knew, that he was in trouble. He had come even to look forward to the kif in the morning, because it did stay to talk; and he had stopped thinking it was going to take a piece out of him without a reason.

But it had not come this morning nor the morning before. And when the door opened, he thought it was lunch, which he wasn't interested in, because his stomach could only tolerate the breakfasts, and no one cared, and no one changed the menu.

So he thought he could lie there on the bunk and not pay any attention and it would go away.

But it didn't. Whoever it was didn't make the ordinary sound of setting down a tray and leaving. Whoever it was just stood there.

He turned over and looked, and saw a kif like every other kif, except its black robes glistened and the border of its hood had silver cording. He could not see all of its face, just the snout. But he had the impression of its fixed stare as he sat up.

"Sir?" He had no idea the proprieties, whether he should bow or stand there, but he decided on bowing. He thought it might be a station officer of some kind. It was even possible it was the kif he had hit, which had gotten him in here. He hoped it didn't want a fight. He was considerably at a disadvantage, and besides, he had gotten in trouble that way in the first place.

"They tell me you're refusing your food."

It was an official of some kind. "It doesn't agree with me, sir. I'm sorry."

"A very respectful hani. Males of your kind have a reputation for violence. For strength—one can expect that. But they say you're such a quiet, cooperative prisoner."

"I didn't mean to hit anybody. If it was you, I'm sorry."

"No, no, not me. I assure you. In fact I've taken the liberty of contacting the governor in your case. A hani ship is in port. I thought it might agree to help you get home."

All at once his pulse was racing. Everyone said never trust such a creature, and it had to want something—kif didn't *do* you favors. Everyone said so. There had to be a catch.

"Who are they, sir?"

"Relatives of the *mekt-hakkikt.* Chanur clan. And they *have* agreed to take you in custody. I hope this is agreeable to you."

Agreeable. He folded his arms to keep from shaking. "Yes, sir. Absolutely." Chanur. Gods, oh, gods, if it could possibly be true . . .

"You wonder why one of my rank would be interested?"

"Yes, sir."

"My name is Vikktakkht. Can you say that?"

"Vikktakkht."

"Can you remember it?"

"Yes, sir."

"You understand gratitude."

"Yes, sir."

"Then do me a favor. When it occurs to you . . . repeat my name where it seems appropriate."

"I beg pardon—?"

The kif came close to him, and laid a black-clawed hand on his arm. It was as tall as he was, and he had a most uncomfortable look within the hood, into narrow, red-rimmed eyes that gazed deeply and curiously into his.

"Go with the officers. Cause no trouble. Remember my name. Never forget it. At some time you will want to ask me a question."

Sheets dropped into the printout tray. One . . . two . . . three . . .

. . . ten . . . eleven. The thing was a monster.

. . . forty nine . . . fifty . . .

My *gods*, was the printer on a loop?

. . . one hundred . . . one hundred one . . .

Out of paper. Tarras reloaded the bin and Hilfy sat and stared glumly at the stack. She *refused* to start reading until it was done.

. . . two hundred twenty six . . . two hundred twenty-seven.

The ready light went off. The binder whirred. She extracted from the bin a contract almost as heavy as the cargo it represented and flipped through the minuscule print.

The computer started into the translation program then, and started displaying the result. She was looking at the stsho script, page after closely written page.

The intercom blurted out: *"Security is here, captain."*

"Get outside," she said to Tarras. "Get a check on those papers. Tiar knows what I mean."

"Security?" Tarras asked, ears up again.

"Delay the offloading for an hour. You're going to query station on this one."

"What's security got to do with it?"

She was trying to read stsho script. On this screen it was a challenge to the eyesight. "I committed an act of mercy. The gods' penance for fools." The translator was already querying for conflict resolution. And *she* had to do it. Tiar knew enough stsho to handle customs. Tiar didn't read the classical mode. Which this was.

And when you had a contract, you by the gods read it. Demand it in hani? Better to pin down the contract-giver in native expression—or *gtst* could claim deception on your part. Better to be able to claim deception by them against you. The courts did give points for that.

Was there a non-performance clause? And on which side was the penalty?

Was there a contingency for breakage? For war and solar events and piracy?

Did it cover personality alteration? And gender switching? Stsho *did* that, under stress, and in trauma.

Did it cover death or change of the designated recipient before accepting the object?

Did it provide a sure identification for the object?

The translator kept interrupting, begging resolution. She foresaw a sleepless watch, and irritably split-screened the display, stsho and hani versions.

One did *not* translate a formal stsho contract into Trade tongue: it only developed ambiguities. One did not tell the translator to solve its own conflicts. The first wrong logic branch could start it down the road to raving lunacy.

"Captain. Sorry to interrupt you. They say we can't access the legal bank without an authorization from admin—"

"Get it. Call the governor's aide. Tell them the difficulty. Tell them I've just spoken to *gtst* excellency and been assured this would not happen."

"Aye," Tiar said cheerfully, and the com went out.

Did it stipulate a deadline for delivery?

Did it set damages and arbitration?

"Captain."

Gods. "Tiar?"

"The station office won't put the call through without an authorization from you."

An addendum to the contract. Access. For every last member of the crew.

"I'm going to shoot the kif. Tell them that. Tell them . . ." No, she was not going to invoke aunt Py's name or her perks or her reputation. "Tell them I'm putting the call through. Personally."

"Aye, captain."

She did it. Very patiently. She resolved a conflict for the translation program, then punched through to station com, and drawled, "This is captain Hilfy Chanur, *Chanur's Legacy,* to No'shto-shti-stlen, governor of Meetpoint, and so on—fill in the formalities. Excellency: some individual in lower offices is obstructing your orders. —Relay it! Now!"

"Chanur captain."

"Yes?"

"Chanur captain, let us not be hasty. Can this person assist?"

"Possibly." She took on far sweeter tones. "If you can get a copy of that entire dossier my crewwoman just requested, *and* relay us an affidavit that the case in question is settled as of this date . . . in case something proliferates through files at some other station. Should we be inconvenienced by this, in doing a favor for the governor? I think we should not."

"Notable captain. —A matter of moments. A formality only. Every paper you want."

"In the meanwhile—hold that message ready to send. One quarter hour, to have those papers on the dock, at our berth. This should have been done, do you understand that? This was No'shto-shti-stlen's own order!"

"Esteemed, a quarter hour. Less than that!"

"The quarter hour is running now, station com. Good luck to you."

There was the clause regarding payment. 1,000,000 haulage and oversight. And there was the clause regarding delivery of the cargo, to a stsho in the representative office on Urtur Station.

So far so good. She read through the succeeding paragraphs.

"Captain. We got it."

"Good. *Thank* station com."

"Captain. His clan is Meras. But he's off a Sahern ship."

Her head came up. The translator was stuck again. She ignored it. She had ignored the situation with the boy—not wanting to walk out that hatch and deal with a party of kif and a hostage. It wanted a cooler disposition than she could manage at the moment.

But *Sahern,* was it?

Not friends. A clan with whom they had a centuries-old, formally filed feud.

Thank you, gods. Penance for mercy indeed.

"I'll see him."

She solved the translator's problem, let it run and read until she heard the hatch cycle. Then she leaned over and killed displays, swung the chair around toward the door.

Boy, she had said. So many were, that had gone to space. But he was older than that. He had his full growth—at least in height; had to duck his head coming through the door. His shoulders were wide enough to put the consoles in jeopardy. *Handsome* lad—a statue had to notice: and a spacer crew months out on a run was going to notice. Shy, scared, all those things a young man might be, dropped in the midst of a strange clan, and him in the wrong—it took a moment before he decided he had to look at her.

"*Na* Meras. Welcome aboard."

"Thank you, *ker* Chanur. I'm very grateful to be here."

"I don't doubt. I hesitate to ask why your ship found it necessary to leave."

"I don't know, *ker* Chanur."

"Captain will do. And don't you?"

Ears lowered. The boy found a spot on the deck of interest. "I don't remember what I did. They say I broke some pottery. And hit a kifish gentleman."

"A kifish gentleman." The boy *was* delicately bred.

"I don't remember that part," he said. Add *new to drink and bars.*

"You weren't in communication with your ship."

"No, captain."

"Not since?"

"No, captain."

"And you've no notion why your captain suffered a lapse of memory either."

"No, captain."

"*Na* Meras, that answer could get very tiresome over the next several months. Possibly even by tomorrow."

"I'm sorry, captain."

"What's your *name, na* Meras?"

A glance up, ears half-lifted. "Hallan, captain. From Syrsyn. —I—I met your aunt once, on Anuurn dock. And *ker* Haral . . ."

Her ears went down. She remembered a dockside, at Anuurn, too, a parting with the crew. A handful of bitter words.

There was absolute adoration on the boy's face—not, she was sure, cultivated on any Sahern ship. And sensitivity enough to realize he had just trod on dangerous ground. Bewilderment . . . confusion. He had the sense to shut up, give him that.

"Are you married in Sahern, lateral kin, . . . what's the relationship?" It was a measure of how often and how long she had been downworld that she did *not* track the lineages any longer. He could be related to the Holy Personage of Me'gohtias for all she knew.

"No relation," he said, managing to locate that spot on the deck again.

So a tasteful person would stop asking. Look at the boy. Figure a kid wanted a berth. And Sahern gave him one.

She shot a glance up at Tiar. "I think the lad could stay in passenger quarters."

"I can work maintenance. I have my license."

"That's to prove. In the meanwhile—" Practicalities occurred to her. "I don't suppose you came with baggage."

"Everything—" The boy made a despairing gesture. "Everything's aboard the *Sun.*"

"*Sun Ascendant? —Tellun* Sahern?"

"Yes, captain."

More bad news. "We'll get you caught up to your ship, or drop you where you can make connections . . ."

"I want to stay *here.*"

"On Meetpoint?"

"No, captain. On this ship. I want to stay with *you.*"

"The *Legacy* has a full complement. No berths." She saw the ears go flat, the frowning attitude of not quite resignation, and ticked down a Watch this boy, a little sense of resistance there. Of . . . one was not certain what. "You want *my* long-term advice? Ship home. Go back, work insystem cargo if you're so dead set on space."

"*No,* captain."

A little flare of temper. A set of the mouth. Gods-rotted fool kid, she thought, and glared. What did I do to deserve this?

Chapter Two

The stack from the translator was 532 pages thick . . . counting the alternative translations successively rendered. That was the first pass the comp had made. The legal advisement program advised that its analysis of the translation would be 20588 pages in length and did the Operator want it simply to summarize?

"Apparently the thing is a vase," Hilfy said. Four hani faces, four worried hani faces, stared back, and blinked in near unison.

"A ceremonial vase," Tiar said. "Somebody's grandmother buried in it?"

"Not from what I figure. I've run *oji* through every cognate and every derivation I can find. It means 'ceremonial object with accumulated value' and it's related to the word for 'antique' and 'relic.' Its transferred meanings and derivatives seem to mean 'ceremonial object with social virtue,' 'communal high tea,' . . ."

"You're kidding."

". . . and 'inheritance.' "

"No'shto-shti-stlen's going to die?" Fala asked.

"Who knows?" A shrug was not politic, but it was close company, here. "Maybe *gtst* is designating a successor. Maybe the old son *is* going home to die."

"They do that," Chihin said. "Stsho won't die in view of strangers. Bad taste."

"It's pay in advance. *Gtst* can't change *gtst* mind."

"That's for certain."

Hilfy stared at the stack. "Pay in advance. Gods, it pays. You just keep asking yourself why."

"What can go wrong?" Fala asked, and got a circle of flat-eared looks and a moment of silence.

"There's an encyclopaedia entry," Hilfy said, "under *oijgi*, related substantive, to the effect that an object like that can't be paid for, that it just transfers, and money can't touch it directly. Mustn't touch it directly. It's all status. Of some kind. It could account for the extravagance."

"We could outright ask somebody," Tarras said.

"No. Not when we don't know what we're dealing with—or how explosive it is. No'shto-shti-stlen has ears in every wall in this station."

"Electronically speaking," Tiar said.

"I certainly wouldn't bet the contract against it."

"So you're leaning toward signing?"

"Once every quarter hour. Elsewhen I'm inclined to take our cargo on to Hoas and forget I ever heard about it. Why in a mahen hell does this thing have to go rush-shipment to Urtur? Why not a slow trip via Hoas in the first place? Does the governor have to be difficult? Does the thing explode on delivery?"

"You want my opinion?"

"What?" she asked.

"I say *if* we take the contract, we get all our cargo buys nailed down in advance. And stall signing to the very last moment. Gossip's going to fly the moment that check hits the bank. They'll jack the prices on us."

"Give the old son *no* time," Tarras said, "to frame us for anything. Because you can bet the next trip's take that bastard No'shto-shti-stlen is thinking how to get that money back before it hits our pockets. On *gtst* deathbed *gtst* would make that arrangement. *Gtst* isn't the richest son this side of space for no reason."

"Trouble is," Chihin said, "—we've got to take certain cargo *for* Urtur if that's where we're going. And unless old No'shto-shti-stlen's been uncommonly discreet, there are stsho on this station who know what the deal is; and if they know, security's already shot. If we're going to deal, we'd better deal fast, because I've got a notion if this thing is that important to the stsho, it could be important to No'shto-shti-stlen's enemies, too. If it is, figure on spies reporting what we buy, and what we deal for, and what we've got contracts on—if we sneeze, it's going into somebody's databank and right to No'shto-shti-stlen's ears for a starter."

"And elsewhere simultaneously," Hilfy said. Aunt Py had dealt with the stsho. And still did; what was aunt Py's expression? Never trust the stsho to be hani? They weren't. They wouldn't be. No more than hani would play by stsho rules; or mahen ones; and the stsho had been cosmopolitan enough to know that single fact before the *han* or the mahendo'sat ever figured it out. Add to it, that a hani who happened to be fluent in stsho trade tongue and its history might deceive herself in special, personal blind spots related to the interface between languages and world-views.

"I want," Hilfy said, extruding claws one after the other to signify the items: "an estimate on a list of things I've left on file, under 'Urtur.' I'm betting on goods that originate from beyond Meetpoint, that no one's going to bring in from the other direction. Things we know Urtur's short on. And I want a search on the manifests for ships going out of here. We can't account for what might come in from Kshshti—so let's concentrate on stsho and t'ca goods."

"Gods, not another methane load."

"It pays. It pays and they have their own handlers."

"It's who else might be interested in it worries me," Tiar said.

"It's a straight shot to Urtur. If we just do a fast turnaround here, and get ourselves out of port . . ."

Tiar made a visible shudder, and waved a hand in surrender. "It pays."

"So we agree?"

A murmured set of agreements. Hilfy watched the expressions, wondering whether they might be agreeing against better judgment, because of kinships, because of loyalty.

"I want *opinions!*" she snarled. "I want someone to disagree if they're going to disagree!"

No one moved. She waited. And no one said anything.

"No opinions to the contrary."

"No, captain," Tiar said, with a flat, unmoved stare. And added: "I'll check methane ship departures. See what their trade's been. If it looks like there's a niche for us, aye, we do it. We'll pay out the ship on this run. That's worth a chance."

"Do it tomorrow," she said, with the weight of the day on her shoulders. "I want that Hoas cargo done, too, who's going out we can dump it on. Again, quietly."

"I'll check on that," Chihin said. "We'll just pull a big general dataload from the station . . . costs, but nosy neighbors can't tell anything out of one big request."

"Do that," Hilfy said. Specific records-searches *would* tip off the curious. 15,000 credits. Minimum, for that datadump. But they could re-sell it at Urtur, get back five, six thousand, as moderately comprehensive information. Maybe 10,000. They stood to own the highest currency of information coming in. With a full dataload. She found herself thinking, with increasing solidity: *at Urtur.* Not Hoas, as they had been bound. At Urtur. They had the advantage of having just been through there, they had the uncommon situation of having the funds to buy their own cargo. That meant the profit was *theirs,* not some shipping company's.

And Hallan Meras still had a chance to catch his ship. Gods. One more problem than they needed.

"You're not staying on watch," Tiar said.

"No."

"I'd better."

"Get some sleep, I said. I want a crew with brains tomorrow. Good night."

" 'Night, cap'n." From Tiar. At the door, hindmost. Still registering objection, in that backward glance. But Tiar went.

Tiar was right. If they were half practical they would keep one of them on watch from now on until they parted company with Meetpoint. If they had enemies, things would develop in files on their off watch and proliferate through their sleep. Anyone who had prospects had trade rivals here, and they could have plenty, if No'shto-shti-stlen's shipment was general knowledge . . . which, of course, they could not ask to find out.

But all that had proliferated into their files thus far was mail, the stack of which, even from ships that had long since left port, equaled the translation. And with the comp set to rouse them for fire, collision, and interstellar war, she reckoned they knew enough. She added one more alarm word from her console: *contract,* and on a stray thought, added *No'shto-shti-stlen.*

And headed for her own quarters and for bed, tired, gods, yes.

Until her back met the mattress and her head hit the pillows. Then every detail of the day wanted to come back and replay itself behind her eyelids.

Kifish guards. That brought her eyes open, and she tried to think of something else, anything else, bright things, full of color, like the clan estate on Anuurn, with the golden fields and green forest and rolling hills.

But that did no good. She wound up thinking about family politics, remembering her father, *wishing* that the timestretches that spun out her star-jumping youth had somehow reached planetside, and extended Kohan Chanur's life. But the years had caught up with him—not a fight with some upstart, thank the gods. His daughter and his sisters and his nieces had kept the young would-bes away, had given him a peaceful old age. No one but time had defeated him. He had just not waked one morning.

Meanwhile *her* husband, *na* Korin nef Sfaura, thought *he* was going to move into Chanur. Pick a husband with brains *and* muscle and you got the hormones that went with it, you got a husband with ideas, and Hilfy Chanur had spent sleepless nights telling herself there were reasons to abide by the old customs, that shooting Korin Sfaura, while a solution on the docks at Kshshti, was not a solution on Chanur's borders, with a neighboring clan.

Not unless one wanted to crack the amphictiony wide open, and see war on Anuurn.

Gods-rotted bastard he had turned out to be. But the male-on-male fighting men learned for territory had a few things still to learn from Kshshti docks. Korin had limped out of Chanur territory, half-wed and vowing revenge, and by the time he'd made another try, cousin Harun had come in as lord Chanur . . . big lad, Harun. Rhean had searched the outback to find him and get him home, out of his wilderness exile. Best fighter they could find, best lord of household, for a clan taking a lot of challenges. Of all the lads that had come home at Kohan's invitation, and some of them even settled inside Chanur walls, Harun . . . was not one of that liberal, easy-going number. Ask any of the males he had sent packing, including the ones born to Chanur. A hani of the old school—hair-triggered—thick-skulled . . .

But it had taken him to rid the clan once for all of what *she* had brought home, and detest and despise *na* Harun Chanur as she did, and know, as she did, that Rhean had brought him home precisely to counter aunt Py's influence . . . she had to think that he might be the right hani for the times; because Pyanfar's gallivanting about and Pyanfar's naming *her* head of clan had certainly raised the hair on a number of conservative backs. Change happened and you thought it was forever, and immediately there were all the enemies of that change making common cause and meeting in the cloakrooms.

And there were all the victims of that change—dead, like poor bookish Dahan Chanur, who had died for nothing more than wanting to collect his notebooks. Gods-rotted thick-headed Harun had ordered him out, Dahan had said something about his notes, headed back for his room, and Harun had flung him into a wall.

That was the lord of Chanur now. And she had done Rhean's daughter out of the *Legacy*, and some didn't forgive her for pulling rank and spending her ascendency as clan head as an absentee.

Truth be told, she was guilty of everything they said at home. Aunt Rhean was disgusted with her. High and wide she'd fouled it up, mate-picking and house-running . . . parted company with aunt Py, that day on Anuurn docks. And aunt Py . . .

Ex-clan-head Pyanfar Chanur had said, being lately hailed grand high whatever of everywhere civilized, and leaving Anuurn's dust for good.

Aunt Py had said, *Responsibility, Hilfy*. Jabbing her with an attention-getting claw. *I can't go down there again. It'd be war. And every enemy I have—listen to me!*

Another jab, and a grab, because she'd tried to walk out on Pyanfar, and nobody did that.

Every enemy I have on Anuurn will try to break the clan. That's the only revenge they can get on me. I want you to go down there, take the responsibility I gods-rotted carried, do your marrying . . . Kohan's not going to hold out forever . . . and get somebody in his place that can hold on to what he helped build. Do you hear me, Hilfy Chanur?

Gods-rotted right she'd heard her. Pyanfar talking about Kohan as if he was already dead, just to be written off; Pyanfar telling her to go down there and make a baby or two, when Py's own offspring in Mahn had been trouble from birth . . . tell *her* about handling her responsibilities to the clan, when Pyanfar was off with her ship and her crew and everything in the universe that mattered to her.

Py wanted her off her ship and away from Tully, was the bare-faced truth. Go fall in love with your own species, kid. Tully's all right for Chur and Geran, and Haral and Tirun and anybody else who wants a roll in the bunk, but don't even think of the heir of Chanur in that picture.

Go make babies downworld. Go find some muscle-bound, ambitious son of a clan you trusted, that you have to get some other muscle-bound dimwit cousin to get rid of. It's a tradition.

It's a gods-be tradition we kill the ones like Dahan and keep the ones like Harun.

And all the lost young lads who believed in Chanur's taking men onto ships, all the hundreds of young lads who with stars in their eyes had begged and bribed their way up to space, where they'd be free of tradition . . . what did they meet, and where were they, and what became of them, on the ships they'd gone to?

She tossed over onto her face and mangled the pillow, thinking about a human face and a place she didn't want to think about, ammonia-stink that she still smelled in her dreams. Sodium lights and kifish laughter. And Tully'd collected the worst of it, because Tully was a novelty. Tully'd escaped them once and they had something to prove. . . .

They'd come through that, and come through war and fire, and Pyanfar had said . . .

You'll only do him harm.

Damned if Pyanfar knew that. Damned if Pyanfar cared whether she knew what had gone on between them: Pyanfar had cared whether she took up the burden of the clan, and Chanur's politics downworld said there'd been scandal enough—Chanur's heir had to be something the old women downworld could deal with, and accept, and politic with.

She couldn't deal with it. She wouldn't deal with it. The hypocrisy gagged her. And the hypocrisy of *We have to change our ways*, and *Men aren't educated to make decisions*, and *This generation has to pass*—

So Dahan was dead and Harun was lord Chanur, and a hani ship took a naive kid aboard and *left* him, at the farthest point hani traded, because he wasn't *educated* to think and wasn't *educated* to handle strangers, and because every species in the Compact believed that hani males were helpless, instinctual killers.

Gods *rot* the way things worked! Gods *rot* the old women

who made the rules and the captain that had pulled a ship out with a crewman in kifish hands! Gods *rot* Pyanfar Chanur, whose powers extended to every godsforsaken end of the Compact and beyond . . . and who couldn't do justice in her own clan!

She pounded the pillow shapeless, she thought of the kid she'd received out of the hands of kifish guards, she thought of a big, good-looking lad who'd probably paid the obvious for his passage, and she thought bitter thoughts of what was probably going through her crew's heads . . . months away from home port and the sight and sound of a male voice.

She hated to make an issue. She probably should give a plain and clear hands-off order: Don't scare the kid. Don't crowd him. Where he's been—

She flung herself out of bed, crossed the room in the dark and found the bathroom door cold blind. Washed her face in the dark, washed her mane and her neck and her hands and stood there with her ears flat and her nostrils shut and told herself it was her cabin, her own ship and she had no need to *think* tonight about that place, or to remember the stink and the look on Tully's human face.

She did not need the light. She felt her way to the shower and shut the cabinet door behind her, turned on the water and let the jets hit her face and her shoulders, hit the soap button and scrubbed and scrubbed, until she could smell nothing but the soap and her own wet fur, until she was warm through and through and she could stand a while against the shower wall while the heated, drying air cycled.

She could forget them, then. She could forget that place, and tell herself the lights if they came on would be the spectrum of Anuurn's own yellow sun; and the voices if she should call on them would be those of the *Legacy*'s crew, cousins and kin she could rely on, kin from Chanur itself, and Chihin and young Fala Anify, Geran's and Chur's cousins, of the hill sept.

Not unreasonable women. Not fools, not political, not planetbound in their thinking, not any of those things she had met downworld. Believers in Pyanfar's ideas . . . gods, could she ever escape them? But trust her crew? With her life, with her sanity. Lean on their advice? Often.

Risk their lives, on this wild hope of proving Rhean and the rest of them wrong, paying out the *Legacy*'s costs and putting the clan on a footing financially that owed not a gods-be *thing* to Pyanfar Chanur? If she signed that stsho contract, there was a chance that she might go back to Anuurn solvent and independent of debt.

A chance, too, that she might so compromise herself that Chanur could not redeem her, not financially, not in reputation.

Hilfy Chanur did not intend to come home begging for resources. Hilfy Chanur did not intend to make her way on her aunt's influence, her aunt's reputation, or her aunt's decisions. That was what she decided.

Sign the contract. Take the chance. What would aunt Pyanfar do?

Far more foolish things. Far crazier chances. Aunt Pyanfar had risked Chanur and everything they owned for a principle.

Was that not mad . . . when no one else of her acquaintance gave a damn—and hani did as hani had always done?

He had not slept, truly slept, in very long; and having a comfortable bed and only the whisper of air from the ducts, he had hardly needed do more than lie down and shut his eyes before he was gone.

He tried to think about things, but they escaped him. He tried to worry about where he was and where he was going, but he simply fell unconscious.

He waked after that in the disorientation of some unfamiliar sound and an unfamiliar cabin—he found he had left the lights on, and wanted to do something about it, but his eyes shut again and he burrowed under the covers and forgot about it on the instant. The next time he waked, he lay thinking about it, and realizing his eyes were tired of the light, and thinking that he ought to get up and do something, but he threw the covers back over his head and was gone again.

The third time he realized someone was in the room, and he took fright and lifted his head.

"Sorry," the crewwoman said—one of the senior two, his scrambled wits could not recall her except as Chanur clan. His fright did not go away. She seemed friendly enough, but he was in strange territory, with strangers he had to get along with.

"Go back to sleep if you like." She opened the closet, took his breeches off the hook and took a quick several measurements while he blinked stupidly at the embarrassing proceedings and decided it was something about the clothing he didn't have.

"Going to need a special order on this," she said. —Tiar was the name, he could recall it now. Tiar. Chihin. Hilfy Chanur. Someone else he couldn't recall, the small one, the young one . . . "Do you some kifish outfits, stsho, whatever you like, no trouble. Even mahen stuff. Not hani. I can't even swear we can find blue. I'll do the best I can."

"Thank you," he said uncertainly. Something seemed called for, however awkward the circumstances. And it got a pursing of the mouth, a twinkle in the spacer's eye.

"Hey. You're safe here. Relax."

He wanted to think so. He remembered Pyanfar Chanur. He remembered every time things got truly bad, that *she* had taken time to talk to him, and *she* had encouraged him.

It was a Chanur ship. That was the realization in which he had fallen asleep, and the reality to which he waked. It had all the attributes of a dream, that it was improbable, it arrived out of nowhere, and it promised him everything he couldn't likely have and couldn't hope for.

He truly wanted Tiar Chanur to like him—most of all, to think of him as a spacer. He watched the door shut, and thought that he shouldn't lie here like a lump, he should get up and make up his bunk and be ready to do something around the ship. He wanted to make the best impression he could on Hilfy Chanur. So he got himself out of bed, hoping no one would open the door unannounced, and showered and dressed in the only pair of breeches he had, everything else being on the *Sun.* He made his bed meticulously.

But when he went to go out, the door was locked.

He tried it a second time, to be certain. His heart sank, and he debated whether to try the intercom and appeal to be let out, but they knew he was here and they surely knew why they had locked the door.

So, with nothing to do, he sat down on the carefully made bed and stared at the furnishings, listening to the sounds that a ship had even when it was at dock, the rush of air in the ducts, the thumps and occasional cyclings of hydraulics. He had no breakfast. Which he supposed they might omit, thinking he was still asleep. But he had looked forward very much to familiar food. He had thrown up most everything they had given him in the jail, and there was nothing available here but water—which at least did not smell of ammonia, there was that to be glad of.

He listened to the sounds of the cans moving out of the hold. He heard the hatch cycle more than once. Finally he lay down and stared at the ceiling, trying not to despair. He did not want to think about his situation. It was like the jail. It was better if you didn't think there, either, or wonder about things.

He did not need to wonder about his ship. He had every certainty where it was, in hyperspace, bound for Hoas. He had every certainty why it had left him, and he supposed now he should not have been surprised. If he were back on Anuurn, he would have had to quit the house, because when boys grew up, they had to leave. They had to go out into the outback to live, learn to hunt and to fight each other and if boys lived long enough they could come back and try to drive some older man out into the outback to die. If the man's wives and sisters didn't beat him to death before he got a chance to challenge one on one.

That was what he had been headed for. That had been the order of things forever. There were always too many boys and most of them died. But Pyanfar Chanur's taking Khym Mahn into space, her moral victory over the *han* and its policies, and her outright defiance of the law and the custom . . . had given him a chance at the stars, at . . . freedom.

Well, it was freer than shivering in the rain and killing to eat and to live. Freer than getting beaten off and driven off and told he was crazy because he was male.

He didn't think he was crazy. He thought he did a fair job of holding his temper. He hadn't *meant* to hit the kif. He'd only wanted away.

Probably, though, the captain had heard the story from the police and the station authorities, and that was why the door was locked. So he could get out of this. He just had to be quiet and patient and not cause any trouble, and prove to the captain that he'd learned something in his apprenticeship aboard the *Sun.*

Hilfy Chanur was Pyanfar's niece. She was one of the crew that had fought at Anuurn. She was one of the ones that had changed the world. She wouldn't do what wasn't fair. She wouldn't judge him without giving him a chance. She wouldn't just put him off somewhere, or send him home.

He would rather die than go home. Not after . . . after all he'd learned, and worked for, and seen existing just outside his reach.

Granted he hadn't fitted in. The crew of the *Sun* had accepted him, slowly—well, they were on the way to accepting him. He tried to outlast their opinions, and they were almost, sort of beginning to take him for granted once they'd gotten used to the idea of having a male aboard. He'd gotten them to show him things, he'd done the best he could, he'd studied everything he could get his hands on, and he'd been getting better, in spite of the growth spurt he'd put on.

He hadn't lost his temper. They'd played jokes on him, but that was just to see how he would react, it was just because he was there and he was different, and he'd proved he could take it. He'd only slipped up the once—

On the docks. Which was bad. That was really bad, and the captain had a right to be mad. But he'd gotten control of himself. He'd not hit anybody else, not even when they arrested him.

Truth was, he'd been scared, not mad. He'd been dreadfully scared. And that feeling was back with him as if it had never left.

The translator was on the fourth from-scratch pass. The legal program was on its second. If this kept up, Hilfy thought, they were going to have to put in an order for another carton of paper. She *hated* the hand-slate. You took notes on it and it just got messier and spread the information you were working with further and further apart. And you couldn't punch marks in it or turn down the corners or take notes on the back.

Paper, she keyed to the Do List. The thick stuff. It massed more but it didn't fold up while one was reading or note-making. And she had done a lot of reading this morning, while the loaders were clanking and thumping away under Fala's and Chihin's supervision. Meanwhile Tarras was tucked down with the datadump from station files, looking for information—who might take the transship cans, who had what for sale and what the futures list and the methane-folk routings looked like.

The party initiating the contract requires of the party accepting the contract that in the event of the activation of Subclause 14 Section 2 the party accepting the contract shall perform according to the provisions of Subclause 14 Section 2, notwithstanding this shall not be construed as negating the requirements of Section 8 parts 3-15, provided that the party receiving the goods be the person stipulated to in Subsection 3 Section 1, and not a Subsequent of said person; if however the party qualified to receive the goods be the Subsequent of said person or Consequent of the Subsequent named in Subsection 3 Section 1, then the conditions set forward in Section 45 may apply.

She had a headache, and sipped gfi and put a purple clip on the side of the paper for *performance* and a blue one for *identity*, took another sip and winced as something hung up in the

Legacy's off-loading system. A new ship had glitches in common with an old one, systems with bugs in them.

One of the bugs was in the out-track, the very simple chain-driven system that should take one of the giant container-cans smoothly from the hydraulic lift to the hydraulic loader-arms. They had tried lasers to find a fault in the line-up, they had tried carbon-coated paper to turn up an imprecision in the teeth, they'd marked the places on the chain that jammed and the places on the wheel that jammed, and no joy. She had preferred the system because it was what *The Pride* used, it was old, it was tested, it was straight-forwardly mechanical, cheap to repair, but that gods-rotted chain was going to break and kill somebody someday. Every time it jammed like that she flinched.

A small problem, the outfitter swore. Easy to fix. Just pinpoint the problem, and we'll make it right.

The loader started up again. So nobody was killed. Hope it wasn't the mahen porcelain they were hauling. But the chain was intact. She heard it working.

If the party receiving the goods be not the person stipulated to in Subsection 3 Section 1, and have valid claim as demonstrated in Subsection 36 of Section 25, then it shall be the reasonable obligation of the party accepting the contract to ascertain whether the person stipulated to in Subsection 3 Section 1 shall exist in Subsequent or in Consequent or in Postconsequent, however this clause shall in no wise be deemed to invalidate the claim of the person stipulated to in Subsection 3 Section 1 or 2, or in any clause thereunto appended, except if it shall be determined by the party accepting the contract to pertain to a person or Subsequent or Consequent identified and stipulated by the provisions of Section 5 . . .

However the provisions of Section 5 may be delegated by the party issuing the contract, following the stipulations of Subsection 12 of Section 5 in regard to the performance of the person accepting the contract, not obviating the requirements of performance of the person accepting the contract . . .

Another sip of gfi. A chase through the stack of paper after subsection 12 of Section 5. She could Search it on the computer but that meant moving the output stacks, the notes, the reference manuals and the microcube case that was sitting in front of the screen.

Somewhere in Library there was a reference work on Subsequents, at least as far as mahendo'sat understood stsho personality changes. She would have the computer look it up. When she found the monitor screen.

She took another sip of gfi.

The Rows were the open market at Meetpoint—anything you wanted, you had a chance of finding scattered on the tables of a hundred and more smalltime merchants, stsho and mahendo'sat . . . stsho and mahen hucksters shoving things into your attention and claiming miraculous potency for unregulated vitamins and curious effects for legal and peculiar compounds, offering second-hand clothes and trinkets, carvings by bored spacers and erotic items peculiar to mahendo'sat and curious to everyone else.

But to a hani in a hurry, with specific measurements and business already in the hands of a mahen tailor in a real established Rows shop, with a pressure-door and every indication of permanency and respectability, the glitter and gaud and traffic of the market were an obstacle—and Tiar tried to make time against it.

Though an honest hani watching her waistline *could* get distracted here, because among the glitter of cheap jewelry and real gold, the echoes of argument and the twittering of doomed kifish delicacies—came the smell of baked goods and spice; mahen pastries. And a number of worldbound hani might turn up their noses at sweets, but she was cosmopolitan in taste: truth was, there was a good deal about mahen sweets she found to like.

And maybe the kid did. And certainly Tarras had the habit.

Well, maybe a dozen. The captain liked some sweets. Fala might. Chihin favored salted things. She could manage that.

And if they were in a mortal hurry and did not get back to

the market on this rare stop at Meetpoint (she had asked the tailor to deliver, at soonest) . . . she could take a small detour.

She bought two dozen of the sweets. And decided, well, there were the fish done up in salt crystals, a crate of those, deliver immediately. And the smoked ones. Practical, and a welcome change in the menu aboard. The stsho merchant offered samples, and, well, a box of those. And there was the herb and spice section, right adjacent, where a hani could inhale her way along, collect a bottle or two—she did no small bit of the cooking, and she felt inspired, here.

Then she thought, with her arm considerably weighted with parcels, well, the poor kid had come aboard with nothing in hand. He could use a few toiletries—such things as a young man might like. Brushes, yes. A couple of combs. A mild cologne, something clean and pleasant.

A pair of scissors. A file—it was absolute hell to be without that, and have a claw that snagged. Toothbrush. Of course. Creme for hands and feet—Meetpoint air was dry by hani standards, and he had been in it for days. A good conditioner for all over, while she was at it, not spicy, something like sweet grass. Any young man would like that.

A kit-case to hold it all. Second-hand, with real silver ornament. Never mind the inscription was in mahen script, and probably some love sentiment, it was a nice piece and if nobody but mahendo'sat could read it, who cared?

"Hani officer. A word?"

She looked around, at a brown mahen belly; and up, quite a distance up, at a sober mahen face.

"*Legacy?*" the mahe said, laying a hand on his chest. "Friend to Chanur, I, long time, follow the Personage."

Gods, another one.

"Look . . ." Tiar shifted the packages in her arms and suddenly realized she was far along the Rows, she had spent longer than she intended collecting her odd items, and a mahendo'sat with religious enlightenment or a crackpot scheme either one was not going to get her home any sooner.

"I know, I know, too many come you ship talk crazy. Not

me." A hand larger than her head applied itself to approximately a mahen heart. "*Good* friend, name Tahaisimandi Ana-Kehnandian, ship name *Ha'domaren,* dock right down there–"

"I'm late. Cap'n's going to skin me as is. Send a message."

"No, no." Said mahen hand landed on her arm, and it was drop the packages or listen. As a third alternative, she laid back her ears and stared up at the owner of said hand, who protested, "Important you listen."

"Important I get back, mahe."

"Call me Haisi."

"Haisi. Get the hand off or I'll give it to you on a plate."

"Very serious! Listen. What you name?"

"Never mind my name! You got a message for the Personage, save it for her! My captain's got her own troubles!"

"You take stsho deal?"

She shouldn't have reacted. But she had, she did, and she stood staring at the mahendo'sat.

"Where'd you hear that?"

"Got ears."

"Got ears. Great. You want a word with the captain? I'll *get* you a word with the captain, you just go right down to berth 23 and use the com, like any civilized individual."

"What you name?"

"Tiar Chanur."

"Ah! *Chanur* officer!"

"Chanur officer, gods-rotted right, Chanur officer! You want to *stay* friends with the Personage, you get down to 23 and say what you've got to say–"

"I carry package for you."

"I'm doing fine! Get! Don't walk with me! We got enough gossip!"

"You lot worry, Chanur officer. All fine. Name Haisi. *Respectable,* long-time come and go this station."

"Get!" She aimed a kick. Haisi escaped it. But Haisi went.

* * *

"So where did you hear about this deal?" Hilfy asked, as the mahe sipped expensive tea and lounged in her shipboard office, foot propped. "*When* did you hear it?"

"What deal you want know?" A large mahen hand balanced a tiny cup, and the mahe regarded it closely. "Nice porc'lain. Tiyleyn province, a? You got good taste."

"What do you want?"

"You so ab-rupt. So ab-rupt. How you deal with stsho?"

"I don't think you know anything. I swear to you, if you've talked your way onto my ship for some gods-rotted sales pitch, you can take yourself right out—"

Hand on throat. "You insult me?"

"I'm too busy to insult you! I have a ship to turn around, I have cargo all over my dockside because I can't get enough gods-rotted transports! If you know something, spill it!"

The mahe leaped to his feet. "I leave! I don't sit be insult!"

He might be serious. She regretted that, just long enough for him to reach the door and look back.

"You stupid hani let me walk out."

"I stupid hani let you sell me some damn deal! All right, all right, sit down, have another cup of tea."

"You say nice."

Rubbing salt on it. She pursed her mouth in pleasantness, pricked up her ears and made a gracious gesture toward the abandoned chair. "Do sit down, Ana-kehnandian."

"Nice." The mahe, gods rot his hide, sauntered over to the chair and sat down again, leaned far back and crossed his foot over his knee. "Nice you ship, hani captain."

"What deal?"

"You so sudden. I like more tea."

"Sorry. My entire staff of servants jumped ship at Hoas. The pot's right beside you."

A mahen grin. Only humans and mahendo'sat did that. It was life-threatening on a hani ship. And Tahaisimandi Ana-kehnandian took his time.

"So," Ana-kehnandian said, with a sip and a sigh. "You want know how I know?"

"I want to know *what* you know."

"You got fat deal, stsho with stsho. No'shto-shti-stlen got kif work for him. Same Urtur stsho. Lot big thing with kif. You tell Personage she need take quick look."

"Easy to propose. Not so easy to do. Why should the Personage be interested?"

"What word *hotai?*"

"Bomb. Explosion."

"Explos'. Damn right. Explos' like hell. I tell you, make good deal with you, you let us look this cargo."

She had felt a skip in her pulse from the instant the word *kif* came into the conversation. And this mahe was probing for information, playing a little information as if he was in it up to his ears. Let him look at this cargo indeed.

"Where did you learn about it, Ana-kehnandian?"

"Call me Haisi. We friend."

"Haisi. Where did you learn about it?"

"Cousin on Urtur."

"So this isn't exactly unexpected."

"No. Long time expect."

"Tell me."

"You let me see cargo."

No spacer. Not any merchant captain, if he was a captain, which she suspected: *Ha'domaren,* Tiar said. And that fit: top of the line ship, fire-power concealed by panels, capable of dumping cargo and moving fast, with all the engine capacity of a freight-hauler. She'd seen mahen agents operate when she was with *The Pride,* and she folded her hands now easily on her middle, assuming a studied relaxation.

"Which Personage are you working for? Not my aunt. She'd not be so coy about it. And if you aren't working for my aunt, why should I let you look at anything?"

"You assume lot."

She pursed her mouth into a smile. "Gods-rotted right I do. Who *are* you working for, and is it anyone I should trust?"

"Absolute." Give him credit, cornered, presented with the

case, he shifted directions. Which meant he had some authority from someone.

"Name?"

"Paehisna-ma-to."

Didn't tell her a thing. And if the mahe had good research on aunt Py's clan, he might know she had a slight sore spot about kif in general. So tell her the kif were interested.

But if the mahendo'sat were interested, and kif got wind of it, they would be sniffing around the situation. It was their nature. Like breathing.

"So who is Paehisna-ma-to?"

"Wise woman."

"I'm glad. Tell her Hilfy Chanur keeps her contracts. Tell her if there's anything untoward about this contract, her representative should tell me before I sign the thing."

"You not sign yet?"

"Maybe I have, maybe I haven't."

"Don't do!"

"Maybe will, maybe won't. Right now I'm busy. No more time. Unless there's something else I should hear."

"My ship *Ha'domaren.* You want talk, you send. Don't call on station com."

"I gathered that." She stood up and walked the mahe to the door and down the corridor toward the hatch, her crew being otherwise occupied—listening, and armed with a stranger on board, but occupied. "You give my regards to your wise woman."

"Will," the mahe said, and bowed, and strolled off down the corridor to their airlock.

She stood there until she heard the lock cycle.

"Is he gone?" she asked the empty air.

"*Down the ramp,*" Tiar said via com from the bridge. "*Watching him all the way.* Sorry *about that, captain. I thought you'd better have a face to face.*"

"No question," she said, and stared at nothing in particular, thinking how the most secret plans couldn't remain a secret once anybody talked to anybody at all. Suspect anyone. The aide, the kifish guards, most especially them. Stsho refused, since the war, to take their ships out of stsho space, or to trade anywhere with the younger species, except only at Meetpoint. But there was a stsho ambassadorial presence on Urtur. There was a stsho presence even at Mkks nowadays. There would be one at Anuurn, if the *han* would permit it, but the *han* let no one in, secretive and protective of the homeworld, with recent reason.

Certainly whatever was going on between No'shto-shti-stlen and the stsho supposed to receive this whatever-it-was at Urtur had attracted someone's attention, or leaked at one end of the deal or the other.

Point: Haisi was here. He had come here from elsewhere at sometime—and Urtur was as good as anywhere. While chance and taking advantage of a local leak of information might have brought him to their ship, it was just as possible he was telling part of the truth—and he had known it and come here knowing it.

Which meant others might.

They were offloading canisters as fast as the *Legacy* could cycle them out; and by tomorrow they had to be taking others aboard. They had to know as early as next morning whether they were going to pass over the Hoas cans and let another ship take the Hoas load. And that meant making a decision . . . that meant signing or not signing.

That meant solvency after this trip . . . or *still* being involved in the deal even if they turned it down, dammit, because being Pyanfar's niece, if she took the stsho object aboard, it said one thing; and if she refused, and it was some crazy stsho religious thing that brought down a friendly governor at Meetpoint—that was disaster.

For once she wished she *could* ask Pyanfar.

But if leaks were happening, they would proliferate. If the mahe agent knew, his crew knew something; if his crew knew something, it could get to the docks; if the kifish guard knew, the kif they might be in collusion with knew; and if things had gone out over station com, then the com operators in station control might know, and so might their associates. . . .

In which case if she didn't sign it and didn't take the deal, and left here for Hoas, there were die-hards who would never believe they hadn't the object aboard, and that it wasn't all a ruse. So the minute one Haisi Ana-whatever knew anything about it—they were tagged with the stsho deal and the stsho object whether or not they actually had it.

At least if they signed the deal and took it, they got paid.

"Who we got to take the Hoas stuff?" she asked on com, when she got back to her office.

"We taking the deal, captain?" Chihin asked.

"Looks as if. Who do we have?"

"Mahen trader. *Notaiji.* Just in, reputable ship. Regular runs to Hoas. Plenty of time to make the schedule and looking for a load. They don't usually bid, just take what's going and ship when they're full—but this is up to their cap. Good deal for them."

She considered that an unhappy moment and two. Of course a mahen ship was all there was. Where was another hani ship, when a little obfuscation might have served them?

"There are kif outbound. And a t'ca may be. But I didn't consider them as options."

"No," she said. Almost she had rather the t'ca. But getting the address and the disposition of cargo straight with a matrix brain was an exercise in frustration.

And it might send the cans to O'o'o'ai, for all any of them could tell. It didn't bother a t'ca shipper, so far as anyone could figure out their economics. But it played hell with one's reputation with oxy-breathers.

Chapter Three

The kid *hadn't* had breakfast. He attacked the meat and eggs like a starveling, between trying to appreciate the kit, and the personal items.

"Thought you could use them," Tiar said, standing by the door, and due to be on other duties. But Hallan Meras was alternately shoving food in his mouth and opening packages. She had brought in nothing contraband, so far as she could figure, nothing he shouldn't be let loose with. The captain hadn't said anything about any restrictions, or given any impression she feared the kid would sabotage them. The captain hadn't thought overmuch about the kid, by what Tiar could tell, not delegated anybody to get him breakfast, even if the captain had remembered about the torn trousers and sent her off to the market to do something about his wardrobe. Small wonder—but still . . . where the kid sat, it hadn't been a good morning.

"Everybody thought you were still asleep," she said, by way of apology.

"I got up to work," he said, and swallowed a hasty mouthful, looking at the silver-trimmed box. "It's beautiful. What kind of writing is it?"

"Mahend. Formal. Probably lost in some dice game. Maybe

in a mahen bar. Then down to the Rows. Somebody needed cash. Anything you want, you can find it in that market, that's what they claim anyway. Anything you ever lose—ends up here eventually."

"I got to see it," the kid said.

"Got to see it, huh?"

Hallan's ears dropped by half. "That's where I got in trouble."

"Swung on somebody, what I hear."

"I didn't intend to!"

"Yeah. The police probably hear that one a lot here."

"I didn't! *Ker* Tiar, . . . I wasn't drunk. They said I was drunk, but I wasn't. Somebody just started swinging, I don't even know who."

She found herself disposed to believe the boy—at least that he believed what he was saying; many the hani novice that had lost count of the cups. She could recall such a time. Or two.

"I want to work," the boy said. "I do. I have my license. I used to fix the farm equipment. . . ."

"That's not exactly qualification."

". . . before I shipped on the *Sun.* I mean I learned mechanics. I can run the loaders, I can do anything with cargo. . . ."

"Not that we can't use a hand, but part of the deal with the stsho was getting you off and out of here. I don't think the captain wants you on the docks attracting attention."

The kid's countenance fell, his shoulders slumped. More than disappointment. It was a need of something, there was no time, and Tiar told herself she was a fool for asking.

"Upset you. Didn't mean to. How?"

The kid shook his head. Interest in breakfast and the packages seemed gone. He didn't seem articulate at the moment, so rather than embarrass him she answered her question with a question.

"You want *out* there for some reason? Kid, it's romantic, but it's hardly worth your neck. There'll be other places."

He gave her a hurt look. So it touched on the nerve but didn't quite press it.

"Somebody you want to meet out there?"

Shake of his head, no.

"Something you want to find out there?"

Another shake of his head. Further and further from the sore point.

"You want to talk to me, kid?"

Third shake of his head, and a stare at the wall.

She never was able to walk away from a problem. She stood there, set hands on hips and looked at him a long, long time, figuring he'd collect himself.

"I want to work," he said finally, without looking at her. "I'll do anything."

"I hate to bring this up," she said, with the feeling she still hadn't heard what she was after, and might not, now. They had circled somewhere away from the substance. "But you know we're sort of ancestral enemies."

"Not with Meras!"

"But with Sahern."

"I know," the kid said faintly.

"Hey, it's not as if it's active. A couple hundred years since. We've got no present grudge. We'll get you back to your ship. We can be real civil to them, just let you off and wish them well. If we can't do that, we'll drop you at some station where they're due."

"How could I live? And I don't *want* to go back to them!"

It was a question, how they were going to install a hani male on anybody's quiet space station. Never mind he was a quiet, mannerly kid, the reputation of hani males for violence was well-established and the fear was there. And if anything did happen . . .

"Well, we'll think of something. Don't worry about it."

He did worry. He looked at her as if he faced an execution. Then looked down and shoved his breakfast around the plate.

They'd locked the door on him. They hadn't been certain of his disposition to stay put, or to take orders. They hadn't been certain his sojourn in the station brig hadn't been justified and they still didn't know that.

But she had some judgment of the situation. And the captain might have her hide, but . . .

"What's your skill entail, son? Your license says tech. You do anything else?"

"Cargo. Maintenance. Galley. —I want to stay with Chanur."

Stay with Chanur. An unrelated male. Nobody's husband. —Same mess he'd been in on the Sahern ship, to tell the embarrassing truth, and she wasn't going to ask. Young kid like that, too anxious and too gullible, who knew *what* his skills had entailed?

"I can *prove* I know what I'm doing," he said.

"I haven't said you didn't know what you were doing. I'm sure you do."

"Then let me work!"

Plain as plain, his hope to impress hell out of them, to prove himself in some dazzling display and have the whole crew beg him to stay. And who wouldn't rather a Chanur ship than Sahern? Perfectly reasonable choice. Perfectly engaging kid. She'd had two sons—had cursed bad luck, that way. They were probably dead. She hadn't stayed planetside long enough to make it worse than it was. Had had them, one and the other, but the disappointment was there from the time the tests had shown they were male. Lot of women wouldn't have carried them. She didn't know why she had, tell the truth, but she was old-fashioned, and she had problems about *that.* Had regretted it for years. And here came this kid, about the age of her younger boy, in space, trying to overcome what Pyanfar Chanur and a lot of her own generation called stupid prejudice, and what a whole string of other generations from time out of mind called nature.

She wasn't sure where she stood on that. If Pyanfar was right her boys had gone out in the outback and died for nothing.

If Pyanfar was right—it still made problems. Because the kid was unattached, he had a face you wouldn't forget, particularly when he looked at you like that and stirred feelings that weren't maternal at all. She tried to think about her own boys, telling herself it was Pyanfar's new age and she was not supposed to think thoughts like that about lost, scared kids some clan had let stray out of a cloistered life to deal with people who hadn't had to exercise their moral restraint in a long, long time.

"Tell you what," she said, because she *was* ashamed of herself, "we got some mop-up to do, and if that fits your notion of work . . ."

"Anything that needs doing."

"You finish that breakfast. Door's unlocked, I'm right down the corridor, in the operations center. We're calc'ing trim and we're going to be taking on a fuel load. Sound familiar?"

"I can learn." The animation that had left his face was back, his eyes were bright, his whole being was full of anxious energy. He looked strung tight, probably so scared he hadn't been eating, scared now, too, of the word no.

"Eat your breakfast. Take a right and a left as you leave the room. You'll know it when you see it."

"Back again," the kifish guards observed.

Hilfy had no comment for them, except, "I'm here to see *gtst* excellency."

"Of course, of course, fine hani captain. This *way,* hani captain. We would never give offense to the great—"

"Shut up," she said. And regretted losing her temper that far. But she had a bad feeling all the way to the audience hall.

"Tlsti nai," the secretary said, with a lifting of augmented, plumed eyebrows. It might not be the same secretary. The pastel body paint looked subtly different. But it was hard to tell. *Gtst* gathered the contract and the requisite gift into *gtst* long fingers and performed three increasingly deep bows.

"Tlistai na," Hilfy said, bowing once. "I send it by your undoubtedly capable hands. There is no need to disturb the excellency."

"So gracious. Bide a small moment, most honorable."

She bided. She felt her stomach upset—felt an insane and

thoroughly impractical urge to charge after the secretary and retrieve the contract before *gtst* passed the curtains.

But the deed was done. She thought after a moment that she might successfully escape back to the ship, but in that moment the secretary returned through the curtain to wave at her and to beckon her to come ahead. No'shto-shti-stlen wanted to see her, perhaps to hand the object into her keeping on the spot, for all she knew; and she was not eager to have the responsibility crossing the docks. An order to move the bank to action, on the other hand . . .

She had far rather the million on credit in her account, because there were cargo cans irrevocably destined for the *Legacy*'s empty hold; while the Hoas cans, already on their carriers, were scheduled for *Notaiji*, a very happy, very grateful *Notaiji*, who could not quite believe the good fortune that had landed in their laps, from 'the good, the great hani captain.'

So they had stepped over the brink. Figuratively speaking. As she walked into the audience hall.

"We are exceedingly pleased," said No'shto-shti-stlen as she seated herself.

"We have concurred with your excellency. We are pleased at our agreement on the contract and look forward to continued association with your illustrious self."

"Your response is gracious. The elegance of your utterances and your circumspect behavior is a credit to your species."

Then why are you back to using kifish guards? occurred to her, but stsho had rather elegance than truth.

"I am honored by your confidence," she murmured instead; and bowed; No'shto-shti-stlen bowed, everybody bowed again, and No'shto-shti-stlen inquired whether she had time to take tea.

Two teas was a monumental sign of favor.

"Of course," she said, with lading piled all about the *Legacy*'s cargo bay, with transports in scarce supply, thanks to the Hoas load, with a mahendo'sat scoundrel and probable agent of some power swearing to her that the contract was a supremely bad deal, and offering, of course, his services.

A tea in full formality, in the audience hall, in the bowl chairs, with stsho servants this time, and No'shto-shti-stlen reciting poetry:

White on white.
The distinctions thereof are infinite.
Upon white snow the eyes dream in pink and gold and blue.
Nothing is.
Everything might be.

Or something of the sort—in classical mode. Hilfy sipped tea and pricked up her ears and laid them flat in deference when it was done.

"Extraordinary view of a delicate perception," she said. "How extraordinary to be afforded such an honor. Are you the poet, excellency?"

No'shto-shti-stlen positively glowed . . . for a stsho. Painted lids fluttered over moonstone eyes and long fingers made wave patterns. "I have that small distinction."

"I am touched to the heart by such an honor. Would it be indelicate to ask your excellency for a copy?"

"Not in the least!" Fingers ripped at the aide, who fluttered off in a cloud of gossamer drape and nodding plumes. "You inspire me to thought. And . . ." No'shto-shti-stlen produced the gift box from among *gtst* gossamer robes, and delicately lifted the lid, on a little item she had brought from Anuurn—from Haorai, a carved alabaster box, and within it a single carved *ua* stone ball. And within that—another ball and another and another.

No'shto-shti-stlen opened it; and *gtst* crest flattened and lifted.

"An *oji* of sorts. The ball and box have passed hand to hand for a hundred sixty-three years since it left the artist, of Tausa, in Haor, in Sfaura's eastern sept, on Anuurn. There's a small card that traces its provenance, if your excellency finds it of interest."

"Extraordinary!"

"Each is unique. One bestows the stone on ceremonial occasions. This stone came into the hands of Chanur and thus into mine as clan head—a Sfaura clan object, as the design indicates. Luran Sfaura had it made for her fifteenth birthday celebration; and it passed at her decease to her daughter, and so down to the end of that line in Haor; thus to Sfaura's western sept, part of the unsecured gifts—the explanation is on the card—which has gone back and forth between Sfaura and its tributaries at weddings, oh, a hundred years before it came to me, as a birthday gift from my prospective husband." It was white and it had a history, which she had written up in florid and dramatic detail. It had last been her late husband's, and such historical trinkets impressed the stsho.

Clearly No'shto-shti-stlen was pleased. The creature bowed numerous times where *gtst* sat. Hilfy felt constrained to bow.

And there was, necessarily, yet another round of tea, after which she bade farewell for the second time, and walked out with the kifish guards and out into the foyer and took the lift down to the docks.

Feeling rather pleased with herself, truth be known. She had scored with that gift. She knew the stsho, in a way most hani did not. The governor had given her something monetarily valuable and ceremonially valuable in the cases of tea. But she had given *gtst* something ceremonially and personally and *historically* valuable—so there, she thought, walking out onto the dockside. So there. Remember *me,* stsho, remember *me* and my crew.

She was in such a good mood she decided against taking the public transport. It wasn't that far, down to the *Legacy*'s berth. She was still in a good mood when she threaded her way through the maze of loaders and cargo transports to reach the *Legacy*'s personnel access. She walked on up the rampway into the yellow, uncertain tube, with its coating of frost, and she walked into the *Legacy*'s lower decks and operations area in an expansive, happy mood, after what she had had to do. She had at least an assurance it was going to work.

Then she put her head into ops and saw Hallan Meras.

"What in hell is he doing here?"

"Captain," Meras said, standing up at once.

"Not bad, actually," Tiar said; and Chihin, managing the number two console, said, "Begging the captain's pardon."

"Get him back to his quarters!"

"Aye," Tiar said. "But he is a licensed spacer. And we are short-handed."

She was not in a mood for reason. Disasters were still possible. "He's not been out on the docks, has he?"

"No, captain," Hallan said at once, and got up from the chair he was occupying, very respectful.

Which made her the villain in the case.

"Gods rot it, he's not crew! He goes back to quarters!"

"Aye," Tiar said. "But he's a help, captain."

"Not right now!" she said. Gods, they had outside messengers likely coming aboard. They didn't need Hallan Meras underfoot. Even with that soulful look in his eyes.

"Captain," he said.

"Don't 'captain' me! You're a passenger on this ship. Chihin, take him back where he belongs."

"I—" he was still saying.

"Kid's done all right," Tiar muttered, as Chihin took him by the arm and drew him out the door. "He's not had a good day, cap'n, go easy."

"He's not had a good day. We're going with the number 1 load. Skip the alternates. Berths full of kif. Snooping police. I want the gods-rotted deck clear out there, I want the fueling done—we've got three loads coming in tonight and we're going to be working straight through the watch!" She was on nervous overload, on her own way to the door. "I'm going to run the nav-calc, I want it checked and triple checked—we're hurrying, if you haven't noticed. We haven't got time for shopping tours and mahendo'sat with a deal and stray boys who'll be reporting our ship cap to Sahern, next thing we know, keep him the hell out of stations!"

"He doesn't want to go back to Sahern."

She swung around, hand on the door frame, finding herself

in the middle of somebody's completely foreign dealings, that possibly went against her own. "He says. Don't cut him any deals, cousin! You don't know what he did, you don't even know he isn't a total mistake—'Take this poor lost boy,' the stsho say. In the same gods-rotted conversation with their deal—and *I* don't know what connection if any the two have, I don't know why they didn't give this deal to Sahern except their boy was out breaking up the station market, I don't know what connection it has to anything, and maybe it doesn't, but gods rot it! let's not complicate matters. We get to Urtur, he goes off the ship, he waits for whoever he likes, his ship, somebody else's ship, a passing knnn trader, I don't care, but we don't need to activate the feud with Sahern, and we *will* if we keep him—"

"How's he going to live?"

She had not gotten that far. Not at all.

Tiar asked: "What's he going to do? Urtur isn't going to let any male hani aboard. Do we give him to the police to hold till his ship gets there? That's no better than he had."

She hadn't exactly put *that* together either, in her concentration on the contract. "They can't arrest him without cause."

"They'll find one."

"Hell. —There'll be a hani ship there. There always is. . . . Don't make him any promises, don't let him near our boards, don't complicate our lives, d' you hear me? He's going off this ship!"

"Aye," Tiar said, which didn't mean a thing, except Tiar heard her.

"I have to lock the door," Tarras said, looking apologetic, and that was better than had been this morning, at least. Hallan told himself so, and told himself that politeness was obligatory.

Even when he was shaking mad. He kept his ears up and murmured a thank you.

"Ship's just real busy," Tarras said. A smallish hani with a wavy mane that said eastern blood, from the viewpoint of someone from west of the Aon Mountains. Tarras had one ear notched, and a lot of rings that meant a lot of major voyages . . . you only got those when you'd risked your neck on a trip. Which meant Tarras for all her slight size was a person to respect. "Captain's a little quick-fused just now. We'll sort it out with her."

"I appreciate that," he said, and tried to quit shivering and most of all not to have Tarras see that he was. Women were allowed to have a temper. If he did, he was unreliable and a danger to everyone around him. "I'm not Sahern. I'm not related to them. Even by marriage."

"Wouldn't matter. Captain took you aboard. She would have if you'd been Sahern head of clan. So would we. *Don't* try to talk against Sahern. You won't impress us."

"I'm not!" Gods, everything got twisted. "I never said that. I never said anything against them."

Tarras just looked at him a moment, making him wonder if she believed him.

"How'd you get arrested?" Tarras asked. "The straight story."

He wondered how much *was* in whatever report they had gotten from the kif. "I was fighting."

"That's nothing new. Doesn't always get you arrested. What was the fight about?"

"Me. Being there. In this bar."

Surely she could get the idea. Maybe she had. He didn't want to volunteer more details and he hoped she wouldn't ask. He didn't want to remember them.

"Captain wouldn't leave you in any foreign jail," Tarras said. "She's pretty brusque sometimes. But you being here was her idea. Wouldn't leave anybody where you were. You copy that?"

He had, already. He wasn't willing to think badly about Hilfy Chanur. He knew that, being Chanur, she was inclined to believe he had a right to be here. Chanur was the clan that stood up for his right to be here. Only, even in Chanur, the attitudes weren't universal, the change hadn't changed every mind; and he was used to that. He had to be used to that. Things as they were gave him no better choice and no court of appeal.

He said, while Tarras was there to listen, "I'd not do anything against Chanur. Ever. Tell the captain that."

Tarras didn't say a thing, just shut the door. And locked it.

Pumps were thumping away, pouring water and other liquids into the *Legacy*'s reservoirs. Fueling was in progress. Tiar slid a cup under Hilfy's inert, poised hand. And reaching the fingers after it seemed a move too much. Hilfy extended a claw, snagged the handle, and dragged it into her weary hand.

"We made it," Tarras said, dropping her bulk into a chair, gfi in hand. "Every gods-blessed one of those babies."

"Course comped," Tiar said.

"Got to be the one that makes it. Pay the ship off and go into the profit column."

"Somebody feed the kid this time?"

"Fala's seeing to it."

"What's our launch, cap'n, we ever get 'im clear?"

"First watch, topside. We take her through, we get our rest at Urtur."

"Gods, that's brutal."

"Mahendo'sat sniffing around us, this hardship case turns up and No'shto-shti-stlen just happens to want him out of here. I don't like it. I don't like it and I wish I hadn't agreed to take him on."

Tiar's ears flattened. "What do you think, he's some deal of No'shto-shti-stlen's?"

"I think the old son knows more about why he's here than *gtst* is saying. I'm not doubting *gtst* wants him off this station: the stsho don't want trouble and he's trouble. I don't know whose, that's the problem. I don't know who's behind him."

"There are coincidences, captain."

"They become increasingly less when the mahendo'sat show up with deals. *That's* what I don't like. 'Let us look at it!' That bastard's on someone's payroll."

"Not *ker* Py's."

It was a thought that had occurred to her. "If he was hers, why not say so?"

"Good question," Tiar said. "But I don't think the boy's involved. It's perfectly understandable."

"What? Leaving him in the brig?"

"Understandable that he doesn't *like* Sahern clan."

"That's what he says. Sahern is *not* our friend. Other interests aren't our friends, for my aunt's sake, for reasons that have to do with decisions she's made that affect things we have no way to know about. We don't know who could have hired her, we don't know who could have hired him, we don't know what side this Haisi person is on, we don't even know that No'shto-shti-stlen's on the up and up or what *gtst* is up *to*. The news got to Urtur and this Haisi person had a chance to get here and offer us a bribe for a look at the object. So why hadn't the news the time to get to Sahern clan, and maybe Sahern lay out some game that would inconvenience us? Ha?"

"Why would No'shto-shti-stlen give you the boy?"

"Because hani aren't as frequent here as they used to be. Because if *gtst* has had a political object dumped in *gtst* lap, No'shto-shti-stlen is going to want rid of it in the way most guaranteed to absolve *gtst* of responsibility. *Gtst* couldn't dump him on aunt Py, *gtst* couldn't return him to Sahern, and here we come, Pyanfar's close relatives, just so convenient to hand him to . . . I don't know that's the case, but thinking about it is going to cost me sleep, this trip, it's going to make me uncomfortable until he's off our deck and out of our lives, and I *don't* want him loose gathering data at our boards, hear me?"

"Let me understand—you think Sahern *planted* him here?"

"I think it's a possibility. Maybe to create an embarrassment, maybe it's something else. I think it's a possibility there's something more to him than he's showing us . . ."

"Captain, he's a kid!"

"I don't like where he was, I don't like anybody dropped into a kif-run jail and I don't like Sahern dragging him clear to this pit on the backside of the universe to drop him, where, if they wanted rid of him, they could at *least* have dropped him at Urtur. It smells to me like a captain with a god-complex, but I don't swear that's the case; there are all the other possibilities, some of which aren't pretty and aren't conducive to good sleep, but that's the way I see it, that's the way I know how to call it, and that's the only way I know to keep this ship out of trouble. We've got enough problems going, let's not take any additional chances, shall we?"

"Trouble?" Fala asked from the doorway to the little galley.

"No trouble. I trust you locked that door."

"I locked it. I don't see, begging the captain's pardon, why he's—"

Hilfy leaned her forehead on her hand.

"Tell you later," Tarras said.

"We're in count," Hilfy said, leaning back and looking at the clock. "Load's got to be finished by 2300. Gods, I want out of this port."

"Have we got a problem?" Fala asked. Something ticked over, like a piece in a game falling. A roll of the dice. "I want an instrument scan."

"What?" Tiar asked.

"I want a thorough read-out, I want a camera scan on the hull, I want to know if any skimmers have approached us during our stay here."

A solemn stare from several pairs of eyes.

"Is something going on?" Fala asked.

The camera scan turned up negative. Nothing had approached their hull. Station skimmers always came and went, on such business as external inspections, catching the occasional chunk of something that escaped a ship's maintenance systems, things nobody wanted slamming into their hull or catching on some projection, to be accelerated with the ship and boosted to lethal *v*. Trouble was, such skimmers had legitimate business back by one's vanes and engines and up near one's hatches; and if a ship with legitimate reason to worry didn't have cameras to prove where such little tenders had access, that ship had far more reason to worry.

But being the Personage's niece had convinced her before the *Legacy* was outfitted that the camera-mounts were a good idea and that motion-sensors and tamper-alerts were mandatory. So they didn't have *that* to worry about—at least so far as they opted prudently to use them.

There wasn't, of course, a way to monitor everything. But they were sure it was water that had gone into their waterlines and that that water was Meetpoint ice-melt, the sensors above the valve had proved it or that valve would have shut. *Being* Pyanfar's niece and having shipped aboard *The Pride*, she had been in ports where one had good reason to wonder about the lines; absolutely right, being sure was worth the cost.

Unfortunately having solved all the high-tech means of sabotage, one still had to worry about the low-tech means at an enemy's disposal. Certain things one could solve by carrying all supplies aboard, and by not refueling and not taking on water at certain ports: but carrying extra mass cost a ship, if one wasn't paying somebody else's freight plus station-cost getting it to the station. If it was local, you were financially ahead to buy it. If it wasn't, and it massed much, you were ahead to freight it, and that was the sum-up and pay-out of it: if you operated otherwise you weren't competitive, in a tightly competitive market.

But even if you did all of that, and even if you absorbed the cost of being as self-contained as possible, you were still vulnerable to your own cargo and to the legal claim of your ship to use a port and the station's legal right to charge you for being there, and, after that was said, to a bank's obligation to honor the claim of other banks on the funds you had in that all-important record you carried that the bank alone allegedly could access.

But banks themselves were not without their compromised accesses, where stsho were concerned, since stsho had set up the banking system, all through Compact space: stsho technology, stsho procedures, stsho rules of accounting and the stsho system of transfers and debits.

Hilfy Chanur preferred an old hani tradition: cash . . . and cargo; and as little as possible of the former, since it was not going to be drawing interest for the month you were in transit, but your goods were acquiring value during that transit, simply by moving closer to where they were in shortest supply.

Which left you vulnerable to piracy, but you always were; and at least that answer was in your own hands, and in the quality of the armament you carried and your skill to use it.

The hose connections clanked free, and that was one less problem on Hilfy's mind. The *Legacy* was on its own power, cargo in its hold, and the cash from the station bank was on its way . . . hand-carried, the bank insisted, since the bank did not trust any outsider either, and wanted a signature *at* the *Legacy*'s lock *by* the *Legacy* captain that said the money had transferred, all outstanding debts were paid, and the bank was legally absolved of claims against Chanur clan.

And at the same time, they were conveying the Cargo, the *oji*, No'shto-shti-stlen's precious object, along with the funds. Logical enough.

So . . . about time to get one's self down to the lock, looking presentable.

She dusted off her breeches, clawed her mane to be sure no hair was standing on end, and took a wet-fingered swipe at the mustaches and the (cursedly) juvenile beard. Impressions counted, especially with the banks, *which* one could need some dark day. Knees were clean, belt was straight. She picked up Tarras and Tiar for escort, and was still fussing with the beard when they cycled the lock and a blast of chill air from the temperature differential came rushing up the rampway and blew her fur and fluttered the fabric of her silk breeches—

Just as a kifish guard was about to punch the call button outside, within the tube, a scant pace from the *Legacy's* own deck. She did not snarl, did not acknowledge the presence, which she vaguely registered as bowing respectfully in realization of her arrival, she simply focused on the stsho approaching in the frost-coated tube and ignored the dark-robed guards . . . fancy, the stsho were, the group from the bank, with the tablet the nature of which she recognized at a glance, and the group with boxes and cases, in one of which might be—surely was—the precious Object. One could hardly pick out any outline, so extreme were the garments in that lot, a drift of pearlized gossamer, of white fronds and feathers. She bowed, they bowed, her crewwomen bowed, everybody bowed again, even the kif. It was supremely ridiculous.

"Of course the esteemed captain's word would suffice," the banker was constrained to say, in pidgin.

"We can only regret that your honor did not have sufficient time to take tea," she answered, *not* in the pidgin, and augmented eyebrows shot up and the stsho in question clutched the signed tablet against *gtst* heart, or thereabouts, within *gtst* robes.

"Your most esteemed honor is inadequately recompensed in the press of time which requires our most distressing haste. At another moment we would achieve distinction by accepting your honor's offer."

"Your honor has impressed us with outstanding courtesy."

"Allow us however to present the honorable Tlisi-tlas-tin, most esteemed adjunct of *gtst* excellency No'shto-shti-stlen. The excellency has afforded us the most extreme honor of conveying *gtst* adjunct and the preciousness of *gtst* entrusted burden to this ship and into your most capable hands. We are abundantly satisfied of your honor's most excellent character and elegance."

The leader of the second band of stsho came fluttering across the threshold into the airlock, with an engraved case clutched to *gtst* heart—anxious, by the pursing of *gtst* small mouth, and the three increasingly agitated bows.

"We are so inexpressibly relieved, most honored captain, that you speak the civilized language. We have far less anxiousness to entrust ourselves and this preciousness into your ship."

"What's this 'ourselves'?" For an instant all command of stshoshi language deserted her; but Tiar and Tarras hadn't understood a word thus far. Only that. She said it in stsho: "Would your honor clarify the matter regarding one's illustrious self and one's presence on my ship?"

Another bow. "As *gtst* excellency's most honored representative, of course, as guardian of the preciousness which foreign hands must not touch." A wistful curtsy. "I do hope the excellency did not omit the doubtless inconsequential matter of this absolute necessity, and that some provision has been made for my lodging and my meals of sufficient taste and decorousness not to offend my status as the excellency's emissary."

Possibly she did not control her surprise. Certainly her vision suffered that tunnel focus her ancestors used in hunting, and at the same instant the stsho officials and escort backed an identical number of paces—while in the gray fringe of her vision the kif reached for weapons. Consequently so did Tiar and Tarras.

But she did smile, a hani pursing of the mouth, not to show the teeth. And her ears did not flatten, nor her claws extend. Nor did her escort or the kif, fortunately, open fire. She said, sweetly, because they had the contract, and they had a hold full of cargo bought with its proceeds, "How extraordinary the excellency's trust in our ability to adapt to unusual situations. How much baggage do you have?"

Chapter Four

There was an amazing lot of coming and going next door, when Tiar had called down on com maybe an hour ago saying they were going to undock soon. Hallan put his ear to the wall, then backed off as someone began hammering and banging. It sounded as if someone were tearing into the paneling, and maybe taking the whole cabin apart.

That was a peculiar kind of thing to do, on a ship that was supposed to be in count to undock. He began to wonder if they had a malfunction of some kind, and if maybe the access to the conduits or something more critical was there.

But it was certainly an odd place to put an access.

Something had leaked, maybe? The plumbing had given way?

It kept up a very long time. He heard them moving equipment in, he heard thumping and banging and hammering and hissing. He listened again, thinking maybe the whole compartment had flooded. Maybe—

His door opened. A very dusty, contamination-suited Tiar Chanur put her head in and raked her hood back. "Kid?" All of Tiar came in and shed white dust on the floor. He had had his ear to the wall and could find no plausible excuse for himself standing in the corner.

"Captain's compliments and we got a very important passenger right next. She really wants me to impress on you be careful."

He shoved his hands in his pockets. "I understand." He was used to the idea foreigners were afraid of him. Every foreigner he had met was.

"Kind of short on space," Tiar said. "We'd like to sort of move you. Except it's not quite as comfortable. But there's facilities."

"All right," he said, wanting to be accommodating. Really it didn't matter that much. It would be nice to have another set of walls to look at.

"It's kind of—minimal," Tiar said.

"That's fine. —There's nothing to do here. There's nothing to look at. I'd really like some books or something."

"We can get you books," Tiar promised. "I—don't suppose you have to pack."

"This is it. Except the kit."

"The clothes came. We have those. We just haven't had time—"

"That's all right." Anything was all right if it made them happy. And if it proved to the captain that he was obliging and knew how to take orders.

"You want to come with me? We're between coats. I can set you up."

"Sure," he said, and went and got the kit she had given him. When he reached the corridor, Tiar had shed the contamination gear, and there was still a great banging and clattering coming from the closed door of the cabin next door.

"Stsho passenger," Tiar said. "Important deal. Got to change the color, change the sleeping arrangements . . ."

It must be an important passenger, for sure. He followed Tiar past that area, and into the main downside corridor, and to a door there, which Tiar opened.

He truthfully had expected more of a cabin. At least a cot. It did have more to look at. And a blast cushion, with a swing track against the after wall. Otherwise it was a kind of a—

laundry, he supposed. Or bath. There were facilities. That was about all. Bare conduits. Water-pipes. Whatever.

"Gods," Tiar said, and pulled his shoulder down. "Watch your head."

"It's all right." He was used to being tall, on ships built for women.

"There's blankets," Tiar said. She opened the wall locker and there certainly were, the whole ship's supply, it must be. "I'll get you a reader and some tapes. Gods, I'm *sorry* about this."

"It's all right," he said. "It really is."

Tiar stood looking at him, and finally shook her head. "The captain's got a lot on her mind. She honestly does. You don't understand."

"Ker Tiar, I *understand.*"

"Then *I* don't," Tiar snapped. And went and locked him in.

The blast cushion was one of those arrangements that let down and changed angles, according to which axis the ship might move, one of those emergency station affairs that you had to have in every corridor, in case. So he pulled it into level with the deck as was, and got himself a couple of blankets to prop himself with, and one to throw over him, because the thermostat must have only just been reset, and breath frosted. He was not actually uncomfortable once he settled down with the blanket over him. There was more to look at, all the lockers and pipes and such. He could keep his mind busy figuring out all those. He supposed he could warm the compartment up faster by showering, but it might not warm it that much, and he was not sure they were through coming and going in here. So he sat and tried to read the locker labels from here, hearing the thumping still going on that meant they were redoing things for the stsho.

Stsho wouldn't like to meet him at all. People wouldn't, everywhere he went. That was the biggest shock he had had when he got beyond Anuurn's atmosphere, that it was the same Out There as it was at home, that no matter what Pyanfar Chanur said and no matter how you really acted, nobody waited to find out if you were the way they thought, they were just afraid. Even Hilfy Chanur didn't know what to do with him. And he was glad to hear from ker Tiar that things were going on that didn't give the captain time to consider his case. That was reasonable. He could understand that. He really could. It was just so important to him, and he told himself that Hilfy Chanur wouldn't really sweep him aside without listening, he just had to be patient and quiet and prove his case by that. If he was patient and quiet they would notice. If he cooperated they would be appreciative. Ker Tiar had noticed.

But he waited and he waited, and the thumping and the carrying of things down the corridor went on, but Tiar didn't bring the books. She didn't even bring lunch. It would be easy at this point to feel really sorry for himself, but that got no points, either.

Just be patient when you wanted people to notice you. That was what his mother had always told him.

(But she always noticed his sisters, who weren't. She always gave his sisters what they wanted. Which was natural, he supposed. Daughters stayed with the clan, and sons went away and didn't come back unless they were attacking the lord of the clan or stealing something. So it was good advice, the Be Patient thing, because he hadn't attacked his father; and he hadn't come back and stolen the livestock. His sisters had thought enough of him to talk him onto an offworld shuttle, which had led to everything hopeful in his life. He just wished patience got better results in the universe outside. Because nobody had ever taught him any other way to be. Just crazy mad. Or patient.)

The stsho aide put a satin-slippered foot into the newly-paneled room and wiped long fingers on the door frame. This passed. *Gtst* ventured further, onto the newly elevated white decking, to the white bowl-chair sunk into it.

Gtst crest lifted and sank several anxious times and lifted to half. *Gtst* looked all about, turned full circle, making little flutters of *gtst* hands.

"Adequate," *gtst* said in Trade-tongue. "I will inform the honorable."

Whereupon *gtst* retreated from the room and up the corridor, with *gtst* own stsho attendant.

The crew said not a word. Ears were flat. But they had said not a word about the contract.

Neither had Hilfy Chanur. She escorted the stsho out and up to the topside lounge, where the honorable Tlisi-tlas-tin sat sopping up cup after cup of tea and giving orders to Fala, whose ears were valiantly upright.

The stsho conferred, informed *gtst* honor the quarters were adequate, they now dared leave the honorable alone in hani keeping and could assure *gtst* excellency No'shto-shti-stlen that Chanur had taken at least austere care of their charge.

Whereupon the honorable Tlisi-tlas-tin wearily aroused *gtst*self from a chair ill-suited to *gtst* spindly legs, and with a flourish of voluminous gossamer, announced *gtst*self willing to go below with the Preciousness.

Which traveled in that box, apparently, which had its appropriate customs seals as, simply, *oji*, and no *hint* of its shape or nature.

"Honorable," Hilfy said, with, she hoped, an expression as diplomatic as Fala Anify's . . . "may I ask your honor to favor this person whom *gtst* excellency has trusted with your person with a viewing of this most distinguished . . ."

"No!" Tlisi-tlas-tin said. Which might be the most direct sentence she had ever heard from a stsho. *Gtst* gathered up the small box and wrapped it within the gossamer folds of *gtst* robes. *Gtst* gave them collectively and sundry a burning look of *gtst* moonstone eyes. "The Preciousness is not for display."

A practical *and* an academic education in diplomacy did not encourage one to seize *gtst* by *gtst* skinny white throat. Being Pyanfar's niece did; but Hilfy recovered from the fog of anger and her ears were still up and her mouth was still smiling. "Please convey yourself and the Preciousness to your cabin before some incident offends you. My aide will escort your honor to your quarters and show your colleagues to the airlock."

And lock the gods-be cabin door on *gtst* honor afterwards, she thought. The crew was exhausted. They *hadn't* let mahendo'sat workmen do the job, invade their ship, look at their interior, take notes on their systems. Gods-rotted certain they hadn't had kif. And stsho of the *laboring* class didn't exist outside stsho space. So that left themselves—and they had blisters on their hands and panelboard dust up their nostrils, they had broken claws and missing fur, not to mention the captain had dropped a large panel corner on her ankle and taken the hide off.

The captain was not, consequently, in a good humor. The captain was sweaty and ached from head to foot. They were two hours past their scheduled undock, and presented an enigmatic silence to Meetpoint docks, hatches sealed (once the supplies had arrived) hoses uncoupled, com completely silent, their own power plant supplying their needs while they underwent "technical adjustment."

Tarras came up from downside, saying something about the shower downside being occupied, and her having to use the one topside, poor put-upon dear, and Hilfy glared at her, thinking it could be the end of a family friendship if Tarras opened her mouth on the matter of subclauses at the moment.

"Do that," Hilfy said sweetly, with as great a control as she had left. "I've a few things to see to. We've got to recalc our outbounds."

Tarras took the hint. "Want help?"

She thought about it, a second run-through. Thought about particles floating through the filter systems. "Shower first. We *all* will. We'll just give station last-minute notice of our undock." Satisfying notion. "Let *them* do the scrambling. The *oji* has priority. Doesn't it?"

The banging and hammering had stopped. The hatch had cycled. For a long time there was quiet. Hallan decided the ship might be headed for undock, but people tended to forget him.

So he decided it was a good idea to put the blast cushion in order, just in case, and to take a couple of blankets out of the storage lockers, because the heat still had not caught up, and also if they went out very hard or very long, one could want something to stuff in the unsupported spots. They didn't make flight cushions his size either. Or chairs. Or most anything on a ship.

But the ship didn't go, for a long time. He tucked up with his blankets and tried to calculate what he knew about Meetpoint and exactly what *v* they were going to carry if they were loaded full and going, the way the captain had said, to Urtur—which, as he understood, most ships couldn't do without going to Hoas, unless they dumped all their cargo. And they were carrying cargo, he'd heard the loaders, which he was relatively sure sounded inbound. So the *Legacy* must have the engines for it, or they were in a lot of trouble—like lost in hyperspace, forever. Truth be told, he was scared, and a little suspicious that even Tiar had been having a joke at his expense.

If it really was Urtur they wouldn't come in fast or close to the star, because of the dust. Urtur was a dreadfully dirty system, most of it in the disc, but not all of it—

And a pity they couldn't see their own fluorescing trail. Riding on light. Bathed in it. At home, he had had a picture on his wall, a photo someone had caught of a mahen ship coming into Hoas. And he liked to imagine them doing that, every time they made system drop. But you couldn't see it yourself. He had asked about it; and the *Sun's* crew said it was a stupid question. Everybody was busy when you were coming in, and if you ever did see something like that they were too close and you were real busy real fast.

He had ridden through jump himself a lot of times, the last two years in the *Sun Ascendant's* ops center. He thought through all the moves Dru would be making, if he were in ops, if Dru were sitting by him. Dru said he knew what he was doing. Dru was the one who'd gotten him a license, so she could take a break and leave him with the boards, she said—which was undoubtedly true, but she also said he really deserved a license, in a way he could never get the rest of the crew to admit. Yet.

"Hallan?"

Tiar, he thought, on the intercom.

"Yes?"

"Just checking. Are you all right down there?"

"Yes. I'm fine."

"Gods in pink feathers! The books!"

"That's all right."

"No, it isn't. Look. We're about to go into sequence. Are *you all right?"*

"I'm fine, ker Tiar."

On the *Sun,* they didn't use words like Tiar used to him then. He'd never heard them put together that way—and from a very old, very proper clan like Chanur. He didn't understand why she was upset.

But Tiar sent Fala running down the corridor from ops with the nutrients pack he desperately needed for jump and a book, a real, battered, tag-eared book . . . of Compact Trade Regulations.

He was quite touched by that. He really was.

The *Legacy* achieved *v* at a gentle burn. No more energy, in the long haul, to put a push on it—*v* was *v,* and you paid for it, until you ran past your capacity; but the *Legacy* had a stsho aboard, a creature that couldn't take more than 1.5 *g's* without cracking its mostly hollow bones.

Which might be tempting, but they had Tlisi-tlas-tin in charge along with the 'Preciousness,' whatever it was, and the reason doubtless that No'shto-shti-stlen hadn't put the Preciousness aboard a kifish ship was the very well-known habit of kif changing loyalties when unthreatened, unwatched, and seeing a point of advantage.

And likewise for the mahendo'sat—if the Preciousness was in any sense religious, keep it away from mahen hands: the mahendo'sat knew that game too well—and some of them were crazier than others.

The methane-folk? Who knew? The stsho, maybe, knew, who had dealt more with the methane-breathers than anyone. And if the honorable Tlisi-tlas-tin had to go with the Preciousness and the honorable had to breathe oxygen, then maybe that answered that question in a very practical way.

Which left hani—since stsho traders refused to take their own ships beyond Hoas. Stupid hani. Credulous hani. Hani who hadn't been in space until the mahendo'sat (with no one's leave) landed on Anuurn and pitched them from wooden exploration ships into star-faring trade.

For mahen reasons, of course, some of which were sane and some of which were not.

She flipped switches to check working stations, heard Meetpoint's thin voice in her right ear. "Coming up on jump," she was able to declare at last, and opened channel 3 and said in stshoshi trade, "Your honor, kindly take position for jump. We trust you have your medical kit at hand."

Silence.

"Your honor. Kindly advise us if you have done what we request for the preservation of yourself and the Preciousness."

Fry that dimwit!

"Honorable captain?"

"Are you ready, honorable?"

"We are ready."

"Steady, cap'n." From Tiar, at her right elbow. "Murder's not in the contract."

"Don't say that word."

"Hey, we'll be free of it. Shove the Preciousness and *gtst* honor right out the chute and be damned to them."

"Not allowed. Subclause 3."

"They tell you about this Tlisi-tlas-tin character, cap'n?"

"No."

"Didn't think so."

From Tarras: "Do I get to pitch *gtst* out the lock?"

"Negative. Negative. Subclause three point two. No pitching of the Preciousness."

"What *is* this thing? Do you figure?"

"Not a bit. Religious or something. Who knows?"

"That's a blip." From Tarras at scan. "We got somebody away from station."

"Ha'domaren."

"How'd you know that?" Tarras asked.

"How could I not guess? I want a readout on every ship that's left Meetpoint since we've been there."

"No problem. I got it. You want it now or otherside?"

"Any kifish ship?"

"Two kif, one t'ca. All Hoas-bound, last few days."

"That son's going to move. Lay you odds."

"After us?"

"Lay you any money you want that's a mahen agent, for some gods-rotted personage we don't know who, with an empty hold. It's politics, it's politics, it's some one of Pyanfar's rivals . . ."

"Possible," Tiar said.

"It's going to come," Hilfy said. "They'll try. There's never been a dearth of Personages. . . ."

"Coming up on mark," Tiar said.

"Advise our passengers."

"Got that," Fala said from belowdecks.

The numbers ticked down, everything automated, more so than *The Pride.* Progress. And more things to go wrong. She still watched the lines, and compared the numerical readout, scary large numbers. She'd done it on *The Pride,* with her aunt's hand or Haral Araun's on the controls. These days it was Tiar's. She wasn't a pilot, never would be. She could just ride it through.

"Here we go. Suppose we got that mass calc right?"

Ship dropped. Everything went hazed.

—You could dream in jump.

—Sometimes you even knew you were dreaming, if it was an old dream, an often dream.

Dream of gold hair and a human face.

Waiting there. He always was. Even if he was on a ship fifty lights away. Hello, he said, most times, though he was always distant. He had been, since they had parted company at Anuurn. Clearly Pyanfar had talked to him. Told him the practicalities of things. Laid down conditions.

Hello, kid.

But she wasn't the kid any more. Things had changed. She'd been married. And widowed. Thank the gods there were no offspring to promote permanent ties with Sfaura.

Give No'shto-shti-stlen the gods-be puzzle egg. And good luck to *gtst* with it.

Meanwhile there was a human face, a human presence, distant and shadowy, a comfort in her traveling.

You have to take care, Tully said to her. He had never gotten that good at hani speech, that she knew of. But that was years ago.

I always take care, she said.

You trust this deal you're in.

Let's not talk about business. She knew what she wanted to do. Exactly what her aunt frowned on her doing. But Tully was evasive. He walked away from her, with his back turned.

And the lights dimmed, and there were bars about—ammonia, and sodium light.

She took alarm. "Tully?" she said, and he looked at her, scared as she was. She didn't want to be here again. She didn't want this part.

He came and held on to her. He had then. He did until the kif came and then he went with them because they threatened her. The whole thing passed in a kind of haze, the way the hours had in that kifish cage. There were sounds to hear. She chose not to hear them. She could govern the dream now—she had learned to do that, and she kept saying, over and over again, Tully, come back. Tully, listen to me. I don't want to remember that. What do you go there for? I don't want to see that—

Come back and talk to me.

"Tully!"

He came back then, just a shadow. And wouldn't talk to her.

"He knows better," Pyanfar said, out of nowhere and uninvited. "He had his choice, go or stay. He understood. You wouldn't. You still won't."

She did. That was the trouble. She loved him, enough to make them both miserable. Go have babies, Py had said. Thank the gods that had failed. And maybe Korin had never had a chance, maybe he'd sensed that, male-wise, sullen, quarrelsome, and unwisely set on running domestic affairs. Maybe that had set up the situation from the first day he moved in. Maybe—

Maybe in some remote way that had set up everything else, because *she* had come home with violence, with anger, with the habit of war and the indelible memory of a kifish cage. Korin couldn't have imagined that place. He'd made assumptions, he'd made assertions, he'd struck out to make her hear him—

And she couldn't have cared less . . . what he thought, what he wanted, who he was. The only thing she'd wanted—

—was kif in her gunsights. Korin dead. And Tully, on her terms.

"He's not your answer," aunt Pyanfar said, in that brutal, blunt way Py had when she was right. "Look past your gods-cursed selfish notions, niece, and ask *him* what's right to ask of him, and don't tell me it's helping you outgrow him."

That day she'd swung on Py. Not many people had done that and gotten away unmarked. But Py had just ducked, and faced her, the way Py did now, hand against *The Pride*'s main boards.

"Meanwhile," aunt Py said. "Meanwhile. You have a ship to run."

That wasn't what Py had said. Maybe it was her own mind organizing things. The brain did strange things in jump. It dreamed. It worked on problems. At times it argued with itself, or with notions it couldn't admit wide awake.

Most people forgot what they dreamed. It was her curse to remember. Mostly, she thought, she remembered because she wanted to be there. She wanted to be back on *The Pride*, before the kif, before anything had happened.

"Time to come back," Pyanfar said.

* * *

—Alarm was sounding. Wake, wake, wake.

They were in Urtur space, with the alarm complaining and the yellow caution flashing. The computers saw dust ahead.

"You there?" she asked. "Tiar?"

"I'm on it. We're close in. Going for secondary dump."

—You can be a gods-be fool, aunt Py was hanging about to say. Because there's no way you're not being followed.

"Ship out there," Tarras said, on scan.

"Ha'domaren?"

"Sure the right size and vector."

She reached after the nutrients pack, bit a hole in it and drank down the awful stuff. They were, as their bodies kept time, days away from Meetpoint. On Meetpoint docks, on Urtur station, it was more than a month. As light traveled, it was years. And the body complained of such abuses. You shed hair, you lost calcium, you dehydrated, your mouth tasted of copper and you wanted to throw up, especially when the nutrient liquid hit your stomach and about a quarter hour later when the iron hit your bloodstream. But you got used to it and you learned to hold it down, or you didn't, and you didn't last as a deep-spacer.

"You all right?" she heard Fala ask of Meras, below, heard him answer, brightly, *"I'm fine."*

Like hell, she thought. It wasn't fair if he was. The stsho would be coming out from under . . . stsho and humans had to sedate themselves for the trip, whatever *those* completely different brains had in common—though Tully could survive without; had had to prove it . . . once, at least; and was still sane. . . .

Woolgathering, Pyanfar called it, and damned the habit. She didn't have her hands on controls. She'd been ship's com tech, protocol officer, and that didn't have a thing to do with running the ship. But she followed the moves, she knew in her gut when it was time for Tiar to kick in the third *v* dump, and lip-synched the order, tense until Tiar gave it, and then satisfied.

She *could* do it herself. She was tolerably sure of it. But she never bet the ship on it. And certainly not on this jump.

"Fine job," she said to Tiar.

"We're in a little closer than I wanted."

"Still," she said. First class equipment, first class navigator in Chihin and first-class pilot in Tiar. It wasn't any run of the lot ship *could* single-jump as they'd done. The older pilots, the navigators of Chihin's age . . . they'd done it in the war years, they'd the kind of reflexes and system-awareness that could come out of it with a critical sense where they were.

So, most clearly, did *Ha'domaren's* crew. That told you something. That told you, at least, the quality of that crew and equipment, that it carried no cargo, and that whoever was at the helm had done this before.

That they were overjumped, that somebody had actually overhauled and passed them in hyperspace, that said that was one bastard who didn't mind the navigation rules *or* care about the dust hazard in Urtur system.

Chapter Five

Urtur was a smaller port than Meetpoint—heavily industrial. Its star was veiled in murk and dust, a ringed star, with gas giant planets sweeping the veil into bands of crepe and gas and ice; with miner-craft both crewed and otherwise running the dusty lanes in the ecliptic; with refineries and mills and shipyards operating at the collection points—

And the main station, under mahendo'sat governance, devoted itself to manufacture, shipping, and entertainment for the miners and makers of goods. You wanted culture? Go to Idunspol. You wanted religion? Go to forbidden, god-crazed Iji. You wanted iron and heavy metals, you wanted sheet and plate and hydrogen, you wanted a raucous good time and a headache in the morning? Urtur was the place for it.

You said Chanur here, and certain authorities' ears pricked up and twitched—by an irony of things as they were, there were outstanding warrants here that could not quite be forgotten, by mahen law: every situation was subject to change and every administration could be succeeded by some new power diametrically opposed to the last. So charges stayed on the books, something like reckless endangerment, public hazard, speeding, unlawful dumping, and damage to public property. *The Pride of Chanur* had had its less popular moments.

And supposedly the charges included the name of Hilfy Chanur, crewwoman. But she paid no more attention to them than aunt Py did, coming and going as she pleased these days in regal empowerment.

So she ordered the *Legacy* shut down and the hatch opened to Urtur; and she completed the formalities with station control, signing this and signing that—advised station control of the existence of their full-scale dataload and its date of provenance from Meetpoint; and got a bid of 3000, which wouldn't go higher—counting that rag-eared son of a mahen outlaw had beaten them in by eight hours.

But with their fragile passenger and *gtst* fragile object, they couldn't have made it in at anything like that speed.

"That's five thousand that son Haisi's cost us," she muttered. "Maybe eight."

"Couldn't have done better," Tiar said. "Better take it."

"Out of his hide," she said, signaled acceptance, and switched channels to *gtst* honor Tlisi-tlas-tin. "Honorable, we're ready to make contact with your party on Urtur. We're pleased to announce arrival and opening of station business. We will have the distinction to contact the excellency immediately and advise *gtst* of your presence and mission."

"*We acknowledge. We are in preparation. We would like our meal now, if your honor will instruct her aides.*"

"We will, honorable. Stand by." A sigh as she cut the connection.

"*Gtst* could have eaten it when we fixed it," Tarras muttered.

"*Gtst* mission is to be a pain," Hilfy said. "Check on the other passenger while you're at it. Make sure he didn't crack his head."

They'd been up and about for hours. They had had their lunch, but the stsho had been too exhausted and too sick to, as the stsho put it, 'burden the stomach with uncertain and foreign preparations.'

Hell.

Meanwhile she had been putting together a message to advise *gtst* excellency Atli-lyen-tlas to contact her on an urgent basis.

To the most excellent Atli-lyen-tlas, emissary of gtst *excellency No'shto-shti-stlen, the honorable Hilfy Chanur, captain of the hani ship* Chanur's Legacy, *head of the ancient and honorable Chanur clan, sends her respectful greetings and has the distinction and honor to advise and inform your excellency that she has a message of extreme importance for the attention of your excellency personally, which can only reflect well upon the achievement and elegance of your excellency for the future.*

It went out on the push of a button. It would probably take time for a response. The computer was set to listen for a message from *gtst* excellency.

Meanwhile the messages were pouring in. From customs. That had to be answered. From routings. Had to be answered. From the stationmaster. Had to be answered. From name after name of ships and individuals she had no idea who. Anything that contained the name Pyanfar Chanur automatically routed over to the auxiliary stack—otherwise their operations could drown in the deluge, and important operations could stall.

The Pyanfar stack had hit 105 messages and added four more while she checked it for bombs and known names.

Somebody had to read them. After customs. After the stationmaster. After dealing with the freight office and getting on the lists for goods. The futures market had already reacted to the arrival of a ship out of Meetpoint, to the arrival—the sharper traders had surely figured—of a ship that had just come from Urtur round trip; and the knowledgeable types were basing their bids on what they thought she might know, what they thought she might carry, and whether or not they thought by the way the *Legacy* had entered system they were carrying mass. And *she* had the definitive answers, which mahen rules let her give *before* customs—figuring that if a captain didn't like the result of customs, it was only a matter of sufficient fines or sufficient bribes, or court, all of which was fodder for the gamblers on the market. Old mahendo'sat lounged in their station apartments and bet their retirement checks on the system. Hustlers bet on it in bars. Businessmen prayed for it and burned incense to whatever fad religion they thought guaranteed their luck.

And, having that answer, she keyed it through and watched on separate screens as the futures market reacted, as bids started coming in, as customs notified her that she had inspection officers on the way to expedite her cargo in what was clearly a move to stifle disruptive speculation on the reason a hani ship came straight in from Meetpoint.

Tiar's job, handling the inspectors, going through the forms. Meanwhile the bids were looking good. Hard not to let the pulse quicken and the fever set in. But the hani captain that took to gambling on the market herself—that was marginally legal, and ultimately foolish. She watched. She had the computer set to analyze the trend—and she could interrupt at any moment by taking the bid of a particular company; with a bond, before customs, without one, after.

Historically speaking, she preferred after. The market knowledgeables would know that too, and play their serious bids accordingly.

"Felicitations," came a message from the stationmaster, on the more private communications possible now that they had a station communications line physically tapped into their interface. *"You come back much soon than expect,* Legacy. *You got trouble?"*

"No trouble. Personal choice. Felicitations, stationmaster. Chanur's compliments."

"You wait customs before exit."

"I understand they're on their way."

"You come big emergency?"

"No problems, thank you. All fine. On an express run."

"Express run. Who?"

"No'shto-shti-stlen." It was no more than *Ha'domaren* was going to tell them. *"Gtst* excellency wanted a message carried, diplomatic privilege." Freely translated, not legally your business, stationmaster.

"Expensive."

"Yes."

"Congratulation' you safe arrival, Chanur ship. Felicitate you pilot."

"Thank you, sir. I have."

Station seemed satisfied. Meanwhile there was a bleep from the computer, which had found a trigger word in an incoming live communication.

She keyed it in: got:

"H'lo, *you,* Legacy! *What delay you?"*

Grinning bastard. It wasn't worth an answer. Not one she wanted to give over station com.

"Got talk you, Legacy."

She wasn't about to.

"You clear paper with that haul, Legacy? *I got rumor customs got question, back at Meetpoint."*

At *Meetpoint.* In a mahen hell there was a question! "That's the oldest scam in the book, *Ha'domaren!* You try to tie me up with some gods-be lie, I'll have your ears! You know gods-rotted well we have clear papers on everything aboard!"

"On what they see. I got rumor not ever'thing seen. Got stsho arti-fact no papers."

"Diplomatic! It doesn't need papers, you—" It wasn't politic or productive. She shut up. Fast. "Cute joke. Cute joke, Haisi. You still got those charges pending at Mkks, or what?"

"Lot funny, Chanur captain. You want meet for talk business now? You want talk Atli-lyen-tlas, a? I got bad news. Real bad news."

The stationmaster hadn't said that name. She hadn't said that name to anyone at Meetpoint, nor to anyone at Urtur until a scant few moments ago, that she'd keyed out a message for that individual. She had never so much as heard the name aloud on this leg of the trip—but she knew *gtst* as the well-reputed stsho ambassador to Urtur, the addressee in the contract, the intended recipient of the Preciousness.

"You want meet for drink?" the mahe said. *"You going need same."*

* * *

"Atli-lyen-tlas quit," Haisi said, taking a puff of one of those cursed mahen smoke-sticks. And exhaling, what was worse. "Same quit, go—" A move of Haisi's large, bare-palmed hand, a glance of dark mahen eyes about the indefinite perimeters of the lounge—the lounge next the trade office, as happened. Hilfy was not about to go onto *Ha'domaren,* or take Haisi Anakehnandian's hospitality, or be subject to whatever esoteric truth-seekers Haisi might have installed. Haisi's eyes roamed the implied infinite and came back to solidity, to her—the poetic hand returned to lie above Haisi's heart, and Haisi smiled.

"So, so difficult figure alien mind."

"So where did *gtst* go?" Hilfy's ears were flat. She made no pretense of pleasantness.

"You do me small favor."

"What favor?"

"I tell you," Haisi said, "I do work in files, all hours I wait talk with you, you know? What for you got arrest here? I curious."

"I never got arrested here."

"You all same got police record. File on list. Hilfy Chanur. That you? Sound like you."

"Then you just better let it lie there. You go digging in that dirt, you're going to need the bath, because it's nothing Urtur Station wants to find. And how patient is your personage with foulups?"

Maybe she scored one. Haisi took another puff and seemed to think about it, blowing smoke from his nostrils like some brazen image.

"I might call your personage," she said, "and tell her—it is *her,* isn't it? We got one mahe being damn fool. Call him home before he embarrasses you."

"Personage might say, Who you talk fool, Hilfy Chanur? You got thing aboard you don't know what is, you don't know what does, you got stsho play politic, use you name, use you ship . . . Big fool."

"What do you want? Outright, mahe, what do you want?"

"You bring me 'board you ship. You let me talk stsho."

"You want to send a message, I might take it. You let the stsho ask to talk to you. If *gtst* wants to, I'll bring you aboard."

"I tell you no good you come here. Stsho you look for—gone."

"Gone since how long? Since you found out about the shipment? Since you were here last and you learned about it?"

"You not bad guess."

"What is it to you? What do you care what the stsho do with each other?"

"Ask why stsho care what I do."

"Why, then?"

"Maybe rise and fall Personages."

"Which personages? Stsho? Mahendo'sat?"

"Maybe so. Maybe."

"Gods rot you, give me a plain answer!"

"No more you give me, Chanur captain. Which side you?"

"I'm on the side of making a living, I'm on the side of running an honest trade and shipping operation! If somebody's got cargo going, and it's not live and it's not illegal, I haul it, that's all! I'm not a personage, I'm not a fool, I'm a ship captain."

"You think that, you be number one fool, Chanur captain. Wherever you go, politic. All time politic. You want tuck head under arm not see what is, you do. But maybe all same Urtur find old arrest warrant. Maybe search ship . . ."

"You want an incident with the stsho, you go right on and try that. You want an incident with Chanur, you want an incident with the *han*, you want me to sue you clear back to your ancestors, you earless bastard—"

The lifting of an empty mahen hand. "Want no incident. Want know what thing No'shto-shti-stlen send Atli-lyen-tlas."

"What in your ninety-nine hells difference does it make what *gtst* sent?"

"You not know that?"

"I have no interest in that!"

"Then why you ask?"

Murder occurred to her. Most vivid murder.

"Because I got a large hairy fool being a fulltime pain in the—"

"You *know* what No'shto-shti-stlen send? Or you take *gtst* word what you carry? Sloppy way pass customs."

"Until it comes *off* my ship, customs can wonder."

"Unless it univers-al contraband. Like run guns. Like run—"

"I'm bored. I'm leaving."

"You not know."

"Goodbye."

"You want know where Atli-lyen-tlas go?"

"Where?"

"What you give me?"

"I'll look it up in station records."

"Kita. Go Kita Point. Easy jump. You want data on Kita market? Got. Real cheap. Great bargain. Give you break. Get you futures reports maybe two month back."

Futures in a deeper mahen market where the mahendo'sat knew best what they had and didn't. Speculation there was asking for trouble, hired hauling was the only sure thing, and information at the narrow downside end of mahen trade routes wasn't going to tell you what goods might already have arrived there from points upstream.

And there was a worse problem with Kita.

"You want deal?" the mahe asked.

"I'll think about it." She stood up and walked for the door.

"Not real long time think," Haisi said. "You got stsho deal, not good you break promise. Cargo get lost, stuff screw up at Meetpoint . . . Personage not real damn happy with you, Chanur captain. Big mess. You go ahead. You do. You make. Talk me later I see if rescue you worth while."

"You captain?"

"Me? Not."

"*Ha'domaren* your ship?"

"Not. Belong cousin."

"You got cousins everywhere, don't you?"

"Big fam'ly."

"I'll bet." She did walk out, shoved her hands in her pockets and thought how this had more and more the smell of trouble, such that she wasn't seeing Urtur's garish lights, she was seeing what used to be, and missing the weight of the pistol she had worn in those days before the disarmament agreement, before the peace.

It didn't feel like peace. Not at all.

"We got check," the mahen customs agent said, and Tiar jabbed the slate in question and said, politely, "It's on our ship. Until it comes off our ship it isn't your province. That's in your regulations. Until it's offered for sale it isn't merchandise. It's an item in the possession of *gtst* honor under *diplomatic* privilege and it stays on this ship until we find the addressee. In which case you can work out the problems with the stsho delegation. It's not our problem!"

"Got consult stationmaster," the agent said, and flipped his slate closed and walked off. Tiar stood staring after him, and turned and stalked back into the access, up the rampway to the hatch and the lower main corridor.

"Trouble?" Fala asked.

"Gods-be right we have trouble, we have bids breeding like crazy and we can't get the gods-rotted customs to fill out the gods-rotted forms and clear the gods-be-feathered—"

It had been quiet for a very long time. And *Trade in Agricultural Goods* might be informative, and Hallan was willing to learn anything that gave him expertise in anything whatsoever to do with space and trade; but it was uninspired and highly repetitive.

Still, he read on, having had his shower and his lunch and all. He heard crew members going up and down the corridor outside, he listened hard, thinking that he might hear something, but most of all he heard a voice he thought was Tiar's yelling about mahendo'sat and customs and blackmail.

So he thought something bad must have happened.

Then he heard the captain's voice, he was relatively sure,

yelling something about mahendo'sat and blackmail. So he didn't think things were going well.

Probably it was not a good time to ask to be let out of the laundry. Probably he should read *Trade in Agricultural Goods* very slowly and thoroughly and make it last, because it might be all the entertainment he had for a while.

Home again, to read the gods-forsaken contract. To consult the legal program. The translation. The transcription of the original into mundane type, and into phonetic rendition.

7098 pages. Of which the computer identified 20 clauses as of particular application, regarding *Unproven Subsequents.*

And the pertinent dictionary and legal dictionary definition: *Subsequent: a person who in substance whether in whole or in part may be in tenure of the same rights and legal entity as a named individual. See: Subsequent in Identity; Consequent.*

Subsequent in Identity: a subsequent who has the same physical identity as a named individual.

Consequent: an individual who in substance whether in whole or in part is in tenure of legal rights and legal entity as a direct result of contact with or the actions of an individual or gtst *subsequent.*

. . . If the party receiving the goods be not the person stipulated to in subsection 3 section 1, and have valid claim as demonstrated in subsection 36 of Section 25, then it shall be the reasonable obligation of the party accepting the contract to ascertain whether the person stipulated to in subsection 3 section 1 shall exist in Subsequent or in Consequent or in Post-consequent, however this clause shall in no wise be deemed to invalidate the claim of the person stipulated to in subsection 3 section 1 or 2, or in any clause thereunto appended, except if it shall be determined by the party accepting the contract to pertain to a person or Subsequent or Consequent identified and stipulated to by the provisions of Section 5 . . .

However the provisions of Section 5 may be delegated by the party issuing the contract, following the stipulations of Subsection 12 of Section 5 in regard to the performance of the per-

son accepting the contract, not obviating the requirements of performance of the person accepting the contract . . .

"We have a problem," Hilfy said, over gfi, in the *Legacy*'s galley. She was maintaining, she felt, extraordinary control over her temper. Sober faces were opposite her, the whole crew—since no offloading was going on. Meanwhile *gtst* honor was lighting up the com board with requests to go out into the station, and whether Haisi had messed them up with station officials or whether Haisi had only fairly warned them what they were facing—customs had a hold on them.

"Have you told *gtst* honor?" Tiar asked, elbows on the table opposite her.

"Not yet. Haisi *could* be lying through his teeth."

"If he isn't? What about that contract? What's it say, if we can't *find* the bastard we're supposed to give this to?"

She truly hated to say that. She did hate it. She leaned her own arms against the cold surface and regarded a tableful of more experienced traders—give or take Fala. "There's a clause in there about Subsequents and Consequents. That we're still bound to get it to the right party."

"You mean that son of a stsho has transmogrified? Switched personalities? Disintegrated *gtst* psyche?"

"We don't know that exactly."

"We don't know it, so we're not responsible if *gtst* has gone crazy and shipped out of here."

"We aren't responsible if *gtst* does. But we do have a clause in there about finding out if there's a Subsequent."

"Oh, gods," Tiar said, and her hand slid over her eyes.

"It said Urtur," Fala Anify protested.

"It also said—find out if there's a Subsequent. And we—*I*, I'm not passing the responsibility. I should have considered the possibility of *gtst* not staying at Urtur."

"What possibility?" Chihin asked with a rap on the tabletop. "Stsho don't travel once in a—"

"Lifetime," Hilfy said. "Which only holds true until someone spooks it into a new personality."

"So what spooked the ambassador? We were through here,

we dealt with *gtst* excellency at least indirectly to get our clearance for Meetpoint, we didn't see anything wrong, did we?"

"I didn't," Hilfy said. "But I'm willing to bet Haisi has some remote thing to do with it. He was at Meetpoint when we came in, he was in a position to know what No'shto-shti-stlen knew . . ." A thought came to her, a summation, a time-table, that sent an outrageous anger rolling through her veins. "That son of an earless mother!"

"Haisi?"

"No! No'shto-shti-stlen!"

"You mean *gtst* knew we weren't going to find *gtst* recipient here?"

"If *gtst* didn't know, *gtst* had a gods-rotted good idea there was trouble here! *And* wrote that bit into the contract about obligating us to go on a Subsequent-hunt! Gods *blast* that skinny, painted, conniving—he wants us to go running around the immediate universe looking for this character!"

"Where would *gtst* go? Where would *gtst* be?"

"*Who* would *gtst* be? That's the question! Haisi says Kita. But that won't be *gtst* stopping-place—it hasn't got amenities for them. And the mahendo'sat are all stirred up, or Haisi's personage has got a lot of pull here, a *lot* of pull."

"You don't think it's Pyanfar behind his personage."

"I don't know! I don't know not! That's the trouble getting involved in politics, nobody wears a name badge!"

"So what are we going to do, captain?"

Run for it? Haul their load clear to Kita, with no guarantee there was a profit there?

Hope the mahen stationmaster had traded heavily into the futures market here, and took a soaking when they yanked their cargo off the market and ran for it? Break a few regulations that made the speeding violation look like a mahen commendation?

Good way to make lasting enemies, in either case.

But *deal* with Haisi? He might be Pyanfar's bosom friend. He might be working for her overthrow and with a mahen sense of humor, using her help to do it.

Get the truth out of Tlisi-tlas-tin? *Not* outstanding likely. And there was no way to consult No'shto-shti-stlen.

Continuing silence at the table. It was the crew's moral refuge and her moral dilemma: the captain was thinking. The captain was going to get them out of what the captain, who was young enough to be Tiar's daughter, had gotten them collectively into.

"We can pull out. We can stay. We've got two other hani in port with us. That's *Padur's Victory* and a Narn hauler, both slated for Hoas. But they're marginal ships, they're not up to this. If we involve them, they could be in big trouble, so that's no help."

"No threat to them."

"None so far. We could get the kid aboard—"

"The kid's in potential trouble."

"The kid's ship is at Hoas."

"The kid's ship is probably on its way here right now, if we put him on one of them, he'll miss his ship."

It was true. And beyond Hoas, either ship might be on to Meetpoint, where he wasn't welcome—and consequently they might not be.

"Tell you something else," Tiar said. "Captain. That kid's been *on* this ship."

She understood what Tiar was getting at. She didn't particularly want to listen to it.

"If you turn him out on the docks," Tiar said, "the mahendo'sat are going to pick him up. There's no question. They'll assume he knows what they want to know."

"He's also not Chanur, *not* involved with us, he's Sahern crew, they're coming here, and if we're holding him . . ."

"He doesn't want to go to them. He wants to stay with Chanur."

"He's in love with my gods-forsaken aunt! He's a fool kid, light-years from home on a notion—"

"A gods-forsaken ticking bomb," Chihin said. "We have a stsho aboard this ship, a stsho that we daren't upset. We have a kid with healthy hormones right around the corner from *gtst* honor and the Preciousness *we're* now supposed to get to Kita—beyond which, there's precious few choices where we're going, captain."

"If they're Pyanfar's, she'll sort it out. If they're not—and we help them, they'll cut our throats."

"What happens if *our* stsho fragments and decides *gtst* is the queen of the gods?"

"We have a problem," Tarras said, which brought them back to point one.

"Honorable," Hilfy said, not cheerfully. "I have news."

A languid wave. *Gtst* was restoring *gtst* body-paint, carefully brushing a pattern down a white forearm. *Gtst* completed it with a flourish.

In strictest courtesy, Hilfy invited herself into the bowl-chair and sat down.

"There has been a complication," she began.

"Then your honor can surely solve it. Are you not hired to do so?"

"Would your honor care for tea?" She made a slight wave of the hand toward the door, and Fala, with tea-service in hand.

"If your honor sees fit." *Gtst* looked anxious, waving the newly painted arm, arranging *gtst* draperies.

With a species that tended to dissociate psychologically at grievous upsets—five rounds of tranquilizing tea seemed perhaps a good idea. Especially since it was their stsho and their contract, with the Preciousness enthroned in its case above their heads.

Five cups, in which Fala contrived not to spill anything on the white cushions, in which their juniormost acquitted herself with commendable self-possession.

"We hope your honor has been comfortable such as our hospitality has been able to provide."

"We have survived. We are composed. The Preciousness in our possession is unmolested. We could not ask more of your meager circumstances."

Snobbish son.

"May your honor," *gtst* asked, "choose to inform us of the matter which troubles your peace?"

"Regarding the intended recipient of the *oji*."

"The Preciousness."

"The Preciousness. Would it surprise your honor in the least to know that the intended recipient has—em—quit *gtst* post?"

Shocked pale eyes lifted and centered on her face. "Impossible."

So *gtst* did not know in advance. Perhaps her surmises were unjust and mistaken.

"Quit *gtst* post so far as the mahendo'sat have been willing to inform me. Should they have reason to lie? One of them has been quite forward in asking me to allow him access here."

"No! A thousandfold no! This is insupportable. This is *unthinkable!*" Paint spilled as *gtst* jostled the bottle. "Oh, where are my servants? The paint, the precious pigments, —oh, my predecessors, oh, my honor, oh, my reputation, oh, I am wounded! I perish, wai! I perish!"

It was blotting furiously—impossible to tell whether the migration of Atli-lyen-tlas was the shock, or the paint, or the reference to mahendo'sat, but *gtst* was highly agitated, breathing in great gasps, and Fala came running, cups rattling on the tray, all the while the honorable was fighting for breath and clear as clear was the possibility of a dissolution before their eyes.

"Be calm!" Hilfy said, unsure whether to lay hands on the creature or not. "Be calm! Your honor is not in question, most honorable, most excellent! Calm yourself, breathe quietly—"

The stsho did listen. Moonstone eyes gazed at her in shock, a paint-spattered hand clutched a paint-stained fold of *gtst* robe to *gtst* breast, and it shook and trembled and lifted and lowered *gtst* plume-augmented crest in high agitation.

"We are empowered to search further!" Hilfy said, reaching for vocabulary. What *was* the ceremonial deferative singular for "personality disintegration" and was it appropriate to use it? "You are in no wise responsible for this, honorable! There is every possibility *gtst* excellency foresaw such an event—we find it in the contract!"

"In the contract."

"In the contract, honorable."

"But *gtst* excellency should have confided in me, *gtst* excellency has dishonored me—"

"*Gtst* excellency has entrusted you with the Preciousness. Has *gtst* not? Or should we not question that? Should we ask what is in that box?"

Moonstone eyes went wide and horrified. And *gtst* looked up and up and around, where the shipping box sat within its braces.

"Must we not be certain? Would you *recognize* the Preciousness if you saw it?"

"Of course! Of course! Oh, the villainy in your mind!" Tlisi-tlas-tin scrambled to an undignified exit from the chair, trailing paint-soaked robes over the white cushions and the tiles of the floor, *gtst* long fingers sought the shipping latches and undid them, waving Fala's offered help away in indignation. *Gtst* undid the latches of the box itself, and Hilfy held her breath, unbearably driven to reach out restraining hands in case it should fall.

But there in the plush white liner sat a white, carved—vase, one supposed. Is this it? Hilfy wondered; Fala looked puzzled; but Tlisi-tlas-tin sank down with a sigh and fluttered *gtst* fingers, held a hand to *gtst* chest, and muttered,

"I am vindicated. I am vindicated, *gtst* excellency has not lied to me."

"We had no doubt of your honor," Hilfy ventured to say, and stood by as Tlisi-tlas-tin picked *gtst*self up off the pastel-smeared floor, in the wreckage of *gtst* finery. *Gtst* struck as belligerent and proud a pose as a creature could, that a gust of breath could shatter.

"But this is a pen for *animals!* I cannot possibly abide these circumstances! Look at me! The Preciousness cannot abide in this wreckage! My honor! My reputation!"

Hilfy thought of another word, but she bowed with great

courtesy and smiled. "We are of course concerned. We will act instantly to rectify this unfortunate circumstance."

"Immediately! I cannot abide this! Oh, the injustice, oh, the cruelty, oh, the perfidy!"

"*What* perfidy, honorable?"

"I *demand* to see the next highest stsho authority, I *demand* to have access to this individual!"

"Honorable, —"

"I am wronged, oh, predecessors and antecedents, I am wronged, most grievously!"

Fala made a glance toward the overhead. But in space there was no direction for heaven.

And the gods were probably busy with aunt Pyanfar.

Chapter Six

Potential spies everywhere, Haisi blackmailing them for access to the stsho *they* had contracted to protect, and the stsho in question wailing and moaning and lamenting betrayals on the part of the stsho ambassador to Urtur, *and* of the staff of said ambassador, who did not return calls.

And the honorable Tlisi-tlas-tin's quarters were a shambles, *gtst* person was a shambles, *gtst* affairs were a shambles, and in a species that Phased under stress, into new and unpredictable psychological configurations. . . .

The Preciousness might end up in the hands of a completely different individual, for which—Hilfy hesitated even to send the legal program on another search through the contract and the handbook of Compact law looking for legal responsibility. *Gtst* honor was tottering on the edge of dissolution and *gtst* wanted the damage to *gtst* quarters repaired, *gtst* wanted the colors changed, *gtst* wanted new clothing, and a better diet, and entertainments and amenities.

Which meant scouring the market for stsho items, checking through what *they* had in cargo cans; *and* dealing with customs one more time.

"You got problem?" a mahen voice said; and Hilfy turned to find the scoundrel on her track—*following* her, gods rot him.

Maybe not even doing the watching himself . . . just have some underling do it, and call him for the intercept.

"What do you want?"

"Want make deal. Hear you look for stsho stuff. Hear you want make buy stuff like deck tile, like *'vuli* cloth, like . . ."

"How *nice* you got all these things to sell me! Good price, huh?"

"You funny. Amuse stsho?"

She started to walk away. He got in front of her.

"Hear you try talk stsho embas-sy. Not possible. Stsho shut down. Some go Meetpoint. Some Kita."

"You've had yourself a main proper disaster here, haven't you? You try to break off trade with the stsho? Try to screw up politic for my aunt?"

"I *friend* Pyanfar." Hand on chest. "My personage friend with Pyanfar, number one try do good for you." Haisi Anakehnandian glanced about as casual traffic passed, and he made an unwelcome catch at her elbow. "You want stsho stuff, I get for you. Easy done. Stuff all over embassy. Nice stuff, number one stsho furniture."

"Breaking and entering? Pirated goods?"

"Shush, shush, don't make noise ever'body hear. You come. I fix, you get."

"You drove the whole gods-forsaken stsho embassy off Urtur, and you want to help me? No thanks! Go talk to the kif, they appreciate a pirate!"

"Don't be fool. You want clear customs? You want get stuff *on* ship, same deal you got get customs stamp. Customs don't let you trade till you cleared, hani, you got figure how things are."

One could figure how things were. One could figure somebody was in tight with the officials at some level.

"You want stop whole deal for redecorate stsho cabin?" Haisi asked. "That funny."

"Who said?"

"Funny thing you got real white shopping list. Stsho emissary not happy with decor? Maybe lot stress on this person?"

"Go to hell," she said.

And walked off, walked and took a lift and a transport bus to the dockside customs office.

And got the official no. No onloading if there was a hold on offloading.

"So what if a ship pulls in here and doesn't want to sell to you? You're not going to let them buy?" Her fist landed on the counter. "I don't believe that!"

"Not same. Not same. You got hold on you cargo. Not same legal situation. You want deal, you let custom inspector see contraband."

"It's not contraband! It's stsho diplomatic property!"

"Make you appeal stsho mission."

"There *is* no stsho mission on Urtur! You scared it off!"

"Not us scare off. Maybe this object you got scare them."

"No way! News of it got here with *my ship!* No way they know about it. You ask Haisi Ana-kehnandian what spooked them, you ask him what in your seventh reprehensible hell he knows about our cargo and who's pockets he's got access to. I want to talk to the stationmaster, I want to talk to the personage of this station, I want a legal accounting of every paper you've brought against us, and I want my ship cleared!"

"You not yell in this office!"

"I by the gods yell in this office, I yell until somebody contacts the personage of Urtur and *gets my customs slip cleared,* and no more of this talk about invading a stsho emissary's privacy and searching his baggage!"

There was a disturbance at the door behind her. A mahen voice registered protest in some mahen tongue, another joined it before she could even look around. She did look, and there was a handful of mahen spacers *and* Haisi Ana-kehnandian shoving other business out the door.

He shut the door and held it then, with a wall of large mahendo'sat.

She *missed* carrying a gun. Gods, she did. Claws came out. Haisi twitched and she went over the counter, scattering customs personnel left and right. Chairs went over, clerks jammed up in an inner office door and shrieked in panic.

"Hani!" Haisi shouted. "You stop, stop now! You listen!"

Nobody had guns. But they had the door. There were clerks under desks. The group behind her squeezed into the room and shut that door.

"Where's your authority? Where's any proof you're not a pirate, Haisi Ana-kehnandian? Unblock that door!"

"All right, all right." Haisi made calming gestures. "You not break furniture, Chanur captain. You got important relative, no reason break place up. Don't be damn fool!"

"I got important relative, same time got real distrust of people who get pushy, mahe. You want I charge piracy? You want I say you try damn underhanded trick with customs? I want to talk to the stationmaster, I want to talk right now, and no more tricks!"

"Stationmaster indispos'."

"Indisposed like the stsho ambassador? Indisposed like run for Iji?"

"You talk wild, hani. No. Indispos' like not take time talk with every damn' fool got problem."

Damn' fool was close to the point. Something was seriously wrong at Urtur, and the more they suspected she knew the less likely she was to get out of this room, much less out of the port. Far better to have played outraged trader.

"I want my ship cleared! I want customs clearance, I want my record cleared, I want to sell my cargo when and if and at what price I choose, and I want an end of interference with my business."

"You want tell what sort object you carry?"

"No, I don't. It's none of your gods-rotted business! You get out from in front of that door, you get yourself and your crew out of my way! This is a public office. If I don't see a badge, an authorization, or a personage, I'm not giving you anything. And if you try to hold me, my ship—a *Chanur* ship—is going to carry a complaint to the Compact."

"You be calm, be calm, hani. This get to very silly point. You listen to me. You walk 'round station talk about dangerous business, name dangerous stuff, you come in this office make demand in front of witness you don't know by damn who, you try get throat cut?"

"Open that door!"

"A' right, a' right. —Rahe'ish' taij meh, jai."

The mahendo'sat with him moved aside from the door.

"Against the wall!" she said.

"You got damn poor idea who give orders in this room, hani!"

"I got damn good idea you got no authority to give orders. Or *you* can clear the papers. You want big blow-up you just keep going."

"Clear papers. I clear papers. All right!" Haisi spat out a torrent of mahendi instructions, only half of which she could understand, but which got the clerks cautiously out from under the desks and brought the customs agent back from the office in the rear.

The door opened, from the other side. Station police stood there, armed with pistols and ready for trouble. Someone had called them. Probably from the back office.

Fine, Hilfy thought. Great.

"Small misunderstanding," Haisi said, with a wave of his hand. And said something to the police, low and fast. Stationmaster, she caught that word: stsho; and ambassador. And trouble. But she could guess that one.

The Personage of Urtur was ruffled. Highly. The Personage of Urtur found the business too evidently distressful, and abandoned it to her Voice, a towering mahe with a furious scowl.

"You disrupt whole office, you got clerk scare' like bunch pirate, what for you damn' fool action?"

"Ask him! He blocked the door, wouldn't let honest citizens in or out!" You didn't yell at the Personage of Urtur. The Personage of Urtur didn't debate such matters. The Voice did. And Hilfy found her ears persistently flattening. She made every effort to keep a pleasant look on her face, and to keep to logical points, when at the same time the Voice tried to provoke gut level reactions. She wanted to make mincemeat out of Haisi Ana-kehnandian—who sat smoking like a factory, with a frown on his face.

The Voice did ask Ana-kehnandian, evidently. The two of them talked back and forth in one of Ijir's numerous languages, in which the Voice grew quieter and quieter, and even good-humored—which suggested, first, they had no wish for the hani foreigner to understand; and second, they were out of the same district of Ijir, and *therefore* Haisi Ana-kehnandian must be a good upstanding fellow.

This went on and on and back and forth, and in the meanwhile the Personage sat surveying the potted plant on her desk and frowning mightily.

"You make mess in customs office," the Voice then said in the pidgin. "Personage not happy. You make lot public mess, scare people—"

"I take it the Personage understands the Trade. Ask the Personage whether she has given any authority to this person to harass my crew, threaten me, create a riot in customs, hold my cargo for ransom, and ask personal questions about a stsho passenger who's never set foot on this station nor applied for local customs clearance. I feared firearms were present. I went over that desk in protection of my life! This advised innocent persons to take cover, for their personal safety! This fool committed the aggression, by blocking the exit in an aggressive manner, in the clear intent to do violence!"

That prompted another conference, a lengthy one. And more frowns from Haisi.

The Personage then took to pinching leaves off the plant on her desk, and paying no attention to either of them.

"Personage not like speak pidgin. Say 'pologize for distress you. Say customs cleared. All fine."

She had to replay that again to believe she'd heard it. But Haisi looked far from happy with the situation.

"Then thank the Personage on behalf of my ship and my passenger."

"She understand fine. She say, Be careful with stsho. Good luck on you deals on station. You need all luck you got."

"Ask her why."

"Not need ask. Ask you: why be fool? Why make damn lot racket, attract notice? Ask you: what benefit you this stsho thing?"

"Money. *Money*, like making a profit on this trip, like getting hired like any merchant captain—"

"You not merchant. You *Chanur*."

"Gods-rotted right I'm a merchant! What do you think, I'm rich? I travel from station to station for a hobby?"

"You got aunt."

"The gods-be *universe* has got Pyanfar Chanur, but I don't! She can't be head of Chanur any longer, she can't sit in the *han*, she can't hold property and she can't vote on Anuurn—Your informers have been lying down asleep if you think I'm on her payroll! My ship hauls freight to pay the bills and keep our clan's taxes paid. That's all, no politics, no secrets, and no *interest* in secrets. I'm paid to transport this thing and transport it I will, until I can get the thing off my deck to its legitimate owner. But *don't* expect my aunt knows. We don't speak!"

Evidently it was not the answer the Voice or the Personage expected. There was another sharp exchange between the two of them.

Something—she understood two of the mahen languages—about relatives and assumptions and another Personage of feminine gender.

And Haisi was not pleased. "All you papers cleared," Haisi said. "You go. You put stuff on market, quick as you want. Stsho you want go Kita. Wish you luck find same. Suggest you make nice thank you to busy Personage."

"Thank you," she said, and made two successive bows, to Haisi, and to the Personage who had never once looked her in the eyes. There was a small pile of leaves below the miniature tree. The Personage raked them together with a nail, and seemed perfectly absorbed in this activity. The Voice did not exist when the Personage was speaking for herself. And the Voice stood to the side of the room, hands behind his back, with no more to say to her.

So she left. And hoped the Personage of Urtur had more intense words for Haisi Ana-kehnandian once the door closed.

There was all this banging and sawing again. And the loaders were taking things off the ship, finally. Hallan was puzzled by the former, found the latter comfortingly ordinary, and had himself another snack while he read the tail end of *Love in the Outback*.

They had moved in a minifridge full of food and snacks and drinks, a microwave, a viewer, a tape player, and a stack of somebody's tapes and books . . . some of them really embarrassing. But interesting. He really hoped they hadn't known those were in the stack. Tiar had been in a real hurry when she brought them in, and said something about the captain having been in some dust-up with customs, but everything was all right now, and she was sorry, and she wished she could let him out, but they had a very upset stsho on their hands and if the stsho ran into him *gtst* would Phase on the spot. So please forgive them.

With which Tiar ducked out again. And the banging and sawing went on, and the loaders proceeded.

Clank-clank. Clank. Bang and thump.

It would have been very tedious, except if anybody was going to come after him he hoped he got to the end of the book first, and he hoped they didn't catch him actually reading it.

If he were on the *Sun* the book in the stack would have meant one thing.

Here—he was having thoughts he'd never exactly had before . . . or not thoughts, exactly, but feelings. Not about Tiar, actually. Just about belonging. Dangerous thoughts—like fitting into an ancient pattern that he didn't want, that he'd rejected for his dreams of traveling and being free, and here he was reading this stupid book, increasingly confused about what was going on with his hormones and his thinking processes. Try to be independent and put up with any crude thing the crew did, and sometimes go along with what they wanted, and he could do that without letting them really get to him; but now here he was, guiltily reading what he really hoped they hadn't meant to be in the stack, and thinking thoughts that meant maybe Mara Sahern was right and instincts were too strong, and he couldn't depend on using his brains—that ultimately, when he got all his size and hormones kicked in for good and earnest, he wasn't going to be worth anything but one thing until he was as old as Khym Mahn and hormones had stopped making him crazy.

That reputation for violence was why the stsho was afraid of him. That reputation was why everybody on Meetpoint had panicked when he had panicked and swung on the kif. And that reputation scared him, because there wasn't just the kif to deal with, there was *the* Chanur, lord Harun Chanur, who would break his neck if he caught him in Chanur territory, the same as there was lord Sahern to object to his presence on the *Sun*. It was one thing to go to space before he was old enough, quite, to have his adult growth, but after three years he was about *there*, banging his head on the doorways built for female crews, and finding instincts he'd thought he was immune to—worst of all, to think that, over the next few years, he might progressively lose his self-control and his reason. It just was not true. It would not happen to him, it didn't need to happen, it was, what had Pyanfar Chanur said, that so outraged the *han?* —an unscientific belief system; and conforming to it was custom, not hardwiring.

But here he sat on a Chanur ship having thoughts he didn't even want, and wanting to finish the cursed book, and not wanting to, and scared and drawn at the same time.

Was that being crazy? Was that what happened, and was that what had started when he came on board the *Legacy*, among female people he could really want?

He kept reading. He got to the end and he sat there staring at the wall and wishing he knew what was ahead of him, and whether he was a fool or not, being out here, in this foreign place with a crew he . . .

Really, really wanted to belong to, in a very absolute and traditional and gut-level way that that book was about.

Which could very definitely get him killed. Which was stupid, intellectually speaking. But not—not when feelings cut in.

The incoming messages were stacked up.

From Haisi, Hilfy presumed, since it had *Ha'domaren's* header: *You better think who you are. Dangerous you not know.*

From Customs: *Customs approved.* For the third time. They were over-compensating.

From *Padur's Victory* and *Narn's Dawnmaker*, a joint communique: *We are in receipt of troubling news regarding difficulty with customs and station authorities. We request a briefing at earliest.*

That had to be answered, urgently and in the most courteous way, hence the presence of a Padur and a Narn captain in the downside corridor, plain trader captains in workaday blue trousers, out of the midst of their work. And it certainly behooved the bone-tired hani captain in question to meet them personally at the airlock, and invite them into her downside office, and sit down and explain the situation, in spite of the fact she and her sleepless crew were again facing no sleep and snatched meals. Tarras was down there alone, no one was on the bridge, and the offloading was going to go on until the *Legacy*'s holds were empty.

Meaning about 12 more hours.

"There's a ship to watch," she said, "*Ha'domaren.* If you want my guess what's going on, there's a personage with an agent on that ship who's fairly high up in the hierarchy; that personage *assumed* I have a direct line to my aunt—which I don't—and somebody on this station tried to blacklist my ship by bringing up old records about *The Pride.* I wasn't interested in a secret game, I raised a racket, this agent didn't want the publicity, and when the police got involved it bounced the case right where I couldn't get anyone else to send it—straight to the Personage of Urtur, where I said very definitely I hadn't any contacts with my aunt and all I wanted was trade. After which they gave me my customs clearance and the Personage of Urtur gave the agent a reasonably dirty look. That's the sum of it."

"We hear," Tauhen Padur said, with a discreet cough, "there's some sort of politically hot stsho cargo."

"Where did you hear that?"

A shrug, a lowering of one ear. "From my crew, indirectly from the market. Where, specifically . . . I think they'd have said if the source was unusual. Probably just the merchants."

"Same," said Kaury Narn. Old spacer, Kaury was, lot of rings, pale edges on the mane, and a right-side tooth capped in silver—ask where and on what kif pirate she'd broken that one. The Narn captain came from far wilder days. "Whatever the chaff is, it's drifting up and down the market."

"We didn't talk to anybody in the market. There's only one way that information flew in here ahead of us."

"This *Ha'domaren.*"

"And one Tahaisimandi Ana-kehnandian, nickname Haisi, who's operating out of that ship."

"Eastern hemisphere Ijir. At least by ancestry." This from Kaury.

"You know him."

"No," Kaury Narn said. "But the name is eastern. I'll remember it."

"Haisi," Tauhen said. "Which personage?"

"Not the Personage of Urtur. Somebody named Paehisna-ma-to."

"Not familiar."

"Not to me."

"Is there any way," the Narn asked, "you *can* get in touch with your aunt?"

"No. That's the truth." Touchy question, under other circumstances; but this was with obvious reason. "What I hear, she's somewhere . . ." She censored that. ". . . inconvenient;

and I don't know where. Possibly Ana-kehnandian's personage is shaking the tree, so to speak, to see what falls out; certainly somebody wanted to use me to get to her, and I couldn't if I wanted to. So if your trail and hers should cross, let her know. But meanwhile I *hope* I've settled this mahe and got him off my tail. What I want to know—*are* there any stsho hiding on this station?"

"Gone when we got here," Padur said. "And Padur was here before Narn. Rumor is they just boarded ship and took out of here. I won't bet on any holdouts, but by my experience, they'd Phase if they had to hide: they wouldn't do it."

"Which ship took them? Where?"

"The general staff, on *Pakkitak,* to Meetpoint via Hoas. A rumor—a rumor about certain ones going to Kita on *Ko'juit.*"

One kifish ship. One mahen ship, to Kita Point. Not unheard of, for stsho to use either species' transportation. But Padur said it: it was rumor. Everything they knew, was a report they had *from* the mahendo'sat, namely from the Personage and from Ana-kehnandian.

"We've got to find Atli-lyen-tlas. We have a package with that address. Hear anything on that score?"

"The ambassador?" Kaury Narn said. "That *gtst* excellency and one of the staffers went with the mahen ship."

"How sure are your sources?"

"Market gossip, no more, no less." Kaury twitched her ring-heavy ears and settled back, arms folded. "Which means nothing. And if I knew anything else that bears on it, I'd be quick to tell you. I don't know."

Information appearing without source, in a hotbed of gossip both true and false, in a market that sailed and fell on rumors and accusations and public perceptions. Wonderful.

"We're outbound tomorrow," Padur said. "Fueling in the next watch. You're on to Kita, then?"

"Not willingly. Certainly not where I'd like to go. If you do run across my aunt's track—"

"I'll pass it on what's happened, where you've gone." Small

movements, twitches of the ears, shiftings in the chairs, said that two busy captains were anxious to get back to work: news was welcome, but sparser than they had hoped, and it threatened none of their clan interests.

This captain was the same—at least busy and anxious to get back to the market reports—to safeguard her clan interests. Their on again, off again entry into Urtur market and the (by now) famous encounter in the customs office, had sent the prices of goods in their hold up and down, up and down, and (more than one could play that game) she had had Chihin and Tiar buying current entertainment, fine-grade composites supplies, grain, and a handful of mahen luxuries on the market, saying, if asked, that the *Legacy* might just go on to Kita to sell its load. Which was an honest possibility—until she had gotten a fair offer and a fair buy option.

Not that she'd have deceived other hani captains: they'd already concluded their deals before the *Legacy*'s cargo hit the boards; besides that they were coming from the other direction, with different goods; and one being in process of loading and one set for undock, already in countdown.

Dirty tricks on the mahen traders and the handful of kif in port, but traders who relied solely on the rumors that ran the docks were asking for surprises; and those who asked what all of a certain species seemed to be acting on, and how they were selling and buying learned far more. It was the way the game was played, that was all, a stsho game from top to bottom.

Except they had a direct barter offer on the methane load, gods rot the luck: that was the trouble with dealing with the methane docks—they too often wanted to barter, you couldn't always handle what they wanted to give and you couldn't talk to a matrix brain to explain your constraints.

Hani, thank the gods, were much more straightforward.

"What's the situation at Meetpoint?" Padur asked on the way to the airlock.

"Chancy. You want my opinion, if I weren't carrying what I'm carrying, for a rate I can't tell you, I'd do a turn-around at Hoas back for here. Something's going on with the stsho, you've guessed that the same as I have, and I don't have the least idea what, but it would keep me out of Meetpoint if I wasn't paid real, real well. *Possibly* the administration there is in some kind of crisis. Possibly the crisis is here. Possibly . . ." The idea occurred to her on the spot, and she might have censored it, but these were allied captains, of nominally friendly clans. "Possibly it could be a crisis much further into stsho territory. And someone wiser than I am should consider that possibility. I've no way to get a message anywhere, except by you."

Kaury Narn gave her a particularly straight stare. And nodded and left. Padur walked with her down the yellow, ribbed tube, around the curve, the two of them talking together and doubtless more comfortably, with an associate decades older in her friendship than a young upstart Chanur.

Seniority was what they had lost, with Pyanfar out of the picture, and doubly so with Rhean retiring to manage the situation at home. From senior, and important, Chanur had descended to a Who are you? from captains who honestly had to see Hilfy Chanur to know whether they could trust her word or her judgment. Oh, they *knew* her: they'd recall her as one of *The Pride*'s crew, once upon a time; but no few of the captains and worse, the crewwomen, gave her that second look that remarked her youth, and wondered what deals she'd cut to obtain of her clan, at her age, the post they'd worked a lifetime for.

Working *for* her aunt, certain mahendo'sat evidently thought—running the *mekt-hakkikt's* errands and serving as decoy.

Having notions, the old women in the *han* would say of her and of Pyanfar. Delusions of deity. A disdain for Anuurn. A blurring of self—what was hani and what was not. Herself, yes, defiantly she blurred those lines—but blurred lines were definitely not Pyanfar's attitude: that was the first and foremost of the problems between them.

The loader clanked. She held her breath, stopped in her office door, wondering was it going to balk and stick. It kept on. Tiar passed her, paint-spattered, towing a large carrier full of plastic-wrapped cushions, all white.

"For the gods' sake watch the—whatever-it-is. Don't spatter it."

"Won't, cap'n," Tiar panted. Chihin and Fala brought up the rear, with a lamp trailing connections, like some sea creature rudely uprooted. A trail of white dust tracked down the *Legacy*'s corridor, while *gtst* honor sat in sheet-draped splendor in the lounge, making personal purchases on the station market and demanding to be back in *gtst* quarters as soon as possible.

The loader balked again, cl-unk. She looked at the deck as if she could look through it, beseeched the indifferent gods of trade, and the thing limped onward. It worked better on incoming, for some reason known only to those gods. They had the cursed thing on auto at the moment, and trusted mahen passers-by and dockers not to fling themselves gratuitously into the gears and sue while Tarras was working inside.

Impossible. Impossible to get out of here with any dispatch. And a tired crew was asking for accidents to happen.

Wasn't, however, the only source of brute muscle they had aboard. The stsho was topside and little likely to stir.

She walked down to the laundry, hit the door once, and opened it.

Hallan Meras stuffed something away in a hurry, ears flat, face dismayed, and she surveyed the laundry, that now contained pieces of the crew lounge, the galley, and somebody's personal library.

"Captain," Hallan said, scrambling for his feet. He *was* respectful, commendably so.

"Crew says you say you can work cargo."

"Aye, captain."

Sounded sane. Sounded like someone who could take basic orders.

"We've got a problem," she said. "We're in a crunch, Tarras

is working the loader solo, inside, we've got nobody keeping the local kids' fingers out of the loader—I don't suppose you brought a coat, did you?"

"No, captain." Ears flagged. "But I could sort of wrap a blanket around—"

"Unworkable. No boots, no coat, no cold suit, no hold. Can you *behave* yourself on the dockside? We're going late. We're nearly 12 hours behind, we're unloading and we're loading, fast as I can get the buy made and the cans on our dock. Nobody's getting any sleep."

"I'd *love* to, captain. I really would!"

She truly didn't trust enthusiasm in a kid who'd broken up the Meetpoint market. She refused to soften her expression, only stared at him with ears flat and nose drawn. "Hallan Meras, have you lied? *Can* you work cargo? *Do* you know what you're doing?"

"I swear to you, captain."

"You foul up, you break any seals, you scare *anybody* on this station, Hallan Meras, I'll sell you to the kif."

"Aye, captain."

She hated when people she threatened were over-anxious to go ahead.

"At ten percent off," she said. But she failed to kill his enthusiasm. And it made her remember what he *really* wanted, which she wouldn't give, wasn't about to give, gods rot him. She had a smoothly functioning crew, they understood each other, they were relatives, they had everything they needed.

He was also too gods-rotted handsome and too feckless and too *male*, confound him, which was the main reason to get him out of here before more than the crew lounge and the galley found its way down here.

"Get!" she said, shoved a pocket com into his hand, and he got, down the main corridor toward the airlock, at a near run.

Couldn't fault that. She looked for ways. She went into the laundry, looked around for signs of mayhem or misdeed, found nothing out of order except one unfolded blanket, the viewer, the *Manual of Trade,* for some gods-only-knew reason, and . . .

She bent and drew from under the blast cushion the printed book Hallan Meras had put there.

And who gave him *that?* she wondered.

Chapter Seven

You didn't run on the rampway link, you respected that perilous connection, that icy cold passage that gave a ship pressured access to station.

But Hallan walked it very fast, and, via the pocket com, called Tarras to report in: he figured that was the first test, whether he could use it and whether he knew what to do next.

"*What are* you *doing out there?*" Tarras snapped at him, probably cold, certainly surprised.

"The captain said I should, she said you could use some help."

"*Gods-rotted right I could use some help, but don't scare the dockers! Are you on pocket com?*"

"Aye."

"*You keep near the access ramp. And don't be sightseeing!*"

"I'm at the bottom now. Have you got a cam-link?" That, he figured, would tell Tarras he had some notion what his job was. "We've got space for one more can on the transport, we've got a 14 canner moving up. Have we got a destination list?"

"*Your display, code 2, check it out. Docker chief's a curly-coated fellow, and just hold it, I'll call him and tell him who you are. For godssake, bow, be polite, you'll scare him into a heart seizure.*"

"Aye, I do understand. Tell me when it's clear." He used his time taking stock of the surroundings, *feeling* the cold near the access and wishing that he could move away from the draft. The pocket com had a display: keyed, it scrolled the offload, 142 of the giant containers gone to their various buyers, the loader with, one reckoned, 10 more in its grip, outbound, and the transport sitting there with 15, which meant that particular hold was probably approaching empty, and Tarras was going to have to initiate the number two hold, which—

"You're clear," Tarras said. *"His name is Pokajinai, Nandijigan Pokajinai, he speaks the trade, mind your manners."*

"Got it." He spotted the mahe docker chief, flipped the com to standby and strolled over. He saw the apprehensive expression, too, and made his most courteous bow. "Sir." In case they thought hani males went homicidally for anything of like gender. "Hallan Meras. *Na* Pokajinai?"

A nervous laughter from the rest of the dockers.

"Name Nandijigan, call Nandi. You Meras."

"Meras is fine." His father would have his ears. "Ker Tarras is working inside, I'm her eyes out here."

"Not hear Chanur ship got male," somebody muttered. He was undecided whether to hear it or not. He decided not. He simply flipped the com to active and advised Tarras he'd made peaceful contact.

It was wonderful. It was the best thing in all the universe, being out here, trusted, with the smells and even the cold, and the noise of foreign voices—the clangs and bangs of machinery, and the romance of the labels that the docker chief had to give mahen customs stamps to, and write on, and sign for.

They were a lot less likely to have a miscount with one of the *Legacy* crew out here. It was a real position of trust the captain had given him—she *had* listened to the other crew on his case, so there was still hope of pleasing her and becoming indispensable and permanent.

"How's it going?" Tarras asked, breathless, teeth chattering, he could hear the rattle over the com.

"Everything's clear," he said. "Ker Tarras, are you all right?"

"Cold. Just cold."

There were transports coming, a *lot* of them, and there was nobody else loading at this section of the docks. The 16-carrier moved out with a whine of its motor, and the 14 moved in. Another 16-carrier moved into the waiting line and the automated handlers moved can after can out, instantly frosting on the surfaces, internally heated, but the insulation was so efficient they could sit in a cold-hold and keep their necessary conditions within parameters. Tarras had been scrambling about the latticework of walkways in the hold unhooking the connections and the hoses from the temperature-controlled cans. Alone, the captain said. No wonder she was out of breath.

Where had everybody else gone? He had no idea what time it was. He didn't think it was a good idea to ask questions, especially on the comlink, outside—just do his job.

Maybe Tarras would get some relief in there.

Meanwhile he consulted with the mahendo'sat and relayed Tarras' suggestions about sequencing the offload, to minimize shifting the cans about from loader arm to loader arm. *He* was cold. He didn't want to think how it was for Tarras.

Cl-ank. Cl-l-l-l-

Tarras said a word over com you weren't supposed to say on com.

The loader chain had stopped. The loader arm was half extended.

"Can you back it up?" he asked Tarras. "If you can sort of rock it—"

"I know that!"

"It's those 14-can transports."

"What?" Tarras snapped.

"The 14-can—"

"What's that to do with the gods-forsaken chain?"

"The loader arm. When it extends full out."

"What's that to do with anything?"

"It has to. The 14-can jobs, the old ones are a little low. The loader arm has to extend out, it cramps the leads, and it just—ties up. You back the loader arm up."

"Are you serious?"

"It works with the *Sun's* loader, *ker* Tarras. The loader arm tells the driver the chain's hung. But it isn't. The loader just thinks it is. Back the arm up and set it down about a hand short. —Wait a minute. You're going to—"

Bang.

Into the carrier cab.

"Not that far," he said.

"That's where it goes!"

The mahen driver was getting out, yelling in his own language, and when people did that it scared him, like at Meetpoint, like when the fight started, and he didn't want to fight anybody. He made a fast approach to the docker chief, but all the mahendo'sat were yelling, and the docker chief screamed, "Move damn cart! How for park there?"

He thought the chief meant him. He was by the single-can cart, it was no more than a lift vehicle they had to hoist the inbound cans, but they didn't need it yet. He just stepped aboard and backed up out of the can-transport's way so *it* could adjust position with the arm.

"Move damn thing!" the transport driver yelled at him. "Damn stupid park there!"

He didn't know who had. He wanted to save his ship fault in the matter. He whipped it smartly around; and *bang!*—

Brought up short, with a transport there filling his view that just hadn't been there before, a transport that was flashing yellow lights and shrieking alarm, with a writhing shape inside the purple-lit glass.

Methane transport. . . . Explosive as hell.

He tried to go forward. The bumpers were hooked.

He cut the motor. He had that much presence of mind. Lights were flashing everywhere. Sirens were shrieking. The ten-story-tall section doors were moving shut, walling off their whole area of dock.

"Ker Tarras?" he said into the com. "Help."

* * *

"*Captain?*" came the call on all-ship.

"Lower main," Hilfy said, got the message, and something like three seconds later was on the downward access.

Colored lights were everywhere, sirens were blowing, there was a tc'a vehicle and a cargo lifter clearly in mortal embrace, with rescue techs swarming over the scene, and a knot of Urtur station police clustered about Hallan Meras, who was out of his vehicle and answering questions with the gods only knew what legally complicating admissions.

She drew a breath and strode down into the mess, answered the inevitable, "You captain this ship?" with the lamentable truth, and fixed Hallan with a flat-eared look. His ears twitched downward, and he winced, but he did not look down.

"Is the methane truck leaking?" she asked. If the tc'a vehicle was leaking its atmosphere into flammable oxygen, this was a bad place to be standing. Procedure was to evacuate the passenger into a rescue pod, pump the methane atmosphere into a sound container, and get the victim methane-side for medical treatment, rather than to pry the wreckage apart—but nobody had told the docker who was bouncing on the oxy-vehicle bumper trying to disengage it. "Stop that!" she shouted. "Fool!"

The police and the rescue workers started yelling, and maybe the tc'a in the cab was distraught too: it started writhing about, its serpentine body bashing the windows of the cab with powerful blows, and wailing—wailing in a tc'a's multipartite voice its distress. Its companion chi was racing about—a wonder that the convulsions didn't smash the sticklike creature to paste, and the whole cab was rocking, rescue workers were shouting at the tow-truck, something about come on, hurry up.

Then the thrashing grew quiet. The rescue workers climbed up on the cab and peered inside, and Hilfy held her breath. There was a lot of dialectic chatter, a lot of muttering and one of the workers got down off the cab and began motioning the tow-truck to move in.

The police yelled at the rescue workers, the rescue workers yelled at the police, Hallan said, "I'm sorry, captain."

"What," she said in a low voice, "happened?"

"The loader jammed. I backed the truck. It just—turned up in back of me."

Tc'a didn't exactly drive a straight line. It was the nature of their nervous systems. "Do you have a license to drive on dockside?"

"No, captain."

"Do you suppose there's a reason why you don't have a license to drive on dockside?"

"I think so, captain."

The police were coming back. They had the tow truck hitched. "Watch your mouth," she said. "Let *me* do the talking." Out of the tail of her eye she saw Tiar and Tarras on the ramp, and Fala behind them.

And the police were on their way back to them, with their slates and their recorders. Lawyers would be next—if it was an oxy-sider Meras had backed into. One could only wish it was lawyers.

"It reproduce," their chief said, with an expansive gesture involving his slate. "You responsible. Urtur station not."

She drew a long careful breath. "You write your report. I write mine."

"We got take him."

Tempting thought. "No."

"He not list with you crew."

"He's on loan. He's a licensed spacer. I put him on the dockside. I take responsibility for accidents."

"Captain," Hallan objected, brim full of noble and foolish objections—her claws twitched out and her vision shadowed around the edges.

"Shut *up*, Meras. —I'll need a copy of your report, officer, and I'll pay charges on the alarm."

Don't even ask if anybody was injured when the section doors moved shut. Disruption of business, inconvenience to traffic, time and services of rescue workers and police . . .

Say about 200,000 in damages . . . give or take.

She signed the report as Reserving the right to amend or correct, and so on, due to language barrier and lack of legal counsel, etc., and so on. She thanked the officers, thanked the rescue workers, gave the eye to her crew lurking up in the ramp access, and smiled sweetly at Meras.

"He try fix loader," the docker chief said.

Grant the fellow a fair mind and an inclination to speak out. She delayed for a look up at the mahe, and gave a bow of the head, and put the name in memory, Nandi, in the not unlikely event they needed a witness. "He thanks you for your support," she said, in her best mahendi, and gave a second bow, before she took Meras by the arm and headed him up the ramp.

"I feel awful it was pregnant," he said on the way up, and she threw him a disbelieving glance.

"They *reproduce* under stress," she said. "You're a *father*, gods rot you, to a tc'a! What's lord Meras going to say to *that?*"

He looked horrified. Appropriately. About the time they reached Tiar and Fala and Chihin.

"It spawned," she said, shortly. "Probably so did the chi. —Tiar, get up to the bridge. See to *gtst* honor!"

"Aye, captain."

Tiar went, at top speed. That left two. "Fala, down there and take over for Meras. —Chihin, you're on your own with the guest quarters. Get!"

The com was trying to get her attention with periodic, when-you-have-time beeps. She waited until she had gotten Meras into the airlock, and keyed into the ship's internal system. "Tarras. You all right?"

"Aye, captain." Chattering teeth. *"Captain, the kid was giving me a fix on the loader."*

"Fix on the loader." Two and two weren't making four. "You get that gods-forsaken cargo out of there. I'll hear it later." She grabbed Meras by the elbow and steered him through the lock and down the corridor toward her office.

"Captain, I'm really sorry. I'm really—really sorry you had to take responsibility . . ."

"We are in one gods-rotted *mess*, you understand that? You understand me?"

"Captain." From the com again. Tarras. *"I'd really like to talk to you about what happened. . . ."*

"Later!"

They reached her office and Meras followed her in. She sat, he sat, disconsolately, his big frame somewhat overflowing the chair that was designed to accommodate even mahendo'sat. She stared, he looked at the front panel of her desk, or somewhere in that vicinity. The loader had started again. Presumably they had the go-ahead from the port authority. Clank-clank. Clank-thump.

"Meras."

"Yes, captain."

"Do you know what you've *cost* us in fines?"

"If there were any way I could take responsibility—"

"Would Meras like a 200,000 credit bill?"

"I don't think so."

"I thought your captain was reprehensible for leaving you at Meetpoint. I begin to feel a certain sympathy for her, you know that?"

"Yes, captain."

"I don't have a license to drive that cart. Tiar's been out here for forty years and she doesn't have a license to back that cart up. Do you understand me?"

"Yes, captain."

"I want you to understand something. We have a stsho passenger who's already in delicate health. They are *not* a robust species. This stsho is occupying the cabin around the corner from here. If *gtst* saw you, it could tip matters right over the edge. Do you understand *that* fact?"

"Yes, captain." A visible wince. "—Captain,—"

"*Yes,* Meras?"

"I really—really want to do right. I can *do* a good job—"

"Two hundred thousand worth. That's a gods-rotted steep hourly wage!"

"I didn't know about the license! The loader was jammed, and they couldn't move the truck till somebody moved the cart—"

"Until a licensed driver moved the cart!"

"I didn't know that!"

"Well, there's a gods-be lot you didn't learn in your apprenticeship, Hallan Meras, and you're not doing it at our expense. We've got to go on out of here to Kita, from Kita the gods only know where the gods-forsaken addressee has gone to, but *gtst* is on a mahen ship, and from Kita our choices are Not Good. Do you follow my logic? This is no trip and no place for any gods-rotted apprentice!"

"I'm not an apprentice—I've got my license—"

"Got your license—I'd like to know how in a mahen hell you got your license, I'd like to know doing what you got your license, because it sure as taxes wasn't on any dockside ops board, and it gods-rotted sure didn't entitle you to back a cart the length of this office! You're a papa, Hallan Meras, you're a papa to a methane-breathing five-brained colony entity and probably to another chi who's crazier than it is—and mama or whatever you call it when you reproduce when startled is just capable of asking his, her, or its matrix what gods-be *ship* its offspring's papa is working on! Methane folk have this way of turning up in the deep dark empty and saying hello when you don't want to see them. Methane folk have this way of navigating that doesn't respect lanes in space any more than they respect lines on a dock! I've had them come near my ship when they weren't after anything, thank you, Hallan Meras, and I don't want to deal with them when they are! I by the gods sure don't want to meet that mama or its offspring in deep space! Do you remotely understand why I'm upset?"

"I could—I could try to have station get a message to them, station can talk with them . . ."

"That's a myth. That's a thorough-going myth. Station can approximate things like 'Open the hatch,' and 'That's a fire hazard!' It doesn't do gods-be well with, 'Hello, I'm Hallan Meras, I'm responsible for your offspring.' They've been in space long before we were, and we *still* don't know how to say 'Stop it you're in my lane,' and: 'My ship can't perform that maneuver.' You want to see a matrix brain communication? I can show you one. . . ." She got into comp with two jabs of a key and voiced it: "Matrix-com!"

Matrix-com came up, with the typical grid. Five rows across, output of each of five voices of its multiple brains. She hit vocal and knnn-voice wailed over the speaker, like a wind-organ, like pipes, and deep, deep bass vibrations.

Hallan winced, ears twitching with the assault, nostrils working. He shivered visibly. *Then* she remembered she was dealing with adolescent male hormones, which ought to give a sane woman pause—but gods rot it, he insisted he was one of the girls, that he was cool-headed, he wanted to play the game on their terms; and she slammed her hand down on the desk, *bang!*

"Off-comp!"

Sound stopped. And Meras was still twitching, but he hadn't left his chair, his eyes were dilated, but the ears were trying to come upright—he was paying attention, he was listening, he wasn't crazy.

"*Captain.*" Tiar—on the bridge. Magnificent timing.

"I'm in my office, Tiar. What's the problem?"

"*Just got a blip on station feed.* Sun Ascendant's *just entered system.*"

The answer to prayers, it might be.

Hallan looked upset. Shook his head and shaped No with his mouth. Said something else.

"Thanks, cousin. Glad to hear that."

"I don't want to go, captain. I don't want them—"

"You signed with them. You sat at their table, you slept in their shelter, they got you your license, and I don't know what made them leave you at Meetpoint, Meras, but so far as what I've seen they may have run for their lives."

Made him mad, that did. Good.

"If you want to go back to the laundry, you stay there. If you want to go back to the passenger cabins and help Chihin paint and patch, feel free. I'm not turning you over to station police, and being the righteous fool I am, I'm not identifying *Sun Ascendant* to the tc'a. We'll handle it. But I've done everything I'm obliged to do for somebody I gathered out of a jail he by the gods got himself into. I've got 41 messages in ship's files for my aunt at this station; I've got 156 for *me,* most of them from people trying to use me to get *to* my aunt for favors they want; and here comes one of my aunt's devoted admirers who just really badly wants into my crew, because he just really badly *wants* it, that's why. —Well, so does half the universe, Meras. And I'd suggest you give up and go home if meeting my aunt is what you want; or if being a spacer is what you want, focus down and use your head on problems before you kill somebody. I'd suggest you give up on the *Manual of Trade* and start reading the licensing and operations manual. It may keep you out of the next hot spot you land in. —And give my regards to Tellun Sahern. Minute your ship makes port you're going over there."

Ears were flat. Really mad. Better. Maybe he'd *survive* in Sahern, in far space.

"Go on," she said. And he got up and bowed and left.

Which didn't make her happy. Nobody could be happy, who had a 200,000 credit charge pending against her ship, a cargo half unloaded, a distraught stsho dignitary in the crew lounge, and a course change pending to Kita Point, a gods-forsaken dot in the great empty, after which, as she had said to Meras—limited options.

"Ker Chihin," Hallan said, hesitating in the open doorway. "The captain suggested I help."

"I don't need anything backed into," Chihin said shortly, and Hallan winced. The room was all white. The furniture was gone. You walked up steps to the floor and there was a depression full of white cushions.

Besides there was a pedestal with braces going out to it, but nothing on it.

"You can vacuum," Chihin said. "Floor, walls, everything. Steam vac. All the dust. Height could help. Are your feet clean?"

He looked. They weren't, exactly. "I'll go wash," he said meekly.

"Packaged wet towel, right there by the steps." Chihin frowned at him as he sat down on the steps and reached for it. He tried not to look at her face. He felt sick, he had felt sick ever since he had backed into the tc'a, but he couldn't go back to that closed room, he couldn't stand it. So he washed his feet off so no one could complain of a smudge and he looked for a place to dispose of the towel.

"Over there," Chihin said, indicating a plastic bucket. He went and dropped it in. "You know how to use the steam vac?"

"Yes, ma'am." He was too well acquainted with it. It was all Sahern had let him do for his first weeks aboard the *Sun*. He went and checked the prime, checked the water and pulled the filter screen, which he figured he ought to clean before someone else found fault with him. "Is there a sink, ma'am, or should I—"

"Bath's in there. Sink works just like ours—it's the fixture on the left."

He went and washed the filter. It *was* different plumbing. Ordinarily he would have been intrigued, but the lump in his throat would not go away and he just tried to go moment by moment and not to think about what the captain had said, one way or the other. The captain had a right to be mad, gods, he couldn't pay back the damage he'd cost—probably nobody in Meras clan history had ever fouled up so egregiously, so consistently.

But the docking chief had *said* to move the cart.

He put the vacuum back together. He took it to a corner and started there, with a racket that made conversation impossible. But he was aware of Chihin staring at him from time to time: maybe she expected the vac to explode or something; or him to do something she could fault. Of all the crew, Chihin was not in any way friendly, and he supposed by now the rest of the crew was ready to kill him. Except maybe . . . at least Tarras had tried to speak for him. Fala and Tiar had looked upset, as well they might, but they hadn't hated him. Chihin—

didn't want him here. Which was why the captain had sent him to work with her, he supposed. But it was still better than sitting alone in the laundry and remembering backing into that truck, and that *thing* snaking back and forth in pain and battering itself against the windows, leaving bits of skin and fluid on the glass. . . .

At least it hadn't exploded. Nobody had gotten killed. Quite the opposite. Somebody had gotten created. He wondered how the tc'a felt.

"The kid was trying to straighten out the loader," Tarras said. There was still ice in her beard, melting and glistening in the heat of the downside office—Hilfy had called her up, ordered her to trade places with Fala, and the way to the dock lay through the lower main corridor and past her office. So she had both of them, Tarras *and* Fala, arguing with her, the loader was in temporary shut-down, pending the switch, and no cargo was moving. But she figured she might as well listen and be done with it.

"All right," she said. "Voices on Meras' behalf . . . while we're at it." She pushed the call button. "Cousin. Listen in."

"Aye," Tiar answered from the bridge. *"What's up?"*

"The loader jammed," Tarras said, and sat down, while Fala edged a half a step further into the office, in the doorway. "The kid knew the equipment—*Sun Ascendant* must use the same model. Anyway, it pulled its usual stunt, and the kid said it was the 14-can truck, when the arm positions itself: he says it's a false signal, there's nothing to do with the chain, it's the arm overextending. This one model of truck has a slightly lower bed. It reaches down to get it, the arm jams, jams the chain, you back the chain—it fixes it. So if you move the truck a little farther—"

"The docker chief said he's heard of it," Fala said. "It's something they say on the docks but the companies won't investigate. Doesn't happen until the equipment gets a little wear on it, and then it'll happen if the play that gets into the joint works far enough to the right where the sensor bundle runs through, and *that* bias only happens when you get a whole lot of fifteen-year-old Daisaiji 14-canners in a row. Which you get on Urtur, they got more of them than anywhere, because they made them here. And it only happens if some driver parks short. That's why it comes and it goes."

She couldn't help but be interested in the purported solution to the loader glitch, if it was the answer—it sounded iffy to her; but most of all she didn't want to hear it was Meras who had the information. She'd worked up a perfectly good, justified fit of temper, from which Meras could learn something that *might* keep him alive, and she didn't want any extenuating circumstances.

"So the thing jammed," Tarras said, "and the docker crew wanted to move the truck, and somebody'd parked a can-hoist in the way—"

"Probably why the truck parked short," Fala said.

"And the kid said it was the truck, so the chief started yelling about moving the truck," Tarras said. "He was pretty hot, so the kid—just got in and backed it up."

"Without a license."

"Captain," Tarras said, "the length of the truck, it had to move. Isn't a spacer working freight hasn't stepped aboard and moved a hoist a few—"

"I haven't. I don't want my crew doing it. You *let the dockers* do their job, you don't lay a hand on their equipment, we got a special handicap, f' godssake, Chanur's got too many enemies who'd like to sue the hide off us, you understand?"

"Understood," Tarras said sullenly.

"But," Fala said, "it was only cosmic bad luck the tc'a was back there—"

"Luck! Methane loads come in on oxy side all the time at Urtur, and we got tc'a going back and forth on business oxy side, and it had business which is now complicated by an offspring! We can only hope we don't get *company* our next trip out. Luck be damned!"

"Aye, captain."

"Captain," Tiar said, *"begging your pardon, but he's young. Haven't any of us made mistakes?"*

"He can make them on *Sahern's* deck, and welcome to him. Enthusiasm is one thing. We can't afford his enthusiasm. Besides, his ship is here—"

"They didn't do him any favors, cap'n. That's their teaching? They take a kid on for an apprentice, and he's got a little of this, a little of that? I asked him stuff on ops. He knows this board real well, doesn't know how it relates to the main board. That's 'Sit here and watch the colored lights, kid,' that's what they gave him."

"It's not our problem! He's not signed with us, he signed with them."

Silence from Tarras and Fala. Glum stares.

"Aye," Tiar conceded from the bridge, not happy.

So no one was. She wasn't. Meras wasn't. But neither, one could suppose, was the tc'a.

Meanwhile *Sun Ascendant* was inbound, in contact with Urtur control. "To work," she said, and, in peace, composed a polite message for merchant captain Tellun Sahern, to rest in her message file.

From Chanur's Legacy *to* Sahern's Sun Ascendant, *the hand of Hilfy Chanur, to Tellun Sahern, her attention:*

We are pleased to report that—

No, scratch that. Sahern would find a way to take it wrong.

Meetpoint authorities, having dropped all charges against Hallan Meras, requested us to ferry him as far as Urtur where he might rejoin his ship. We will be glad to escort him to your dockside at your earliest convenience or to turn him over to your escort here if that is your wish.

From Sahern's Sun Ascendant *to* Chanur's Legacy, *the hand of Tellun Sahern, to Hilfy Chanur, her attention:*

We trade for a living, we don't take secret money or run without cargo.

It's clear you had a motive in buying him free of the stsho.

As you've surely learned by now, he has no data on our ship to give you. I doubt he could even falsify credible numbers. Chanur has made its bargains. We will not rescue you from your folly.

The message slipped into the tray in printout. It burned on the screen. Hilfy pushed the button to capture to log, took the printout and slipped it into physical file.

The message she thought of sending was: *Earless bastard, I thought your reputation had hit bottom.*

The message she sent was:

From Chanur's Legacy *to* Sahern's Sun Ascendant, *the hand of Hilfy Chanur, to Tellun Sahern, her attention:*

We require a release from apprenticeship signed by you, under Sahern seal, and we will seek passage or assignment for him elsewhere.

From Sahern's Sun Ascendant *to* Chanur's Legacy, *the hand of Tellun Sahern, to Hilfy Chanur, her attention:*

Too late, Chanur. We've been following the news since we entered system. We accept no legal liability for the actions of a fool we left in stsho custody and you conveyed here and let loose on Urtur docks. You bought him. He's yours.

Although I thought your personal preferences lay outside your species.

From Chanur's Legacy *to* Sahern's Sun Ascendant, *the hand of Hilfy Chanur, to Tellun Sahern, her attention:*

Daughter of a nameless father, if this young man wishes to file a complaint against you for desertion in a foreign port, I will swear to particulars.

As to my personal tastes, at least I have preferences.

Possibly she had made a mistake. Temper had gotten the better of her. She should not have offered legal backing. She sat contemplating the screen, and thinking black and blacker and blackest thoughts.

"Captain?" Tiar asked from the bridge. *"We got all that on log."*

"Good."

"Kid never got a fair break, captain."

"The universe doesn't guarantee fair breaks, and I don't want any apprentice under *any* circumstances! Something's gone wrong with this whole business, we've got a nervous stsho on our hands and Kita is no place to take a novice. I want you to contact Narn and Padur—no, never mind. *I* will."

"Captain. Can I say a word?"

"I know what you're going to say, and I'm not listening."

"Captain, on behalf of the crew . . ."

"We're not taking any apprentice! His apprentice papers are over on a Sahern ship, they're not going to give them to Chanur, they're out to cause us whatever trouble they can, the whole radical right is looking for a Cause against Chanur, and I was a fool ever to agree to take him aboard—I *thought* Sahern would be reasonable, but clearly not."

She beeped off the contact, and composed another message—thought about couriering this one over to avoid public commotion and public pressure, and thought about the hazards of sending *Legacy* personnel alone and within reach of station police, angry merchants—or Ana-kehnandian.

No. *No* such chances.

From Chanur's Legacy *to* Padur's Victory, *the hand of Hilfy Chanur, to Tauhen Padur, her attention:*

We have advised Sahern of the presence of their apprentice crewman, Hallan Meras, on our ship. They have refused responsibility for this young man, who has been cleared of all charges which caused him to be detained by stsho authorities, and further, they have refused him access to their ship in harsh terms, preferring to recall an ancient feud with Chanur, no fault of this young man of Meras clan, a licensed spacer, who has traveled under our protection.

While Padur has no obligation, Chanur would be obliged if

Padur could take this young man under its protection and possibly find a berth for him.

From Padur's Victory *to* Chanur's Legacy, *the hand of Tauhen Padur, to Hilfy Chanur, her attention:*

Padur while friendly to Chanur and altogether desirous of maintaining Chanur's good will, under the circumstances of the recent accident on Chanur dockside must regretfully decline to incur the possibility of legal liabilities under mahen law.

From Chanur's Legacy *to* Narn's Dawnmaker, *the hand of Hilfy Chanur, to Kaury Narn, her attention:*

We have advised Sahern of the presence of their apprentice crewman, Hallan Meras, on our ship. They have refused responsibility for this young man, who has been cleared of all charges which caused him to be detained by stsho authorities, and further, they have refused him access in harsh terms, preferring to recall an ancient feud with Chanur, no fault of this young man of Meras clan, who has traveled under our protection.

While Padur has declined our solicitation, we hope and Chanur would be obliged if Narn could take this young man, a licensed spacer, under its protection in any sense whatsoever.

From Narn's Dawnmaker *to* Chanur's Legacy, *the hand of Kaury Narn, to Hilfy Chanur, her attention:*

I have my sister's young daughter aboard: I could not in good conscience expose her or Meras clan to the consequences of taking on this young man. Nor do we have passenger facilities. However, Narn is willing, under appropriate safeguards, and at Chanur's request and assumption of all consequent responsibility to Meras, to convey the young gentleman under close supervision as far as Hoas, where he may await a ship with familial connections.

* * *

Read that: lock him in the laundry and turn him over to Hoas authorities. At least no worse accommodation than he had, and a station where (gods hope!) he had no legal problems. But going to Hoas took him *back* toward Meetpoint, and he would have to come back through Urtur again.

Where that ship might find legal problems waiting for them, unless they could get a release, and she *knew* the mahen politics waiting for them.

Hilfy sat and contemplated the screen; and sent back:

From Chanur's Legacy *to* Narn's Dawnmaker, *the hand of Hilfy Chanur, to Kaury Narn, her attention:*

Thank you for your offer. We fully understand. We will hold your proposal in reserve while we seek other safe disposition for—

—him.

The pronoun itself was unaccustomed out here. Ten, fifteen years ago, you didn't by the gods *use* the male pronoun in a message between clans. It still felt queasy and indecent. It felt indecent to have one's decades-senior aunt ahead of one's self in pushing the conservative limits. When had *she* become the defender of hani propriety?

—the gentleman, she finished. *If we don't get back to you, we wish you a safe voyage.*

And to Padur:

From Chanur's Legacy *to* Padur's Victory, *the hand of Hilfy Chanur, to Tauhen Padur, her attention:*

We are seeking other solutions. Please bear witness that we have attempted the honorable discharge of our reasonable obligations to Sahern and to Meras. Safe voyage.

She sat. And sat.

She *wished* she had not used the com in the approach to Sahern. Aunt *never* used com for clan to clan business if she could help it. Good, on the one hand, that the initial business with Sahern was on public record and overheard by two other clans. She did *not* regret that. But . . . mahendo'sat who did not speak hani certainly had translators. So did the kif, of whom there were fifteen in system.

She had a prickly feeling all down her back, the same feeling the whole atmosphere at Urtur gave her—since the dust-up in customs, and the Personage's too-easy dismissal of Anakehnandian, and every gods-be stsho on the station running for elsewhere when *she* had the Preciousness just itching to be delivered to somebody.

It had the feeling of powers at war, somewhere. And powers at war always went for the soft spots, the joinings between uneasy allies, the bribes, the coercions—the cooperations.

The feuds.

Chapter Eight

Ker Chihin passed finger-pads over the panel surface, stooped and passed the same inspection over the floor, and evidently she found no fault with the job. Hallan put the vac away; and *ker* Chihin inspected that, too, then told him to take it to the laundry and stow it in the number 3 locker.

Then Chihin said, "Good job, kid."

He looked back from the doorway, and bowed, hands full and all. He didn't think he was called on to say anything, just to keep quiet and do what he was told; so he went and stowed the vac.

But *ker* Chihin hadn't said about whether to come back or not. He thought he should; and came quietly back and stopped in the doorway, because Chihin was fixing a case back in the traveling brace, on the pedestal, and it might be fragile.

He waited until she had tightened the bolts and slid the cover off the box, which proved to hold a simple vase. Then he cleared his throat.

"Gods *rot* you!" Chihin cried, with a start, and knocked back into a bucket of construction trash and another of panel clips.

"I'm sorry, *ker* Chihin."

"You didn't see this thing."

"Yes, *ker* Chihin." He honestly wished he hadn't. He thought maybe he was meant to get out, immediately, but Chihin started picking up loose bits and pieces of the scattered debris. He went to help, tentatively, and grabbed up loose panel clips as fast as he could find them, until he had a double handful.

"You be careful you don't miss any of those. If one of those goes whizzing around here under *v*, you don't want to know what it'd do to a body's head."

"I know, *ker* Chihin. I'm sorry."

"It was my foot," Chihin muttered, which was fairer than most ever were to him. He went back after more clips, and searched all around the edges of the cabin, and around the cushions and down in them, no matter how remote the chance.

No more of them. He came back and dumped what he had.

"Boy,—what got into you, wanting to come out here?"

"Captain said I could help . . ."

"I mean *here.* I mean going to space."

That question. It always came up. "I *wanted* to."

"I know that. But what's a nice kid want to come out here and run over tc'a and get arrested for?"

Ker Chihin didn't think he belonged here. He was used to that. And you couldn't argue with it. He shut up and kept his head down, already knowing the captain was going to throw him off the ship, so there was no use in arguing.

"Kid?"

"I wanted to go to space, that's all."

"Think you couldn't have found yourself a spot on Anuurn? Don't think there's some niche you could have carved out? You're a good-looking kid. You'd have gotten somebody's attention."

"I guess. Maybe. I don't know." He'd been through this too many times, with every ship he applied to, with the one that had taken him, with every member of the *Sun*'s crew, in one form or another. Sometimes he'd given answers to make them happy. He'd caught himself lying and sworn off it. But he didn't want to argue with Chihin either. The day had already gone wrong enough.

"So what d' you think?" Chihin asked. "Is space what you expected?"

"I don't know." Same stupid answer. He found a piece of debris and brought it back, thinking, and he said it: his back was to the wall and he couldn't lose any more than he had. "But I don't want to go back. And I'm getting better."

"At what? Parking?" Chihin said, straight to the sore spot. He kept his head down and picked up the container of debris. "You know where to take that?"

"To 'cycling. I guess it's out by the lifts."

"You guess right." Which let him go, so he went out down the corridors and sorted the trash into the right chutes, plastics and metal bits apart, then wiped the bucket down and took it back to the only place he knew to take it.

"Goes in the maintenance locker," Chihin said. "That's—"

"Lower Main 2. Next the lift. I spotted it."

Chihin frowned at him and flattened her ears. He didn't know whether Chihin was annoyed at him or not. "Sharp eyes we have."

"Shall I put it up, *ker* Chihin?"

"Get," she said. He got, back to the area he had just been in. The lift was working. One of the crew coming down, he thought. He opened the locker, stowed the bucket, and was just latching the door when the lift door opened. He looked up, to say hello to whatever of the crew it was.

It wasn't.

He saw the stsho in the same moment it saw him. He stared in shock; it let out a warbling shriek and ducked back into the lift.

He ducked back down the corridor. Fast. And around to where its cabin was.

"Chihin!" he stammered. And when Chihin looked at him: "I think it saw me. The stsho. It was in the lift."

Chihin blasphemed in a major way and told him to go to his quarters. So he went there, and shut the door and sat down on the cushion.

He hadn't thought things could get worse, or imagined that he could find another way to foul things up.

Oh, *gods,* he hadn't thought so.

"Perfectly safe," Hilfy said in her best stshoshi Trade. "I do assure your honor, this is a person who came aboard with references from *gtst* excellency *gtst*self . . ."

". . . *who lied!*" Tlisi-tlas-tin said from the speaker.

Hilfy leaned against the panel, kept her voice calm. "Your honor, occupying the lift is against all safety regulations designed for your comfort and well-being . . ." She was down to quoting the primer lessons in the Trade. "Kindly bring the lift car back to lower decks and open the door."

Gods rot the creature for taking it on *gtst*self to wander about the ship.

"Your honor, do you hear me? This is a civilized and well-mannered young person who was assisting a member of the crew in maintenance."

"An immature male person? This ship has immature male persons performing life-critical maintenance? This ship has entrusted vital functions to persons known for irrational behaviors and distasteful tendencies toward violence toward uninvolved bystanders?"

"This young male person was disposing of refuse. *Kindly* bring the car back to this deck."

"We have been betrayed by all pertinent interests. How do we know if anyone is telling the truth regarding anything? How should we have anticipated this desertion? How can we survive this devastation? We are the prey of strangers and persons without discrimination!"

"Your honor, as the captain of this ship I require you to come to the lower level, for your own protection, your honor, as if there should be an emergency on-station the lift is not a safe place to be."

There was no response. But stsho were not a valorous species where it came to bodily injury.

"Broken bones are possible," she said, "should this station encounter some emergency."

The lift thumped and whirred into motion.

"I think we got the son," Chihin said.

"Don't push our luck," she said.

The lift reached lowerdecks. The door opened. Hilfy pushed the hold button, and bowed to the pale, tremulous creature at the back wall of the lift.

Gtst bowed. She bowed.

Gtst edged outward. And peered past her, cautiously.

"Will your honor view the quarters? Your honor certainly will not want to leave the *oji* unattended."

A slippered toe edged across the line and into the corridor. Hilfy stood well back as *gtst* honor looked over the corridor.

And retreated.

"Your honor . . ."

And advanced again, with a fluttering of *gtst* long fingers about the vicinity of *gtst* heart. Moonstone eyes looked toward the corridor, under feathery brows, and *gtst* honor advanced a pace.

"We are not certain, we are far from certain we can bear this stress. We have been affronted, we have been transported far from tasteful and familiar places, our presence has been assaulted by strange persons of male and violent gender—"

"If your honor please. You will be most favorably impressed by the tastefulness of your quarters. And the Preciousness is absolutely inviolate. Have we not promised?"

Step after step. Chihin backed aside. Hilfy gestured the stsho further and further and around the corner into the appropriate corridor, which *gtst* was willing to enter only after an advance look.

As far as the doorway at least, *gtst* advanced. *Gtst* craned *gtst* long neck around the doorframe to look left and right, and took a step inside.

And another.

"Spare," *gtst* said. And advanced another pace, into a white,

white, white cabin with white treelike shapes and the Preciousness enthroned in its case.

"Elegant," *gtst* said, and sighed and walked further, from object to object, fluttering *gtst* hands and sighing and sighing again.

"A success," Chihin muttered at Hilfy's shoulder.

"A triumph," *gtst* breathed. "How can a colored species have achieved it?"

One hardly knew whether to be complimented or not.

"Is your honor then comfortable?" Hilfy asked.

Gtst turned full about, staring at all of it, no little of which was gotten at bid, from an abandoned stsho embassy and abandoned stsho apartments. And two mixed lots of white paneling, the only white paneling they had been able to find.

"Does this . . . male person share nearby quarters?"

"By no means," Hilfy said.

"Moderately acceptable," *gtst* said. "Our sensibilities are relieved."

The door shut.

"Put him in the lounge," Hilfy said.

"Captain?" Chihin said.

"I said put Meras in the crew lounge! The crew can socialize in the galley! We can't afford another incident!"

"Aye," Chihin said quietly. And went.

"No question now," Hilfy muttered, over gfi, at supper. "Hoas. Narn's not happy about taking him, but they will. Leaving him here's not a good idea. Let them think about it and somebody'll think up a lawsuit."

Faces weren't happy. "I'm against it," Tiar said, foremost. "We have a responsibility, captain, we didn't exactly ask for it, but this isn't an experienced spacer we're talking about. . . ."

"We're *all* against it," Hilfy said. "We'd all *like* to leave him in better circumstances. We'd all *like* for Sahern to behave like a civilized clan and take care of its responsibilities, but that's not going to happen. The only question is whether we throw him off our ship or we send him to Hoas where Narn will throw him off theirs. Maybe I can get a legal release out of the station office that'll make it safer for him coming back through here—I'll try that, in what time we've got, while we're onloading . . ."

"Dangerous," Chihin said. "Rattle a lawyer's door and you get more lawyers, that's what I say."

"I know that. But we've at least got some influence to bring to bear, at least I've got a foot in the door with the personage of this system—not mentioning aunt Py—and the questions we can settle are questions that have to be answered, by any other ship that brings him back through here from Hoas. And Hoas it has to be. We can't alter distances. There's no way he can get back except through here."

"He's still safer with us," Fala said, her young face earnest as might be.

"We're *not* taking him."

"I've backed a loader now and again," Tarras said. "The docker chief was yelling to move it—the boy moved it. There's not a one of us—"

"That's fine. So we're all occasionally guilty. We're leaving the boy with Narn!"

"What if Ana-kehnandian thinks he knows something?" Tiar said.

And Chihin: "There's—ah—a complication."

"What complication?"

"The boy's seen the vase."

"What do you mean, 'seen the vase'? Wasn't it put away? Didn't I order it taken down until we'd absolutely finished knocking around in there?"

"We were. I thought he'd gone back to quarters. I sent him there. I thought he'd stay. He didn't."

"Chihin, —"

"I'm sorry, captain."

"He disobeyed orders?"

"I didn't exactly order him to stay there. I sent him there. He came back."

"Gods. What else? What possibly else can he get into?"

"I don't know," Chihin said. "But—being fair, it wasn't as if he was deliberately doing anything wrong."

"He's never doing anything wrong! I've never met anybody so gods-rotted innocent. Gods in feathers, *why* is Meras wherever you don't want him?"

"It's a small world down there."

"Small world. Small gods-rotted one corridor he was told to keep his nose out of!"

"The stsho took an unscheduled walk too."

"The stsho is a paying passenger. The stsho wasn't picked out of station detention! The stsho didn't create an international incident on the docks and have the section doors closed!"

"What I can't figure," Tiar said, "is why this Haisi Ana-kehnandian wants to know what the object is. What possible difference could it make?"

"Evidently a major one, to someone." She stirred the stew around in her bowl, stared at floating bits as if they held cosmic meaning, and thought back and back to this port, and days when one went armed to dockside. When accidents that happened weren't accidents and you didn't trust anything for face value. It felt like those days again and she felt trapped.

Fool, she said to herself. Fool, fool, fool. One grew accustomed to high politics, one grew used to breathing the atmosphere at the top of bureaucratic mountains, and one's vital nerves grew dull to signals of high-level interest and dangerous associations.

One just didn't by the gods think of it as unusual . . . when any freight-hauler else would have said Wait, go back, why me?

"If we leave him," Tarras said, "somebody's going to grab him for questioning. Or try to."

Of course they were. Give them sufficient cause for curiosity and local authorities might trump up some charge to get the boy off any ship that was carrying him: figure that too. She had rather not have that ship be *Legacy*. But honorably speaking, she could not wish it to be Narn, either.

And *customs* had come asking about the nature of the cargo. Maybe Ana-kehnandian's questions had put them up to it, and maybe the Personage of Urtur was innocent as spring rain. Or maybe she wasn't. Maybe that angry scene with Ana-kehnandian had been only because Ana-kehnandian had produced no results. Because it had gotten noisy, and public, and Ana-kehnandian had had his bluff called in a way the Personage of Urtur didn't like.

She found herself still stirring the stew, like an idiot. And asking herself what Meras could actually say that could do damage. 'It's a white vase?' Stupid piece of information. And what did it mean? What in a reasonable and occasionally logical universe did Ana-kehnandian know or not know about the stsho that could make it valuable or life-threatening or politically important to his Personage, or what in a mahen hell was going on among the stsho? Meras could know something useful or he might not have seen any detail the mahendo'sat could remotely find useful. It might not be *that* it was a vase. It might be the carving on the vase. It might be that it wasn't a doorstop, a bag of dried fish or an antique teapot, for all they could possibly know.

She looked up at four sober faces, four sober stares. Fala's ears went down, Tarras' did; then Tiar's did, one ear at a time. Chihin was the only exception, eye to eye with her.

"My fault," Chihin said. "I thought he'd stay. I *didn't* expect the stsho down the lift. —If we could transfer him to Narn secretly—"

"And say somebody gets onto it, they get him anyway, and they've got help. Say they *might* be within one jump of doing something with the information, straight back the way we came. But the ambassador went to Kita so we have to go to Kita. That's more than one jump from Meetpoint. I wish I knew what in all reason it matters it's a vase."

Chihin shrugged perplexedly.

Hilfy took a spoonful of stew, wondering if history would forget one Hallan Meras if she sent him on a spacewalk, say on their way to jump.

"I'll talk to him," she said, and ate another spoonful. "With any luck whatsoever, divinely owed us these last five years, there'll be a hani ship through here outbound from Hoas on its way to somewhere useful. I've got a hundred lots of cans, a general mail shipment, twenty cans of medical supplies, the luxury goods, the dupe-rights on the entertainment tapes; and that's about the best we can do on short notice. High value shippers are spooked. Can you blame them? Lucky we can get better than pig iron this run. Industrials and a load of foodstuffs and a ten can lot of spare parts for some construction company at Kita. Mostly cold-hold stuff. I know you've been going shift and shift; and we could carry more. But we need to get out of here. I want us out of this port before somebody files suit."

"I'll go with that," Chihin said. "The sooner the better."

"I'll get down to cargo," Tiar said. "I've had the easy stint last watch."

"We're going to push till we're loaded," she said. "Sleep when you're off, do anything we can to get turned around. I'll work hold. Meras can stay in the lounge, *in* the lounge, I don't care if it catches fire, he's not to leave it except on my personal order, do we agree on that?"

Nods. "Aye, captain," from Tiar.

She shoved the bowl back and got up. "I'll talk to him. And I don't care how persuasive he is, I don't care how pretty his eyes are, I don't care how polite he is, I don't want that son out of the crew lounge until we're sealed and we're sure our paying passenger is staying put! Do I hear Yes, captain?"

"Yes, captain," the answer came back.

So she left the galley for the lounge.

The captain came through the door with her ears down and her face scowling. Which might mean something else had happened that was his fault, although, before the gods, Hallan had no idea how or what. He stood up in proper respect and ducked his head.

"*If* the gods are good, a hani ship will come through here at the last moment bound directly for hani space and take you off our hands. If the gods are less well-disposed, you'll be on to

Kita with us. And if—" The captain's first claw extruded. "If you do one more thing to screw up, if you walk out of this lounge without my express permission, if you startle our passenger again, if you *assume* any gods-be need to go anywhere, if you bat your eyes at one of my crew or land in anyone's quarters, you're going to find yourself *chained* in the laundry for the duration of this voyage, which may last another year! Does this order get through to you?"

"Yes, captain."

"Do you believe I'm joking?"

He looked the captain in the face, a very pretty face it was, and a very serious and dangerous one. "No, captain."

"Do you *want* to spend a year down there?"

"No, captain. But if I could help in any way—"

"You don't help!" She jabbed the forefinger in his direction and he backed up. "You don't offer to help me, you don't offer to help my crew, you don't offer to help our passenger. You never saw anything, you will never remember that you saw anything in the stsho's cabin, and if you ever do remember you saw anything you'll forget it forthwith. Do you follow that?"

"Yes, captain."

"With luck someone *will* come through here and I can send you home."

He hoped not. He truly hoped not. He knew that the captain was angry and that she had absolutely good reason.

"I want more than anything," he said, "to help. I don't want to go back to Anuurn. I never want to go back to Anuurn."

"We can do better," she said, "without your help. *Stay out of it,* do you hear me?"

"Yes, captain."

With which she walked out. And shut the door. He sat down again. It was not an uncomfortable place to be. And he didn't get his hopes up. She'd said—there might be another ship. He truly hoped not. He hoped he would have another chance.

He sat down and thought and thought how he might have done differently about the accident; and the stsho; and how he could, still, if he could just get one break, prove to the captain that he was qualified—if they would just let him work cargo. He *wouldn't* back up any more trucks. But they wouldn't believe that. He wouldn't be in any corridors he wasn't supposed to be in. But Chihin had told him go there. So he'd thought it was safe. . . .

Maybe Chihin had set him up. But he didn't want to think so. She'd been fair, about him startling her. She'd taken shots at him, but everybody did. He didn't want to think Chihin had done it to him. And she certainly hadn't been responsible for the truck. That was all his doing.

Tiar brought him supper soon after, which was stew. Tiar asked him if the captain had explained things to him and he said that she had.

Tiar said don't take the captain too seriously, and said that the captain yelled when she was upset, but that she was fair when she calmed down.

"I'm sorry about scaring the stsho," he said, and Tiar said it wasn't hard to scare the stsho, the harder problem was keeping it happy, which they had to do. And Tiar said he'd done all right, except not to take any chances, even if it seemed people were yelling at him—don't let them rattle him or make him move faster than he could think.

In other words, he thought, Calm down. It was what women said to misbehaving boys, stupid boys, who at about thirteen started having shaking mad temper fits, and their sisters said, 'That's all right, just calm down, Hallan,' and papa got irritable and refused to have him around any more, and youngest sister said, '*Try* to think, Hal, just use your head about things, everybody feels like that.'

(Then oldest sister said, after he was sixteen, 'He thinks too *much*. He can't survive out there.' Or at home either: papa had told him get out, the girl his sisters had tried to fix him up with said he wasn't a match for her brothers, and his sisters had spent all their savings to get him a ticket to station, to a place they'd never seen, and hadn't any interest in going to; but it was everything he wanted, and they gave him that very expensive chance—for which he adored them. He couldn't come back and be sent down in disgrace they'd know about, to an exile he'd die in, because he'd trained himself to be *here,* that was all, and he'd rather die here than there.)

He didn't have much appetite for the stew Tiar left him. But he told himself that was male temper too, upsetting his stomach. He told himself stop it and think how he was going to feel in an hour or two; and how if they were going for jump this soon, he *had* to get the food down, as much as he could make his stomach take.

So he finished it down to the last, and set the dishes by the door.

There were vid tapes to watch. There were books to read. He wished they would let him bring his things from below.

But he didn't ask. He didn't use the com. He didn't make himself a problem to them. He found himself a blanket in the storage locker in the lounge and he tucked up and watched bad vids while the loader worked. Clank. Clank-clank.

It didn't stall. So they *had* listened to him. And Tarras at least knew he'd been right.

Chapter Nine

The *Legacy* eased out of dock and away—put her bow to solar nadir in the dusty environs of Urtur system and took a leisurely start-up, a leisurely acceleration at *g*-normal for their stsho passenger. The *Legacy*'s hold was not full, the cargo was light-mass, the crew on watch was minimal to the safety requirements, and as soon as they hit their assigned lane for the outward run, the crew was snug in beds, sound asleep, except for the captain, who had the sole watch, who was propping her eyes open and seeing ghosts in the shadows of the bridge.

She never had done such a turnaround since she came to the *Legacy*, never hoped to do another. And when they had gotten out past the worst of the dust, and the rocks that attended the planetary vicinity, the captain set autopilot, tilted the cushion to flat relative to the accel plane and wrapped herself in a blanket for a rest.

Musing on tc'a and outraged stsho, wandering in a mental wilderness of white on white. . . .

Thinking of *The Pride* and the human aboard her, thinking of a friendly face and eyes of unhani color. Tully wouldn't have turned on her, Tully wouldn't have attacked poor cousin Dahan and broken his head. She hated her late husband; and *hated* cousin Harun. If she'd had her way, Harun Chanur wouldn't be lounging his oversized body in her father's chair, sitting by her father's fire, and slapping the younger cousins around; Rhean would be back in space aboard *Fortune* where she wanted to be; she, for her part, would be on *The Pride*, with Tully, clear of all of it: the gods only knew who'd be managing the clan's business, then. Which showed how impractical it all was.

But she wouldn't be thinking of the Meras kid, then, and thinking how his expression had reminded her all too much of Dahan's, kind and confused, and upset and hurt when she'd yelled at him. She had never thought she agreed on principle with Chihin, she'd stood more with Pyanfar on the question of culture versus instincts; but she found herself with Chihin this time: Meras didn't belong in space, Meras didn't think, didn't think *first*, at least. Like backing the truck, because some mahen foreman yelled do it. That the foreman hadn't meant him just hadn't tripped a neuron in his brain.

Imagine cousin Harun in a position of responsibility. Imagine Harun having to use his head rather than his hands.

Men that did think had gotten killed, for thousands of years, that was the way biology had set up the hani species. Other species were luckier, maybe, and other species might be better at handling politics between the sexes, but hani hadn't been civilized long enough to sort out mate-getting by any other means. Nobody had told her when she was growing up that every attitude and opinion she had learned was going to be obsolete when she was twenty-five. Nobody had told her the whole world was going to be set on its ear and the way hani did business with outsiders was going to change. Evidently nobody had told the rest of the home planet, either, because they were still doing things the old way. Same with the kid in the crew lounge . . . nobody had told him things were going to change, until aunt Pyanfar had lured him off in the promise of a miraculous change in the universe.

(Wrong, kid. It doesn't work that way. Narn won't have you, Padur won't have you, we don't want the complications you pose and the crew that took you aboard in the first place wasn't looking at your resume, were they, kid? Hani are hani. People with power aren't going to give it up. Fair isn't fair, not among hani, not elsewhere. And no sister ever taught you to think before you jump.)

Nice-looking boy. That's all anybody had thought. That's all anybody would ever think. She had no personal illusions about changing the way hani were, or worked, or thought: that was aunt Pyanfar's pet project, not hers, she had never asked to carry any banner for reforming anything, or anyone, except that hani shouldn't be so gods-be xenophobic and so set on their own ways.

And don't say Pyanfar Chanur got beyond biology when it came to personal choices either. Pyanfar had dumped Chanur in her lap and run off to do as she pleased, free as she pleased, with *na* Khym—It's your turn, niece. You go be responsible.

Nothing in her life she had planned had ever worked and no living person she had ever trusted or wanted had ever come her way. Tell that to the jealous rivals who thought Hilfy Chanur got everything she ever wanted at no cost and no effort.

She was on a self-pity binge. She recognized it when she hit the chorus. She tried to get her mind out of the track and stared at lights reflected in the overhead, listened to the small constant sounds of the ship under way, and thought how so long as they were out of ports and so long as she had the *Legacy*, she was safe—how she didn't have to go back to Anuurn ever again if she didn't want to, how space was all she wanted, all she ever had wanted, and to a mahen hell with planets and the attitudes that grew up on them.

So occasionally she ran into other hani ships and had to meet the world-bound mindset out here, in people like Narn, who ought to know better, who ought to be free enough to spit at the *han* and the old women back home—but she didn't, and wouldn't: you couldn't expect it of most of the clans, and you didn't see it taking rapid hold of the spacerfarers. Quite to the contrary, there was a conservative backlash. That was the disappointment.

Which told her how badly she personally wanted to crack heads and knock courage into Narn and Padur, and how badly she wanted the universe to be different, and play by civilized rules, and not by the gods *care* whether a young fool wanted to fight biology and go to space, but things didn't work that way either.

So Meras hadn't asked for what had happened. Neither his upbringing nor his apprenticeship had taught him what he needed to know, and maybe she hadn't been fair with him, either: she hadn't exactly given him any parameters, just a general instruction to go out there and do what he claimed he knew how to do, as if those papers of his really meant more than a license to sit and watch the boards while a licensed spacer took a break.

There were ships that treated apprentices like that. There were ships that treated female apprentices like that—a lot of them, more the pity. *The Pride* had turned her out knowing what she was doing—and most ships never met what *The Pride* had on her tour: there wasn't much she hadn't met or done or seen in the years of running communications on Pyanfar Chanur's intrigue-bound dealings.

The kid hadn't had any such break. The kid was in the lounge watching vids, the only one of them who wasn't falling down tired; they were stuck with him for a little while; and the more she thought about it, the more she felt uneasy with herself for the family temper and an extravagant expectation of an apprentice she'd *sent* onto that dockside, thanks to the lack of a coat—rather than down in the hold, also true, where he could lose an arm or a neck in the machinery. But the dust-up with the Urtur authorities hadn't been entirely the lad's fault . . . he hadn't known his limitations, he'd probably imitated a bad habit he'd seen somebody else do—Tarras was right in that.

And he'd go off the *Legacy* no smarter and no better than he was if nobody knocked the need-to-knows into his head. He'd been the *Sun's* responsibility; somehow he'd gotten to be theirs, and by the gods, she had a certain vanity where it came to the *Legacy*'s operating and the *Legacy's* way of doing business.

Her papa hadn't been stupid. Uncle Khym wasn't stupid. *Young* men were stupid, while their hormones were raging and their bodies were going through a hellacious growth spurt that had them knocking into doorways and demolishing the china. Then was when young men left home, and went out and lived in the outback, and fought and bashed each other and collected the requisite scars and experience to come back formidable enough to win a place for themselves. Seven or so years and a gangling boy all elbows came back all shoulders and with muscle between his ears.

But Hallan Meras didn't seem to have as much of that as, say, Harun Chanur. Light dose Meras had been given. Illusions he was a girl. Trying to act like one and use his head, at his age.

She angled the couch upright, straightened her mane and flicked her earrings into order with a snap of her ears. She punched in the lounge com and called Meras forward; so he came, diffidently, as far as the middle of the bridge, darting glances here and there about the crewless stations.

"Used to the environment, are you?"

"I've—seen the bridge, yes, captain."

"Seen the bridge. You're a licensed spacer and you've seen the bridge? That's remarkable."

"I mean I've seen the bridge on the *Sun.*"

"Not worked it?"

"I got my papers in cargo management, down in—"

"You're a specialist, then. A real specialist. —What's that station?"

"That's scan, captain."

"Congratulations. Ever read the screen?"

"Not actually."

Figured. "Who in a mahen hell gave you your papers?"

Ears flagged. "The authorities at Touin."

"Did they speak the Trade? Did you take a test? Did they interview you?"

"I think they took *ker* Druan's word."

"Druan Sahern."

"Hanurn, actually. *Ker* Druan Hanurn nef Sahern. She helped me. She showed me things."

Aunt Pyanfar had had no patience. Under her captaincy, an apprentice sat every board on the bridge, somewhere before aunt Py signed any application for a license. Emergencies don't wait for the experts, aunt Pyanfar had used to say. Gods-be right you learned every board, every button, and every readout. You could be the only one that could reach the seat. The whole ship could depend on you in a station you didn't ordinarily work.

"I haven't changed my mind. I'm still kicking you off this ship first chance I get. But I don't think we're apt to find a thing at Kita, it's not a place I'd leave anybody, and, by the gods, nobody's going off my ship and having the next crew say we didn't teach him anything. You understand me?"

Ears were up, eyes shining. "Thank you, captain."

"Thank me, hell. Keep me awake. We've got six hours to jump, my eyes are crossing, I'm sore down to my fingertips, I'm out of patience with fools and I want you to sit down over there at the scan station and read me off what you see happening on that board and on that screen."

"*Yes*, captain!" He went and dropped into the seat, and started rattling it off, the numbers and the names and the lane designations.

Not by the gods bad, actually. Most critical first and right along their laid course—which was plotted there, for somebody who could read the symbols.

"Who taught you the codes?"

"I had this book."

"You had this book. What book?"

"The general licensing manual. *Ker* Dru let me study it."

"She let you study it. Nice of her. So you read up on more than cargo operations."

"Everything. I read all of it."

"You remember everything you read?"

"I read it a lot."

Her pulse ticked up. It sounded familiar, sounded by the gods familiar; in the same way, she'd had the manual downworld, aunt Py had slipped her the copy, and she'd studied and studied and kept it out of her father's sight, because *he* had gotten upset about her studying. *He* had wanted her to stay downworld and be papa's favorite daughter; but *she'd* memorized every bit, every chart—memorized boards she'd never seen and operations she'd never watched.

Because she'd wanted it so much it was physical. And some gods-be hormone-hazed boy thought he could want something that much?

"What's in quadrant 3?"

"That's a buoy."

"What buoy?"

"That's the insystemer code."

"Quadrant 4?"

"That's an ore freighter."

"How do you know?"

"Its prefix is a mining designation. A lot of letters."

Brilliant. A lot of letters. But the kid was, essentially, right. That was how the peripheral vision made the sort-out. That was what the system of IDs was set up to do.

"Captain, something's just away from station. I think it's mahendo'sat."

Her thoughts left young fools and proceeded immediately down darker tracks.

"Can I ask comp?" he asked. "Is this the toggle?"

"Below the screen, left bank? Punch it."

"Ha'domaren."

"Of course it is. On our heading?"

"I think so, captain. It looks like it."

"Approximately. Anywhere headed out, Kita vector."

"I think it is. Yes. I'm pretty sure."

So here sat the two of them, watching a mahe up to no gods-be good. Alone, on a mostly darkened bridge. Witness to collusion, intrigue, things that smelled like Personages at war.

But Hallan had no least idea. Hallan Meras gave her a puzzled, worried look and didn't exactly ask what was up, but he must have caught something from her expression. His face grew troubled.

"This isn't a mahe I trust," she said. "This one's been on our tail since Meetpoint."

"Why?" he asked faintly. "Do you know?"

"Meras, do you know what we have aboard?"

"No, captain. A stsho person."

She had to smile. She, gods help her, had to smile. And so few living souls could make her laugh. She gazed at his sober, foolish face, and thought, How in the gods' sweet name could he hope to make it out here? Could a naive boy learn the control boards from a book, and not learn where the power was that runs the Compact, or what betrayal was?

No. He already knew what betrayal was. Betrayal was a ship that left him stranded in a foreign jail. Betrayal was a ship that had signed him on without his best interests at heart, and used him for the menial work, the work somebody had lied about to get him licensed.

And he must not have made the captain happy. The captain had had to make the decision that had stranded him.

"You shouldn't look away from the boards when you're on duty," she said. "You don't do that on this ship."

"Yes, captain. I'm sorry." He turned around immediately, and watched what she had told him to watch.

And she watched him, thinking . . . she was not even certain what. Not thinking about him. Thinking about one Anakehnandian, and what he possibly had to gain. And about the stsho belowdecks who had said something about betrayals.

A white vase. A vase carved over all its surface with nonrepresentational bas-relief, that made sense to stsho, one was certain. Maybe even ancient writing. There was a lot the stsho kept secret. And one was certain not to get any sense out of Tlisi-tlas-tin.

* * *

Meras kept at the scan image for the next hour or so—kept at the post so reasonably competently that she began to believe if anything did turn up he might beat the autoed alarm giving the warning, and do it with at least some sense that certain ships were reason for worry even if they weren't on a collision course. She let her eyes drift shut, dangerous business, against all regulations, considering what she knew about Hallan Meras and his license. But they were autoed. And she did sleep—dropped right into a deep and resting oblivion, so that it was Tiar's shadow that waked her, passing between her and the light.

"You all right?" Tiar asked.

"Fine," she said, blinking at the screens, the five that automated ops delivered to her working station.

"He all right?" Tiar asked.

"Ship hasn't blown up." The rest of the crew was arriving on the bridge, for the last stint before jump. Hallan Meras was ceding his place to Chihin, with apologies that weren't at all in order. Hilfy punched buttons to pass the active boards to Tiar; and, thinking about dismissing Hallan Meras back to the crew lounge, decided otherwise. "Meras can take the observer seat," she said, before she quite thought that that seat change put him with Chihin, at scan.

So, it put him with Chihin. Not the happiest pairing, but not one *na* Hallan could blink his pretty eyes at and overwhelm with stupidity, either.

"Meras, you stay out of Chihin's way."

"Aye," he said, "thank you, captain."

Chihin shot her a reproachful look; and probably took it for revenge for the stsho incident. But *na* Hallan settled in, and Chihin settled at nav and scan; Tarras on his other side, at general ops and cargo; and armaments, if the *Legacy* had ever needed them. Fala Anify slid in at com; and the captain—the captain sat backup to several posts, a selection of inputs to her screens.

"We've got company out there," Chihin said. "That son's still with us."

"Noticed that," Hilfy said. "I don't credit him with any good wishes."

"Not him or whoever sent him," Chihin said.

Switches went to On, lights and more screens flared up, and changed displays at Tarras' switching. The computer locked onto the guidance point. Fala advised their stsho passenger to take precautions and got an acknowledgement. Hilfy took the leisure of being momentarily out of the critical loops to pull up Kita charts and the latest trade figures, figuring that if the gods were good they could do a jump for Kirdu and mahen space, once they'd delivered the *oji*. They had the requisite clearances. No question on that. And Kirdu wasn't a bad destination out of there. Most ships were going the other direction, and you could pick up a major load of mail, bank shipments, and the occasional high-paying passenger, not to mention the items out of stsho space that were fairly scarce at Kirdu port.

Only granted the faint, fair hope their addressee was at Kita and not elsewhere by now . . . or about to be elsewhere. Atli-lyen-tlas seemed to have had a fair head start.

"Set for jump," Tiar said. "Boy, are you all right over there?"

"I'm fine," the answer came back, but he was doing something that wasn't regulation, she could see the activity in the tail of her eye as the numbers spieled down toward a convergence of *v* and distance from mass.

"Kid," Chihin cautioned him.

"I'm trying to get ops echoed," he said. "I want to see—"

"Just enjoy the ride," Chihin said.

"Can we get attention to what we're doing?" Hilfy asked. It wasn't a time for a side issue. "Tiar."

"I've got it, I've got it. —Kid, punch in your 3. Leave that gods-be board alone, it's live!"

"There it is!"

"Gods-rotted distraction," Chihin muttered. "This is a working station. The kid had better learn not to punch buttons."

"I'm sorry, *ker* Chihin."

"Learn it!"

"Yes, *ker* Chihin."

"Belong at home, is where."

"Ease off," Tarras muttered.

"I want to know if he understands about that board!"

"I'm not pushing any buttons, *ker* Chihin. I won't. I swear."

"By the gods better not. That board's got a link to fire controls. Why don't we shoot at the station for entertainment?"

From Tiar: "Just shut up, Chihin, godssakes, he said he was sorry."

"Everybody quiet!" Hilfy said. "We're almost on mark, I'm supposed to be off duty, can we have the crew paying attention for the next small while?"

"Sorry, captain."

"I'm sorry," Meras said, and Chihin:

"No gods-be place on the . . ."

"Shut it *up,* Chihin!"

("She's always like this," Fala whispered.)

"Gods-be zoo," Hilfy said, running her eye down the figures, watching the lines converge. "Shipped with two men and a kif that fought less." She hadn't been able to think about that in years. Certainly not to joke about it. There was something oddly comfortable about the kid sitting there, hulking over the controls that, one had to admit, he came aboard understanding better than *na* Khym had. Certainly better than Tully.

Numbers reached +14 and +14. Lines met, at 0 and 0.

Dead on. . . .

. . . Not bad, Tully said to her. Not bad. You could do worse than that young fellow.

Tully walked away then, down what might have been a dockside. She thought it was.

Wait, she said, Tully. Come back here. You can't leave like that . . .

. . . Stick to your own kind, aunt Pyanfar said. And she:

You're to talk. You work with the kif. You trade with them. In what? Small edible animals?

. . . They were home. Kohan was sitting on the veranda where he liked to sit, in the sunshine. His mane was gold, his eyes were gold. His hide shone like copper. The vines were blooming on the wall. It was the most perfect day of the most perfect year of her life. Papa talked about going hunting. . . .

But there was a shy, quiet kid sitting on the steps, whittling something. Dahan would sit in Kohan's presence and Kohan never cared, Kohan was not the sort that would drive a boy off, Kohan used to sit lazily in the sun and talk to Dahan about hunting, about boy-things. Sometimes Dahan would talk about his books and his notes and the stories he'd heard, and Kohan would talk about science and what he theorized, and about his herds and his breeding, that was a passion with Kohan, talk with him as seriously about house business as if Dahan were one of the daughters, and not a someday rival; while Dahan studied genetics not because he had any original interest in it, but because Kohan did. Dahan was the sort who should have benefited from aunt Py's politics. . . . Pyanfar should have asked him up to station, taken *him* aboard *The Pride,* if only for a tour or two . . .

. . . but Dahan was dead. She'd seen his skull break. She'd seen the blood on the wall.

Things went darker. She didn't like this dream. She knew it too well. It tended to replay. But it was back to the porch again, and the sunlight. "What should we do?" Hallan asked. And her father said, "He's not a fighter, the gods look on him, he's not a fighter, he never will be, I've no reluctance to have him about. But I've got to talk to Pyanfar the next time she's here."

Before then, Kohan had been dead. Before then, Pyanfar's gods-cursed son moved in. Her Mahn half-brother. *Churrau hanim,* the old women called it. *Betterment of the race.* And she hadn't shot cousin Kara in the back. She'd played the game the age-old way. She'd married a challenger, Rhean had found another when *he* proved a disaster. On a civilized world, women didn't shoot fools, no, they let the Haruns and their ilk knock the likes of Dahan into a wall, spatter the brains that had theirs beaten by tenfold. Women made up the deficit. Women had the genes that mattered, they passed down the intelligence and the quickness of wits, they passed down the cleverness they had gotten over generations. A girl got footloose, called her brother and set out for a place she thought suited her: her brother or her husband knocked heads to get it for her, and that was brains? That was the way civilization worked?

Tully, she said, refusing those images, Tully, come back here.

She could control the dreams. She could see him walking away from her the way he had—walking away into this gray distance of gantries and lines, the same as Meetpoint docks where they'd met him. . . .

"Tully," she called after him, spooked by that; and to her relief he heard her and turned and waited to talk with her, alone for once.

"What are you doing?" he asked.

"Following you," she said.

"You shouldn't," Tully said. "You really shouldn't."

That made her mad. It wasn't the truth anyway. Tully never spoke the Trade that well. His mouth couldn't form the sounds. "You don't object to Chur. Or Geran or . . ."

"It's different. It's just different with them."

"It's not different! Don't listen to my aunt! She's trying to run my life. She doesn't know what's good for me. . . ."

"Have you asked what's good for me?" he said, and turned and walked away, leaving her with one of aunt Pyanfar's favorite pieces of wisdom. From him, she didn't for a moment believe it, and she wouldn't *let* the dream be this way. She insisted not. She went walking along the dockside, in that jungle of then and now, and places that were real and weren't. . . .

The kid was there, of course the Meras kid was there, when your mind attacked you with images it didn't go by halves. Tully was acting like a fool and agreeing with aunt Py, and of course here was the kid—

Couldn't be, couldn't be that aunt Py had set it up. No. Py hadn't even known she was on her track. And the kid stood there staring at her, in his bewildered way, and blinked, saying . . .

. . . But she couldn't hear what he said. The alarm was going off. Illusions walked off arm in arm. Cousin Chur could see reality in jump. Or something beyond it. She'd tried to. Her mind just went off into hyperspace and lived in the past; and argued with itself; and with aunt Py and with Things As They Were. And it did no one any creative good. . . .

. . . "Welcome to Kita Point. Armpit of this end of space. Kifish cultural center. Mahen religious objects, three the credit. . . . Stsho ambassadors, bargain prices. . ."

. . . Chihin's sense of humor. Gods save them.

She reached after the nutrients pack, found it strayed and stretched after it, with muscles that protested. Couldn't go on at this pace. The mind was playing tricks. The body was arguing back. She left a smudge of fur on the chair arm.

And the stomach definitely wanted to heave, when the soup hit it unprepared.

"Is *gtst* honor still alive?" Tarras asked.

"Think so," Fala said. "I hear moaning."

"Not to their liking, stringing the jumps like this."

"Hope the ambassador thinks so. Hope *gtst* heaved up *gtst* insides, maybe *gtst* won't have shipped out of here."

"Bets on it," Chihin said. "The Preciousness for our chances."

"Gods," Fala said. "The com could've been open!"

"It wasn't."

"Cut it, cut it," Tiar said, "small mass-point here, we're ready for a double-dump, check your numbers. This isn't a nice one."

Gods-be right, Hilfy thought. She hated this . . .

. . . Bottom fell out of the universe and knit itself back.

"Gods." Male voice. What was that doing here?

Then she remembered.

"Here we go again," Tiar said, and the *Legacy* pulsed its

field and broke the bubble a third time. Energy bled off into the interface. Hilfy gazed at a haze of instruments that informed her the ship was on course, proceeding in toward the brown mass that was Kita Point, at a sedate, manageable velocity.

It wasn't much of a place. The brown dwarf lent energy enough for the collectors that spread like vast wings . . . grandiose scheme. But it worked. The station had grown, within the span of her years in space, from nothing more than a repair and emergency services depot to a utilitarian nondescript can of a supply and manufacturing center.

It blipped at them, they automatically bleeped their identity. "Is that *it?*" she heard Hallan Meras murmur, doubtless confused by the small scale of things. "That's Kita?"

"Guaranteed," Fala said, "or Chihin's aimed us at Kefk."

"I'm never wrong," Chihin said. "When was I ever wrong? Tell me when I was wrong."

"Twice last year," Hilfy muttered, and punched in intraship com: "Your honor, how are you riding down there? Are you all right?"

A stsho muttering came back to her. *"Oh, the unwieldiness, oh, the heaviness . . ."* or some such. It was some planetary language.

"Your honor? We're at Kita. Is everything well with you?"

"With me? With us? With what creature? Oh, the misery. Oh, the discomfort and untidiness. We shall not be fit for viewing."

Gtst sounded normal enough. For a stsho. *Gtst* was alive. The Preciousness was on its perch and unbroken. And she hoped to all the gods respectable and otherwise that *gtst* excellency Atli-lyen-tlas of Urtur was here.

Ha'domaren was here, already at dock. *That* showed on the station schema the buoy had handed them on arrival. *Ha'domaren* had started well behind them again, gods blast them, and gotten in first, figuring Ana-kehnandian had no mundane problems, like cargo or other such inconveniences.

The first over-jump, at Urtur, might have been one mother of a powerful merchant ship.

Might have been just a courier, beating them in.

Not twice, it wasn't a simple courier.

"The devil," she said. "Berth 10. You notice?"

Chapter Ten

There were communications you could make in transit and business you could do in transit, even blind tired and frazzled; even collapsing face-down on the galley table between calls and drinking gfi to stay copacetic enough to do routine business.

Chanur's Legacy *inbound to Kita Point Station, to Kita Point Customs Authority . . . we have items under seal at Urtur customs, therefore internal to mahen space, we don't anticipate a need for prolonged procedure as we are not crossing international borders. Our trading license is in order and we are prepared to present papers. Note also this crew will be resting after dock, due to repairs necessary at Urtur.*

Chanur's Legacy, *inbound to Kita Station, from captain Hilfy Chanur, her hand, to* Ko'juit, *at dock at berth 14: we have an urgent personal message for one Atli-lyen-tlas, passenger on your ship according to records at Urtur. Please place us in vocal contact. Translation is available on board.*

Chanur's Legacy, *inbound to Kita, from captain Hilfy Chanur, her hand, to* Ha'domaren, *attention Ana-kehnandian, chief scoundrel. We don't take kindly to being passed in jump. We have your position on record before and after. Be advised."*

. . . "Captain. Captain?"

Facedown on the galley table, fingers in the handle of the cup, and no memory of falling asleep.

"Sorry to wake you," Tarras said, "but we're heading in."

She grunted, disentangled her fingers from the cup and ran her claws through her mane, eyes shut.

"Couple of meaningful messages came in," Tarras said. "Nothing cheerful. The stsho we're looking for . . . disappeared."

"What, disappeared?"

Tarras laid a paper on the table. She blinked her eyes into focus.

Ko'juit, *at dock at Kita Station, Me-sheirtajikun captain, to captain Hilfy Chanur,* Chanur's Legacy, *inbound. Regret inform you not know passenger whereabouts.*

Ha'domaren, *at dock at Kita Station, Tahaisimandi Anakehnandian his hand, to captain Hilfy Chanur, why you so slow? You want know whereabout Atli-lyen-tlas, we find, you no worry.*

"I'll kill him."

"Nobody's told our passenger," Tarras said. "Figured you'd want to do that. It's not official, though. We can ask station authorities, see if there are any stsho on station at all. . . ."

"Do that," she murmured, resisted the urge to fall flat on her nose, and got up and wandered back to her quarters.

Should have taken the off-watch in her bed. Meras was asleep and harmless. Kita was going to be a disaster. They'd run as far as they could without rest. The crew had gotten half a watch of sleep before jump, but right now the drawstring waist of her trousers was loose, she'd dropped weight in jump, a pass of her hand across her chest turned up a palmful of loose fur, and if she were sane or fully conscious she would have a bath before she hit the mattress.

Wasn't near habitual that she slept through dock. But she was no use as she was. She fell into bed, dragged the safety net back over and locked it, and was unconscious for the next while.

* * *

Kita Point Customs Authority to captain Hilfy Chanur, in dock at Kita Point. We recognize Urtur customs seal, same good trade in mahen space. We clear all fine, only need stamp manifest which same you give at dock. All cooperation this office much appreciate.

Ha'domaren, *at dock at Kita Station, Tahaisimandi Anakehnandian his hand, to* Chanur's Legacy *captain Hilfy Chanur: You want talk? I got information you want. Make you good deal.*

A nap, a shower, and clean clothes didn't make the message more cheerful. "I'm going to talk to the mahe," she said to the assembled crew, Meras excepted. "I'm going to find out what he knows. I'm not going to shoot him no matter what the provocation. We can off-load as soon as we get the customs stamp. Tiar, you see to that."

"The stsho's calling up to the bridge," Fala said. "We keep telling *gtst* you're asleep and nobody can decide. And *ker* Pyanfar's mail . . . is piling up again. Do you want to see it?"

"I'm not available. Tell *gtst* honor we're already aware of *gtst* request and we're out seeing to it, it's our top priority. *Don't* let *gtst* out of *gtst* quarters. Jam the lock if you have to. Drown *gtst* in tea. Tarras, Chihin, I want the cargo out of here. I want the customs stamps clear. I want a list of what's available for transship to any port whatsoever, don't make any deals, we don't know *where* we're going. . . ."

Troubled faces stared back at her. Not a one said to her: This contract is a disaster. Not a one said to her: We may end up in debt because of this. Not a one said: You're a damned fool, captain.

"Take care of it," she said, on her way to leaving.

"What about the kid?" Chihin asked.

Extraneous subject. It was *not* what she wanted to think about. She cast a glance about familiar surroundings and familiar jobs and the thousand and one things that regularly wanted doing. And thought about a young man who had worked through pre-jump, stayed through jump, and was now, given a rest break, shut away again solo in the crew lounge. He wasn't a can of soup that you could stack on a shelf and forget about. He was an earnest stupid kid trying too hard—that was what she had read in their time together; and that enthusiasm was the biggest danger he posed. "He can have the run of the galley, he can do anything on this level he thinks he can do, but check it behind him and don't let him do anything stupid. He *doesn't* go off this level, he doesn't go near the lift, if the stsho gets loose . . . don't insult anybody, but get Meras under cover if you have to hide him in a locker. All right?"

"No problem," Tiar said.

"Gods rotted mess," Chihin said. "There's got to be a hani ship headed off to Kirdu or somewhere."

"Not likely. And I'm not sure he's safe at Kirdu." That came from the gut. From the knowledge of *Ha'domaren* out there wanting a conference.

From things that weren't by the gods right. And she couldn't believe she was taking that position, but in coldest terms, she thought as she headed for the lift, neither Narn nor Padur could have told the Personage of Urtur they weren't giving up a crewman, *most* hani ships didn't have the Personage of Personages for a relative. . . .

Gods forbid they had to turn a hani kid over to mahen authorities, whose system of justice was nothing a hani boy was brought up to understand. He made mistakes? He was pampered by his sisters. He assumed and didn't ask? He hadn't been brought up to responsibility. He didn't think? He hadn't been encouraged to think. Thinking was what his sisters did. Consequences were what his sisters took.

Jumpspace did things to your mind. And the business with Tully walking off from her, that was a nightmare that didn't quite go away. You could get superstitious, you could start to think it was something external to yourself or that you were communicating with somebody across stellar distances, when an educated being knew that there was no such thing, that it was one's own subconscious and one's own inner thoughts.

So what was it with the kid, that she came out the other side of jumpspace with a gut-deep feeling they couldn't desert him?

She punched the call button. The lift door opened and she got in, faced the perspective of the galley-dodging corridor that led to the bridge as the door shut and the lift started down.

They couldn't desert him, because, by the gods, they weren't the scoundrels *Sun Ascendant* crew were, they weren't the sort to take advantage of the kid, they weren't the sort to have run and left him like abandoned garbage, and she wasn't the sort that could have left him locked away in a featureless room. . . .

Lift door opened. She got a breath, set out down the main lower corridor for the airlock.

Another gods-be small space. Which she didn't like to think about closing around her when she was in this kind of funk. She punched cycle and watched the lights run their course, met the different-smelling air of another port and walked the ribbed, lighted tube to the ramp and the dockside.

Where customs was waiting . . . "Welcome Kita Point, hani captain! Sign all form. . . ."

And past that obstacle, just beyond the rampway access, by the control console for the gantries and the lines that were feeding the *Legacy* water and taking off her waste . . .

"H'lo, pretty hani." Haisi waved at her approach like an old friend. "How you do?"

"Hello, you rag-eared scoundrel. What do you know, how do you know it, and why shouldn't I file charges for endangerment?"

The kid *wanted* to do whatever routine maintenance wanted doing, and faced with such self-sacrifice, a body thought of all the things nobody wanted to do . . . like the cursed filter changes, that weren't exactly due, but almost, and if they had somebody that wanted to lie on his back and crawl halfway into the ventilation system, that was fine, let him.

Meanwhile there were the customs people, and, left in charge, with the stsho making calls from belowdecks and the customs papers looking like a mere formality, a sensible person in want of rest might draw an easier breath. Which Tiar drew.

And headed downside to talk with customs in the captain's wake.

"Everything in order," the customs chief said. "All clear with Urtur, all clear here. You captain sign, all fine." There were benefits to dealing with the small stations, the newly built. Luxuries were scarce. Necessities were short. If you weren't armed and dangerous you could get through customs with most anything; and you didn't expect dispute.

But you did have to take the aforesaid customs report and trek to the station office in person to file for various services, and schedule for off-loading.

Which in the case of Kita Point and their berth was a distance off, far enough to be inconvenient on a station too small and too rough to afford a full time shuttle service.

So one walked. And walked, stood in line at the office because Kita Point had no separate line for ships' lading credentials or spacers wanting to certify a live pet for transport, which made a very strangely assorted, unruly and uncomfortable line to be in—a line that snarled and snapped in two instances, and struggled in wild panic in another.

"The hani trader *Chanur's Legacy,*" she was finally able to say, with the waft of kifish presence in her nostrils—two of them were in line behind her, but the mahendo'sat with the wildlife had gone through. She slid the physical papers across, left the mahen agent in peace to survey the requisite stamps, and made out the request for cargo receipt.

"Station load," she said, meaning it was for the station's own use. And that usually got priority. She stood waiting.

And felt something in the back waist of her trousers.

She reached back, suspecting wildlife or an off-target pickpocket.

And found a piece of paper.

She looked around, found nothing but a blank-faced shrug from the mahe immediately behind her in line, and saw a whisk of a white scuttling figure in a gray cloak vanishing around the corner.

Stsho. But no way was she going to leave her place in line to give chase.

"Sign," the agent was saying, and she took the stylus and the tablet and signed, in the several places marked.

"You when want offload?"

"Ready now. Soon as possible." She tried to sneak a look at the paper, but the agent was saying,

"You got volatiles? You need sign form."

"Right. No problem." She got a look. It said, in bad block print, *Help. 2980-89.*

A phone number? An address?

"You sign here," the agent said.

She looked distractedly at the form. She read the variables and signed, collected the requisite form and took the paper with the message with her, on her way to a public phone.

Better *not* involve the captain.

Haisi Ana-kehnandian took a puff on the abominable smoke-stick, blew the contaminated air into the neon-lit ambient, and smiled lazily. "I tell you, pretty hani, you got one bastard lot luck. Just so, Atli-lyen-tlas come here like we know. Then . . . not good news. Atli-lyen-tlas gone kif ship."

"Kif!"

"And four stsho dead like day old fish. Big damn mess."

She didn't want to owe Haisi a thing. She didn't want to have to ask. But the mahe sat there smiling smugly and knowing she had no choice.

"So? Why?"

"Kif big suspect. Or maybe scare to death."

"Residents here or come in with the ambassador. Don't string it out, out with it."

"You so impatient. Got pretty eyes."

"Who were the stsho?"

"Three resident. One secretary Atli-lyen-tlas." Another cloud of smoke in the pollution zone. "I got photo, you want see?"

He reached into his pouch and pulled them out. She leaned over gingerly and took the offering, fanned them in her fingers.

Not a pretty sight, no, especially the close-ups. "What did they die of?"

"Poison, maybe. Maybe scare to death. Stsho deli-cate."

"Where'd you get these?"

"Got cousin in station office."

"You got cousins everywhere."

"Big—"

"Big family. You said."

"Same like Chanur. Big fam'ly. Influ-ential fam'ly."

"I'm a merchant captain trying to make a living! I've got no influence with my aunt, I don't know her business, she doesn't know mine, we don't speak!"

"Hear same. Sad, fam'ly quarrel."

"None of your business."

The waiter set the drinks down. Iced fruit for Anakehnandian and iced tea for her. Intoxicating tea. She sipped hers carefully.

"What's the truth?" she asked. "Who's your Personage aligned with? Who does she do business with? What's her connection to my aunt or does she have one?"

"A. You want I say my Personage business."

"Might increase my trust of you."

Another puff on the smoke-stick. "You long time on *The Pride*, now you not speak? What story?"

"Not your business either."

"You clan head."

"I am. In name. *Ker* Pyanfar appointed me."

"You not forgive her for that, a?"

"Maybe not. What's it to do with anything?"

"Just lot people know you pret' damn good."

"Good for them. I'm so pleased."

A laugh and a puff of smoke. A lot of smoke. Hilfy wrinkled her nose.

"You a lot like the Personage. You same bastard like her."

"Family resemblance. Family temper. You want a demonstration?"

Another grin. Mahendo'sat and humans did that. Bad habit. Could get you killed, on Anuurn.

"You nice. No bad temper. Just hani."

"You're a prejudiced son, aren't you. You want a deal? You tell me what difference it makes what we're carrying. You tell me what difference it makes to the stsho and what's at stake."

"You not know."

"We haul cargo. We're being paid. The stsho didn't hire mahendo'sat to do what we're doing. Don't you think if they'd trusted you very much they'd have let *Ha'domaren* carry it?"

"Maybe they look for damn fool."

Point. "So you know so much: what is it? What significance does it have? Convince me you're our friend."

"Lot status. Lot status with stsho." Puff and puff. Sip of fruit drink. "No'shto-shti-stlen number one bastard, want run whole Compact. Stsho all same lot disturb by give this thing."

"So what does it matter what it is?"

"Same make difference what kind *oji*. Some got big presence. Some got histor-icity. Some got art. Some make suicide."

"Make suicide."

"You get *oji*, you got respond or you lose big. Number one dirty trick."

"You mean they have to equal the item."

"Or lose status big."

"And Atli-lyen-tlas doesn't want to receive it?"

"Maybe." Another sip. "What kind *oji?*"

"Sorry. Not enough information. Why should I help your Personage? She might not be my friend."

"We *good* friend! We number one good friend! Whereby you get idea? Long time mahendo'sat been friend hani. Who get you into space? Who bring ships to you world? Who give you number one help make ships and trade? You damn hani fight each other with sharp sticks two hundred year gone. Now so smart you tell mahendo'sat goodbye, no need help."

"Well, that's not a question you ask a merchant captain. Go tell my aunt what she owes you. Tell my aunt tell me tell you what I know, no trouble."

"You say you don't speak."

"Haven't had a reason. If we had a reason we'd speak."

"How much you want tell me what is?"

"You can't buy me."

"You want know where gone Atli-lyen-tlas?"

She was really tempted. Not to trust this Haisi person. But to trust him more than the stsho. Historically, the mahendo'sat had been more allied with hani than not. But not *all* mahendo'sat were on the same side. "Not many choices out of here. If it's Urtur I'll have your ears. Suppose I said it was a piece of art."

"Need know more than that, hani."

She took a sip of tea. Her last. And got up. "I give you something, you give me nothing. Wrong game, mahe. I'm not playing anymore."

"Kshshti."

"With the kif."

"They *hire* kif. Sit, sit, talk."

She sank back into the chair, leaned her elbows on the scarred table and gazed at the mahe's eyes. Green neon didn't improve his complexion. Green shone on his dark fur, on his uncommunicative, flat-nosed face—on the smoke he puffed out of his nostrils.

"So talk. What kif ship?"

"Maybe . . . *Nogkokktik.*"

"Why?"

"No'shto-shti-stlen got lot enemy. Plenty old, plenty smart. Enemy want *gtst* come home, give up be governor. That enough?"

"No'shto-shti-stlen is an old friend of my aunt. Why should I betray *gtst* interests?"

"No'shto-shti-stlen nobody friend. You know how long live stsho?"

It wasn't a known fact. There were guesses . . . in what she'd read.

"How long?"

"Maybe two hundred year. Hard make figure. Stsho change

sex, change person, change everything, not remember. How you know when born, when change? Nobody sure. But what make stsho care? You Phase, same you dead. You don't got memory who you were. Same like dead."

"Who knows whether they remember who they were?"

"They say don't remember. You don't believe stsho?"

"I believe I got paid. And I get real nervous when people start asking questions about my business or about passengers on my ship."

Another puff of smoke, green in the neon. "You want make contact local stsho?"

"Maybe I will. Maybe I'll use the station com, like any civilized individual."

Haisi grinned. "Maybe you don't get answer. Damn scare' this stsho."

"Who is this?"

"Name not matter. Same aide to Atli-lyen-tlas, got real scare', not go with kif. I got contact. You got *oji.* And No'shto-shti-stlen messenger."

"So?"

"So you stsho make this stsho talk damn fast."

Tempting. "I'm under contract. I can't say what I can agree to. Interesting idea. I'll say that. But I have to go back and take a look at the document I've signed."

"Not safe place, Kita. Mahendo'sat upset, stsho upset . . . kif upset. You want talk new governor at Meetpoint, lot change. Change make money, change lose money. Lot people got lot stress. Bad for health."

It didn't make one feel confident, sitting in a mahen bar, with a mahe with unknown interests bankrolling his ship and making deals through him with unknown parties with unknown intentions.

"I'll get back to you," she said, and got up and left him the bill.

2980-89 *was* a phone number. And an address, that being the system on Kita Point Station. Which made it just about as easy to take a walk to the lift and a ride up to the residential levels, up to Deck 2, Section 80.

Not a bad neighborhood, Tiar said to herself, seeing the immaculate paneling and the neat plastic address plates, and the plastic signs that said, in the universal alphabet, *Silimaji nan nil Ja'hai-wa.*

Meaning, for a mahen maintenance worker who might not speak the pidgin, *Through traffic prohibited.*

No clutter, no smudges, none of the graffiti endemic on the dockside. Pri-cey.

She rang at no. 89, and waited, while optics in the wall doubtless advised the occupants of a hani in spacer blues in the spotless corridor.

"Who? Identify!"

"*Ker* Tiar Chanur, of the merchant freighter *Chanur's Legacy.* I had a notice to call."

Electronic and manual locks clicked. The door shot wide. A stsho was standing there, taller than most, painted in curlicues of palest lime and mauve, about *gtst* plumy crest and moonstone eyes. "Chanur, honorable Chanur. Protect us! You must protect us!"

It was hardly a conversation for a hallway. But she had no desire to let a door close her in some stranger's apartment, either. "In what way? From what?"

Hands waved, trying to beckon her inside. "In, in, the danger, the danger, honorable hani."

"Danger of *what?*" She backed up, evading the white, beseeching fingers. "I don't know you. If you want help . . . come to the ship."

"Most excellent hani! I have little baggage, very little, please, please, you will bring me safely aboard your ship . . ."

"I didn't say that! The captain has to clear any passengers!"

"But if the distinguished captain admits this honest person, where will my baggage be? How shall I live? What should I do? I must have certain things necessary for my existence! All is ready, all is gathered, I need only gather it up, oh, please, *please,* estimable hani, most honorable . . ."

"Get the gods-be bags! Hurry, if there's danger!"

Gtst wailed, *gtst* dashed back as fast as a stsho could move, and, indeed, *gtst* dragged out bags and bundles in feverish haste, from lockers, from cabinets, from various quarters of the pastel room, until it made a sizable pile.

"You can't carry all that."

"This honest person had hoped, had most earnestly hoped that a strong, a most excellent and trustworthy hani would be kindly disposed to . . ."

"Gods rot it." She went in, not without a wary glance about, grabbed up the heaviest bundles by their strings and handles and left the stsho to manage the rest, on her way out the door while *gtst* was still filling *gtst* arms.

"I'll take this lot," Tiar said over her shoulder, "you take the rest and don't look like you're with me, if you don't want publicity. And if the captain doesn't like the look of you, you and this whole pile are out on the dock, hear me?"

"Oh, most clever, most wise hani, most excellent . . ."

"Stow it! Close the gods-be door!" The creature had no concept of intrigue. *Gtst* shoved a note in an alien stranger's trousers and never thought an open door might raise questions.

So might a lift full of baggage, a hani, and a panicked, muttering stsho. A mahe with a child in tow got on at Deck One, and rode down with them. The child bounced around the walls, grinning at its own cleverness, and managed to knock into both of them in the short time before the doors opened on the cold grayness of the docks. Perhaps the mahe meant to space its offspring. Perhaps the mahe hoped someone else would do it. Tiar clutched the bundles and dragged them past the overanxious doors, held them for the weak-limbed stsho, and snarled, "Move, kid!" in such a tone the mahe grabbed the brat out of their path.

The stsho was clearly impressed. *Gtst* pale eyes were very wide. *Gtst* murmured, "Kindly restrain the offspring. It is very annoying," and followed her out.

For a stsho toward a stranger, that was amazing. *She* was impressed. *Gtst* had more fortitude than seemed evident.

"Berth 10," she said, and led off at a moderate stride, a moving obstruction on the docks, in the abundant foot traffic.

She looked back, just to be sure the stsho was still following. And *gtst* was, slogging along with *gtst* swinging, pendant baggage of small bundles, limping on lime-slippered feet.

"Go on, go on," *gtst* panted, shaking *gtst* crest from *gtst* eyes. "We are in great danger. I shall seem not to know you. It will be a ruse. Please, keep walking!"

She walked. There were kif about. There were mahendo'sat. Not another hani, not another stsho. Of a sudden their dissociation seemed exceedingly naive and dangerous.

"Come on," she said. "Hurry it! I don't like this."

She was ever so glad to see the *Legacy*'s number on the display board, and to see the first of the transports already arrived. The hold was open, the ramp gate was showing green for unlocked.

"We're all right," she panted, hoping for the sight of Tarras or Chihin. There was the stsho, valiantly (for a stsho) struggling after.

There were three kif, just standing, watching them.

She was never so glad to walk up the ramp and find the gate opening to her request. The stsho was gasping at the bottom of the incline, trying to gather up *gtst* baggage, the cords of which had tangled with *gtst* robes. One of the kif was headed toward them, with deliberation in its moves.

"Get up here!" she said, regretting the laws that meant the nearest gun they owned was in the locker in the airlock. "Now!"

Gtst stumbled and limped *gtst* way up. The kif stopped, and for a moment looked straight at her, a stare that made the hair stand up on her nape as she shepherded the struggling stsho into the chill of the ramp.

"Oh, the cold!" it breathed.

"Kif," she said. "Move!" She dropped the baggage in the rampway, on the *Legacy*'s side of the doors, and ran for the airlock and the locker. The stsho shrilled a protest at the desertion. She heard it attempting to run, wailing and gasping.

She hit the airlock controls, waited through the cycle and, inside, used her first and third claws in the sockets that opened the locker. She seized the gun inside, clicked the safety off, and scared ten years of life out of the stsho that came gasping and struggling through the airlock.

"I'm going back after the baggage," she said. "*You* stay in the airlock."

Gtst wailed, *gtst* gasped, *gtst* sobbed. "Let us through! Let us through! Oh, murder, oh, vilest murder on us . . ."

Gtst was still wailing as Tiar walked back to get the baggage. The fragile tube was no place to start shooting; but her eye was toward the gates down there, that anyone with a key could open. And if a kif did, he was in dire trouble, by the gods, he was.

. . . it shall be the obligation of the ship's captain to secure the item and to maintain its safety and its confidentiality from all unauthorized persons . . .

. . . the representative of the person issuing the contract shall be the final arbiter of the disposition of the object unless the person who has been the representative of the person issuing the contract shall be determined to be no longer in substance or in fact the same individual entrusted and declared by the contract to be the individual representing the person issuing the contract.

Gods.

Hilfy raked a hand through her mane, stared at the screen. *Final arbiter of the disposition of the object. The representative of the person issuing the contract.*

Meaning Tlisi-tlas-tin representing No'shto-shti-stlen. Meaning ask Tlisi-tlas-tin, as the final arbiter.

She keyed out, got up from the desk in lower deck ops, and went to see the representative of *gtst* excellency . . . who, one hoped, was capable of assuming responsibility, or at least of discussing the matter in a sane and reasonable fashion.

She should tell *gtst* about Ana-kehnandian. She had never contemplated working in any close way with a stsho. *No one* contemplated working closely with a stsho. They were only preferable to the methane-breathers, in reason.

But if she had an ally now who could explain anything it was Tlisi-tlas-tin.

She went to the door and signaled her presence. "Your honor? *Ker* Hilfy Chanur. A word with you."

It took a little for a stsho to respond—a little longer to rise and arrange *gtst*self and walk to the door. In unusually short order the door slid back and *gtst* honor Tlisi-tlas-tin gave a languorous ripple of *gtst* fingers in respect.

"Most honorable captain."

She didn't even have time to break the news. The lock cycled, and a shrill warbling entered the main corridor. *Gtst* honor's eyes went wide and *gtst* ducked back within the doorframe.

"Who is that?" *gtst* cried. "Oh, murder, oh, mischief! What distress is that?"

She had not a thing in her hands. It sounded like murder, and something was in the ship that did not belong there.

Something turned out stsho, and disheveled and woefully frightened, a figure hung about incongruously with parcels and strings and tangled pastel garments.

And behind that apparition, cousin Tiar, gun in hand.

"Refuge!" the stsho cried. Tlisi-tlas-tin's door shut, quickly, and Tiar got between, motioning the panicked stsho to stay still, casting a disturbed and hasty look in Hilfy's direction.

"What's going on?" she demanded of Tiar. Guns, for the god's sake, and a stranger on their deck.

"Kif," Tiar breathed. "Captain, I'm *sorry.* I was out on the docks—this . . . person . . . wanted help. . . ."

Her heart was thumping doubletime. But *seeing* a stsho, finally, proved they did exist here, stsho seemed on the receiving end of the trouble in mahen space, and this one was no threat . . . terrified, rather, distraught, exhausted, at the visible limit of *gtst* resources.

"Help for what?" *Kif* was still echoing in her ears, but if the inner hatch had opened, the outer hatch had shut; and no kif was getting in here.

"Oh, great hani, *kindly* hani person . . . please, refuge from this terrible place, please, violence, terrible violence . . ."

Four stsho dead, Haisi had said.

And beside her the door opened and Tlisi-tlas-tin put *gtst* head out. "Oh, woe! Oh, distress! Is this the person? Is this the one?"

"Captain," Tiar tried to say, but there was too much stsho wailing from both sides, and Tiar gestured helplessly with the gun in hand. "Kif, watching the ship!"

And Tarras and Chihin about to open up the hold for the dockers.

"Have we got a docking crew out there? Have we got any station security on the cargo lock?"

"Just the dockers. . . ."

The intruder had edged forward, toward Tlisi-tlas-tin, babbling and bowing . . . was all but at the door, and that set off old, war-honed instincts. Hilfy put out a warning hand and laid her ears back, by no means eager to let *gtst* near the *oji*.

But the intruder-stsho bowed and bobbed and babbled in manic frenzy, *gtst* moonstone eyes wide and bright, paint streaked on *gtst* face and arms and onto *gtst* pastel robes . . . *gtst* reached Tlisi-tlas-tin, *gtst* honor nothing protesting, with the parcels dangling about *gtst* limbs, but Tlisi-tlas-tin had retreated inside *gtst* cabin, and the intruder seemed overcome, hanging on the doorway and wailing.

Tlisi-tlas-tin hissed and straightened *gtst* robes, a hand on the pedestal of the *oji*. "This is by no means Atli-lyen-tlas!" *gtst* declared. "This is a juvenile! What unseemliness has turned an unformed individual loose without face-saving escort?" . . . or something to that effect. It was a barrage of high stshoshi, indignant and outraged, and the intruder covered *gtst* face and cowered.

"Aide to *gtst* excellency!" *gtst* protested. "I am no juvenile! I am an honorable person, gainfully employed and competent!"

"What," demanded Tlisi-tlas-tin, "what is your wretched and undistinguished name?"

What had *gtst* done? Hilfy wondered, stunned by the viciousness of Tlisi-tlas-tin's attack. Stsho weren't violent. Stsho avoided conflict, and unpleasantness, and *gtst* attacked a stsho *gtst* called a juvenile . . . who hovered in the doorway murmuring,

"Oh, the beauty, oh, the elegance, oh, oh!"

Tlisi-tlas-tin's crest lowered and lifted. *Gtst* blinked rapidly, and the young stsho bowed repeatedly, and turned and patted Hilfy's arm.

"Tell *gtst* excellency, tell *gtst* excellency I am overwhelmed, I cannot remember the unworthiness in the face of this magnificence, I admire *gtst* excellency, please say this!"

"*Gtst* says . . ."

"*Gtstisi*, oh, *gtstisi!*"

Gtstisi. The Indeterminate. The Transitory.

They had a gods-be Phasing stsho on their hands, a personality overwhelmed and disintegrating.

"*Gtstisi* says . . . *gtstisi* is overwhelmed." It was all of it she could construct. It was all that made sense.

But Tlisi-tlas-tin turned *gtst* back and walked a few steps before *gtst* deigned to answer.

And *gtstisi*—assuming it was Phasing—crouched on the floor at the doorway.

"Your honor," Hilfy said, trying to attract *gtst* attention. "*Is* this—" One could not directly refer to the former identity of a stsho in fragmentation—it was abominable manners. "Is this someone with whom your honor might have business?"

Gtst was clearly agitated, pacing and wringing *gtst* long, white fingers. "Excellency," *gtst* had the presence of mind to declare, promoting *gtst*self a notch, for the visitor's benefit, one could think. "I do not notice this distasteful event. If *gtstisi* remains, *gtstisi* remains. Where is Atli-lyen-tlas, what am I to think?"

"Excellency, I have had a report *gtst* moved on, likely to

Kshshti. This could not possibly . . . *possibly* . . . be the identical person, please forgive my forwardness."

"A servant," *gtst* said, at which the intruder wailed and covered *gtstisi* head with locked arms. "Take this juvenile from my sight. It is insane."

One hesitated to make any disposition of the wretched creature. One hesitated to lay hands on it: stsho were fragile, and bones might break. But she took it by a fold of cloth and tugged, wondering what she might do with it, thinking of the accommodation they might improvise out of the remaining passenger cabin next door, and recalling that cabin was dark gray and a definite blue.

It might drive the creature over the edge, or pry its last grip loose from reality. *Final arbiter*, the contract said, of the disposition of the Preciousness. And that was the loader clanking into motion, those hydraulics were the cargo hatch unsealing the *Legacy* to the dockside and the dockers and kifish bandits, by Tiar's report.

"White paint," she said, and cast about desperately after resources of personnel or energy. "White paint. Panels. There have to be some pieces in storage."

"I think there were," Tiar said.

"Get on the com. Advise Tarras and Chihin there's kif out there. Get—" She had the stsho in hand, Meras topside, *gtst* honor in the passenger quarters . . . and *gtstisi* was wilting in her grip, wiping at its body paint and its crest indiscriminately. "Lost, lost," *gtstisi* wailed. "I was someone and I forget, I forget, oh, the misery I have had, and I forget!"

"Get on it!" Hilfy said, and dragged the fainting stsho to the neighboring cabin. "This is temporary," she said. "It has no taste, no distinction. It will change."

"Oh, the despair!" *gtstisi* cried, and slumped inside. "I die, I perish, oh, woe and obliteration . . . where is my name to be? What shall I become?"

"An honest stsho!" she said irritably, and shut the door and locked it.

And leaned against the wall, surveying over her left shoulder a scattered trail of small abandoned parcels. Tiar was not in sight. Probably Tiar would gladly be several lights away at the moment, and the hold was not far enough.

But she could not blame Tiar entirely. Nor blame Hallan Meras for this disaster. This one came of being here, came of kif stalking them, came of dealing with a scoundrel of a mahe who wouldn't tell her what she needed to know.

She had the most sinking feeling that *this* was the stsho Haisi had claimed was still available and knowledgeable, *this* was the source of knowledge still available to them, and *gtst* had just lost touch with *gtst* own mind—was, in effect, dying to the stsho *gtst* had been, and becoming another entity, if *gtst* could pull the bits and pieces of a personality together.

But *gtst* might not remember once *gtst* had made that transition. *Gtst—gtstisi.* Indeterminate, desperately trying to sort out its reality, and locked, within that storage compartment, in an environment that could lend it no cues.

She shoved herself away from the wall, opened Tlisi-tlas-tin's door without *gtst* permission and met shocked, offended eyes. "A mahe named Tahaisimandi Ana-kehnandian has been following us since Meetpoint. He said that some of Atli-lyen-tlas' staff remained . . ."

Gtst honor . . . *gtst* excellency, as *gtst* lately styled *gtst*self . . . flinched. "This is extremely distasteful."

"Because that unformed person *is* Atli-lyen-tlas?"

"No! A thousand, thousand nos. This is a person beneath our tasteful notice. We would not undertake a mission to such an individual. Do not distress us further. This is a juvenile. Atli-lyen-tlas has abandoned *gtst* post and fled in our face. The treachery, the abysmal treachery! I perform heinous insults upon this gift of *gtst* shapeless servant! It will not dissuade me!"

"You mean *gtstisi—*"

"Is surely a servile leaving of *gtst* excellency. Can you look at the magnificence of my surroundings and affront me with that disheveled and untidy person? *Gtstisi* may serve here. The lack of servants offends my dignity, which surely your honor knows. I will accept this individual as resident in my quarters, but *gtstisi* must be clean and respectful!"

"I will inform *gtstisi* of your—ah, excellency's offer."

"My order!"

"Exactly." She kept her expression sweet and her ears up, and bowed politely and went to the neighboring cabin to run *gtst* new excellency's errand. "*Gtst* excellency wants you," she said to the huddled figure inside. "But I suggest you make yourself presentable. There is a thoroughly tasteless place where you may find water and organize your baggage. Follow me."

"Oh, oh," was all *gtstisi* managed to say. "Despair and disaster."

But *gtstisi* followed, through the litter of the abandoned baggage, while thumps and bangs and the action of the loader heralded the exit of cargo from the hold, and, one could hope, not the entry of kifish pirates off the unregulated docks.

She saw the nameless stsho to the washroom, let *gtstisi* gather up *gtstisi* trail of baggage that was strewn from Tlisitlas-tin's door to the airlock, and meanwhile used the com at the intersection of the corridors to call the cargo lock.

"Tiar? Are you alive out there?"

"*Things look quiet,*" Tiar said. "*They're gone.*"

"Are you armed?"

"*Gun's right here in the lock. We're legal.*"

Thank the gods for favors. She called the bridge:

"Fala. Where's Meras?"

"*Doing the filters.*"

"Remind him keep off lower decks. We've got a problem."

"*What kind of problem, captain?*"

"*Two* stsho. One's Phasing. Ours, thank the gods, is still sane. There are kif on the docks, Tiar's working outside, they know she brought the stsho here . . . where's Tarras?"

"*Right here, captain. You need some help down there?*"

"Just be my eyes and ears on dockside. And investigate cargo for Kshshti. Don't agree to anything yet."

"*Kshshti!*"

"I know, I know, best I can do. I'll be on com. I've got a scoundrel to call."

"Aye, captain."

"So can you still deliver what you asked about?" Hilfy asked, and the scoundrel in question said, via station com:

"You number one bastard thief! How you find?"

It was the only pleasant moment in a disgusting day.

"Guess."

"What you propose now, hani bastard?"

"Manners, manners, Haisi. We all lose a few."

"Repeat: what you propose?"

"We might have something to talk about. But now we have the information and you're buying."

There was a moment of silence on the com. Hilfy leaned her arms on the ops station counter, and flicked her ears to listen to the rings jangle.

"What you offer?"

"I don't know. Let me think about it."

"You head for trouble. I number one good friend. Who else you trust?"

"Dear friend. Good friend. You don't want to rush my decision, do you? You want to give me time. We have to maintain good relations."

Now and again there were mahen words she hadn't heard. There followed some. Then: *"Of course. Number one fine. Talk to you later, pretty captain."*

Tarras was looking up cargo for Kshshti. And if they didn't want to be charged with abducting the Preciousness, if they didn't want to pay back a million credit deal . . . Kshshti looked to be where they were going.

And out of Kshshti . . .

Out of Kshshti, Maing Tol, or back to Kita . . . or worse choices. Kshshti lay in the Disputed Territories. It was still a mahen station.

But it was too close to the kif . . . far too close for comfort.

And *gtst* excellency had taken a kifish ship at Kita Point?

Or the kif had taken *gtst* excellency. Certainly the young stsho Tiar had rounded up on station might have told them what the facts were, if the young stsho had not been driven straight out of *gtst* mind, either by the harrowing run to the ship, *gtst* conditions on the station, or the sight of Tlisi-tlas-tin. The fact was, they didn't know and might never know what had been the triggering event, or whether it bore on what had already happened.

So they had to go on. But she would feel ever so much better if she knew how far they were going to have to chase this Atli-lyen-tlas, or into what.

Hallan really, truly did not want to make another mistake. He knew how to clean the filters and maintain equipment, but he had read the manual and the instructions just the same, to be absolutely, unmistakably certain what he was doing. He didn't think speed was going to impress anyone . . . since he was sure they had given him the job to keep him out of the crew's way; and because it *would* save the crew a little time. He wished he could find a disaster in the making, that he could fix, and by that, impress the captain and make up for what he had done at Urtur.

He had nightmares about that. He had nightmares about the tc'a showing up and demanding he come methane-side and parent its offspring. And of strangling in the atmosphere. But there were probably laws to protect him from that.

There were none to protect the ship from the fines it had suffered because of him, because of having to close the section doors, and scaring all those people. . . .

He didn't think he could ever live that down. Sometimes he thought he would be better off to go home and live in the outback and do things the way they had always been done and not be a problem to anyone. He was not really a fighter, he never had been, he was just clumsy, which he daily proved, and his elbows continually found something to bash, or his head to knock into, but there was just no use for being his size on board a ship.

He heard someone come up near him. He did everything as precisely and efficiently as he could. Whoever it was stood there watching. And he finished the job before he looked to see.

"*Ker* Fala?"

"I was just watching."

That made him nervous. He put the tools away and got up, intending to take them to the storage. He supposed he should go to the crew lounge then, because he hadn't any other instructions.

She was still staring at him when he walked away. It made him feel—highly uncomfortable.

The crew aboard the *Sun* had behaved like that too. And he didn't feel the same as he did with Sahern clan, he felt confused, but it wasn't a confusion he wanted to think about. It scared him. He was afraid she was going to be waiting in the lounge when he got back, but she wasn't, she was in the galley making lunch. And maybe he should go help her, and not sit in the lounge as if there were nothing on the ship his intelligence could discover to do, but he didn't want to be alone with her, so he started aft.

But Fala said, to his back, "Want to help?"

And there went his available excuse. "All right," he said, not cheerfully, and came back to the very small galley.

"I think the captain's getting softer," Fala said, with a wink. "If she let you sit on the bridge, she's giving some. You want to get the *cghos* out of the refrigerator?"

He looked. He found it and put it on the counter, and she said, "You can turn on the steamer, it's the red button." She was busy and in a hurry, whacking slices off the lunchmeat with a knife, and piling them onto a plate with the cheese. "You can roll those if you want to, it's just sandwiches. I figure everybody's going to be eating with one hand and working with the other."

"Have we found the stsho we're looking for?" he asked, and Fala gave him a glance.

"Somebody who finds out less than I do," she said with a

flick of her ears and a frown. "No. *Gtst* skipped out ahead of us. We don't know why."

He wondered if she expected him to know. For that moment she sounded friendly and not threatening, and he suffered a moment of panic, reminding himself he shouldn't slip into that kind of thinking, he shouldn't be here.

"Probably Kshshti," she said. "That's what I hear."

Kshshti was a border port. A dangerous place.

"Are we going there?"

A nod. A flick and settling of her couple of experience-rings, that said *she* was a real spacer. "I think so," she said soberly. "You ever seen it?"

"No. No, I never was at the far stations. Except Meetpoint. And Maing Tol."

"I've been there," she said. "You really feel foreign there."

He had slid into a personal conversation. He didn't *do* that with spacers. He tried to stay businesslike. He lowered his ears, looked away and found occupation rolling up the sandwiches and skewering them together.

"Something bothering you?" Fala Anify asked. "You *worried* about something?"

"No," he said.

"Scared of Kshshti?" she asked.

That was next to insulting. He wasn't scared of Kshshti, he hadn't been brought up to run in panic. But he supposed it looked that way to her, and he wasn't willing to explain, he just didn't want to look her in the face and talk to her, because she could really mess things up for him. He had wondered if there was a way he could possibly mess up in this port, and he had found one, that was certain. Because he didn't think Hilfy Chanur was going to tolerate him getting involved with the crew, especially the youngest of the crew. Chihin was safer. At least she was less complicated.

"We'll be all right," Fala said, as if Kshshti were the center of his problems. "The captain knows what she's doing. On *The Pride,* she was in and out of all kinds of situations. And we're armed, the *Legacy* is, if we ever run into anything that needs it, we've got it. The captain knew when she set out that a lot of people could think of getting at *ker* Pyanfar through us . . . so we're outfitted for most anything. We're not a ship anybody should mess with."

"That's good to know," he said, and flinched when Tarras put her head in and asked,

"What have we got here, a romance or a lunch?"

He could have died. On the spot.

Fala's ears went down, flat, in complete embarrassment.

Chapter Eleven

There was tea, while the loaders clanked away. The galley annex that had somehow gotten established in the lowerdeck laundry had found another use, now that *gtst* excellency Tlisi-tlas-tin had acquired a . . . staff . . . fit for *gtst* station in life.

Meaning the nameless servant had acquired an interim name: *gtstisi* was *Dlima,* which meant something like Scant Necessity: not a flattering designation, in Hilfy's estimation, but one could have settled any indignity on Dlima in the present state of affairs, and *gtstisi* could not on the one hand protest it, or, on the other (by all she had read on the matter, written of course by non-stsho) could not integrate it into a meaningful reality. In *gtstisi* condition, experiences fell randomly, and had no order. *Gtstisi* would follow orders, to be sure—mahen scientists suggested (and stsho were tastefully silent on the matter) that *gtstisi* actually required orders, so that *gtstisi* had a hope of discovering structure in the events that tumbled in apparent chaos.

So, distressful as it might be to outsiders, outsiders were advised to ignore their personal scruples and to be as arbitrary, as harsh, as demanding as a stsho of rank might be, because, contrary to mahen expectation, and, as it happened, contrary to hani attitudes, the stsho in question would not hold a grudge, would scarcely remember, and would probably benefit by the experience.

So they said.

So she settled into the cushions, accepted the tea, ceremoniously served, at the foot of the pedestal on which the Preciousness rested, while the loaders worked and the cargo left their hold.

While Haisi was doubtless scouring the station for answers he might suspect she had. And while Tlisi-tlas-tin was discussing the poor but essentially necessary service *gtst* had acquired, "by the good offices of the esteemed hani captain."

"Has this individual discussed . . . hem, . . . any smallest detail of *gtstisi* former life?"

A distressed waggle of fingers. "I should never accuse the esteemed hani captain of a lapse in taste, but I really cannot discuss these distressing matters. Obviously this life contained affairs which *gtstisi* could not organize in any tasteful or useful fashion. These are . . . iiii . . . *biological* matters. Is enough understood?"

Hilfy thought; and thought; and thought in widening circles . . . with the confusions that came of studying alien language and custom much of her life, and not least among them the stsho. When everything else failed, the maxim ran . . . ask the alien how to ask the question.

"Then," she said carefully, and paused while Dlima poured; and paused further while Dlima served Tlisi-tlas-tin. "Then how shall I ask what information you might have gained in this port?"

"Nothing is easier."

"How shall I ask? I wish to benefit from your unquestionable good taste and elegant gracefulness. You have shown most extraordinary virtues . . ." *Never* attribute exact words like frankness to a species which might not value it. ". . . in dealing with the stresses of this voyage. And I am moved to wonder if your resourcefulness and intelligence might have gained information which would make your person far safer if the captain of this ship should learn it."

Moonstone eyes blinked several times, and the tiny mouth sipped at the delicate cup. "You have discovered a graciousness uncommon in your species."

And other species could be, by other species' standards, great boors. But she smiled and kept hani opinions behind her teeth, as invalid in this venue, even on her ship. "I thank your honor."

"As to the answer to your question, I think it very clear that the nameless person of no distinction was at one time a close associate of a person who has behaved tastelessly. Whether this abandonment was intentional or not, it is equally clear that this movement is not coincidence. The designated recipient of the Preciousness has gone to Kshshti."

"Could your excellency possibly enlighten me further as to the doubtless impeccable reasoning that has led your excellency to that conclusion?"

"Kif are involved. They would not readily convey this person closer to mahen centers of power. They had rather seek areas where circumstances are more favorable to them."

Meaning the border, the Disputed Territories that were still, despite aunt Pyanfar's good offices, a matter of disagreement between kif and mahendo'sat. She had no quarrel with that reasoning. She was only glad to hear it confirmed.

"But, enlighten me again, excellency: how has this individual known we were coming? How has *gtst* managed to evade us not once but consecutively? Or is this *gtst* doing?"

Tlisi-tlas-tin carefully set down *gtst* cup, with that twist of the wrist that signaled an end of tea, and a seriousness approaching severe.

"I cannot say."

"I have trespassed. But may I ask: do you advise us to continue as we are, and pursue this individual to Kshshti? And is there reasonable likelihood that there we may discharge our responsibilities and increase our respectability?"

"We must continue. We must go to Kshshti. There is no question."

"I thank your excellency for your most extreme good will. I am always enlightened and invigorated by your discourse. As your excellency knows, there is a mahe pressing us closely, who has offered us bribes and threats in his insistence to view the Preciousness. . . ."

"Unthinkable!"

"I take it our refusals of this individual are wise."

"Villainy, utter villainy. Avoid this person!"

"He thought he could lay hands on your excellency's servant and extract information. The foresight of my crewwoman prevented him doing this. I therefore suspect he does not have the full cooperation of the directors of this station, or he could have laid hands on *gtstisi.* I think that he knew of *gtstisi* existence here, but not the exact whereabouts, nor could he discover it before we did . . . quite unexpectedly and by the forwardness of this juvenile person, and thanks in no part to the mahe in question."

"Most impressive." Tlisi-tlas-tin gave a slight glance aside to the servant. "Most desperate."

"I understand from this mahe that stsho were murdered here, most recently. He implied this was connected to the disappearance of Atli-lyen-tlas."

"Distressing. Most distressing. Is there other information which may be tastefully asked?"

"He implied that the sight or even information about the nature of the Preciousness might enable him to make a critical judgment of its meaning."

Gtst crest fluttered, lifted and lowered. "Unmitigated and unjustified arrogance!"

"I take it your excellency does not approve of his proposal."

"I perform indignities upon his graceless proposal."

"Is he possibly telling a falsehood?"

"In a most shameless fashion. This is a trading style well-known among mahendo'sat, this obtaining piece after piece of what one wants."

"A mahe could not possibly understand the meaning in the sending of the Preciousness."

"You are far more tasteful than he and you do not comprehend."

"Most certainly so, excellency."

White fingers reached for the cup again, and turned it. The conversation was ended. "A symmetry of information has been reached," *gtst* said. "Do you agree?"

There were a handful of questions she would ask that would not get answers—questions like: what part are the kif playing? Are they working for anyone but themselves?

The stsho might think they were. That was the trouble. Everything was the stsho's estimate of what was going on . . . and the stsho had had their fingers burned before. The stsho might be the last to know what was going on. The stsho might be the last to know that they were understood by the mahen scientists who wrote treatises on their psyche.

Gtst excellency said that no mahe could comprehend the nature of the Preciousness—but Haisi chased them from star to star trying to learn what it was?

One *could* conclude that a mahen Personage might not be the only player in this contest . . . that the information Haisi wanted might be going to someone who *could* interpret it.

"I have a thought, excellency."

One did not break the symmetry of a conversation. Tlisi-tlas-tin's brow knit and *gtst* mouth drew thin in displeasure.

"Would a stsho *hire* a mahe to ask us about the Preciousness?"

The frown deepened and lifted.

"Or enter into collusion with some mahe for that purpose?"

Another frown settled on Tlisi-tlas-tin's brow.

"These are disturbing questions," *gtst* said.

"Are they wise questions, excellency?"

There was no immediate answer.

She cleared her throat. "Graceless as it might be, I might purvey him false information, and I would for your excellency's protection do so, if it would not offend you. But I would not know what falsehood might be believed by whoever hired him."

Tlisi-tlas-tin's respiration increased markedly. "These are most distressing ideas. I must consider them."

That the stsho would deceive . . . was well-established. But lying was not a word one tossed about carelessly, dealing with other species. Some species did. Some didn't. Some would, individually. Some would, collectively. And what some called lying others called an answer for indecent curiosity. Meddling with reality *or* its perception was, at least among oxy-breathers thus far studied, what intercultural scientists called a potential flashpoint—a ticking bomb in any interspecies dealings: the more alien, the worse in potential.

"I take my leave of your excellency. I entrust matters to your wisdom and discretion. Should I fail in elegance, I trust that your grace and most excellent sense will advise me to a more proper course."

"Most gracious."

"Most excellent and enlightening."

She *hated* bowing and backing. It wasn't hani. And she didn't do it all the way to the door, not quite. Being hani.

No question then where they were going—and since they had missed that wretch Atli-lyen-tlas twice due to *gtst* damnable haste in going wherever *gtst* was going (one suspected now, away from them) speed might be of the essence. Which meant no delay in loading cargo, no great mass to what they could take, and no time to fuss about the niceties of what they took.

"Got a few possibilities, captain," Tarras said. "Kshshti not being an unusual destination out of here." Meaning that they couldn't be too picky on that account either.

Hilfy read the list. It was a matter of figuring what they could load quickly, and one of the best answers was something light and valuable and easily disposed of in a port that bordered kif territory (she shuddered to think, and refused to carry small edible animals) and likewise lay on the receiving end of two lanes coming out of mahen territory, and one port away from stsho space and tc'a.

Methane load, maybe, which she hated almost as much as the small edible animals.

Or pharmaceuticals. She read the latest market reports from a ship inbound from Kshshti, ran it through the computer program that could spot the relative bad deals and bargains compared to markets elsewhere, factored with points of origin for the goods in question, plus a set of keywords like shortage and various diseases and rise and fall of prices in the business news. It advised, at least, it read news faster than a mortal eye could scan it, and it liked the pharmaceuticals possibility, the radioactives (another load she was not fond of, since one was at the mercy of the company in question's packaging practices, inspection was not easy, and some of them were appallingly naive about what a loader did to cans.) But Kita was an importer of such materials, while Kefk, one step further on from Kshshti, was a moderate exporter of said materials and reasonably would be shipping them to Kshshti . . . figuring trade possibilities was a headache on a border, because you *couldn't* get thoroughly accurate information across said border: traders lied, governments lied, and the black market flourished, but a well-known ship was ill-advised to play that game.

You wanted something . . . something that *you* knew about that the rest of the universe didn't. And the only thing they knew about that the rest of the universe didn't was the exact nature of the Preciousness, and (at least as regarded the average trader) that they carried some sort of stsho psychological . . .

. . . event.

She punched in data with sudden energy and factored in *political uncertainty* and *instability: stsho* . . . and even, thinking about Tahaisimandi Ana-kehnandian and his meddling personage . . . *instability: mahendo'sat.*

The computer silently worked and worked, and came up with a whole new set of projections. Under those conditions, a person wanted essentials in store and a government or a station wanted information and strategic necessities in greater abundance than ordinary. And it projected price rises and scarcities in different patterns.

The only difficulty with that scenario, the glaringly clear difficulty, was that inside information didn't do you a bit of good if the people making the decisions to buy weren't *also* privy to it. It was good for playing the futures game. But perfectly smart investments could bankrupt you if the secret stayed secret. As, contractually, it was supposed to.

Strategic metals, strategic materials, and out of a place like Kita, which was a quasi-star of so new a generation it hadn't heavy elements and wouldn't exist except that it provided services and repairs, and that those services and repairs had employed people who wanted first food and then luxuries to ameliorate their barren lives, and then employees who served up the luxuries, and then food to feed the purveyors of the unnecessary, an ecosystem of elegant simplicity beginning to run to the baroqueries common to civilization.

All of which told you, as every trader knew, that Kita was a place that imported as much for its own use as it could afford to have, and exported surplus luxuries, which it might well have; surplus necessities, which it was more reluctant to release; surplus people, who wanted out of Kita Point; and finally the final layers on the developing economy of a new station, Kita served penultimately as a cheap warehouse for speculators to store what could be imported from its neighbors and unloaded at a more advantageous time, at a higher price; and most baroque of all, it *manufactured* things out of the pieces, parts, and materials which the speculators warehoused; and employed workers who in turn began to want luxuries, and so on, and so on . . .

Dreadfully crazed, a developing economy. But Kita did produce some of the damndest things, geegaws, items in incredibly bad taste, the product of idle minds and fertile imaginations, and occasionally, just occasionally, some product that actually had unanticipated popularity in some other port.

She scanned the lists for materials in future necessity, for materials all species tended to hoard in time of trouble, and idly, finally, for odd items that might prove an inspiration to some local merchant . . . least reliable: *never*, as a throughpassing trader, gamble heavily on fads.

But you never knew what might lurk there, and along with the life and comfort necessities . . . a methane-side curiosity, a compression-jewel that, exposed to oxygen and water . . . blossomed and ablated unpredictably.

Perhaps she'd been dealing with stsho too long. Perhaps she'd been *speaking* stshoshi too long.

But there was a word: *niylji,* art-by-irreproducible-chance.

The image of the exploded object was . . . white with pale mineral stains.

And the legend said you didn't know what you'd get until you uncased it. Or detonated it, as the case might be. An electronic fuse. Pull the tab to admit oxygen, and run for your life.

Art by explosion.

How *big* were the things? Palm-sized. The finished—pieces—were unpredictable. Some went to fragments. Some just puffed up to about the size of one's head.

Done on methane-side, under pressurized oxygen, they mostly eroded to a fist-sized mess. Done on oxygen-side, they absolutely . . . flowered. Somebody on Kita must have found it out the hard way, because it was certainly the first time she had seen the offering. The picture and explanation of the exotic was intriguing, although you could expect the entrepreneur who had actually *dealt* with methane-side (an accomplishment) to get the globes manufactured there, had picked the biggest of the lot.

Certainly worth a try . . . *they* had the franchise. It was a mahen company, trying to market them as geological curiosities, cross-listed under collector's market. They were willing to enter a partnership agreement with a company that could deal in a can lot . . . gods, that was no small number.

Inexperienced entrepreneur. They *hadn't* found any takers. Kita got mostly kif, tc'a, and, mostly, mahendo'sat in the trades associated with industrial companies, and traders, a lot of traders.

Call the fellow. See if he'd deal.

The merchant ship Chanur's Legacy, *captain Hilfy Chanur, to Ehoshenai Karpygijenon. In exchange for exclusive trading franchise under your patent of creation we meet your price and will contract with you for future shipments based on sales and returns, patent holder to assume legal liabilities relating to manufacture and compliance with Compact safety codes. We are at dock for the next 12 hours.*

That was a short time frame. But either the seller had the merchandise or he didn't. Either the seller had been waiting long enough with his funds tied up . . . or he hadn't. If it was inexpertly packed, they were making very low-*g* passage, for reasons other than that cargo, which most merchant carriers would worry about.

The merchant ship Chanur's Legacy, *captain Hilfy Chanur, to Tabi Shipping. Order for purchase: item #2090-986, 4 cans. Item #9879-856, 10 cans. Please confirm availability. Order valid for delivery within 12 hours or cancel.*

That would hurry them. But it was a fair-sized order.

The merchant ship Chanur's Legacy, *captain Hilfy Chanur, to Aisihgoshim Shipping. Order for purchase . . .*

And so on, with three more companies.

Then she called Haisi.

"Haisi?"

"I hear, pretty hani." It was not a cheerful mahe. *"What fine double-cross deal you got?"*

"By what I can figure," she said, "you're right."

"What you mean 'right'? What mean, 'right'?"

Agitated, he was. "You know and I know you know. So let's not play games, Haisi. We're headed out, you know we are, and I've got a list of futures I'd recommend to you if you want to play the market."

"Want talk."

"I'll bet you do. Safe voyage, Haisi. See you."

Drive him crazy, that would. She had not an inkling *what* Haisi knew. But aunt Pyanfar always said, If you're up against a smart opponent, make him *think* himself to death. . . .

Com came live, an excited, effusively grateful Ehoshenai Karpygijenon, who spoke very little Trade interspersed with an obscure mahen dialect.

"Find same one time go bang I unload geo-logics. I say why

not sell, lot people want like collect, like make go bang, like real lot many. . . ."

And more like that. The entrepreneur in question was a dock worker who'd sunk his whole savings into buying this can of rocks from a tc'a trader and hiring tc'a to assemble them into tolerably high-pressure methane/nitrogen globes. Detonators came separate. Put them on with double-sided tape. That was very nice to hear. The mahe was not an utter fool.

And, yes, oh, yes, the mahe was ever so excited to learn that a relative of the great, the esteemed Pyanfar Chanur was indeed in port and had expressed an interest, and of *course* the mahe would be delighted to franchise his product via Chanur's well-reputed trading company. . . .

Well-reputed at least where hani bankers weren't taking a close look at the amount of debt Chanur was carrying.

But for a dock worker who'd had a geological grenade blow up in his face, gambled his life savings and had sudden interest from a Chanur ship, after months of advertising in the list at ruinous rates, gods, the fellow offered her everything but a pledge of marriage, and called on mahen divinities to look on Chanur with outstanding prosperity and confusion upon Chanur's enemies unto a thousand thousand generations . . .

One would do, she thought. But the franchise offer was absolutely to the mahe's liking, he was completely thrilled, he was sure the Chanur name would lend respectability to his enterprise . . . she could have *had* the marriage proposal if she'd written it in. Her proposal to put him in for a percentage of sales thereafter was, he professed, full of such real business terms he knew he was in honest hands. . . .

Gods protect the fellow, Hilfy thought. Real business words, indeed.

For the rest she was sure Haisi was investigating every deal she'd just made, and drawing conclusions about the degree of her understanding based on what she was buying.

Which meant Haisi's personage was going to learn in short order, plans might well be laid in accordance with Haisi's best guess about what she had learned from the stsho, and so much the better.

Aunt had used to din into her juvenile and unwilling ear: Trade isn't about goods. Trade is about information. Goods sit in the warehouse until information moves them.

Gods, she hadn't felt so alive since she was a teenager. She was in a situation up to her ring-bedecked ears, and by the gods she felt . . .

She felt something she hadn't felt in years. She felt . . . as if she had suddenly understood what her aunt had been trying to make her feel, talking about responsibility to the ship and the responsibility of the merchant trade and things that had just gone into an over-hormoned young brain and out the other ear . . . she outright *shared* something with Pyanfar Chanur, over the absent years and across light-years of space.

A feeling aunt Pyanfar had given up, for . . .

For what aunt Pyanfar had sworn she despised—politics. Gods-rotted politics, Pyanfar had used to say, cursing the practitioners thereof.

And then she went and joined the forces.

Led them—was the truth. And why?

Hilfy began to see a certain sadness in that. Even to have *sympathy* for aunt Py, and to think that maybe having *na* Khym with her was a necessary consolation. . . .

And what was she doing wandering down tracks like that? What in the nine or so mahen hells was into her? And *why* had she called Haisi back to rattle him and make him do desperate things, when Haisi going away was what she wanted most?

Pyanfar-nerves, that was what she was experiencing. She'd learned from a past master at chicanery and if she weren't convinced she was half-crazy, she'd say she'd waked up, come alive . . . that she'd challenged Haisi Ana-kehnandian because she was Pyanfar's niece, not Kohan's well-behaved daughter.

Gods, she'd just contracted for a can of exploding rocks. And a franchise on them.

She'd just sent a very dangerous mahen agent wandering through station computer records to ask himself *why* she'd bought what she'd bought, and why station life-support chemicals, basic foodstuffs, and exploding rocks nobody in Compact space had wanted to buy . . . all interested her in the light of what she'd learned from a stsho Haisi didn't know had Phased out of *gtst* former identity and out of *gtst* sanity.

Did hani Phase?

She wondered. She wondered about mahendo'sat.

And listened to the sounds of the *Legacy* giving up cargo to create space for the deals she'd just made.

"I was terribly embarrassed," Fala said. "I'm terribly sorry," and Hallan, cornered in the crew lounge, with no excuse to leave, murmured what he hoped was a polite agreement and tried to think of somewhere else to look but Fala Anify's face and something, anything, that could look like an assigned job.

"Tarras just jokes," Fala said.

"I know," he said.

"You're awfully nice," Fala said.

He tried desperately to find occupation in sorting through the tapes in the rack.

"Tarras and Chihin both joke a lot. It's just their way of being friendly. They really like you."

That didn't exactly help.

"Where is Meras, exactly?"

"Ruun. Near the mountains. It's a real small clan."

"I ought to know. But I wasn't at all good in geography. I can astrogate. That's fine. But I just wasn't interested in planetary stuff. My aunts went with *The Pride*. They used to send me things when they were in port." She bounced down to sit on the end of the couch, which made it harder not to look at her. He must have sorted the tapes beyond twice. He looked stupid, he knew he did, and his ears twitched like a fool's if he tried to keep them up. So he had to look like he was sulking, and that might make her mad.

She asked, in his silence: "Meras isn't a spacing clan, is it?"

"No. No, it isn't."

"How come—?"

"I just wanted to." Gods, they were around to that.

"Anify's up in the mountains. My uncle's a lump and my aunts walked out on him and I think they sort of drifted into *ker* Pyanfar's business. But I'd get presents from space and Anuurn just didn't matter to me. I wanted it so bad, to go to space, my mother used to box my ears about my lessons, and finally she just told me spacers had to know this and spacers had to know that and if I didn't do my divisions and my tables and my geometry and my biology and my Compact history no ship was ever going to want me. But she couldn't make me believe it about agronomy and geography and classical poetry."

He liked classical poetry. But he could understand what she was saying.

"I just nattered my sisters into helping me," he said. "They got me a ride to station. They said I wouldn't last the first winter in the woods. They were right. I was a scrawny kid. And I don't have any aptitude for politics or farming. So if somebody *handed* me a niche in the clans I'd foul it up."

"I think you could do anything you wanted to."

"You could learn geography. If you wanted to."

He hadn't thought that was particularly clever. But she started to laugh, until the all-ship blared out:

"Fala? Where's that systems check? We're in count, gods rot it!"

"I've got to go," she said, and scrambled for the door. But she stopped there and looked back. "Can I bring you anything? Gfi? A sandwich?"

"No. No, I'm fine."

"Fala!"

She ran for it—*not* using the com unit by the crew lounge door. The door shut. He found himself exhaling a pent breath and feeling as if he should adjust the cabin temperature.

So they were in count for leaving this port. That was fast. That was very fast. And he was anxious to get out in space where there was something maybe the captain would let him do, so he had an excuse not to be cornered.

They were in count and the clanks and thumps of offloading cargo kept going. That was a first too, so far as his experience went.

But usually crews wanted to take a few days' rest and liberty on the docks. And the *Legacy* had urgent business, very urgent business, with *two* stsho aboard, now, one of them crazy and the other apt to go that way if *gtst* met him again.

He was absolutely, resolutely, positively resolved he was not going to make one single more mistake on this voyage and he was not going to do anything the captain would disapprove of. . . .

Which meant not getting caught with Fala Anify in the crew lounge. The door opened. Fala put her head in. "You have the *prettiest* eyes," she said. And ducked out.

He dropped his head into his hands. His career in space hung by a thread, he had nothing to think about but stupid tape dramas and the aux boards manuals he was *trying* to din into his reflexes so he wouldn't foul up the next chance the captain gave him, and he had a junior and Chanur relative trying to get his attention.

Gods, *please* let the captain keep her busy.

Chapter Twelve

"Well, there's *Ha'domaren.*"

That from Chihin, at scan. Four hours out from Kita docks and they were approaching jump.

"I don't think I'm surprised," Hilfy said, pursing her mouth. "I *wonder* what he made of the rocks."

"One real happy mahe," Tarras said. "Karpygijenon, I mean. Not our Haisi-lad."

Laughter on the bridge. It was a good sound. Except it was a slightly off-color joke, involving Haisi's morals, and *na* Hallan was probably mortified.

Well, let him be. He could adjust. He would have to.

"You know," Tiar said, "whoever's backing him has got to wish he'd carry cargo."

"I wouldn't bet *where* his mass is. He's shorting his jumps. He probably could do Urtur-Kshshti direct."

"Unless he's carrying a mortal lot of armament," Tarras said–their own gunner . . . if, the gods forbid, they ever had to use what they carried.

Propulsion stuff, Tarras was implying. And that jogged a very bad thought. "Heavy stuff is all government issue."

"So they've got a permit?" Fala asked.

"If they're running with a heavy missile load."

"I wish," Hilfy said, "that we had a source for this Paehisna-ma-to that son claims he's with. I'd like to know if she's in the government."

"If she is," said Chihin, "she's a whole different kind of bad news."

"Probably he's just shorting the jumps," Hilfy said. "Doesn't want to show off to the locals."

"They've got to ask," Tiar said, "the local officials, that is . . . why this ship doesn't offload or onload."

"Gods, no, they're not going to ask," Chihin said. "That son reeks of influence. That ship's probably real well known here and there."

"Suppose *ker* Pyanfar knows him?" Fala asked.

"Wish *ker* Pyanfar would come get him," Tarras said.

"I *don't* like the idea he's got government ties," Chihin said. "If the mahendo'sat go unstable . . . and the stsho already are . . . that's not good."

"We're out and away," Hilfy said, "and I'll tell you how I'm betting. We're bought into staples and strategics, and as soon as sell it, I'd rather warehouse it on Kshshti for a sale when the stsho do go crazed . . . *or* find some reseller I can talk into taking the whole lot at enough profit."

"Rocks and all?"

"Are we serious about the rocks?" Fala asked plaintively. People put jokes over on Fala. Long, elaborate and sober-faced ones. And Fala wasn't willing to fall for another one.

"They're tc'a eggs," Chihin said. "That's what they really are."

Wicked dig at *na* Hallan, that was. Hilfy looked in the reflection on a dark screen, and saw Hallan Meras trying to look as if he were utterly absorbed in the boards.

"No tc'a jokes!" Fala said.

"Was that a tc'a joke?" Chihin asked.

"*Ker* Chihin," Fala said sternly.

Getting serious, it was. And Fala hadn't the rank. "Chihin," Hilfy said.

"Aye, captain. No tc'a."

"*Na* Hallan?"

"Aye, captain?"

Kept his temper, he had. She saw his reflection looking at her, ears at half mast, then pricked up respectfully as she delayed answering.

"You may hear about tc'a from time to time. Do you take jokes, *na* Hallan?"

"Yes, captain."

"Can you make them?"

"I—don't think of one, off-hand, captain, I'm sorry."

"Tc'a," Chihin said.

"Chihin!" Fala said.

"I was just suggesting."

"Chihin," Hilfy said, and saw Chihin dip her ears and lift them again. No gods-be way to stop her but an AP at point blank range. Or losing her temper, which didn't work with Chihin Anify, no more than it had with her cousins.

"Tc'a," Hallan said gravely, and Tarras sneezed, or laughed. Chihin scowled, and Fala grinned at her boards.

"I think that was a joke," Tiar said.

"You've got to tell me," Chihin said.

"That was a joke," Tarras said dryly.

Chihin's ears twitched. Chihin's mouth pursed into what might have been a smile. You could want to kill her. But Chihin was as ready to take it as give. Not from strange men, be it noted. Not from men in general, that *she* knew. Or most wouldn't try: definitely old school, Chihin was, and radiated her willingness to notch ears. Not unlike her cousins.

Fact was, Hilfy thought suddenly, and for no particular reason but many bits and tags, *Chihin* was pushing in a very odd way, for Chihin. Gods-be patient, she was.

And she *knew* the looks young Fala threw in *na* Hallan's direction.

It could get down to a sticky situation trying to get *na* Hallan's highly attractive self off the ship. Which by the gods she was twice determined to do. They had a smoothly functioning crew. They got along. The ship didn't need the scandal, Chanur didn't need the gossip, Meras didn't need it, and if she had her hands on *ker* Holy Righteousness Sahern at this moment she'd give her a lasting remembrance of Hilfy Chanur.

The crew was nattering at each other again. Quibbling over the jump, which was all right—exactitude saved fuel and saved money.

But they were coming up on the mark.

"Stow it. We're away, on the count. Are our passengers set, Fala?"

"*Gtst* excellency says they are."

"On the mark. How's our shadow?"

"Just blazing right along. I *wish* that son'd give us more room. We don't need to bump him in the drop."

"That son or his pilot is probably just too gods-be good. He could jump that ship onto a dinner-plate, you want to lay odds? They don't give just any captain a hunter-ship. And that's by the gods what it is."

"I'd lay odds our stsho passenger might know more about that son than *gtst* is saying."

"I'd lay odds our other stsho passenger did know more than *gtst* is sane enough to say. But we've no guarantee *gtstisi* is going to sort out anything like the stsho that was."

"Spooky," Tarras said. "Spooky lot. *I* wouldn't want to go through jump with a crazy person."

"I wouldn't want to be a crazy person in jump," Tiar said. "Can you imagine?"

"I'd rather not," Hilfy said. "Are we watching where we're going, please? We're coming up . . ."

The coordinates blinked.

She punched the button. The *Legacy* . . .

. . . dropped out of Kita Point space . . .

. . . "Well, well," Pyanfar said.

"Go away," Hilfy said. She didn't *want* her aunt. It frightened her that it *was* her aunt who kept disturbing her dreams—and it was beyond any doubt a dream, it was that comfortable thing the mind did when it didn't want to handle space that wasn't space. Except her gods-rotted aunt wouldn't stay out of them lately. Maybe it was the political stench about the *Legacy* on this voyage. Maybe it was her good sense trying to tell her she'd made a mistake. She wasn't superstitious about the illusions.

Not much, anyway.

"You're indulging yourself," Pyanfar said, sitting on something or another—furniture and rocks materialized when you wanted to sit. And Pyanfar usually sat down when she was going to meddle, parked herself like a gravity sink and insisted on affecting things around her. "Woolgathering's a bad habit, slows your reflexes, fogs your thinking. . . ."

She tried to imagine Pyanfar into the encompassing gray haze.

Pyanfar said, obstinately present: "You *live* in jump, don't you? Just your own little place where you can have your way with Tully and nobody can object. Not even Tully."

Her subconscious was getting vicious.

"Try living in realspace," Pyanfar said. "Try living where you are, Hilfy-girl. Try your own species, for starters."

"Gods rot your interference!" She was as mad as she'd been in years. "If you'd stayed out of my business I wouldn't have married that gods-cursed fool—"

"You're not listening. This isn't a life, niece. Life's not this. Your cousin Chur doesn't time out. Your cousin Chur *sees* the stars in a way I almost can. And you spend your time wishing for what wasn't. *Wasn't,* niece, wasn't ever, and wouldn't be, and couldn't be in a thousand years, and if you want me to say more, I will."

She didn't. That rarely stopped Pyanfar Chanur. But her aunt tilted her chin up in that lock-jawed way she had when she knew she'd won a point, and changed subjects.

"That's a hunter ship out there. And it wants what you've got. It could blame things on the kif. It could be rid of you, get hold of your passengers and the *oji,* pin the raid on kif pirates, and *still* show up in civilized ports smelling like a spring morning. Think about that. They could be lying silent when you show up at Kshshti. They could clip a vane and strand you, for a least thing they could do. Kshshti's not going to investigate. You *know* what Kshshti is. . . ."

She was on Kshshti docks—red lights flashing, black-robed shadows closing in on them in some trading company's dingy freight access, fighting for their lives, and Tully going down—

She didn't want the rest of that memory. She tried to come out of it. She hadn't flinched at going to Kshshti when she'd known she had to, she hadn't let what had been affect what would be . . . she wasn't a coward, she hadn't been and wouldn't run scared. She'd *go* there, she hadn't given herself time to think and none to recall the jump out of there, the absolute black despair of a kifish hold. . . .

Kshshti was where it had started. That was where she had made the worst mistake of her life, when the kif had been waiting for nothing so much as a chance at any of them.

Leave it to the kid.

She'd been younger then. Hormones in full spate. A fool.

A kif leaned close to the cage, and talked to her, its speech full of clicks from inner and outer rows of teeth.

A kif reached into a cage and devoured small live creatures that squealed and squeaked pathetically. Kif were delicate eaters. Their appetites failed, with other than living food. And nothing went down their gullets but liquids—of whatever viscosity.

She wanted out of this dream.

. . . But it was forever before she heard the beep of the alarm, telling her they were making the drop . . .

. . . here and now.

"That's first dump," she said. And remembered the huntership. "Where's *Ha'domaren?* Look alive! Can you spot him?"

"Got the buoy," Fala murmured.

And from Chihin and a deeper voice almost simultaneously, a set of coordinates, as Tiar's switching sent the buoy system-image to her number one screen.

She was relieved to know where that son was, damned sure.

Meanwhile Fala was talking to *gtst* excellency, who seemed to be alive, and Tiar was handling a message to station.

"Rocks didn't blow," Tarras said.

"That's nice. Advise *gtst* excellency we're going down again."

Pulling the dumps close together. But they'd come in close. Showy precision. She pulled a nutrient pack from the clip and downed it in three gulps.

"Kshshti Station," Tiar was saying, talking to a station central that wasn't going to hear them for another hour. "This is *Chanur's Legacy*, inbound."

Not *The Pride*. Now wasn't then. Maybe on Kshshti docks a stsho was running for cover. Maybe they'd caught Atli-lyen-tlas this time, maybe *gtst* hadn't had time to get out of port. A stsho didn't have the constitution for consecutive spaceflights. *Gtst* had to be feeling the strain of the chase by now. *Gtst* had to be saying to *gtst*self that maybe running wasn't worth it.

Gods-for-sure certain no *kifish* captain had provided *gtst* the comforts they'd given Tlisi-tlas-tin. That kifish ship held the dark kifish eyes preferred, the sullen glow of sodium lights, the perpetual stink of ammonia . . .

. . . on anyone who dealt with them. . . .

A stsho couldn't flourish in the dark. *Gtst* sanity would go.

On the other hand . . . considering Kita Point . . . maybe it already had. Maybe there *wasn't* an Atli-lyen-tlas by now, just a body, and compliance to kifish orders, and no knowledge who *gtst* had been.

Disquieting thought.

One she refused to deal with until she had found their recipient.

They traveled at insystem *v* now, good, peaceful citizens of the Compact. They had the output of the buoy computer that, constantly updated by real events in its vicinity and events transmitted from Kshshti Station, maintained a time-warped reality of its own, shading from the truly real and contemporaneous, or at least minutes-ago truth to the many-minutes-ago truth of Kshshti station.

The station schema was, at the time they got it, some 52

minutes old. That was a benefit of the peace: stations were no longer so paranoid as to think that two enemies might go at each other in full view of a station—or with one linked to its fragile skin. Kshshti Station showed *Ha'domaren* ahead of them . . . where else? And a ship named *Nogkokktik*, captained by one Takekkt, at dock since yesterday.

Closing the gap, by the featherless gods.

Hani traders didn't even *go* to Kshshti. But there were sixty-seven messages, for aunt Pyanfar here, one outstanding legal paper suing for information, and a stray package pickup (from a mahen religious foundation?) postage due.

Meanwhile the kifish ship *Nogkokktik* remained at dock—wasn't *talking* to anyone except station, and claimed, through station communications, not to know anything about any stsho passenger.

Likewise *Ha'domaren* received their salutations, welcomed them to Kshshti, and, no, Ana-kehnandian was not available. Ana-kehnandian was in his sleep cycle and could not be disturbed. Amazing how the watch officer's command of the pidgin declined as soon as he'd said that.

And was there a stsho ambassador or anything of the sort on Kshshti?

No. The ambassador had taken ill and died last month.

"Gods *rot* it!" Hilfy cried.

"There's something," Tarras said, "going on."

Notable understatement. She gave Tarras the stare that deserved.

"I mean," Tarras amended that, "major."

A long breath, slowly exhaled; unwelcome reminiscence of ship stalking ship, the chill of hearing a safety go off behind one's back. Of seeing a ship die in a silent fireball, and hearing the voices over com . . .

She didn't want those days back again. She didn't want to be in this port playing tag with a kif.

But gods be. She hadn't the habit of giving in. Not even to

her aunt. And never in a mahen hell to outsiders, notably not the kif.

She sat with her chin on her hand, thinking through their options, since no one was talking. Kshshti authorities were no reliable source of help—unless someone had come in here and swept out every official who had ever taken a bribe, and she had never heard that that had happened.

Of resources they had . . .

"Deal with customs," she said. "Offer the cans for sale . . . except the rocks. We're keeping the rocks."

"Keeping the rocks," Tarras echoed. "Right."

"If we get a decent offer, let me know. If we don't get a decent offer, look us up an honest warehouse . . ."

"At *Kshshti?*"

"Best we can do. I want everybody on Kshshti to know what we're carrying; and that we're willing to warehouse it if we don't get our offer."

Tarras gave her a curious, thoughtful look.

"Why would a Chanur ship come in carrying strategics and staples, and insist on warehousing . . . if we don't get a top price?"

A line developed between Tarras' brows. "You'll panic the market," Tarras protested. "Captain, . . . begging your pardon . . ."

"They know they're dealing with Chanur. The dockside bartenders probably know we're carrying an important stsho object. We're in this to make a living, cousin. So are they."

"You'll shove the market into a war scare. It'll proliferate. Captain, people can get hurt."

"There's nothing they'll buy they won't need. And that's the market, isn't it, cousin?"

"Not starting gods-be rumors!" Tarras cried, and immediately lowered her voice. "Captain. This isn't right."

She scowled at Tarras, at disloyalty, at a clear challenge to her methods, her character and her ethics. They had had doubts under aunt Py's command, too, there had been scary, sticky moments, a good many of them here at Kshshti, but, by the gods, the whole crew had stood by her.

Py had a few more gray hairs, be it known. Py and the four senior crew had been in tight spots before they had ever gotten into the mess at Kshshti, and they'd known Pyanfar was smart enough to think her way through it.

But Tarras didn't know that about her. Tarras knew she'd gotten the captaincy because she was Pyanfar's niece, that was what Tarras knew about her, the same thing all Chanur's rivals knew about her.

"If we let this loose," Tarras began.

"It's already loose, cousin, it's already part of the record, what we got at Kita, what we're doing, who we're carrying, where we're going . . . People *watch* us, people rake over everything we do . . . that message stack is in our files because every gods-be station *assumes* we're in thick with Pyanfar's doings, and all right, why don't we just call up station central and tell them who we've got aboard, what we're carrying, what we think Haisi's up to, why don't we just stand out there and see what happens then, cousin? So we lie to them, so we flash a few pieces of information and let whoever's out there wonder if they've got the picture. If we told the gods-be truth they'd go insane trying to figure out which part of it was a lie."

"I'm not for creating a war scare! I'm not for throwing the whole commodities market on its ear because we've got a problem!"

"So what if there *is* a war? What if, at least, the mahendo'sat and the stsho are maneuvering for position and somebody's going to double-cross aunt Py and the whole glass house is going to come down? How many people are going to get hurt then? How fast will some kifish *hakkikt* appoint himself to grab power? The market's a small casualty, cousin. A tick or two in the price of grain's something the smart traders will ride smart and the amateurs are going to get stung with, but I'm not responsible for that. I can't do anything about small investors' mistakes, I'm trying to keep Chanur afloat, I'm trying not to let this blow up in aunt Py's face—which it could—or let Chanur's troubles with the *han* erode her influence to keep the peace, that's where my thoughts are running, because if you're right, Tarras Chanur, a good many more people can get hurt if the peace goes, than if the market bobbles."

"We don't know what side the stsho is on!" Tarras protested. "We could be doing harm rather than help for all we know!"

"People who do something can always make a mistake. So can people who do nothing."

"That's all fine. Do we know what we're doing?"

"We rattle a few doors and see what puts its head out, cousin. And if you'll do what I ask and publish us on the list, I'll go rattle one in our own basement."

"The stsho?"

"They'd better find out their ambassador here's dead. And the other one's missing. People have already gotten hurt, if you want the morality of it. They're all stsho . . . but they still count. They're still dead. Somebody was willing to kill them. And we've got a piece of the puzzle on our deck."

"*Aye*, captain."

So maybe Tarras was easier in her mind. She wasn't. She walked out of the bridge and past *na* Hallan, who was doing a scrub-down and inventory of the galley cabinets, past Fala, who was doing a life-systems check, and got furtive stares from two eavesdroppers who'd probably rather be in the cold-hold.

Amazing the industry that appeared. She punched the lift button and rode down to lowerdecks, heard the clanks that meant Tiar and Chihin were busy in ops . . . their refueling and their readiness to move was the number one priority, ahead of cargo, ahead of customs, ahead of any other business.

Gods, she hated politics, she couldn't believe she'd said what she'd said up there . . . no wonder Tarras was confused.

She walked to the passenger corridor, signaled her intention to open the door, but while she was listening for a response, the door opened, and Dlima, quite nicely painted, gossamer-robed, quite gracious, bowed and let her in.

"Your excellency," Hilfy began, "how have you fared?"

Tlisi-tlas-tin reclined in the bowl-chair, a cup in hand, and *gtst* beckoned her closer, quite at ease, quite pleased with *gtst*self and life in general, as seemed. "Will you take tea, captain?"

"Honored." It was the only appropriate answer. She stepped in and settled herself as Dlima brought her a cup and filled it with graceful attention. "Most elegant."

Dlima fluttered, and subsided, tea in hand, to snuggle up to *gtst* excellency, no trace of the confused person abandoned at Kita Point.

So, so, and so, Hilfy thought. *Gtst* excellency was not suffering. One wasn't so certain about Dlima's mind.

"Tell the captain," Tlisi-tlas-tin said, with a gentle nudge of *gtst* elbow. "Or shall I?"

Feathery white lashes veiled moonstone eyes, and *gtstisi* squirmed deeper into the nook against *gtst* excellency. "I have the rare pleasure to make your honor's acquaintance."

"This is Dlimas-lyi," Tlisi-tlas-tin said, with *gtst* arm about *gtsto* and a look of thoroughly foolish contentment on *gtst* face.

Good, living gods, Hilfy thought in despair.

"*Gtsto* is a person of such inestimable quality, such wonderful refinement. . . . beyond a consolation. I am beyond fortunate."

So Dlima was something like male . . . as Tlisi-tlas-tin *gtst*self was something no other sapient species on record had.

"I am ineffably honored by the event." One didn't refer to gender in polite conversation. What she was seeing was intimacy verging on the indecent, by every book on stsho etiquette she had read. How did one deal with stsho in this condition?

Don't refer bluntly to the integration, the books said.

Don't use the *gtsto* pronoun without clear permission. Use the universal *gtst*.

Don't refer to mating.

Don't act embarrassed.

"That *gtst* excellency has discovered such happiness as my guest," she added desperately, "is a delight and an exquisitely unexpected honor to our hospitality."

Gods rot it. She had business to discuss. Urgent business.

But *gtst* was pleased. *Gtst* sipped *gtst* tea and *gtsto* was quick to refill the porcelain cups.

"Such excellent kindness," she said, and *gtsto* fluttered with pleasure. A spidery white hand reached out to stroke her probably frazzled mane, and she valiantly refused to flinch.

"What a curious and unexpected texture."

If *gtsto* proposed a threesome she was going to run for it.

"Dlimas-lyi," Tlisi-tlas-tin said gently. "Would you absent yourself? There is such tedious business at hand."

Dlimas-lyi bowed, and bowed, on the retreat from the bowl-chair. Tlisi-tlas-tin sipped *gtst* tea and Hilfy did the same.

Thank the gods . . . the third gender was the one that dealt with outsiders, business, and stress.

But outsiders didn't *meet* the sexed genders—or most rarely did.

"I am vastly moved by the trust *gtst* excellency has bestowed."

"Your tastefulness fulfills my extravagant expectations of a foreigner. If I had not come on this voyage I should never have met Dlimas-lyi. As a result of your hospitality I have . . . iiii . . . no, I shall be daring . . . affected a person of such exquisite worth as I could not dream of. *Gtsto* was the offspring of Atli-lyen-tlas, *gtsto,* ruthlessly abandoned, *gtsto,* hitherto *gtste* . . . who most valorously hid from *gtst* enemies until Chanur had come to port. Then, seeing my magnificence, and surely to afford me comfort, *gtstisi* became *gtsto.* . . ."

So Atli-lyen-tlas' daughter had hid from assassins, and, attracted to Tlisi-tlas-tin had become . . . call it male. It didn't bear offspring in this hormonal condition. If she presented what *gtst* had said to the universities at Anuurn or Maing Tol, she could justify a second certificate in Foreign Studies. Scholars would kill, to hear what *gtst* confided to her . . . but scholars were not going to hear it. That was the other thing you learned in Foreign Studies—not to sell out your source.

And in Protocols . . . never to let your source know you had.

"I am overwhelmed," she said honestly. "You are a most

gracious guest. Admiration of your virtues has compelled me to personal efforts to fulfill our promises. And I must tell you—we are again frustrated in our attempts to reach Atli-lyen-tlas. The kif ship is here. It will not give us any information about passengers. But we have not abandoned effort."

"They are offensive individuals."

"I concur. Also the mahe about whom I spoke, Anakehnandian, aboard *Ha'domaren,* is notable by his presence at this station and his clear intention to meddle in your excellency's affairs."

"What does your honor propose to do about this annoying person?"

"This is Kshshti. We have no confidence in the authorities to do anything. We shall attempt creativity. Has your excellency any advisement? We would receive it with all attention. Or had your excellency rather wait on further information—" *Never* press a stsho for decision. "—we should certainly attempt to obtain it."

"As a hani, are you contemplating . . . iiii . . . violence of some sort?"

"By no means! But we *are* dealing with kif. Therefore it is a possibility, if instigated by them."

"The Preciousness must be safe!"

"At all costs."

"I am then willing to wait on your wisdom."

Gods *rot* the son.

"I have one other . . . em . . . distressing piece of information. Your ambassador here is dead."

"Wai! This is beyond all coincidence!"

"Is there possibly any advice your excellency could impart?"

"I will think on it."

"Perhaps . . . your excellency could step into that lately vacated place, and advise station authorities from that authority that you disapprove the silence of this kifish vessel?"

"Ambitious."

"But within your excellency's scope. Well within your abilities."

Gtst moon-pale eyes blinked, and blinked a second time, and *gtst* expression never changed.

Until *gtst* took a deep breath. "What would your honor do?"

"I admire the extraordinary graciousness of your excellency to consult a foreigner and understand your excellency is merely curious. I would deliver a message to the station of extreme displeasure, assuming the authority of the late ambassador, without leaving this ship, and demand that information on Atli-lyen-tlas be forthcoming at once."

"This is a very sudden step."

"It will startle them. But no more tasteful approach could gain notice from the authorities of Kshshti."

"A bold venture."

"You have been bold in defense of propriety before this."

Tlisi-tlas-tin's eyes were wide. *Gtst* nostrils flared in rapid breathing. "You instill in me a most curious excitement, distinguished captain."

Emotional imbalance, the book said, is to be avoided at all costs.

"I have never before perceived elegance in such reciprocity of hostility. I feel a poetry in it. Dare I take such advice?"

"Modified of course by your excellency's own wisdom."

"No, no, these are foreigners! And I have confidence in your honor's elegance. Convey such a message. I am most displeased with such behavior. I shall certainly relate their answer to the authorities at Llyene!"

"Your excellency most certainly has the right words. Shall I provide your excellency a communications link to station central?"

"Absolutely! I shall execrate their offspring and their dealings!"

For a stsho, Tlisi-tlas-tin was acquiring very hani sentiments.

For a hani, she was acquiring a very curious empathy for a flat-toothed, group-following stsho.

Gtst excellency certainly rattled the appropriate doors.

"I am outraged to learn of the demise of *gtst* excellency and *gtst* staff! This is villainy! I demand recompense! I demand the immediate cooperation of station authorities! I demand serious inquiry into the kidnapping of *gtst* excellency of Urtur! I demand serious action against the harassment perpetrated against us by the mahen ship *Ha'domaren!* Failure to comply instantly will jeopardize trade with all stsho!"

Strange to say, the Voice of the Personage of Kshshti immediately surrendered the mike to the Personage himself.

And strange to say, the Voice was quickly thereafter on the com, in person, to expedite customs for the *Legacy,* and to declare that officials were on the way to make serious inquiry into the issues raised by *gtst* excellency.

"*Most* efficacious!" Hilfy said, and restrained herself from slapping Tlisi-tlas-tin on the back, *gtst* was so pleased with *gtst*self . . . positively beaming as *gtst* leaned back from the ops room com console.

"Let them reflect upon the consequences I have named! Nothing is idle threat!"

The futures market, on the number two screen, showed an immediate five point rise in strategics and necessities. One could predict an active bidding for the *Legacy's* cargo.

One could also predict a message from *Ha'domaren* . . .

"You damn lot ignorant hani! You don't listen, this *no* place to act like fool! I want talk! Now!"

"I'll bet you do," she said, stroking her mane into order.

Old nightmares, old sounds, remembered smells . . . now and then traded places in rapid succession. Kshshti docks hadn't changed that much. It was still a raffish, rough place of bare metal, cheap plastics, leaking pipes and condensation that made rainy weather in the high cold chill of the towering overhead, obscured in the multiple suns of the lamps—hydrogen and sodium spectra that gave everything multiple shadows in bilious colors. It might have been years ago. It might be *The Pride* at dock behind her instead of the *Legacy,* and it might be those dark and dangerous times.

But it wasn't Tully walking beside her, it was Tiar, who hadn't said a word about old history, or anything of the sort, only pounced on her in the airlock with: "You're not going out there alone, captain. And you're not meeting that son by yourself."

So she hadn't gotten away. Orders be damned, Tiar would follow her. Two of them wandering around out there solo was asking for trouble. The dockside office, Haisi had finally agreed—which was line of sight. Haisi refused to come to the *Legacy*, she wouldn't come to *Ha'domaren*, not even close to it: the registry office, where one of them had to go anyway to get the loaders scheduled, was as close a compromise as they could arrive at, and she didn't have that much to say to Haisi anyway.

A couple of lines, like Stay off my tail, and Tell me who you're working for or we're through talking.

"More bars than restaurants," Tiar muttered.

"By actual count, probably." She was trying not to let her nerves get the better of her. It was her personal nightmare, this dockside: kif waiting in ambush, an alley that promised safety turning into a trap . . .

They'd fought, she and Tully had. But there'd been too many of them. And they'd ended up on a kifish ship, a prize aunt Py had to buy back at cost—

—at a cost that might have changed the Compact forever; or might have had no bearing on the outcome: she could never reason it out. Her wits went down too many tracks when she even tried to figure it, and it was more than meeting a mahen agent that brought her out of the *Legacy* and onto this dockside: she had to go. She had to walk out here and see the place again, and, now that she was here, she could tell herself it was a place no different than other places, and that if things were equal, they would take a liberty here, disgrace their species in several of the bars, and leave Kshshti as they left any port in the Compact, maybe better, maybe worse.

Nothing mystical about this place, at least. And nothing that remarkable about the tall mahe who stood with arms folded outside the station office.

"Go on," she said to Tiar, "take care of our business. I'll talk to this son."

"Bad language," Haisi said. "Shame. Shame you lie."

"Got you, did they?"

"No, just make damn mess."

"Listen, mahe bastard, you ride my tail one more time in jump I'll have your ears! I don't care how good your pilot thinks he is—"

A hand landed on Haisi's dark chest, fingers spread. "I. I pilot."

"Fine! I'm glad to know who I'm insulting! You're a damned fool, I've seen better, and I by the gods resent your taking chances with us! I don't care who your Personage is, you have no gods-be right to risk my ship!"

"No risk. I damn good."

She jabbed a claw at said chest. "I mean it! I'll sue you for endangerment. My passenger will sue you!"

"Where damage?"

"My nerves, mahen bastard! I'm carrying a stsho and you by the gods know it! You don't do it again!"

"Maybe same you use sense don't make trouble with stsho. Maybe now you talk deal what kind *oji.*"

"No deal!"

"Oh, now we big confi-dent! Now we got make trouble honest mahe station—"

"*Gtst* isn't kidding, mahe! You want trade shut down, you want that on your Personage's doorstep, you push me."

"You damn fool! You listen me! You want make friend kif? I think you got same real dislike with kif!"

"Kif aren't giving me any trouble right now. You are!"

"Kif give you big lot trouble a'ready. Who got Atli-lyentlas?"

"You, for all I know."

"Not true. Kif got."

A blunt mahen claw jabbed *her* in the chest, and she batted at the offending hand. "You listen," Haisi said. "True No'shto-shti-stlen send Tlisi-tlas-tin go you ship?"

"So?"

"True you go visit No'shto-shti-stlen?"

"So?"

"True same got kif guard?"

"You got a point, mahe? Get to it!"

"You *like* kif guard?"

"I said get to it!"

"All same No'shto-shti-stlen got lot kif. Kif got No'shto-shti-stlen. Same in bed like old friend. No'shto-shti-stlen want be number one stsho and here come stupid hani—" A wave of a dark, blunt-clawed hand. "Believe everything *gtst* excellency got say. Take *contract.* You hold damn *grenade,* Chanur! Thing go bang in you face."

"Same like be friend with damn mahe reckless no-regard-for-life!"

"Same like be smart mahen accent. Chanur *protocol* officer not damn polite."

"I'm always that way with navigational hazards. I have an allergy to fools!"

"You calm down. You listen. You want go bed with kif, you like fine No'shto-shti-stlen. You listen! You aunt be damn fool, all time 'ssociate with kif bandit. Oh, real polite, real nice. But same call you aunt *mekt-hakkikt,* great leader, like real fine . . . All same kif pirate. All same kif steal, kill, lie, I no got tell Hilfy Chanur about kif—"

"You can sit in your own *hell,* mahe, you're way past the limit with me. What I am and what I know, what I did and what I'll do . . . aren't your damn business, they haven't been your damn business, and I absolutely *resent* your trying to manipulate me! No luck, *no* luck, mahe, and you can tell that to the Personage that sent you to maneuver Chanur against itself."

"I try help, hani fool!"

"Stay out of my way!"

"You listen—"

"No."

"You *listen,* hani! You want kif be number one power in the Compact, you keep go what you do!"

"Fine. What's my choice? A smart-mouthed mahe?"

"Don't be fool!"

"I wasn't born one and I won't be made one. Good *afternoon,* Ana-kehnandian. And our regards to your Personage. Maybe she'll send someone polite next time she wants favors from a hani!"

"Fool!"

"Twice a fool!" Shouting was drawing an audience . . . mahendo'sat, a wall of brown and black, no sign of the stsho one might have expected here. "This isn't a place to discuss anything."

"Fine, we go my ship."

"I don't go near your ship. And it's no good you coming to mine because you're not going to get what you want. We're drawing a crowd. Forget it!"

"Hani!—"

"Forget it, I said!" She walked away, shouldered a couple of mahendo'sat on her way to the registration office door, walked through into the brighter light—with some satisfaction in Haisi's discomfiture at being what no hunter-ship captain ever wanted to be: public.

He didn't follow her in. There were stares all about them, mahendo'sat, mostly, and the inevitable (at Kshshti) clutch of black-robed, cowled kif, whispering in their own language of clicks and hisses.

Hani, was one word her ears caught. Chanur, was another.

Tiar was at the desk. She walked up to Tiar's elbow and waited while the mahen clerk processed the information.

"Not a real happy mahe," she muttered into Tiar's canted ear. "He claims he pilots that ship. Cocky son, says *he'll* miss us, we don't have to worry about collision."

"What did he want?"

"Oh, the usual, warn us about a plot to take over the universe, that sort of thing. What else is new?"

Tiar's ear flicked. "Captain, somebody might speak hani."

Dear, literal-minded Tiar. For the first time in a decade she felt alive, felt—

—by the gods, ahead of the situation instead of chasing after it.

Didn't know what she was going to do, precisely, but she knew what she was doing—and whoever was against them, didn't: that was the name of the game; and quite comfortably she turned her back to the counter, leaned her elbows there, and simply stared back (smiling pleasantly, of course) at the mahendo'sat and kif staring at her.

Crazy as the rest of the family, she thought. It probably onset with age. Aunt Py had been relatively stable until she became captain of *The Pride.*

The business at the desk concluded, Tiar putting in her bid for loaders to their dockside, no, they hadn't *sold* the cargo yet, but they'd put in a destination when they agreed with the loaders, so much per section the load had to go around the rim of Kshshti, and no, they didn't need provisioners soliciting them. Everything was fine.

Meanwhile she watched the room in the remote but not impossible chance someone might turn up with a weapon or some sort of trouble might come through the door.

Somebody like Haisi. Somebody like a few of his crew. Probably Haisi was thinking hard what to do about troublesome hani. And if he was connected to anyone responsible, gods rot him, he could have produced credentials from people she knew. She didn't need any, to prove to him who *she* was.

"I think we're ready," Tiar said.

"Let's walk back," she said. "Sort of watch it."

The crowd at the door moved and let them out onto the dingy, multiple-shadowed docks. "Haisi's left," Hilfy said under her breath.

"Wasn't highly helpful?"

"You could say that." Another time-flash, on the smells and the sights and the sounds of the dock, a bus passing, on its magnetic guide strip, rattling the deck plates at a service access. And not a hani in sight . . . just not a place hani had gotten to, lately. Peace might have brought prosperity . . . but merchant ships tended to establish quiet, regular routes. There weren't the disruptions, the wild incidents, the rumors, that tended to send the timid running and the foolhardy kiting in on the smell of profit: and, absent those motives, a merchant ship tended to carve out a route it followed and stick to that route for fear of someone moving in to compete . . . from a cooperative, rumor-trading free trade, they'd become misers, close-mouthed on information, jealously protective of their routes and resentful if somebody moved in on them or undercut their prices—a mercantile age, it was, a greedy, tight-fisted age.

And what was a hani ship saying by *being* out of its normal route these days, or what was a mahen hunter ship doing sniffing about? That there was something different about them? That, being Chanur, there was something other than trade on their minds?

That murdered stsho were significant?

Trust Kshshti to spread the rumors it got. That little business with Haisi was already spreading on a network more efficient than the station news, bet on it.

"Ever been on Kshshti?"

"No," Tiar said shortly. Tiar had an anxious, distracted look. And she *knew* Tiar hadn't been here: aunt Rhean hadn't favored this area of space. Aunt Pyanfar had been the one to run the edges, preferentially, using her experience of foreigners to make *The Pride* profitable.

But aunt Pyanfar hadn't spoken the languages with any great fluency. And *she* could. She'd gone into that study to give herself an edge in getting into the crew, she'd had an aptitude for words, a mind quick to grasp foreign ideas, and a tongue that didn't trip on stshoshi . . . best bribe she could have offered aunt Py, who couldn't say Llyene without dropping an essential l.

And where had it brought her?

A car swerved near them. "Gods-be *fool!*" Tiar exclaimed.

"*Na* Hallan would be right at home here," she said—nasty joke; but *na* Hallan wasn't here to hear it, and she was in a joking mood, crazy as it was. Maybe it was discovering Kshshti was a real place, and debunking it of the myth of nightmare . . . she hadn't flinched from coming here, hadn't let herself, but by the gods, maybe she should have come here years ago, walked the docks, had a look at the place and told herself . . .

"Kif," Tiar said suddenly, and her eyes spotted them at the same moment, a handful of them standing about in the shadows near the *Legacy's* berth.

Her heart was beating faster. She told herself there was no reason for panic, the station was civilized enough these days that an honest trader could get from the dock office to her ship's ramp without a gun; and that calling on the pocket com would be an over-reaction.

One of them was walking toward them, strobed in the multiple shadows of the lights and the flash of a passing service truck. The matte black of his hooded robe was only marginally different from the skin of the long snout that was all of him that met the light. She couldn't see his hands, and while what had once been gunbelts were mere ornament these days . . . knives weren't outlawed.

"Captain, . . ." Tiar said.

"If something happens, break for cover behind the number two console, call station on com, I'll take the number one, call the ship . . ." She monotoned it, under her breath: her mind was on autopilot, her eyes were on the kif . . . all the kif. They were predators, highly evolved, and *fast* over short distances. And no weapons ban covered teeth.

"Good day, captain. What a rare sight . . . hani back at Kshshti. How pleasant. Captain Hilfy Chanur, is it?"

"We might have met," she said flatly, ears back and with no pretense at friendliness. "Have we?"

"That unfortunate incident. I assure you I was light-years away and not involved. Let me introduce myself. My name is Vikktakkht, *ambassador* Vikktakkht an Nikkatu, traveling aboard *Tiraskhti.* Perhaps the *mekt-hakkikt* has mentioned me."

"I doubt it. If she has, we haven't been in the same port in years."

"Ah. And your companion, your chief officer, perhaps."

"Tiar Chanur."

"Another name to remember. How do you do, captain? And I won't ask you such a meaningless question as why you're here. I know why you're here. I know where you're going."

The hair prickled at her nape. The last she'd seen there were only mahendo'sat back there in front of the office, but there'd been those inside. And she had no inclination to wait here through kifish courtesies. "Nice to meet you, give my regards to the *mekt-hakkikt,* and excuse us if we don't stand about. We're running a tight schedule." She took Tiar's arm and started around the obstacle, but there were more of them beyond him, between them and the consoles and the ramp.

"Captain," the kif called after her. "Tell Hallan Meras I'd like to talk to him."

Dangerous to turn her back. It wasn't *Pride* crew she was with. "Watch *them,*" she snapped, and turned to see what Vikktakkht was up to.

"Just tell him," it said, with a lifting of empty, peaceful hands. "We're old acquaintances."

Smug. Oh, so smug.

"Good day, then, Vikktakkht an Nikkatu."

"You have a very good accent."

"Practice," she said succinctly, and turned her back and swept up Tiar on a walk for the ramp access, past the kif who attended Vikktakkht.

The bastard thought she'd panic. The bastard thought she'd still twitch to old wounds. Wrong, kif.

Dangerously wrong.

"What's he want with *na* Hallan?" Tiar asked, glancing over her shoulder. "What's he talking about? Do you know him?"

"Not yet."

"What's the kid possibly got to do with him?"
"That's what I want to ask *na* Hallan."

They were down on several spices, they'd run low on tissues, and they were out of shellfish, but they certainly had enough staples from here to Anuurn.

"*Ker* Chihin," Hallan said. "*Ker* Chihin, I've got the—"

Straight into the captain's presence.

"—inventory," he said. But by the captain's frowning, ears-down look, by Tarras and Tiar Chanur standing behind her likewise ears-down and frowning, he didn't somehow think they wanted the inventory. He didn't *think* anything he'd done in the galley could have fouled anything else up, unless maybe he'd messed up the computer somehow.

Maybe dumped their navigation records . . . something that bad. . . .

"Vikktakkht," the captain said, and his heart skipped a beat. Or two. He remembered the jail. He remembered the kif he'd talked to every day. He remembered the richly dressed one who'd said . . .

. . . said, "Remember my name. . . ."

"Meetpoint," he managed to say.

"Where on Meetpoint? Was he the one you hit?"

"I—don't know."

"But you know this name."

"He said . . . 'Someday you'll want to ask me a question.' "

"What question?"

"I don't know." He shook his head in utter confusion. "That was all he said. I was in the jail. And that was what he said."

"You know him from there."

"The day they . . . brought me to this ship." He didn't know whether what he'd answered was enough. He tried to think if there was anything else, any detail he could dredge up from memory, but nothing came clear to him, nothing had made sense then and nothing made sense now.

"That's all he said, captain. I didn't know what it meant. I still don't. I don't know what question he's talking about. I don't know what he wants."

"What *would* you ask him?"

"What he means. What he wants. I don't know!"

He was scared, really scared. He hadn't thought about the jail. He had put that place behind him. He trusted them, that there was no way he was going back to that place. But he'd found the way to foul up, it seemed. The captain just stood there looking at him, and finally said, "Are you willing to go out there, Meras?"

"Yes, captain," he said. But the prospect scared him of what else he could find to do wrong. "Whatever you want."

"It's what *he* wants that worries me. Go back to work. I've got some calling around to do. I'll let you know."

He was through with what they'd assigned him to do, but it didn't seem a good moment to bring that trivial matter up with her. He said quietly, "Aye, captain," and took his list and his pocket computer back to the galley to create something to do.

Chapter Thirteen

"Captain?" Fala slid a cup of gfi under Hilfy's hand, and she murmured thanks without looking. Her eyes were on the screen, while the search program located the most recent of the letters for Pyanfar, the ones that had just missed her at Meetpoint, the ones that had been backed up at Hoas and Urtur and Kura and Touin. A lot from mahen religious nuts who wanted to tell the *mekt-hakkikt* about prophecies (one never understood why they were never good news) and a handful who had an invention they wanted to promote, which they were sure the great Personage of Personages would find useful (no few hani were guilty of this sin.) There were a few vitriolic communications from people clearly unbalanced. The prize of that lot was from a mahe who had "written four times this week and you not answer letter. I tell you how solve border dispute by friendly rays of stars which make illuminate our peace. You make power color rainbow green and make green like so . . . when Iji orientate in harmony with rainbow color red with orange. Please take action immediate." (With illustrations, and important words underlined.)

But nothing, so far, no hint of aunt Pyanfar's business in this stack.

A question Hallan Meras would like to ask Vikktakkht.

There *was* no question that she knew of . . . except the whereabouts of Atli-lyen-tlas.

And had the kif known that would be a question, back on Meetpoint, before a kifish guard handed Meras over to the *Legacy?*

Or was it some other thing, something Meras didn't remember or was afraid to say? Pyanfar had passed through Meetpoint not so long before: No'shto-shti-stlen had said so, and the huge stack of messages assumed she would come back through that port.

Hilfy sat, and sat, sipped gfi and stared at the blinking lights that meant incoming messages. The computer was set for the keywords Atli-lyen-tlas, stsho, ambassador, Ana-kehnandian, *Ha'domaren,* Pyanfar, hani, and Vikktakkht. She figured that should cover it.

But a quick scan of what arrived in the priority stack were mostly inquiries from various mahen companies asking about conditions at Kita. Not a word from the kif. If kif were talking to each other out there, they were not talking to her. Possibly they were occupied with the local investigation. Possibly they were couriering their messages to each other around the rim, not using com at all.

"Fueling's complete," Tarras reported from downside ops. *"I've got a good bid on the goods. The market could go a point higher, could sink a little. My instinct says take it."*

"Do it. Very good. —Tarras, when the loaders get here, go ahead and open the hold, but keep someone monitoring the cameras. Whoever's going out, wear a coat, stuff the pistol in your pocket, never mind the regulations."

She still wasn't panicked about the threat, and she kept asking herself whether she were really this calm, or whether she was operating in a state of flashback. Kshshti was the site of her nightmares, and things were going wrong, but she found herself quite cold, quite logical. She could wish aunt Py were here, she could wish her crew had had some experience beyond the years-ago skirmish at Anuurn. Out there on the docks—her one split second of panic was realizing she had to tell Tiar which way to look: *The Pride*'s crew had known, at gut level, which side to step to, who would do what, who was likeliest to cover whom. They'd done it before. They'd worked out the missteps. Paid for a few of them.

But aunt Py wasn't here. Sorting the mail stacks, even with computer search, for some answer to what was going on . . . could take weeks: the people with the real information were less likely to dump their critical messages in among the lunatic communications the stations collected in general mail, unless there was some code to tell *The Pride*'s computers to pay attention; and she didn't know what keywords to search. Meanwhile it was her ship, her crew. It was her responsibility to get them through alive, and that included telling them when to break the law, violate the peace, the treaties, and the laws of civilized behavior.

It was up to her to decide a course of action on a kif who had gotten his claws into someone on her ship—before they signed the contract. Surmise that the stsho contract was the kif's interest: if it was, surmise that it had known about that contract, it had expected them to get it, and that it was up to its skinny elbows in the disappearance of Atli-lyen-tlas.

They had guns enough aboard—only prudent, never mind where they had bought them, or how, but it had involved a mahen trader; while weapons were such a cultural necessity among the kif, such a part of life-sustaining self-esteem, that the Compact peace treaty had had to except knives and blades from the weapons ban, figuring that kifish teeth were no less dangerous, and that it was far better to have the kif signatory to the peace than not. . . .

Of course, it had taken considerable efforts in translations and cross-cultural studies to explain the word *peace* to all the several species. Granted, *war* did not translate with complete accuracy; but kif had understood neither idea. Kif weren't wired to understand war, since they were at constant odds with each other, cooperated when hani least would, betrayed when hani would be most loyal, and hit the ground at birth competitive, aggressive, and (some scholars surmised) having first to escape their nest before they were eaten.

As to the last . . . that was speculation. But she did understand their minds better than most hani. It wasn't to say she was forgiving. The kif weren't either. Circumstances either changed or they did not. They had that in common.

She got up from the console, she walked back to where *na* Hallan was puttering about in the galley, and said, with a queasy feeling,

"*Na* Hallan,—how do you feel about talking to the kif?"

"If you want me to," he said.

"You take orders?"

"Aye, captain." Dubiously.

"You foul this up, Meras, and I'll shoot you myself. Lives are at risk, yours, mine, more than that, do you understand? You go out on the docks. And I'll suggest a question you can ask this Vikktakkht—that is, if you can't think of one of your own. Nothing comes to you yet, what he might have meant?"

"I've been trying to understand what he meant, captain. I don't. I can't imagine what he's talking about. It doesn't make sense. It didn't then."

"What would be important to ask him?"

"I don't know . . ."

"Like in the myths, Meras. You get one wish. What would help us?"

His ears went down and lifted again, tentatively. "Knowing where the stsho is. Getting hold of him. . . ."

"*Gtst.* Not him. They're quite touchy on that score. But, yes, that's the question—unless you think of a better one."

"I'm sure I wouldn't—"

"I'm sure if you think of one, you'll tell me. I'll find this Vikktakkht. And if we meet him, if knives or guns come out, you take orders, and you don't act the fool. Do you hear me? Do you absolutely, beyond any question, understand?"

"Aye, captain," he said faintly. But if she had said the local star is green, she had the uneasy feeling that *na* Hallan would have agreed.

Give him credit, he would have tried to see the star that way. But it didn't make Yes the best answer. And it didn't tell you what he'd do when the shots started flying.

She stared at him long enough to let him think about it. "I'll see if this Vikktakkht is by any chance in touch with his ship."

"You," Hilfy said to Fala, in the lower deck main corridor, "work the hold. Can you handle that?"

"No trouble," Fala said, "but . . ."

"No 'but.' I *need* you handling the loader."

Ears went down. "Because I'm the—"

"Because I have things on my mind, Fala! Gods!" She headed down the corridor toward the airlock, where, if Chihin and Tiar had gotten Hallan downside, their expedition was organizing.

The dockers had lost no time: the *Legacy*'s cargo lock was open, and Tarras, in the requisite coat, was out there going over the final customs forms.

There was no graceful way for a hani to wear a cold-hold coat on dockside: Tarras could justify it by going back and forth inside, and perspiring by turns. But they couldn't. So that meant the lightest arms, lousy for accuracy, but they fit in a formal-belted waist with no more than a slight bulge . . . and it was their office-meeting, formal reception best they wore.

Except *na* Hallan, who went in ordinary spacer blues. But when they walked down the ramp to the dock, there was no question where the stares went—straight to the hani a head taller than any of them, the one with the shoulders and the mane that matched.

Work stopped. A transport bumped the one in front with a considerable jolt. Hallan watched his feet on the way down. She watched their surroundings and said, under her breath, "I don't expect it, but watch left and right and say if you see anything untoward. *Na* Hallan, if there should be trouble, you do understand that getting your head down doesn't necessarily cover your rear. There's a lot of you. Wherever we go, I want you to have somewhere in mind that you could get to that would be a solid barrier; and where you'd duck to if you had to fall back. I want this whole dock to be a map like that in your head, do you follow me?"

"Yes, captain. I do, thank you."

He might. Boys learned hunting, bare-handed; boys learned tracking and hiding and all such games as fitted them for defending their lives. It was heroics she worried about. Boys learned to show out, and bluff, and trust the other side most often to follow the rules, although *na* Kohan had said once, reflectively, that men learned to cheat in the outback, because some did, and once that was true—you couldn't assume.

So with Chihin and Tiar. The rings in their ears meant a lot of ports and each one of those rings a risky situation, in space or on the docks. But they weren't *Pride* crew, and they hadn't studied this together. She just trusted they were thinking now, better than Tiar had been when she had felt that cross-up of signals.

They walked through the traffic of transports and past the towering gantry that held the power umbilicals, took that route for the next three berths, before they tended around the off-loading of another ship, mahen, as happened.

There were stares. Hallan cast an anxious look back at them and stumbled on a power cable.

"Feet," Chihin said.

"Sorry," he said.

There was the kifish trade office, number 15, opposite berth 28, as listed—an unambitious and functional looking place, conspicuous by the orange light behind the pressure windows; but beyond the section doors was a district where that lighting was the norm, where kifish bars, restaurants and accommodations mingled with gambling parlors where kif played games no outsider would care to bet on, and where blood-letting was not an uncommon result, at least . . . it had been that way. Maybe they had cleaned it up. One reminded oneself these were civilized times.

But that might be fatal thinking.

"This is the place. If there's trouble, have your spots picked and don't look after anyone but yourself—at least you know what you're thinking and where you're going."

"Too gods-be close to the kif section," Chihin said.

"We're dealing with kif," Tiar said.

Now she was nervous. Now the hair down her backbone must be ridged, and her claws kept twitching in their sheaths.

But not notably scared. It was like sleepwalking, saying to herself, I've done this before, this is the life I chose for myself, this is the way the Compact is, not—

—not the safe, law-hedged half-truths the treaty made. Safe, as long as you're within twenty lights of Anuurn, civilized, as long as it's only hani you deal with, altruistic, as long as you're not dealing with species who have to have that word explained to them.

A methane-breather wove past, in its sealed vehicle; a bus followed, humming along its mag strip. Never *could* convince the tc'a to rely on the magnetics. Something about their sensitivities. You couldn't get that clear in translation either.

That was the truth out here. It wasn't law that got you by. It was good manners. It was giving in on a point that wasn't fatal to you, and might be to them.

There were kif about the door—not unnaturally. And it said something strange, that these kif showed less surprise at them than the mahendo'sat had done . . . these kif simply made soft clicking sounds of attention and backed away to allow them the door. There had been a time when kif didn't share information, when one kif knowing a fact didn't guarantee that other kif did.

Was that a change Pyanfar had wrought, the *mekt-hakkikt*,

the leader of leaders, the power over powers, that had unified the kif for the first time in their existence?

Maybe they were all Vikktakkht's. Those were the kind of kif to watch out for, the ones that came in large, strongly-led groups.

The doors opened. They walked into dim sodium light, into ammonia stink that stung the nose, and Hallan did sneeze, loudly in the silence. Black-robed kif kept nothing like a mahen office. It might have been a bar, a restaurant. There were tables, and one was in among them, and at the end of the room a kif with a silver-bordered robe beckoned to them.

That was Vikktakkht. She would lay money on it. As she would lay money there were guns beneath no few of these black robes.

They walked that far. "Good day," the kif prince said. "So pleased you could come."

"Admirable fluency on your side too."

"I even have a little hani. Not much. But enough to resolve differences."

It was disturbing to hear her own native tongue slurred over with kifish clicks and hisses. And one who learned your language might not be doing so for peaceful reasons.

"This is—" she said, "Chihin Anify. And Hallan Meras you know."

"Delighted. Kkkkt. *Na* Hallan."

"Sir."

"You've done as I hoped—served as my introduction. My character witness, I believe your term is. I behaved well toward you, did I not? You've no cause to complain of me?"

"Not of any kif, sir."

"Not of any kif." A soft snuffling that set Hilfy's nape-hairs up. Kifish laughter. Kifish mockery. They knew no other humor, that she had found. "You're such a soft-spoken hani. Yet they do insist you're quite aggressive."

"No, sir, not by choice."

"Don't try him," Hilfy said sharply. "You don't understand

us that well. Between species, one can make fatal assumptions. What do you want?"

There was a soft clicking, a stir of cloth, all about them. The orange light glistened wetly on an analytical kifish eye, black as space and as deep in secrets.

"I said that you would want to ask me a question," Vikktakkht said quietly. "Kkkt. Do you have one, *na* Hallan?"

"Yes, sir," Hallan said. "What are kif doing, transporting the stsho ambassador?"

Hallan's question. Her wording. Don't give the bastard a question he could answer with yes or no. And Vikktakkht made a soft hiss and wrinkles chained up the leathery snout.

"Following *gtst* request," the kif said. "And I will be more informative. I will answer a second question. —From *na* Hallan."

Gods rot the creature. It was his territory, his terms. And if he spoke hani he likely knew what he was doing, insulting Meras, insulting Chanur.

Hallan stayed silent two, maybe three breaths, and she opened her mouth to say they were leaving; but Hallan said,

"What do you gain by doing that?"

Gods, good question, Meras.

"The good will of the stsho ambassador. Next question?"

Another small pause on Hallan's part. Hallan might have exhausted the permutations of the question she had suggested. And *she* was curious what he would ask.

"Is that—all you want?"

"Kkkt. It would be very valuable."

"But," Hallan repeated quietly, respectfully, "is that *all* you want?"

"No," the kif said. What else could a kif say?

But then Vikktakkht added: "The ambassador is at Kefk. Next question."

It was beyond bizarre. In honor, she ought to object and pull *na* Hallan out of this game. But Hallan did not seem to need rescue.

"Are you a friend of the *mekt-hakkikt?*"

Gods, that was a mistake. Kif had no word for friend.

"My alignment, you mean? *With* the *mekt-hakkikt.* Next question."

"What are you asking my captain to do?"

"To go to Kefk, where *I* have allies. There, I will have custody of the ambassador. There, you may ask me one more question."

Hallan flicked an ear in her direction. It was not a time to dispute the matter. There was silence all around them. This is a dangerous kif, she thought.

"Yes, sir," Hallan said.

"Chanur."

"*Hakkikt?*" Hilfy asked, sure that was what she was dealing with.

"You flatter me."

"I doubt it."

"Kkkt. You're free to go. At Kefk, Chanur."

There were arguments possible with mahendo'sat. None with this. A quality called *sfik* was life and death. And *sfik* in this case meant swaggering out of here on equal terms.

"At Kefk," she said, that being the only choice. She turned abruptly and walked out, praying to the gods her crew did the same, and that *na* Hallan, good heart that he was, didn't linger to push a point.

All the way the kif were estimating them, testing them with soft clicking sounds, the threat of their presence, and cleared their path only at the last moment. They lived as far as the door, and as far as outside, and no one had said anything and no weapons were out. They crossed the traffic pattern of the docks quickly now, toward the cover of the gantries and the shadows beneath the structural shapes.

"Was it all right?" Hallan asked. Now she could hear the nervousness in his voice.

"Good job," she said. "Good job, Meras." Because it had been. It still was. They were out of there.

But in the shadows, in those places where the girders and the double lights overhead made eye-tricking shadows, it was too easy to imagine black, robed figures.

"Kefk," Tiar panted, distressedly.

Kefk was across the border, kifish territory. If they were anxious here, doubly so there. Hani were theoretically free to use that port, theoretically safe there, the way kif were theoretically safe at Anuurn, but neither hani nor kif had tested the treaty in regular trade.

Ally of Pyanfar's, was he? Kif could lie. Kif were quite good at it.

"I tell you what," Chihin said. "We sell *our* stsho to the kif."

"I could be tempted," Hilfy muttered. Chihin didn't say the contract had been the stupidest deal they had ever gotten into. Chihin was being polite.

But it was true. And there was no way out of it, at this point. To cut and run wasn't even a remote option, that she could see, not if they hoped to have a reputation left, not if they hoped to have their trading license, not if they hoped the whole godsbe Compact would hang together. Threads were unraveling. Two, now three, mahen stations had lost their whole stsho population to violence.

And they were in it up to their—

Something popped, with that nasty sound of exploding tissue. Chihin stumbled against her, and she yelled, "Cover!" on a half a breath, trying to hold on to Chihin and drag her out of fire if she could figure where it had come from. She saw the red dot on a girder, knew it was from across the dockside, and flung herself behind a pump housing, Chihin actively trying to tuck her legs into shadow and to get up on an elbow.

"How bad?" Hilfy panted.

"Don't know," Chihin said. "Arm. Feels like I was punched; but it works. Sort of." The shock was setting in, and Chihin's supporting arm began shaking, her breathing to shorten. Hilfy had her pocket com out, made a breathless call to the *Legacy:*

"Tarras! Sniper fire! Get to cover."

She was shaking now, light tremors, which was no good. She put a hand on Chihin, and risked a look out where they had been, where none of her party still was, which was good news. Everyone had made cover of some kind.

"Tarras!"

"Aye! I hear," the welcome voice came back. *"I'm calling the police!"*

Police, for the gods' sake! "Tiar, Tiar, do you read?"

"I'm here," a breathless voice said, thin and distorted by interference.

"Don't give position!" she said, and caught a breath of her own. "How are you doing?" she asked Chihin.

"All right," Chihin said thinly. "Give me a minute. We can run for it."

"That's a sniper. Laser targeted. Light arms, but they can cut us up piecemeal. —Tarras, I think the p.o. is the business frontage. Hang on . . ."

She leaned to get her gun from her belt, plain projectile weapon, with a vid display, and she drew a bead on the suspicious alley . . . couldn't get vid resolution. Couldn't go firing blindly down there: she could hit some poor mahen shopkeeper. But she sighted the structural supports where the laser spot had showed, and calculated the angle of fire across the dock. It had to be coming from that alley, that narrow nook between two freight company offices.

"Can we get an ambulance out here? Chihin's hit—don't know how bad. . . ."

A flurry of footsteps arrived out of the shadows. She rolled on her hip and saw red-brown hide, not black robes—a scared, almost too large for cover Hallan Meras.

"What do we do, captain?"

"We keep our heads down."

He was making as small a target as he could, arms locked about legs.

"Ker Tiar's over there," Hallan said, nodding toward the other console.

"Good." A movement and a crash from the *Legacy*'s area. A truck had started up and hit a can. It kept coming. "Tarras! Is that you in the truck?"

Fire hit it and blistered paint. The sniper didn't think it was on his side. She let off a few shots at neutral real estate to keep the sniper pinned. A neon sign. That blew with satisfactory fireworks.

"You see the son?" Chihin asked, squirming for vantage.

"No. Stay down!"

The truck bashed the gantry console and clipped the girder, crash-clang! It reversed and hooked a bumper.

"Gods," Hilfy groaned. Hooked solid. And it wasn't Tarras driving, it was Fala Anify. Fire pasted the vehicle. It rammed forward and jerked the bumper half off, then it hit the gantry console where Tiar was.

"Tiar!" she yelled into com. "*You* drive!"

There were sirens somewhere distant, under the electric whine of the truck as it backed. Hilfy sent a few more shots into the sputtering neon display, figuring only fools hadn't found cover by now.

And the smoke picked out the source of the opposing shots as they pierced the cloud. Chihin had her gun out, firing at the same area. The truck whined away and backward.

Bang!

Hit another truck.

"Gods in feathers!" Chihin moaned. "What are they doing?"

"They're stuck," Hallan said.

"Most gods-be embarrassing mess I ever . . ." Hilfy began, and a shot blistered paint on the girder just past their position. She leaned an elbow on the decking and put another round after her last, then fished in her waist after the spare clip. The truck was still backing and maneuvering, and she shot a distracted look at the situation as it clipped a control console and shot free, leaving the bumper clanging on the deck plates.

She sent a covering fire across the traffic lanes, and saw an open-sided pedestrian transport lumbering along the dockside, oblivious. "Gods!" she breathed. And to the com: "Hold fire, hold fire, there's bystanders out there!"

It wasn't the only vehicle coming. It rolled through. So did a couple of transport trucks thank the gods not carrying volatiles, and a cab. Then fire set up again, with a smell of blistered paint from the other side of the console that provided them cover.

"They made it," Chihin breathed. Hilfy looked; and ducked her eyes behind her hand.

Bang.

Into a loader arm.

"Fifty thousand," Chihin muttered under her breath.

"Where are the gods-be police?"

Another volley hit the console.

Cars passed, wheels thumping on the deck plates, traffic oblivious to the invisible barrage of laser fire and the pop of small caliber weapons.

She leaned painfully on her elbow, a new clip in her gun, with no desire to hit a passerby.

And saw a bus coming from the other direction.

She pointed to the dark. "Hallan! *Carry* Chihin! Run for those shadows!"

"I don't need—" Chihin began, and yelled as Hallan obeyed orders, grabbed her and darted, brave lad. Hilfy ran behind them, cast a look back as their bus outran their diagonal, and fire popped after them.

Good for the smoke. She pasted rounds back, four of them, and dived for the cover of a girder.

"Keep going!" she panted. "Ramp shadow!"

"Gods be feathered!" Chihin gasped, but Hallan's shoulder cut off her wind, and he ran.

Hilfy fired another shot, darted back one way from cover and ran the other, after *na* Hallan.

A shot burned her arm. That was how close it was as she skidded over the deck plates in a slide for the shadow of a truck.

The far-side tire deflated with a hiss. The mahen dock workers stared back at them out of the shadow with dismay writ large on their features.

Then the police transport pulled up, with yellow-flashing emergency vehicles, ambulances, civil vehicles . . . repair trucks. She put the gun away, out of sight, and looked at Chihin, who had gotten a knee on the decking, *na* Hallan still holding on to her with both arms. Chihin shoved her gun into her belt, out of sight of the police, she had that much presence of mind, as they began swarming around the vehicles. Hilfy started to get to her feet to deal with them, safely behind the cover of the slightly tilted truck.

A shadow turned up next to her, around the truck's back end: Haisi reached for her arm to help her up. She snatched the arm back and got up herself, glaring.

"I try warn you," Haisi said. "I say, watch you back, I say don't deal kif. You got be damn big hurry. . . ."

"Big damn *help*, mahe!"

"You want help? Easy deal. I help carry . . ."

"No!" She barred his path to Chihin, who was bleeding on Hallan. "We got enough help."

"You number one stubborn hani."

"Get away from my ship!"

"Also crazy."

"I said leave! This is *our* business!"

"Maybe better you ask stsho, ask, You want die, you want take ride with kif? Maybe you listen somebody know who friend and not friend."

"Police!"

Haisi cast a look over his shoulder. Police *were* moving in.

"You got answer their question. You got answer, Hilfy Chanur? I got."

"Like you gave me an honest warning! —Officer, this mahe is a gods-be nuisance! I want him off my dockside! Now!"

Haisi said something in dialect, the police officer said something back, put a hand on his shoulder, and the two of them stood in close conference for a moment.

Maddening. But it was what you got, in another species' port. The medics were looking confused, and she motioned them toward Chihin. "There's a surgery on my ship. She goes *there!* Fala, Hallan, stay with her."

"We got regu-lation."

"I got a surgery. There. Go, gods rot it! No argument!"

"Captain?" The com had been nattering at her for the last few seconds. *"Captain? Are you all right?"*

"All right," she said, glumly watching the medics confer with the police and Haisi Ana-kehnandian. "We're coming in. Just keep monitoring."

The Personage of Kshshti to the hani ship Chanur's Legacy, *attention captain Hilfy Chanur.*

We not responsible this fool incident. We do investigation high priority. Hope you not take us do this. Hope well soon your crewmember. We do no charge medical service.

Bill for truck and loader arm attached. Also store sign and panels. You sue party responsible recover damage.

The hani ship Chanur's Legacy, *captain Hilfy Chanur, her hand, to his honor the Personage of Kshshti.*

We thank the police and emergency services for their response. We assure the Personage we took all precautions against endangerment of bystanders, and urge that the party responsible when discovered be prosecuted to the full extent of the law.

We accept the bill for damages and request that, when responsibility is fixed, the suit be lodged by proxy by your office and monies forwarded to us.

Like your honor we are very glad that no bystanders were injured and ask your honor to extend our personal apologies to affected residents. We did not seek or provoke this assault.

The hakkikt *Vikktakkht an Nikkatu to captain Hilfy Chanur, the hani merchant* Chanur's Legacy, *at dock: Our congratulations for the damage inflicted on your enemies and may you eat their hearts.*

Tahaisimandi Ana-kehnandian, mahen ship Ha'domaren, *at dock, to captain Hilfy Chanur, the hani ship* Chanur's Legacy.

You one damn stubborn hani. See what kif do if you not got respect. They try make you scare. I make guess. They tell you go Kefk, yes? Damn stupid. You go Meetpoint. You can do Meetpoint if you carry no cargo. I escort you Meetpoint.

You friend try look out for you, you all same got arrogant mouth.

You deal with kif you got kif problem. How good now?

Repeat same offer. You want ally, you ask. Number one good friend. You call say help, I do.

Chihin called it a patch job. The mahen surgeon, operating in the *Legacy*'s small medical station, called it a close call and wished Chihin would check into hospital.

Hilfy called it a lucky thing it had hit the arm and missed anything irreplaceable. And she was mortally glad to get the dockers furloughed over the next watch, the station medical team off her deck, the airlocks sealed, and the situation down to manageable.

Thank the gods the station had turned a blind eye to the gun law violations.

Thank the gods no sharp station lawyer had yet suggested they'd foreknown there was a risk . . . or they wouldn't have gone out on the docks armed.

To their credit they'd at least advised station that they'd been harassed. To their credit they were Pyanfar Chanur's relatives, and they had special and real reason to worry. As they need not argue with the Personage of Kshshti, *if* the Personage wasn't friendly to Ana-kehnandian's personage, which was yet to be proved. She *hadn't* liked Ana-kehnandian's friendliness with the police.

And she didn't like the feeling in the pit of her stomach.

It was all right on the bridge. There was too much potentially to do to let the mind settle in old tracks. There was just trained response and a bucket of water on every fire that popped up . . . in fact, there were gratefully few of them; but that left an old *Pride* hand wondering where the rest were smouldering.

And when she walked back to her quarters to wash the blood and the sweat and the ammonia smell out of her memory . . . when the steam of the shower was around her and sound was down to the hiss of water from the jets, then the thoughts came back, then the mind went time-wandering and couldn't remember then from now—except the shower was fancier and the responsibility was hers. All hers.

With a crew who'd, admittedly, made only one less mistake than the sniper had made, in opting for a silent and invisible weapon on a moving target. *Not* an outstandingly well-informed or accurate attempt, all told.

And that was worrisome . . . that was just naggingly worrisome, because it didn't add up, except to a random lunatic.

Which almost excluded the kif. Kif slept with their weapons. Kif lived and died, among themselves, by their weapons. And a mistake like that wasn't the style of a Vikktakkht an Nikkatu, unless he gave orders to miss.

It wasn't the style of a mahen hunter captain, in a mahen port, with all sorts of resources, either.

Certainly wasn't the stsho, unless a stsho hired some other species to do the deed. *Could* be stsho: they weren't connoisseurs of violence. They couldn't judge the competency or the honesty of the guards they hired. They only paid them well enough that most wouldn't risk their job.

The same as a stupid hani taking a cargo full of stsho trouble, for a price too good to turn down.

They were in it. That was the fact. They were in it and on the dock out there, with shots flying, they'd made mistakes that weren't going to let her sleep tonight, that threatened to replay behind her eyelids and that stacked up ready and awaiting the idle moment, the dark, the unfilled silence. They'd deserved to lose their lives out there. Every time she thought back through it she found a new mistake—theirs, hers trying to cover them, layer upon layer of foul-ups, from the minor glitch to the decision to walk it and not take a taxi.

She scanted the dry cycle, went out damp and sat down on the side of the bed, staring at the locker, within which was a box, and within which was a ragged printout she wasn't supposed to have, and did. Pyanfar likely hadn't even thought about the ops file in her possession when she told her go downworld; or at least, the level of bitterness between them hadn't gotten that high, that Pyanfar had ever asked if she had more than the printout she had officially turned in.

She'd taken it to learn from it, to understand it, and maybe, in her mind at the time, as a slice of Pyanfar to analyze and figure, when no other clues had served. She still resorted to that printout now and again, when captain Hilfy Chanur had wanted to figure out what Pyanfar had done on some point and what Pyanfar's rules and policy had been on some obscure matter of dealing with certain ports—a compendium of experience that Pyanfar had gathered over a long number of years—some were procedures she'd laid down after certain close calls. Some were just universal good sense; and she had borrowed some inoffensive bits of it to cover the gaps in the *Legacy*'s own freer, easier-going rules, rules that didn't have a lot to say about firearms or being shot at. A lot of that manual her own procedures contradicted, because a lot of it was Pyanfar's own perfection-driven convictions, and some of it just didn't apply in the peace Pyanfar had built.

But a lot of it the *Legacy*'s written rules didn't cover, or didn't mention for one important other reason, because somewhere at the bottom of her resentment she was still Chanur clan-head, and *The Pride*'s operations, secretive as they were, and likely dangerous as they were, still relied on those procedures. Things she knew about *The Pride*'s standing orders, *The Pride*'s policies and tendencies and biases and likely choices in an emergency . . . were in that book; and one of them was that you didn't talk about that book existing, you didn't take that printout off *The Pride* and you didn't discuss those policies anywhere but on *The Pride*'s deck, because there were agencies and individuals that would kill to know what was in there.

But she didn't have time to reinvent everything. She didn't have time to modify a system that wasn't working. She'd nearly lost lives out there because she hadn't breached *The Pride*'s security to tell them. They were peacetime traders. The crew hadn't come in with the close-mouthed wariness *The Pride*'s crew had. Tiar wasn't a Haral Araun, she was a good-humored spacer with a pilot's hair-triggered instincts about survival and a common sense about the information flow. Tarras was a canny trader and she scored highest on the simulations with the weapons systems—Tarras had been hours on the simulators, but that didn't say the *Legacy* had ever launched one of its missiles or fired a gun, or done more than drills. The captain had. Gods-rotted right the captain had. And Rhean's crew had handled sidearms and done the drills and given a fair account of themselves in the battle before the peace, so it wasn't that Tarras had never fired a missile in her life; and it wasn't that Tiar and Chihin hadn't run coordinations or been back-up pilots under heavy fire . . . but too many ships had died at Anuurn and Gaohn, of mistakes *The Pride* hadn't made.

Because of The Rules. The by the gods Pyanfar Chanur way of doing things, which *wasn't* the exact way every hani ship ran its business and which she dared not have her peace-time crew talking about when they were home, or complaining about in a station bar.

And maybe in some remote part of her brain she didn't want to think in those terms any longer. The Compact having changed, peace having broken out—hani wanted to get back to their own business, and take their own time, and not worry about wars, and not hurry more than they had to. The crew was all right, they got along, they were still, after their few years together, making adjustments to working together: they had their operating glitches and they yelled at each other, but no serious glitches, absent hostile action. It was a different age, and instincts dimmed, and fools could steer a ship or a planetary government: precision just didn't matter any more.

Medium was just all right.

Till you rusted or some amateur assassin nailed you for a reason you wouldn't ever find out.

Mad, she was. That son had shot at her and hit Chihin.

That in itself was a sloppy presumption. Aunt Py would say.

If aunt Py were here to lecture . . . or to haul a young captain out of the mess she'd contracted herself and her crew into.

Not *experienced* enough for a captaincy, they said in the *han*, and behind her back.

More by the gods experienced than some—especially in the *han*. And a crew that was getting smoother as time went on.

But there wasn't time to let Hilfy Chanur figure out her way. There hadn't been time for Hilfy Chanur to figure things out, all her life.

She got up, took the printout from the locker to her office and scanned it in.

She edited off all the references to *The Pride*. She searched the crew's names, and subbed in her own . . .

And she came to a dead stop on the matter of Hallan Meras, on the auxiliary post.

Lock him back in the laundry?

Forbid the crew to discuss ops with him, whatsoever?

Why had Vikktakkht wanted him? Why had Vikktakkht insisted to speak to him, except to get a less wary answer, and because Vikktakkht understood hani well enough to know they'd protect him. Meras was a vulnerability in their midst that her own curiosity had made available to the kif, and she couldn't deny that. She had a certain ruthlessness, a certain deficiency of pity, a certain willingness to run risks with other people's lives . . . she had discovered that in herself. Or maybe it was just that nobody planetside understood the things she'd seen, and the experiences she'd had . . . nobody who'd only been a merchant spacer could ever understand . . . and she grew angry, *impatient* with people who were naive, and people who were safe, and protected, and innocent. . . .

But that she'd taken Meras with her . . .

There'd been a good reason. There'd been a kif offering information they had to have. There'd been a kif who could have gone off with what he knew and refused to tell them . . . (in a mahen hell: Vikktakkht wanted them to know what he'd said) . . . but at the time, she hadn't known what Meras' possible connection to Vikktakkht was, when she'd taken a young man into that place—she had, who above all knew what could happen to him. And it wasn't all the good reasons for doing it that upset her stomach. It was the *angry* reason for doing it. That he wasn't Tully. That he was hani, and male, and blindly naive as every charge-ahead brat of a mother's son was brought up to be, worse, he was a feckless fool of an innocent like Dahan had been, and the world wasn't kind to them, the old ways aunt Pyanfar had sent her back to didn't by the gods work, and she didn't care what her biology nagged at her to do. *That* didn't work either.

And she hated . . .

. . . hated a wide-eyed, good-natured, handsome kid looking at her with worship in his eyes, reminding her what she'd lost, what she'd compromised, and what she'd let Pyanfar Chanur . . .

. . . strand her planetside to do.

She was by the gods mad. She was still . . . that . . . mad . . . .

It still hurt. She could look at Hallan Meras and see her junior over-eager self, and be perfectly forgiving and understanding; but when she looked at him and *felt* anything . . .

She got mad, just cruelly . . . mad . . . at things unspecified.

That was a problem, wasn't it?

Py had cut her off from Tully, cut her off from her dearest friends in the entire universe, and sent her home . . . where Py couldn't go again. Ever.

That also . . . was a problem, wasn't it? It was Chanur's

problem. And Py sent her to solve it, and washed off Chanur, and Chanur's politics, and everything to do with the clan—forever, at that point.

Direly sad thought . . . for aunt Py.

Py had gotten hot when she'd said no. Py had said things . . . maybe because Pyanfar Chanur was feeling pain, who knew? Pyanfar wasn't ever one to say so.

So bad business had happened at Kshshti, so she'd had a rough few years and she hated her unlamented husband with a passion.

But *why* was she so shaking mad? *Why* in all reason was she sitting here at her reasonably well-ordered desk upset and wanting to do harm to a young man who'd had no connection with Py except a conversation on a dockside years ago. She was a self-analytical person. She had sore spots and she knew where they were: she might have nightmares that made her throw up, but she didn't let them dominate her waking life, and she didn't let them sway her from what made business sense . . . gods-be right she'd deal with a kif if he had a deal she needed. She'd felt no panic at going to Kshshti. She could contemplate going to Kefk, clear over the border into kifish territory, and as it seemed now, they *were* going.

So she didn't have a problem, outside the occasional flashes on the past. She was free, she went where she chose, she had no problems that a financial windfall and peace in the family wouldn't cure.

So why did she feel that way about Hallan Meras?

Instinct? Something that deserved distrust? Something that threatened them? She hadn't read that between him and the kif. And she generally understood her own behavior better than that.

Attraction? She'd noticed he was male. So? She was also exhausted, distracted, and too harried by petulant stsho, pushy mahendo'sat, and a ship with potential legal problems, to think about any side issues.

She just didn't figure it—being at one moment perfectly at

ease face to face with the lad and then, in the abstract, when he wasn't even at hand–

Enough to make you wonder about yourself, it was, what sore spots did go undiscovered, and what that one was about. But it wasn't about Hallan Meras personally. No. He was just a problem–

A security problem where it concerned the manual. Tell *na* Hallan to keep a piece of information to himself forever, and she honestly had every confidence he'd try. But this was the lad who'd fathered a tc'a by backing a lift-cart.

And, no, she wasn't going to accept him in the crew. Maybe that was what made her mad: that they weren't *The Pride,* but that given time to work together, their way, her way, they might have become their own unique entity, nothing complicating their lives, no family divisions and feuds, no favoritisms. No mate problems. No jealousies.

And now there wasn't a chance for that to happen. Now she had to do something different, in the incorporation of aunt Py's ideas, aunt Py's personal notions, that there wasn't time to take part of.

Maybe that was why the Hallan matter touched her off. Maybe it was watching things go to blazes and knowing that Hallan's slips weren't harmless, that while they were trying to keep his skin whole and interrupting their life and death business to do it, he had become first a vulnerability, and now an obstacle to shaping her crew into what *she* wanted.

That might be it. That might be why she wanted to kill him, because a part of her had been seeing all along that he was that kind of danger.

And with the ship utterly still, the loaders silent, and the only sound the air whispering out of the ducts in the medical station . . . she called in all of them *but* Hallan Meras.

"Come in," she said to Tarras, who hovered at the door. "Sit down. –Chihin, *don't* sit up. Don't push it."

Chihin muttered and stuffed a pillow under her head, one-handed. "Nothing said about not sitting up."

"Orders," she said. "Mine. Nice if someone obeyed them. Just a wistful thought, understand."

There was general quiet. A respectful moment of general quiet. But it wasn't blame she wanted to start with. "First," she said, "the assassin made more mistakes. None of us are dead. The truck—"

"I'm sorry," Fala said faintly.

"It did work," Hilfy said. "It wasn't a stupid thought. Nothing we did was a stupid thought. But the unhappy fact is that we didn't win because we were good. He lost because he fouled up—*if* he lost. We don't know that he didn't accomplish what he wanted. He certainly made a lot of noise. And he's made us have to assume from now on that we're somebody's enemy." She had the thin manual printouts in her possession. She handed them out. "This is procedure from now on. Eat and drink it and sleep with it, but don't talk about it, don't joke about it. *Na* Hallan's not to get this. He's not to know about it. No copies go off this ship, in any form."

Fala was frowning. Chihin was trying to leaf through hers, one-handed, the booklet propped on her knee. Tiar and Tarras gave theirs a dubious look.

"A general change?"

She didn't intend to tell them, she hadn't intended to admit it. But she didn't intend to claim it for a daughter either, and you didn't just rip away everything an experienced crew knew and tell them do differently without saying why. "It's *The Pride*'s ops manual. I'm not supposed to have it. You're not supposed to know it exists. Read it. Follow it. We can talk about it. And maybe we can think of better ways. But we've got to live long enough. This fixes responsibilities, it talks about how many decimal places in the reports, it mandates when we do certain maintenance, it talks about some technical details that are just Py's idea, but let's don't quibble about that for now. She's a gods-be stickler for some details you're going to call stupid and you're going to find some procedures in there that were illegal even before the peace. But my word is, memorize this, understand it, don't mention it in front of outsiders, and I pointedly include *na* Hallan: he's not staying on this ship and he can't take this to another crew. Questions?"

"Are we *going* to Kefk?" Tarras asked.

"Very possibly," Hilfy said. "I don't see anything else to do."

There weren't questions beyond that. Maybe there was just too much reading to do.

"Dockers are on paid rest until 0600. I'd suggest you catch some sleep."

"I'm going to be fit tomorrow," Chihin said.

"You're going to be sore and impossible," Hilfy said. "You can sit watch in the morning. Run com."

"The kid, you know," Chihin said, not quite looking at her, "didn't do too badly out there."

"I noticed that." Of crew, she began to understand Chihin was angry too, in the same way she was, only more so. But Chihin, owing *na* Hallan, was being fair. Chihin set great personal store on being fair, even when it curdled in her stomach—for exactly the same reasons that were bothering her, she could surmise as much and not be far off the mark.

"No reason he can't sit station," Hilfy said. "No reason I don't trust him. He just doesn't know everything. Doesn't need to know. That's all." And Chihin looked somewhat relieved.

So they were going to Kefk. And the captain declared a six hour rest, come lawsuit or armed attack, which made the ship eerily quiet after the clangor and thumping of the loader and the irregular cycling of locks.

Hallan gazed at the ceiling of the crew lounge, faintly lit from the guide-strips that defined the walls and the bulkhead, and listened to that silence.

Fala had said, "It was terribly brave what you did."

Chihin had said, "You drive worse than *na* Hallan." But he couldn't take offense at that, because Chihin, the one who didn't like him, had also said, to him, "Thanks, kid."

She was honest, and she did mean it, even if it choked her;

and he *liked* Chihin—he liked her in a special, difficult way, because Chihin was one of the old guard who was willing to change her perspective on things. You could find people sitting on either side of opinions who were there just because things had landed that way and they went along with it; but Chihin didn't just land, Chihin probed and picked at a situation or a person until she could figure it, and she didn't let up. And she made jokes to let you know what was going on with her. And she made them when you deserved it.

Fala—she was younger than he was, in experience. She'd done what none of her seniors had been in a position to do. And backwards across the docks was faster and it didn't expose any different surface to fire; which wasn't stupid . . . even if she didn't go a very straight line.

She'd said to him, "Oh, gods, I'm glad you're all right. . . ." in a way that made him go warm and chill and warm again, all the way down to his feet. He'd stood there like a fool, not knowing what to say, except, "You too."

Because a feeling like that was what you got in families, and what a boy always had to give up, and couldn't count on finding again anywhere: you couldn't count on it in the exile you had to go to and you couldn't count on it from whatever clan you fought your way into. If you were stupid and your feelings for some girl led you to fight some clan lord you couldn't beat, it mostly got you in trouble.

That was what was wrong with this going to space, that *na* Chanur wasn't here, *na* Chanur who was also overlord of Anify hadn't the least idea he existed. It was like in the old ballads, like in that book, the young fools meeting in the woods, and things getting out of hand and the clan lord not knowing about it. Only when he found out, *na* Chanur was going to want to kill him, and *na* Chanur and in particular *na* Anify was going to be upset with Fala, which was going to make her sisters and her mother mad at her, which was going to set the family on its ear, at the least, and get *na* Chanur after *na* Meras, who wouldn't be happy with him at all, or with his sisters, for helping him get to space, and creating a problem with Chanur that *he* might have to fight over. Not to mention *na* Sahern, who wouldn't like the publicity of a truly famous incident.

Love was all very well in ballads. It was nice to think that it was possible, and maybe it happened in legitimate relationships, like Pyanfar Chanur and *na* Khym, who had to love each other, besides being married. But in real life it got you killed and messed up families, and he and Fala both had been shaky-kneed from rescuing Chihin, and he'd been wide open. The rush of action, that kind of thing. A moment, an incident, that wouldn't be the same tomorrow, if *he* kept his wits about him. . . .

But the feeling just wasn't going away tonight. He really wanted to go off with Fala somewhere and if he did that, and the captain had *na* Chanur to think about, it just wasn't going to help his case. If he did that, it could make it absolutely certain Hilfy Chanur would get rid of him, and that—

—that, in itself, began to have an emotional context it hadn't had, because he couldn't deal with the idea of not being on this ship. He couldn't lose that. He couldn't risk losing this ship or these people, and he didn't know when he'd begun to feel that way.

Oh, gods, he was in a lot of trouble.

I'm saying get out of here, get out, I won't live with a gods-be fool!

But it wasn't Korin Sfaura, it was a pillow Hilfy found herself murdering, and she rolled onto her back in a tangle of bedclothes, sorry she hadn't killed him herself—and gotten him out of her repertoire of bad dreams and stupid mistakes.

She'd gone at him in a blind rage and at a vast disadvantage, that was all—though she hadn't been concussed, as Rhean said she had been, as Rhean was in a damned hurry to say, bringing in cousin Harun for what amounted to a power-grab, and a takeover of Chanur's onworld business.

Which Rhean did all right at. And she was rid of Korin without offending Sfaura, which it would have done if she'd done what she wanted to do. Politics. Korin Sfaura was dead. And that business was forever unfinished, and she carried that anger, too, but she wasn't sure all of it was at Korin, who'd been a pretty, vain, brute-selfish fool. And she wasn't sure why she waked dreaming about a man she wouldn't waste a waking moment thinking about.

Fact was, she'd picked him. Her judgment had been that bad. She still tried, on bad nights, to figure out why it had been that dismally bad, or what failing was in herself. And "pretty" about covered his assets. Maybe "stupid" had been another one—because deep down she had wanted a piece of furniture, something decorative, something you didn't have to justify anything to or argue with, because when her father had died she hadn't wanted anybody in his place, no *real* lord in Chanur, just something that would get heirs and not interfere in the politics between her and her aunts.

Only Rhean, who'd been furious at aunt Py going off from the clan, had had her own ideas how Chanur should face the new age, and what was important, and maybe—no, probably—Rhean had been right: Rhean cared, and Rhean had given up her command and come home and done what needed doing. Mauled her in the doing, granted. She'd been mad as hell about that, and about *na* Harun, and stung by Rhean's reaction to her. But truth to tell, Rhean hadn't been happy to go downworld either. No more than she had been.

The power . . . Rhean liked that. It was a warmer blanket than the husband Rhean couldn't bring home to Chanur, and couldn't likely get to that often. A continent away was a good political alliance, and what was a continent but a half an orbit when Rhean had come in from space, but things were different now.

A lot was.

And she wasn't coming home often, herself. Could marry again, but had no enthusiasm for the institution.

There was Meras. Who was on one level like Korin: pretty face, no source of opinions. Amazing how attractive that still was to her. But not fair to a kid with brains; and he'd shown with the kif that he did think, thought right well for a young man, and clearly enough Fala was taken with him, Tarras and Tiar were. . . .

But, but, and but. It was the middle of her sleep cycle, thoughts like that were a credit a hundredweight, and gods rot it, she didn't want to go through the husband business again. He was bright, he would get ideas, and the politics involved at home were already difficult.

Besides, he'd made irrevocable changes in their operations, he was a liability the kif had used to get her into a face to face meeting with unforeseeable consequences. She'd been mad enough to kill him a handful of hours ago, she and Chihin both.

She grabbed the pillow and buried her head under it, looking for some place void of images.

Chihin understood what was happening, Chihin had seen it coming before she did, Tiar and Tarras were too good-hearted to space him and Fala was suffering a late puberty. She didn't know what to do with him, she didn't know where she was going to unload him—Kefk, maybe. Let him bankrupt the kif.

At which thought she saw that room, smelled the air, felt the ambient tension kif generated with each other, and remembered there were creatures in the universe to whom the highest virtue was the fastest strike and who didn't lose a wink of sleep over blowing a shipful of living beings to radioactive dust. There wasn't evil. She'd studied cultures too thoroughly and learned too many languages to believe in evil. She just knew that she'd tried to arrange her life so she didn't have to deal with the kif at all . . . and here she was again; and there it was, the kifish offer . . . deal with us, learn to strike faster and first, learn to think our way, because we aren't wired to think yours, we can't understand hani thoughts . . .

You always hoped they could. You were always tempted to believe they might cross that uncrossable gulf and deny their own hardwiring, turn off the triggers that led from impulse to action, the way a hani could turn them on, the way a hani could use instincts that *were* there, if you wanted to tear up the stones civilization laid over them, worse, you could get into the game, dealing with the kif—the very primal-level game, that had its very primal rewards, that competed with civilization.

Hilfy Chanur had delved a bit too deeply into kifish minds. Hilfy Chanur had become expert in the language, to understand what she hadn't understood when it was her alone and Tully, and kif had talked outside the cage. She'd learned words she couldn't pronounce, lacking a double set of razor teeth, and words she couldn't translate, without resorting to words of psychotic connotation in every other language she knew.

But you didn't say crazy, you didn't say evil. They weren't. No more than outsiders were what kif would say, *naikktak*, randomly behaving, behaving without regard to survival.

Which said something about how kif thought of hani . . . and about the frame of mind in which Vikktakkht had asked *na* Hallan to ask him questions.

Asked a hani male, who was notorious for unpredictable and aggressive behavior.

Respect for the aggression? Possibly.

Curiosity? Possibly. Kif had a very active curiosity. Kif could be artistic, imaginative, and curious. All these dimensions. They valued such attributes.

But Hallan Meras . . .

Using him as bait to get her closer, that made sense. That was very kif.

But refusing to talk to her, insisting *na* Hallan do the business they'd clearly come for . . .

It snapped into focus. Gamesmanship. Provocation aimed at her.

Why?

She was Pyanfar's relative, but kif didn't understand kinship, not at gut level. They weren't wired for it. They'd understand it as potential rivalry, but the ones that knew outsiders were too sophisticated to make that mistake. That wasn't what Vikktakkht was doing. It felt too gods-be *personal.*

She rolled onto her back and mangled the pillow to prop her head, staring at the profitless dark. *This* was what she did instead of sleeping, too many hours of free association. Why couldn't the mind come to straight conclusions? Why did she have to think about Hallan Meras, her unwarranted temper, and *kif*, all rolled into one package with Vikktakkht's odd gods-rotted motives? Her mind was trying to put something together out of spare parts. And it wouldn't fit together.

What was the kif—

—*after*, by the gods?

Hunt. Prey. Run or fight and you got their attention. Stand still and you got eaten.

She'd escaped the kif. That story was probably famous among kif. But this kif had been right there at Meetpoint, set up with a prisoner guaranteed to get a hani's attention . . .

In jail for hitting a kif. One wondered how far *that* was a set-up.

Any hani might have done. But he'd just missed Pyanfar, who'd just gone through there. Pyanfar went through, the Preciousness suddenly became an urgent matter that No'shto-shti-stlen *had* to get to Atli-lyen-tlas, and Atli-lyen-tlas ran off with the kif while the mahendo'sat ran in panicked desperation to find out what No'shto-shti-stlen had sent.

No'shto-shti-stlen was guarded by kif. So Vikktakkht had either had access to information or had been pointedly excluded from information.

Atli-lyen-tlas had either run to the kif for transport or fallen into their hands as a prisoner. And who even knew *which* kif? Allies of Vikktakkht? Allies of Pyanfar Chanur?

It was No'shto-shti-stlen who'd rather urgently wanted Hallan Meras in her hands. That urgency might have been stsho anxiety about having a hani male on their hands—stsho didn't understand hani touchiness about their menfolk (stsho were no more constitutionally certain what 'male' meant than hani were about the stsho's third gender) but an old diplomat like No'shto-shti-stlen certainly understood that they were touchy, and that it was an issue that could come back and cause trouble of unforeseen dimensions.

So had Vikktakkht given Meras that odd promise at No'shto-shti-stlen's urging . . . or had he outmaneuvered the stsho to get into the jail and set a trap for her?

And had he set it up for *any* hani ship they could get, or had the fact that a second Chanur ship had shown up . . . either suggested to Vikktakkht a connection between events that wasn't connected, or had it offered him a second chance to involve Chanur in this mess?

He certainly would know who she was. He certainly would know she'd had an experience with kif. That she'd survived and come back to Meetpoint with a ship meant, in kifish eyes, she'd increased in rank, not diminished. In kifish eyes, aunt Py hadn't thrown her out, she'd promoted her or been unable to prevent her rise. She was Chanur clan head, and one could bet the average kif knew what she was.

So Vikktakkht had ignored her in that interview and let himself be interrogated only by *na* Hallan. If she were kif, she might have casually shot *na* Hallan and insisted he talk to her. That would have gotten his respect. But he was too sophisticated a kif to expect a hani to do that, or to consider it in purely kifish terms that she didn't. He was sophisticated enough, like the Meetpoint stsho, to know that hani didn't tolerate affront to their menfolk, and probably to know that it was indecent for hani males to deal with outsiders, except when sex was directly at issue.

So was it some bizarre kifish joke? Or the careful playing of a Chanur's desire for specific information against her awareness that if she interrupted the game or refused his rules she might not get everything he would give if she didn't?

Interesting question.

She punched the pillow, battered it with her fist and tried for a comfortable spot in the tangled bedclothes, on a mental hunt through tangles of information. Too many weeds and not enough substance. The merest shadow of what she was looking for. Clearly enough, the kif wanted her to cross the kifish border.

Another punch at the pillow, which refused to take a convenient shape. She wanted to sleep. Please the gods, she could dump it now and not think through what just didn't have an answer.

But what in a mahen hell made all these various pieces add up?

Chapter Fourteen

You could manage to read printout and work cargo. The cold-suit mittens had a spike on the thumb next the first finger that you could use to turn pages, and Tiar read on, with the loader banging and booming overhead, the giant cannisters fuming from their passage out of the cold-hold into the pressurized so-called heated hold, on their way to the docks.

Chihin had the dockside post, with her arm in a sling and a button-fuse on her temper. ("Gods-rotted nit-picking doesn't gods-be make a *difference*, half this stuff! She says she's going to enforce this? She's serious?")

That was somewhat Tiar's own opinion, but: "Whatever we're doing we better all do it," was her second one. And Chihin, who had read the whole thing, had muttered a surly, pain-infected obscenity and declared *The Pride*'s crew obviously had to bolt everything down and double-check the readouts because *The Pride*'s captain was crazy.

But that was the ship's-manual ops section, and every spacer in the clan knew Pyanfar Chanur was a stickler for neatness, double and triple checks, and logging every sneeze. The part about arms maintenance, about who went armed and where and when and when not to fire, who in a group was to watch what and who was to break for help, what the ship would stand good for and what the captain would not tolerate . . . all that, in Tiar's estimation, was a piece of good sense. The instructions might violate five separate Compact laws and two Trade office regulations Tiar could immediately think of, not mentioning local ordinances, but it was comforting to think that there was a standing order for a rescue, that station police no matter with what warrant were not going to take a crew member from the dockside for any reason whatsoever, and that the ship would seal up and leave dock at any moment to protect its crew, disregarding cargo and disregarding station central control. That was against the law. That would get them barred from trade unless they had a good story for the tribunal.

But Hilfy Chanur said that the new rules were the rules and she was going to follow them. It was a major lot of trouble if they ever had to do what was set down here: lawsuits, blacklisting, the various fines and penalties and loss of license Compact law threatened them with evidently didn't matter, if they had another incident like the one yesterday—because *ker* Hilfy said that was the way it was, and in Tiar's experience, Hilfy meant it, come fire come thunder. *Ker* Chanur had no few faults, but if she promised something this drastic, she wouldn't back down if it went operational.

No wonder they didn't want a copy leaving the ship. They weren't trade rules. They were a manual for . . .

A manual for, it occurred to Tiar Chanur as she thought about it, a *hunter* ship, an outright privateer . . . as, at least in the speculation of some in Chanur clan, that was what cousin Pyanfar had been for certain forces in the *han*, for years before it became official and war broke out and the *han* tried to bring her under control.

If we ever do any of these things, Tiar thought, we'll go over that same edge. At that point we'll no longer be a trading ship: ports won't treat us as one. We might get into port—but no knowing who'd trade with us.

And if the *Legacy* goes over the edge, if Chanur has two ships operating like this . . . how can we claim we're still just another clan? The *han* won't stand for it.

She wasn't sure how she felt about that. The captain was upset, she'd picked that up clearly enough. She'd seen it in Chihin, who was in pain, and had a right to be, but she could read Chihin, and it was more than the pain in the wounded arm, Chihin was rattled, ambivalent about this business, and mad as she'd seen her in years.

Because the kid had saved her neck? Maybe. Chihin really, honestly, didn't approve of the boy being here, particularly on this voyage . . . even if Chihin had grudgingly called him a nice, cooperative kid– ("Too gods-be nice," Chihin had put it. "Mincemeat in a month, at home, at his age.")

So it probably wasn't the kid, probably not even the stsho. Chihin was walking around this morning with a head of steam built up and a set to her jaw that said the pain was only an aggravation, she was holding it in, and the wise wouldn't cross her opinions.

Cargo was getting moved—Hallan Meras was back working on the dockside, where Hilfy had sworn he wouldn't be, but Chihin was out there, unstoppable as a star in its course, and Fala was working the pre-launch checks and Tarras was making calls after cargo, running comp and turning a page now and again, a frown on her face.

That was all right, Hilfy thought. She didn't expect expressions of delight when crew found out they were getting less sleep and more work. And that the standing orders amounted to outlawry. She went back to her office to fill out forms for the station legal office, not something she had rather do, but if they had a hope of recovering what they'd just paid out, those forms had to get in before any undock.

Which might come sooner than later.

And there was the matter of the contract, which now, in printout, could fill three of those cabinets. She'd given up on printout. She asked the computer to search *borders/international* and *flight/unwillingness/refusal.*

Search borders/international *negative,* it said with idiot cheerfulness.

And reported . . . *In the event of the refusal of the party accepting the contract to deliver the cargo to the designated recipient . . .*

She knew that part. Double indemnity.

It came up with three similars and a couple of other irrelevancies. Then: *End of search.*

Tarras put her head in the door, with the same worried expression. "Captain. I have a question."

Crew was touchy, crew was upset, crew had a right to be. It wasn't convenient, she was trying to logic her way through subclauses and obligations and Vikktakkht an Nikkatu's behavior, but crew was a priority above priorities. It had to be.

"About what?" she asked, and Tarras eased her way through the door, the Book a rolled-up and well-thumbed set of pages in her hands.

"First off, I was calling the police yesterday. I was trying to get them in there . . . that's why I didn't answer you right off. . . ."

"This thing isn't to assign fault. You weren't at fault. The police got there. That's not what this is aiming at. Absolutely not. If you think I'd better have a word about that . . ."

"I understand what I should have done, by this. But if I'd done that, if I'd threatened station . . ."

"You're *authorized* to threaten station. That's in there. It doesn't mean you open with that bid, cousin. You use your well-known sense. I don't fault you that you were talking to the police. I hoped you were talking to the police. I'd rather you were talking with them, I was a little gods-be busy at the time."

"If we did this, we'd be outlawed. It breaks the law, captain. We'd be blacklisted in every port. . . ."

"We'd be alive."

There was silence in the office. A shadow in the corridor. So Tarras hadn't quite come alone. Fala was listening, too, juniormost and without Tarras' disposition to ask the dangerous questions.

Tarras was thinking about the last one, and maybe thinking alive and outlawed wasn't the career she'd planned for herself.

"I'm not qualified," Tarras said, "to make a decision like that. I'm not a lawyer, I'm the super-cargo."

"You're also the weapons master. Don't tell them you're a lawyer. Tell them you're the gunner and you're left in charge and if somebody doesn't do something you will . . . if I were stationmaster, I'd listen."

Another silence. "You mean bring the weapons up."

"If you have to. Yes. And there's no stationmaster going to enforce a warrant on you. That's not a thing we'll accept."

"There's treaty law! There's the treaty Chanur helped make, Chanur can't break it—"

"You're right," she said, "you're *not* a lawyer. You respect a treaty. They won't."

"I didn't sign on for this!" Tarras said, which she supposed might mean Tarras was resigning, which she would regret to the utmost, but Kshshti was the wrong place to do that. Then Tarras said, in a quiet voice, "Are you under Pyanfar's orders? Is that what we're doing?"

Far leap of logic. But Tarras wasn't a shallow thinker. And couldn't be led off.

"Honestly, no. I don't say Pyanfar's not crossed the path of this deal, but there aren't any orders, I don't know where she is—No'shto-shti-stlen, may he rot, said she was off in deep dark nowhere, and *would* we take this boy and *would* we take this marvelous deal he had? It was my judgment to take it. It looked reasonable at the time. It isn't. But that gods-cursed thing has a double indemnity clause, for value *and* shipping fee. We're stuck. We are quite thoroughly stuck, Tarras, it's my fault, my bad decision to deal with that son, *knowing* he's a canny old stsho and a politician, and here we are. If we get out of this alive and unbanished, I'm taking no contracts but steel plate and frozen foodstuffs, I'm through with exotics, and you can write that one down to the captain's youthful foolishness. I don't want to lose you. I for gods-rotted certain don't want you to walk off the ship here: it's not a safe place."

Tarras stood there looking troubled, ears sinking to a backward slant. "I'm not walking out," she said, as if she'd been misunderstood all along. "I'm not complaining about the deal, I just wanted to know if there was something we didn't know."

"I'm not Pyanfar's. I never was Pyanfar's. Does the crew think that?"

"It was my question. I don't say you'd want to lie to us. But, yes, there's been a little question. In some quarters."

"How I got the command, you mean."

"I didn't say that."

"Py's guilty conscience."

"Huh?"

"How I got this ship." Things came clear to her even while she was talking, absolute clear insight. "She trained me. She knew how I'd react. She wanted me as clan head, at least enough to counter Rhean, who's good where she is." She was perfectly aware she was talking to one of Rhean's former crew. And maligning a closer kin to Tarras than she or Pyanfar was. "I'm a radical lunatic. Rhean's solid conservative. She hates the *han* but she'd back it against the universe. And I've peculiar foreign tastes, Anuurn knows that. As long as I'm clan head, the *han* knows Chanur's led by a depraved young radical. They cooperate with Rhean. Anything, so long as Hilfy Chanur doesn't come home." She shrugged. "Rhean and I get along fairly well, actually. We agree on finances. We agree I should be out here. That's quite a lot."

Tarras might have taken umbrage at that. Tarras merely tightened her lip in irony, acceptance of a Situation neither of them could mend: that was the way Hilfy read it, and she generally could read Tarras.

"Aye, captain," Tarras said. "That's all right."

"I want you," she said, lest there be any mistaken doubt whatsoever. "I *need* you, Tarras. But I respect your other obligations."

"I'm all right," Tarras said. "The rest of us are. It's just—we needed to know we know."

* * *

Ker Chihin was hurting, Hallan could tell that. But she wouldn't stay out of action on the dockside. She kept walking back and forth, overseeing everything, talking to the mahendo'sat in the pidgin, which Hallan couldn't speak, beyond a few words.

He only tried to anticipate what she was going to want, and what was right and what was wrong. He personally, with gestures and his lame command of the Trade, insisted the loaders park on the mark, and the loader kept going without jamming. That was the best help he knew how to be, and *ker* Chihin didn't disapprove it. She finally sat down on the rampway railing and watched, and he took over watching the mahen foreman's check-off on the manifest—brought it back for her approval when they had completed the number two cold hold, and Chihin looked it over minutely and cast looks at the cans last on the truck.

"All right," she said grudgingly, signed it, and he took it back to the docker chief and the customs representative, full of the excitement that came of *doing* something real and useful, and actually dealing with the mahendo'sat himself, talking and being talked to by outsiders—a very queasy, scary situation, if he believed what he'd been taught at home; but it was what he had to do if he ever hoped to find his place among spacers, and the *Legacy* gave him his first real chance.

"You not damn bad," the docker chief admitted. "Not crazy."

"No, sir," he said. "I'm a licensed spacer."

They said something among themselves. Not all of them spoke the pidgin. But they didn't laugh at him, so far as he could detect. And he felt it a delicious wickedness, to be actually making sense to them, and answering a point of debate, which ordinarily a sister would step forward to do in his stead.

He took the completed form back to Chihin and then went back and told them to signal the next load, which was the number three cold hold, and listed for . . . he could make it out . . . Ebadi Transshippers. "All fine, do," the foreman said without quibble, and shouted at his workers. He trekked back to Chihin to say that was what he had just done—she growled at him, but not angry at what he had done, he felt that, only at being asked a needless neo question.

"You're going to wear a track in the deck," she said. "Sit down. They're doing all right. They understood you about parking on the line."

"You speak it?"

"I understand it," she said, and indicated the spot beside her. "Sit. Stay out of their way."

He sat. Chihin didn't sound annoyed, only tired. She said, "We've got cargo coming in. It's Kefk we're going to. You know about Kefk?"

"I know it's on the kifish side."

"It's not a good place. I've never been there. But it's not a place I ever wanted to go."

"I'd go anywhere," he said, consciously pleading his case with her. "If there's a chance I won't come back . . . that's better than home."

"Is it?" Clearly Chihin didn't think so.

"I'm not a fighter. I'm really not. Not for—for what I'd have to fight for if I stayed on Anuurn."

"Is this better?" Chihin asked. He was surprised at Chihin talking seriously with him at all. But it wasn't asking if Chihin was going to reason long with him. He said only the short answer.

"I want to be here."

Chihin was quiet after that. He thought he had exhausted her patience and his welcome, and he should get up and go be useful, somehow. But Chihin reached out and caught his wrist with the hand that worked.

He didn't know what she wanted. He stared at Chihin for what felt like a long, uncomfortable time, and Chihin said,

"You kept your head. You did all right under fire."

"Thank you, *ker* Chihin."

"I don't like your being here," she said bluntly.

"I know that."

She let go his hand. She didn't say anything for a while. Then: "What do you want? What do you really want?"

"I don't understand."

"You want to be out here? You want to spend your whole life running from port to port, with debt at your tail? Or did you think you were going to get rich and be lord of the spaceways?"

"If I knew I could be lord Meras, it wouldn't matter. I don't want what's down there. I want to be here."

"You're a fool."

"They've told me that. But I want it. I don't mind being junior. I am. I just want to be here."

"You tell me that the other side of Kefk."

"I will. I promise you I will, *ker* Chihin. There's nothing ever going to change my mind."

"Kid. The captain wants you out of here."

It hurt. He'd almost hoped. He kept a polite expression all the same.

"Most ships," she said, "are going to want you out of here."

"I'll find someone," he said.

"You can't work dockside. Stations aren't going to want you."

He shrugged, said, with a leaden feeling, "I'll find a way."

"It's sense to go home."

"No, it isn't. I don't want to go back there. It's not sense to do what you don't want."

"Ships have their ways of getting along. Hard enough for any outsider to come in. *The Pride* was . . . under duress. You've got to understand. We get called to station, sometimes in the middle of the night, you haven't got time to dress . . . I mean, it's a thousand things like that. . . ."

"I don't mind."

"Yeah. Well, others do. People talk. And heads have to be cracked for it, I mean, you get no respect if you let somebody make a remark, you know what I mean."

"Yes."

"Yeah. *Yeah,* that's the problem. Shit. —Look at you, your ears are flat."

He brought them up with a mindful effort, started to get up

to excuse himself and get back to work, but Chihin took hold of his arm.

"You understand what I'm saying?"

"Yes, *ker* Chihin."

Chihin's ears went down and then to half. She was looking him in the face and he stared right back.

" '*Yeah*, Chihin,' " she said.

"Yeah."

She had let him go, having made her point. He started a second time to get up, and a second time she stopped him.

"Kid. I don't know it will do a bit of good, but I'm going to talk to the captain, say maybe we should do a wait-see. Mind, she might not go with it. But in my book you earned a chance at it. Not because you hauled me out. But because if you hadn't, a couple more of us might have been fools."

With Chihin you often had to replay things to figure out if they added up to favorable. And it seemed that way. He didn't know what to think: she was canny and she was sharp and he was afraid of her jokes.

"You probably could be lord Meras," she said. "If you wanted to."

He shook his head. "Not me. No."

"Your papa approve what you're doing?"

Another shake of his head.

She patted his leg, which he wouldn't have liked, but it was more like a dismissal: Go away, kid. Behave yourself.

He liked Chihin more for that. He got up and went back to work, feeling her watching him, weighing what he did, approving or disapproving. And, gods, he wanted to do just competently well—flashiness didn't impress Chihin. She'd made that clear, about the rescue. Just common sense. Just doing what you were supposed to do, consistently right. And it made sense to him, the way no one else in the universe had, not *ker* Hilfy, not Tiar, not Fala nor Tarras nor his mother or his sisters. Just do your job and be right.

He thought he could do that. He had a real hope of that, if that was the mark he had to reach.

* * *

. . . If the party receiving the goods be not the person stipulated to in Subsection 3 Section 1, and have valid claim as demonstrated in Subsection 36 of Section 25, then it shall be the reasonable obligation of the party accepting the contract to ascertain whether the person stipulated to in Subsection 3 Section 1 shall exist in Subsequent or in Consequent or in Postconsequent; however, this clause shall in no wise be deemed to invalidate the claim of the person stipulated to in Subsection 3 Section 1 or 2, or in any clause thereunto appended, except if it shall be determined by the party accepting the contract to pertain to a person or Subsequent or Consequent identified and stipulated to by the provisions of Section 5 . . .

It didn't read any better now than then. And subsection 3 section 1 and 2 and clauses thereunto appended made it abundantly clear: the Preciousness went to Kefk.

And the captain went down to the lower deck, to *gtst* excellency's quarters.

She made her presence known at the door. She received no word from inside. She stood waiting.

There were enough disasters. She opened the door, stsho willing or stsho not, and stared in momentary bewilderment at the drapery spread above the bowl-chair.

It was decidedly occupied. It was decidedly not the moment to call a conference. Stsho were notoriously touchy in personal matters.

That *gtst* excellency and *gtst* companion Dlimas-lyi were bound for Kefk was a matter *gtst* excellency might care to know about. But the captain decided *gtst* excellency could find out about it later.

The captain prudently closed the door, mission not accomplished, question not asked.

Is there a plausible lie I can tell Haisi Ana-kehnandian?

So let Ana-kehnandian wait to be told anything. He was loading up the message board, demanding to speak to her directly.

But the captain had things to occupy her. The captain had to get them out of port before the lawsuits started, as they could, the mahendo'sat being a litigious lot.

That they'd used firearms surely had circulated in the rumor market; and a lie was an unreliable weapon—*gtst* excellency's weapon, if *gtst* chose to use it; and a very dangerous thing in the hands of a hani with no notion what it meant.

She had never thought she might look on Kefk as a refuge.

Everything was ahead of schedule. The loader hadn't jammed, *ker* Tiar was insisting she could keep at it, she was getting used to the ice, and she could go into the heated observation room, seeing that the loader was running without a glitch. The cans just kept locking through the rotary platform and the arm kept picking them up and putting them on the chain and the chain kept rolling, delivering them to the arm that delivered them to the waiting trucks.

"I think you fixed this gods-be loader," Tiar said.

Hallan was very proud of that. *Ker* Chihin was going to talk to the captain, Tiar said he'd actually solved something instead of destroying something, and he *knew* Fala would vote for him. And Tarras had tended to. He had real hope, *real* hope. He just prayed the gods of every persuasion not to let anything happen, just let him finish one job that didn't blow up in his face.

Then a one-can truck showed up, with its load, coming back to the *Legacy*'s dockside. The mahen driver got out and talked with the foreman, talked with customs, mahendo'sat (it was always the species name when you were talking about more than one) were waving their arms and saying not a word he understood. *Ker* Chihin was on her feet, but he was closer, and he had the tablet which might tell the story. He didn't think a proper spacer would hang back and wait for his supervisor, it wasn't a male/female business, it was a can trying to come back as damaged or wrongly addressed or not cleared or something, and he didn't want Chihin to have to solve a problem he'd created. He walked up to the shouting mahendo'sat with his tablet and his manifest list.

"Excuse," he said. "Got list. All right, not all right, why?" He was reasonably proud of that sentence.

But they waved arms and shouted at him. He looked at the frost-coated can, number 96, lot 3, and he looked at his list, about the time Chihin walked up, asked, "What's the matter? —What matter, here?"

More shouting. Something, when the mahendo'sat recovered their command of pidgin, about the can being a mistake, that the contents didn't somehow match the manifest, that the contents were listed as grain, the buyer had stipulated dried fish, and there was a complete foul-up.

"Load wrong at Kita!" the customs agent said. And the truck driver shouted, "Off my truck! Not my fault what got!"

"*Na* Hallan," Chihin said wearily.

"*Ker* Chihin," he began, with reference to the checklist, but the mahendo'sat thrust an arm past him and began pointing to numbers and trying to clarify what they meant, he supposed, loudly, in his ear.

"Quiet!" he said, louder than he intended to. But they got quiet, all at once.

"Dangerous," the customs agent said, retreating.

"He's not gods-be dangerous!" Chihin shouted, and Hallan folded his tablet against his chest, calling out, "I'm sorry, *na* mahe, for the gods' sake!"

More shouting, then. And the mahen truck driver saying he was going to offload it, now, here, and they could handle it.

"Now wait," Chihin said, but everything was getting confused. He said, "*Ker* Chihin, . . ."

Chihin paid him no attention. The trucker was getting up on the truck bed, threatening, evidently, to roll the can off and let them handle it; which wasn't a good way to treat a heavy canister, and the dockers were yelling.

"*Ker* Chihin," he said, and nobody at all was paying attention.

He shouted, "*It's not our can!*"

And everything was breathlessly quiet after.

"Not our can?" Chihin said.

And everybody started shouting again, but Chihin was looking, while he was trying to point at the manifest entry, which showed a different local weight.

"Make mistake at pickup!" the foreman said. "Got no pilfer here."

"Open can," the customs agent said.

"No," Chihin said. "You take it, you open it. It's not our can. You get it off our dock!"

"The can is list dry fish," the customs agent said. "We open. Find out."

"We've had one gods-be incident!" Chihin said. "Hallan, get off the dock. Now."

"But—"

"Get!" Chihin said, and waved her good arm at the docker crew. "Bomb," she said. "Blow up. Explosive. *Boom!*"

He was horrified. So were the mahendo'sat, who looked dubious, then in one mass, took out across the dock. The truck driver left his truck and ran for the far side of the dock, while the customs agents hesitated beside the suspect canister, big enough to hold a lift-car full of people or a godsawful lot of explosive.

He knew better than to disobey orders. But Chihin was still there, talking on the com to the ship, and he ran back toward her and met her as she started toward the ship, running and trying to cushion her wounded arm.

He didn't ask. He just grabbed her around the waist on the good side and hauled her up the ramp, as the *Legacy*'s outermost gate and cargo lock began to seal.

"Gods rot!" Chihin gasped.

Up the curving yellow tube, and he was dragging her, now. He stopped to snatch her up and ran as hard as he could, for the airlock still open for them.

He set her down there. Chihin had the presence of mind to slam her hand onto the Close plate, and it sealed in a rush. Then she leaned against the wall, and he did, panting from the run, trying to be sure she didn't fall.

That meant an arm around her, and hers around him, and as

she caught her balance, all the way around him. He held on, she did, and since the universe failed to end, it ended up with Chihin patting him on the shoulder, and him feeling—very short of breath, very, very short of breath, and her likewise, and then both of them with their arms about each other.

Then it wasn't a thought-out thing at all, they were just holding on to each other, and the bomb still hadn't blown up. Tarras was asking, via com,

"Are you all right? Chihin? Na *Hallan?"*

But holding on seemed more important than making sense, and breathing more important than answering, and Chihin was all right, that was what he kept thinking, Chihin was the senior officer, she ought to answer if she wanted to.

"Chihin? Na *Hallan?"*

He hadn't any breath at all to answer.

"They look all right," he heard Tarras say, almost off mike.

And someone else, a younger, outraged voice: *"Gods* rot *her!"*

He knew he was in trouble then, he didn't want to make Fala mad, but he didn't know how to extricate himself, he didn't even try—he wasn't thinking quite clearly, and knew it.

"Is it a bomb?" the captain's voice said, off mike.

"I think they're calling in the bomb disposal people. The customs agent left."

"I think we're going for Kefk."

"Now?"

"We're off-loaded all but two cans. We call the dealer, say we're unable to deliver those two, we deduct the price, we get our tails out of this hellhole, right now. Advise gtst *excellency and* gtst*—whatever. —Can you get those two fools out of the airlock?"*

The captain was up there. Fala was. Tarras. Everybody. There was a bomb on the dock as large as a country haystack and the ship was going to leave. And all he could think of was the face, the very mature face of someone he couldn't believe was attracted to him.

"Got to get inside," Chihin said. And he was scared of the ship going or the can blowing up outside, but more vivid was the thought that Chihin was too different and too common-sense and too steeped in spacer morals to realize he cared for her, he truly, really cared for Chihin—who, with every prejudice she had, honestly made the effort to understand him.

"You gods-rotted idiots, get topside, report in immediately, do you hear me?"

That was the captain. Chihin said a word his sisters never said, then with the rake of a claw through his mane, breathed, "We better do it, kid. Or she'll make us hike to Kefk."

Chapter Fifteen

It was one way to get out of station—station traffic control couldn't rightly refuse an emergency undock, a fire squad had their last two lines shut down, and they were on their way.

With empty holds and running light; with *Ha'domaren* and the kif still at dock and trying to get clearance, Hilfy was sure: one could imagine the messages flying back and forth. If they hadn't a stsho aboard, if they weren't for other reasons reluctant to demonstrate to the universe at large what the *Legacy* could do unladed, they could kite out of here.

As it was they put as much push on it as they dared use and listened to Kshshti try to solve its problem.

With nervous ships trying to bolt, the doors of that section of dock shut, and the whole population of Kshshti under seal-failure warning . . . station police were looking for the driver, who had disappeared, the truck was registered to a warehouse two sections away, no one they'd dealt with, it was stolen, so far as the manager claimed, and the can, which could match almost any ship's ink-written sequence-number for the manifest, didn't match anyone's serial numbers in the embedded ID, that a laser reader would pick up: the manufacturer was Ma'naoshi on Ijir. Mahendo'sat. But cans scattered from their point of manufacture, by the very nature of carrying freight.

It could be anybody's; and being a cold-can, and being handled only by robot and by gloved personnel, any exterior biological contact could go all the way back to the day of manufacture, or to some truck driver on Gaohn station three years ago.

"Probably some load of frozen vegetables," Tarras said.

"Funny thing they haven't cleared anybody to leave the station," Tiar said. "I'm surprised they cleared us."

Station hadn't been at all happy when they declared themselves outbound. Station had threatened them with legal action. But station was silent on that point now that they'd entered the all but vacant traffic pattern and declared course for Kefk.

"We're getting the traffic advisories," Tiar said.

"Guess they've decided not to sue," Chihin said.

There was a markedly subdued atmosphere on the bridge—*na* Hallan hadn't said a thing, Chihin had been remarkably quiet, and Fala maintained a business-only report on the comflow.

One could say one had foreseen this situation, one could toss *na* Hallan off the bridge and lock him in the laundry, except if anyone deserved to be locked in the laundry the senior scantech ought to be first for that accommodation.

"They're saying," Fala said with a sudden edge of alarm in her voice, "they're saying there's something electronic in the can. They're taking it real seriously. Wondering if they should jettison it out the nearest lock."

"Could be a pressure trigger," Tarras said. "That's a cold-hold can. Could be vacuum sets it off, could be thermal. . . ."

"Thermal's the better bet," Tiar said, "rig it through the environmental sensors. Think they want advice?"

"They've probably thought of it," Hilfy muttered, "but gods know . . . relay that, Fala. If they're going to kick it out, better they maneuver it out sunside. . . ."

"Thing could be thermonuclear for all we know," Chihin said. "Somebody's out of their godloving *mind.* They didn't think we were going to let that thing aboard."

"Enough if it's sitting on our dock when it . . ."

". . . goes off. Plain gods-be timer fuse. They should quit messing around and kick it out of there."

Fala was relaying that, too, she could hear the gist of it. It was useless. Kshshti had to know its possibilities, a few more, maybe, than they could think of.

But the perpetrators had to be on the station or on one of those ships still at dock.

"Methane ship's hit system."

"Gods, that's the brick too many on this load."

Add the confusion of an inbound methane-breather to a stationside catastrophe and there was no telling what could happen.

"They are going to jettison the can," Fala reported. Station wasn't answering its traffic inquiries, wasn't acknowledging calls, evidently . . . station's internal calls were probably reaching crisis proportions. What was coming back to them was the ops channel station made available to nervous ships at dock.

"*Tiraskhti* is breaking dock. The kif have given station five minutes to shut down their lines. Station isn't happy."

"One gets you ten *Ha'domaren* is next."

"Won't take that bet," Tarras said.

"Oh, good . . . *gods* . . ."

Number two screen. A white light flashed on Kshshti's side, flashed and died.

Like a lot of innocent station workers.

There was quiet on the bridge. Station ops com was dead. Then some other channel came through, reporting a major explosion, the decompression of sector 8, ordering Kshshti citizens to remain calm and stay put, ordering ships not to complicate matters by launching.

"Those sons are going anyway," Chihin said. "Gods rot it, there's—"

"Methane-breathers are going out," Fala said. "They're talking to the one inbound, I'm not getting any sense on the translator—all that comes clear is *destruction* and *hani* and *stsho, kif* and *mahendo'sat.*"

Chilling message. You could read a methane-breather's

many-brained matrix output in any direction at all. And it all said the same thing.

Chihin said, "Got more than you bargained for, *na* Hallan. Nice quiet trading voyage . . ."

"Let him alone," Fala snapped.

"Touchy. Touchy."

"Cut it out," Hilfy said. "You want to end up as a dust cloud, let's just have an argument in ops."

"She—" Fala began.

"I don't care!" Hilfy said. "I don't care who did what. Shut it down! People are dead back there. Let's have attention to what's *important*, shall we? The ones that did that don't by the gods care who else they kill. Does that fact reach you?"

"*Tiraskhti's* away," Chihin reported. "Going slow. No real hurry. Tc'a are away. Two of them. I'm looking for ID on our station chart. Station's not giving good output, I think they're confused. Hallan, double me, I've got my hands full."

"I want those gods-be ID's," Hilfy said. "Hallan! Acknowledge, rot you!"

"I'm watching, captain."

"*Ha'domaren's* delivered an ultimatum to station. They get the lines shut down or they let them fall. . . ." Fala was back on the job. With her whole brain, hope to the gods.

Vectors were shaping up. *Tiraskhti* for Kefk, no question. *Ha'domaren* . . . *Ha'domaren* was going askew from that.

Meetpoint, Hilfy thought, about the time Tiar said it and Tarras swore.

"What's he up to?"

"I don't know." They could *do* it, unladed as they were. They could burn off *v* and go the other direction, as *Ha'domaren* was headed. They could arrive at Meetpoint with their contract unfilled, in debt for money part of which they'd spent, and have No'shto-shti-stlen suing them, along with Kshshti and Urtur. Or they could go to Kefk, alone with the kif.

"Fala. I want to talk to that son Haisi."

"Aye," Fala said. And made the try. It took a while. They were not cooperative.

Then Fala said, "They say he's not available. He's asleep."

"And I'm the Personage of Iji. Tell his crew I had a message for him, but it's not available either."

Fala did that. Of course they offered to take it.

"They—" Fala said.

"No. I'll talk to *him.*"

There was a delay. And they were still headed for Kefk.

Then Haisi came through, loud and clear. "*You damn fool, hani. What message?*"

"What's the matter? Tired of our company?"

"*You not learn lesson? Go kif? Good luck. Have nice funeral. What message?*"

"What message? Regards from *gtst* excellency. What was it you wanted to know?"

"*You chief number one bastard, you* know!"

"By the gods right I know, mahe! I know you didn't level with me. So I know and you don't. Good luck yourself."

What followed was mahen dialect, and the gist of it was not polite. It was Haisi who broke off the contact, with: "*I don't tell you go hell, Chanur. You already got course set.*"

"Not happy," Tiar said.

Out of Vikktakkht's ship, *Tiraskhti,* not a word.

"Tc'a!" Fala said, and matrix-com shaped up on the number 4 screen.

Tc'a	**tc'a**	**tc'a**	**chi**	**hani**	**hani**
birth	**chi**	**rescue**	**birth**	**go**	**go**
danger	**danger**	**danger**	**danger**	**danger**	**danger**
see	**join**	**make**	**divide**	**danger**	**danger**

"What's this 'birth' business?" Tarras muttered. "I don't like that."

Neither did she, all considered. "Urtur," she said, of the inbound tc'a. "That son's from Urtur."

"Mama," Tiar said. "Not son. That's *mama.*"

* * *

The hours ran on, and the tc'a sent the same message, over and over, an accusing presence on the number four screen persistent as the presence on the scan display. No one said any more about it, but they didn't have to. It was in the tail of Hallan's vision, and the scan display showed the tc'a moving on their heading, not accelerating, but definitely tending toward a meeting of the incomer and the two local ships, and all three tc'a vessels transmitting that same message again and again.

It's my fault, he thought. They blame us.

He had heard how the methane-breathers would attach themselves to a ship, and how they could change vector in jump, which physicists couldn't explain, but tc'a and knnn could do; and chi, who always traveled with the tc'a, aboard their ships, but no one knew whether they were allies or pets. . . .

The captain had warned him. The captain had said he was a fool and the ship could be in danger. Now it was in danger, from the methane-breathers, in addition to everything else, and the tc'a might follow them into hyperspace, where the gods only knew what might happen—if they could change directions, they could *do* things in hyperspace, and having them attack the ship there, he didn't want to think about. . . .

Besides which there was the station back there with a hole in it; and Fala was upset with him, he could see it in every move she made . . . not that he'd done anything or promised anything. But *she* thought he'd insulted her—which he hadn't meant to do. And the crew was feuding with each other, just the way they said would happen with men on ships.

Besides which—gods, he only had to think about Chihin to think how he'd felt down in the airlock, and that was just *stupid*, he didn't want to do what he'd done, he didn't want to feel what he felt, he wanted to use his common sense and straighten things out . . . probably nothing was even wrong in Chihin's eyes, except for Fala: Chihin probably didn't think it meant anything more than the crewwomen on the *Sun* had thought it did. But Chihin was like them and unlike, so unlike and so different in the way she dealt with things that he knew the spacerfarers he'd thought existed, both tough and kind, did exist . . .

And she might not care. That wasn't as important as her existing.

"Stand by for jump," *ker* Tiar said.

They were going. This part always scared him. And the tc'a were still there. The kifish ship *Tiraskhti* was pacing them. People were still dead back there.

". . . here we go."

Fala said, "Why was I so unimportant? Is there something wrong with me?"

He didn't know how to answer that. But Chihin did.

"Nothing but youth," Chihin said, "and time cures that, if you don't make fatal mistakes."

"Let me alone!" Fala said.

He was dreaming. He knew he was, and he could make it stop. He wanted Chihin and Fala not to quarrel. He looked away.

But he could see the ship around him as if it were made of glass. And a shadow of a ship rode close beyond the hull.

Serpent bodies moved and twined within that ship, transparent as their own. He heard sound too low for sound. It quivered through deckplates and through bone, and shrieked until it passed above hearing.

Another ship came dangerously near them, within the proscribed limit, wailing. He leaped up, passed behind Chihin's frozen shape and reached past her shoulder. There was a warning button on that console and he pushed it.

Lights flared red. A siren wailed.

"Go away!" he shouted in this dream, as the shadow loomed larger. It was coming at them. Foolishly he waved his arms to warn it off.

But it swept right through them, with a dimming of the lights, a rumbling of sound, a feeling unlike any heat or cold he remembered.

Then all the ships were beyond them and retreating, the

rumbling gone fainter as they became a triple shadow against the stars, smaller and smaller and fainter.

He dropped into his cushion, breathless and numb—raked his fingers through his mane and caught a frantic breath.

People had dreams in jump. That was surely all it was.

". . . Welcome to sunny Kefk," Chihin was saying. "A friendly sodium burner, no planet, but then, we can't have every convenience. . . ."

"Look alive," the captain snapped. "Where's the tc'a?"

"There's *Tiraskhti,*" Chihin said, and Hallan saw that, and murmured so, but, searching the scan for the tc'a ships . . . nothing showed. An alarm had gone off in hyperspace. One of those anomalies, Chihin called it. Sometimes things happened.

There were things she'd rather lose track of than a clutch of methane-breathers bearing on their tail at three quarters light. "Gods-be snakes could drop out right on top of us," Hilfy muttered, when scan persistently showed nothing but their kif escort.

"With real luck," Tarras said, "they'll drop on *Tiraskhti.*"

"Don't count on it," Tiar said, and toggled a screen change, view of the mass itself: Kefk, sullen apricot orange.

Then it was real to her. The wan sun evoked that reflection on steel bars, that spectrum cast triple shadows on the decking of a kifish prison, lit distant objects in a deathly imitation of sunlight, recalled the clangs and clash of doors and the working of machinery. And over all the smell of it . . .

Sunny Kefk, Chihin said—leading edge of kifish territory, first of a nest of same-generation suns they favored. Pirate territory, before the treaty, space no other species ever wanted to see.

Well, so, this is an experience, Hilfy thought to herself. The young kid that had come to space with Pyanfar had longed after the strange and the dangerous. And found it once. And now again.

You fool, she said to herself—you utter fool, Hilfy Chanur.

* * *

It must be all right, Hallan decided. Everything was normal on the boards. He felt after the nutrients pack. His hands were shaking. He'd never come out of jump so dehydrated or so wobbly. He could scarcely handle the pack without sticking holes in it, he couldn't make his fingers work.

Truth was, he was scared—because there was nothing he could do for himself, because there was, beneath the ordinary and necessary chatter the crew made, a grimness that hadn't been there on the jump before this. And it might very reasonably be because it was a kifish port and their lives were in imminent danger, and they'd lost track of the tc'a ships, all of which was very good reason to be upset.

But there was just this subtle turning of the shoulder Fala did toward him, and somehow she avoided looking at him or at Chihin at all. Everybody was upset with Chihin, the captain had been angry on the starting side of jump, and tempers might be a little cooler on this side—time passed, in hyperspace, a lot of time; and you didn't come out of it as intense about most things as you'd gone in, even if it felt like only an hour later. It was a lot more than that, the body had had a chance to cool down, and the angers and the fears had a chance to settle and evaporate if they had no reason to start up again on this side of jump.

But he'd made a public scene; and as soon as people weren't busy they were going to remember it, the same as Fala already did, as his fault.

He wanted to say something to Fala, he wanted to do something to set it right, but Chihin was sitting between them out there, and his brain was still caught in that sugar-short haze that deprivation created in jump. He was doing well to get himself to his feet when the captain told him: Go fix breakfast, be useful; and his trousers started a slide he only just stopped with a grab at his waistband.

Thank the gods Fala was busy on the bridge and the captain didn't send her too. He couldn't deal with it now. He could scarcely walk. He felt his way into the galley, which was next to the bridge for very good reasons, and giddily, wobbily, started locating the frozen dinners, keeping a hand sort of near safety holds, because a ship coming in from above a sun could find some other ship dropping in too close to them, even yet, and the ship could have to maneuver without warning.

But you didn't plan for it. And probably you couldn't really hold on if it did. Most times the off-duty crew began to stir about just now, only the *Legacy* didn't have that many hands, and they took their breaks close to the bridge, where they could answer a sudden recall. People took breaks as they could, did necessary maintenance on the bridge and thereabouts . . .

And snacked, if they could keep it down. He popped another nutrient pack and shed fur over everything. He *wanted* a bath, but that wasn't possible till they'd reached the inner system boundary: he'd asked for duty and he had it.

Crew was up and moving. Chihin went through, and gave him some kind of a look he didn't dare meet; and came back through again, with her face wet and her mustaches dripping.

He was scared to death she was going to speak. But she didn't. He had some chips, galley's privilege, to keep his stomach from heaving, and it didn't help much. He followed it with cold tea, from the fridge. And he thought he was going to be sick right there, he was cold from the drink and shaking and his stomach was trying to turn itself inside out. He leaned on the counter trying just to breathe, wondering if he should go for the facilities, or if jostling wasn't the right thing to do just now . . .

A hand landed on his shoulder. "You need some help?" Tarras asked, and when he stood against the counter: "You all right?"

"Fine," he managed to say. And prayed to keep his stomach still, while Tarras wandered around and looked in the oven and put a pot of gfi on to brew . . . the smell was almost more than he could take.

"Looks like you've about got it," Tarras said, and came and leaned against the counter beside him. "Hits you hard sometimes."

"Yes," he said.

"You want to go back to the bridge and sit down?"

"No," he said, monosyllabic, desperate. No, he did not.

Silence for a moment. Then: "Prickly situation," Tarras said, and he felt his stomach knot a little tighter, *hoping* she was going to talk about the kif and the ship out there or anything else but–

"You and Fala have something going?"

"No!" He kept his voice low, hoping to the gods they didn't carry over the noise of the fans. "She's just nice, is all."

"She's a good kid," Tarras said. "You're the most attractive thing she's seen in a year. The only. But that's beside the point."

"I didn't–" He didn't want to talk about this. But he was cornered. And Tarras might be on Fala's side, but Tarras was easier to talk to than Fala. "I didn't want to upset her."

"Chihin's a full-time pain. It's her aim in life. You're not obligated to put up with–"

He didn't like Tarras saying that. He didn't want to hear it. He shoved off on his way to the crew lounge, as the only refuge he could think of, and Tarras caught his arm, caught it with a claw, and it hurt, but he kept going.

She caught him again. Most wouldn't. Nobody ever had, on this ship. But he'd learned on the *Sun*, that defying orders meant getting dumped. So he did stop. He didn't have to look at her.

"Oh, gods," Tarras muttered. *"Chihin?"*

So Chihin joked. He knew that. It didn't change the fact he felt it in the gut when she walked past him. It didn't change the fact he liked her, and it didn't change the way he'd felt, and the way he still felt.

Tarras let out a breath and leaned against the wall. "Kid, Chihin isn't the most serious-minded soul in the crew."

"That's all right," he said without looking at her.

"Ow," Tarras said, and after a moment of silence. "Look, *na* Hallan. She's *not* a bad sort. –Gods, I've landed in it, haven't I?"

He didn't know what to say. He wasn't mad at Tarras. He

wasn't mad at anybody. Mostly his stomach was upset and he wished Fala wasn't mad. The oven timer went off, to his vast relief, and he said, "It's ready."

"I'll call them," she said, and ducked out while he took the dinners out.

And burned his fingers.

Something about *na* Hallan and Chihin . . . Tiar didn't wholly pick it up on the first hearing, with Tarras leaning and whispering into her ear.

And then she didn't believe it. But Tarras said, "It's serious."

She unbelted and got up; and went over to the captain and whispered, "The kid and Chihin? We got a problem."

Hilfy turned her head, looked at her nose to nose and said, ominously: "Problem?"

Tiar made a glance back toward the galley, another to Chihin and Fala, working side by side. An unnaturally quiet Chihin.

"She hasn't said a word."

The captain evidently added the same chain of figures. *Chihin* was deathly quiet. Not a joke. Not an ill-timed jibe about the situation. A lot of efficiency out of her, this last hour, but seldom a word, since the first.

And Fala—Fala was talking to the kif, but not to Chihin.

"I want this straightened out," Hilfy said under her breath. "Good *gods,* we aren't in a place we can afford this! Grow by the gods *up,* can't we?"

"I don't think it's Fala," Tiar said as faintly as she could, and got a second furious look from Hilfy.

"I don't *care* what's going on," Hilfy hissed. "This is deadly serious, cousin. The kif aren't playing lovers' games out there. Breakfast at stations, nobody's getting a break."

Good idea, Tiar thought to herself, and went and relayed the order out loud: "Stay at your posts. We've got a situation shaping up. We're in an ongoing caution, here, we can get the food out, but we're not taking any breaks, got it?"

Let them *think* she and the captain had been consulting on

the kif. Give them something outside the ship to worry about. She went back to the galley. "General alert. Get the trays out here, keep them clipped down, no open hot liquids. Tarras, arms board shakedown."

Tarras' ears went back, and sobriety happened fast, in a hesitation between the oven and getting back to her post.

"Get the trays out," Tiar repeated, to the young gentleman at the center of the storm, and he wiped the scowl off his face and started snatching, ignoring singed fingers.

"That's the way," she said. "Let's move! Get in those seats and get belted. This isn't Anuurn system."

She took her own tray back, grabbed a drink and settled in while Tarras and Hallan were passing out trays off the stack and drinks out of a box.

The captain started giving system check orders. The captain ordered a condition three on the armament. And that was the first time the *Legacy* had ever brought the weapons board up full. There was a different kind of quiet on the bridge when that order came down, and various stations had to crosscheck with targeting.

Hope to the gods it was a test. The fact of the weapons got to her nerves too, even knowing it was a calculated distraction. The war memories came up along with that long-silent board. Her reflexes wound themselves tight as a spring, and her heart beat a little faster.

Because now that she thought of it, kif being kif, the arms computer on *Tiraskhti* was probably completely live. And probably had been, from the moment the kif went for jump toward his own border.

There were mining craft. There were construction pushers. They looked, except the major kifish ships at dock, like ordinary miners and pushers in any system in hani or mahen space.

Well they might, Hilfy thought. They were probably stolen.

But the ships at dock at Kefk had no look of honest traders. Huge engine packs. Cold-haulers that could release their cargo or blow off their mass with the flip of a toggle: hunter-ships, clutching cargo cans in their clamps, like many-legged insects; purported tankers, whose tanks probably were false mass.

"Captain," Fala said, "Vikktakkht."

"I'll take it," she said, and a clicking, soft voice said,

"Chanur captain. You'll go first and we'll dock beside you. For convenience' sake."

"Understood. And do we understand this trip is worth our time?"

"Put Meras on. I find him amusing."

I won't talk to you, that meant. "Later," she said shortly, and punched out. "—Tiar, I want one course laid out for Meetpoint, and courses for Kshshti, Mkks, Harak, Lukkur, and Tt'a'va'o. . . ."

"Tt'a'va'o!"

"If we go out of here with kif on our tail, *better* the methane folk than Lukkur. But we take any vector open and deal with it when we get there."

"Aye, captain."

"Their prices aren't bad," Tarras said.

Tiar said: "Gods, load their cans aboard, after Kshshti?"

"I was kidding," Tarras said. "Kidding, cousin."

The *Legacy* still had the option to run, Hilfy thought. She could do a sudden break and sight on Meetpoint and get the *Legacy* out of here.

But you didn't run from kif. If you ran, they were wired to chase—sometimes literally; sometimes, more dangerously, they merely wrote you down for weak and apt for more abstract predation.

A Chanur—if she ran—would weaken Chanur clan in the eyes of all kif. It would prompt ambitions. It would encourage seditions. Assassinations, to which aunt Pyanfar was all too vulnerable.

But rational as everything had seemed the other side of jump—they weren't just the only hani ship in system, they were the only foreign ship anywhere: not a mahendo'sat, not a stsho, not a methane-breather showed in the revolutions of the station. Not even a ship that was clearly a merchant ship.

"Those are hunters," Tiar said. "Every one of those are hunters. What's building here?"

"I don't like this," Fala said. "I really don't like this."

"Don't panic," Hilfy said quietly. "Never panic with them. It's a guarantee of problems."

"Chanur," came the kifish voice over her earpiece, *"you're clear to dock now."*

"Thank you, *hakkikt."*

The schematic flashed up, glowing lines channeling their approach and their mandated velocity.

Scary enough on a small station. But the numbers, the indicators, were kifish characters, base 8.

"They're offering automated approach," Fala said, in a voice a little higher than her wont. "They say they have translation programs."

"So do we and No. No input from them to our computers. Absolutely not. Just calc it."

" 'Just calc it,' " Chihin muttered in a tone of desperation. 'Calc it' was herself and Tiar and their computers, in rapid cross-check calculation. While they were aimed at Kefk Station like a missile.

But numbers started popping into the display of their own instrumentation, distance to dock, rate of spin, moment of contact.

"Fine it down," Hilfy said. "That's a stand-down on the weapons board, Tarras."

"Confirm, captain. Standing down and locked."

The kifish station was protesting their irregular approach. The Kefk control center wanted, they *demanded* computer to computer contact. They ordered them to brake and abort. The emergency flasher was on the station output. And if there was a time *Tiraskhti* could be absolutely certain weapons were at stand-down, it was now, preparing for dock. If there was a time *Tiraskhti* could get a shot that might miss their own station, it was in the next few minutes.

"By the book," Hilfy said calmly, and kept her claws out of the upholstery of her seat. "Extra decimals. Let's not have a repair bill at this place."

Station was still objecting. From *Tiraskhti*, moving in just behind them, there was silence that meant, one hoped, observant respect, waiting to see whether they could justify the defiance of station control, respect that grew or died a dangerous death on the skill with which they touched that docking cone.

And bet that the station wouldn't be quick to warn them of an impending mismatch.

"Rotation shutdown," Tiar announced, and the next queasy part started, as the *Legacy* gave up its own internal *g* and the ring coasted into null. They were coming very slowly, at a tangent to the station's scarily rapid spin. This was the point where panic could set in, and a point where, as an insystemer, you were either licensed to do this or you linked to tenders who were, and got cabled in.

Or you docked, like the ore carriers, in null at the mast.

A long hauler didn't have either option. Just the mobile cone that gave you a little guide and a tangential approach, and took you up at a distance that wouldn't let you crack the bulkheads, before the grapple snagged you and the docking assembly took you into sudden 1.2 *g* sync with the station's rotation.

Tiar made a lightning reach: the *Legacy*'s portside thrusters shoved her one way and then braked that motion null. A quick flurry of small adjustments truing up with the calculated appearance of the cone. You didn't track the cone until the last moment, didn't see it until it was too late to brake: and station computers weren't talking to theirs: theirs was just talking to their engines, now that it had the intercept plotted.

There was the cone. The last correction to put the probe right down its throat and a brisk shove from the mains that put the *Legacy* into the guide zone at intercept with the station's rate. The jolt of capture rang through the bow; the contact moved the whole passenger ring for a stomach-wrenching second and pressed them down in their seats. Grapples banged, the braces touched and boomed against the hull . . .

"And we are *in,*" Tarras declared.

In. At a kifish station. Solo. Wonderful. "Good job," Hilfy said in the collective breath that followed. "Good job. The crew earns one for that."

By the Book, Fala was already sending her fueling request, arguing in the Trade with the Kefk dock authority.

And by the Book, by aunt Py's lately sacred and mandated Book, there would be no bending on that point: fueling and offloading of wastes before the *Legacy* ever opened an airlock, aunt Py's procedures, in places Pyanfar didn't trust; and a very good idea, in Hilfy's present estimation—but meanwhile a kifish *hakkikt* would, publicly, be compelled to wait on his hearing until that fuel was in, and that was a dangerous slight, in a game of volatile egos: *sfik,* kifish elegance, was life: offend it, and expect attack, as they expected a move of you under like circumstances. Kif were much on etiquette . . . their own etiquette, to be sure, a pricklish protocol of arms.

An air of competency, of hauteur, of willingness to take extreme action . . . with the firepower to back it up: those were assets; while generosity was the gesture of a superior to a servant; kindness fell in the same category; and loyalty lasted as long as a leader had *sfik* intact.

Courage? Fierceness in a fight was a plus. But so was deviousness. Self-preservation was the highest virtue, and risking one's neck could be self-preservation—if it demonstrated an arrogant competency to potential rivals.

A whole other universe, Hilfy thought to herself, a very solitary, dark, and aggressive universe. You could do anything you could carry off with style—or at least with sufficient firepower on your side. That counted.

Come to Kefk, Vikktakkht had insisted, certainly aware that she had been a prisoner among his kind, and perhaps, as many kif were surprisingly educated, aware that hani minds, prone to emotional might-have-beens and what-ifs entirely alien to his species, might come adrift from what was, and wander into delusion . . .

Vikktakkht might hope for that.

But there was a benefit to fluency in other languages. She could *think* in kifish: see things from kifish perspective—and, so doing, feel the shift in her heartbeat, the change from twice a month hunter to hair-triggered, hard-wired round the clock predator.

If they expected her to have balked at coming here—not likely.

To panic at being here—she had yet to reach that state.

Here I am, *na* kif. What am I thinking? What will I do? Do you know me that well?

You made me half crazy. If I'm here alone, I must be one tough bastard of a hani.

And you know I don't like you much. So *you're* taking the chance, *na* kif. You'd better pay off. Because by your rules—if you cross me, I can only start a war by *not* blowing you to hell.

"They're going to fuel us," Fala said. "They say they want payment transferred at the same moment they start pumping."

"That's fine. We'll transfer it bit by bit. They reach an eighth of our load, they get an eighth of the payment. In international trading certificates, and *they* can run courier and check the authenticity. *No* computer links to their bank. And we're not talking to Vikktakkht or anybody of his ilk until those tanks are full." Gods, did she know this routine! In her sleep, along with the nightmares. "—Tarras, get a bid on the data dump. We're still traders, that's what we're here for, let's not give them any other ideas. And everything in cash."

Hallan, quietly: "There's some sort of light keeps blinking on com."

"That's the incoming mail," Chihin said. "It's autoed. Com incoming isn't feeding to any computer that's connected to anything; it's deloused before it's available to read and it won't store. Don't worry."

Hilfy keyed up the file list, wondering what in all reason messages could be waiting for the *Legacy* at Kefk.

Pyanfar's mail.

Of course it was.

Chapter Sixteen

The hoses coupled on, the pumps started their heartbeat thumping. Are we safe to do that? Hallan wondered nervously, as he'd begun to worry about every contact with this station. But the crew was busy, there were probably safeguards engaged he didn't know about, and if the ship had to refuel, it had to, for them ever to get out of this port; and there was no use asking stupid questions in that department.

Na Vikktakkht had invoked his name again, and meant to talk to the captain through *him,* and he didn't know why. Maybe it was something to do with the incident on Meetpoint. Maybe they just wanted to get him off the ship where they could arrest him, after which . . . after which he had heard very gruesome stories about kifish habits.

But maybe he wasn't as scared of that as he ought to be. And maybe he shouldn't be upset about what Tarras had said about Chihin. Chihin wasn't upset. She explained things to him where he was ignorant. She acted as if everything was all right. Fala was still ignoring him, but Fala was too busy to pursue a feud, and he didn't know whether she was madder at him or at Chihin. Fala was somebody who wanted anybody; that was the way he read her, fair or not. While Chihin didn't *need* anybody, Chihin didn't expect favors, either, she just did what came into her head and she was honest, it didn't matter that he wasn't the most important thing that had ever happened to her, he was just—

—out of his gods-cursed head when he thought about her being beside him; and he didn't know why, or what the logic was. It was certain enough she could live without him, he never doubted that. It was—

It was that Chihin just didn't expect to have anything, and people didn't get close to her, because of her jokes, and if somebody told her back off now, she probably would.

And *if* she backed away, he couldn't stand seeing her every day, and putting up with Fala, who'd have been . . . nice, if there wasn't Chihin just out of reach.

It was going to take hours to do the fueling and all the coming and going, and he didn't want to confront anybody about anything, and he didn't want to be around Chihin, in case she *was* making a joke, and was going to make a bigger fool of him before she was done—she didn't always know when to stop.

He wished they'd hurry and go talk to the kif, and he could go with them, and maybe—maybe just have a whole new set of worries besides this one. The kif *might* want him. If Chihin didn't, maybe that was better than living here.

Maybe the captain would just say Fine, all right, good luck. Hoping he'd foul up with *them,* and cost them money.

"*Na* Hallan," the captain said, "filter check, lifesystems check, don't drag your feet. We don't know how much time we've got. We could have to go out of here at any minute. With no undock procedures."

"No undock" got his attention. "Aye, captain," he said, galvanized into movement; he went to do that, obscurely relieved that the captain found something useful for him to do besides slit his wrists.

He could be mad, if he really wanted to think about it. He could really be mad, and he didn't even know who to aim it at, not Tarras, not Chihin, not Fala. Not the captain, who might be rough with him, but who'd given him chance after chance after he'd fouled up beyond all reasonable limits.

Certainly not Tiar, who had done nothing to him but good.

Maybe he was just mad at himself, for not being better, or smarter, or more able to handle things. He hoped to redeem himself. He did. He tried to think of the best question he could ask the kif, since the kifish lord had said he would have at least one more chance.

But he had no inspiration, no understanding that would help him. And maybe after all, it wasn't the real issue. Maybe it never had been. The kif had drawn the captain in by curiosity and used him, and maybe it was nothing but that same ploy again. The kif had the stsho, or the stsho was dead, and they were in a place surrounded by a very dangerous species.

He just hadn't been much help to anyone.

"Your excellency?"

Silence.

"Your excellency?" They were alive inside. Hilfy signaled intent to enter the cabin, waited a moment for decency, and opened the door.

The sleeping-drape was still over the bowl-chair. Completely over the bowl-chair. There were two lumps under it, and they moved.

They weren't sick. The tea service beside the pit that had not spattered itself into bits and pieces during dock proved someone had been up and about, undoubtedly Dlimas-lyi . . . was *gtst* excellency going to bestir *gtst*self to work? Not in her experience.

She cleared her throat. "Your excellency, I have the honor to report our safe arrival at Kefk. Does your excellency require anything? We will negotiate with the persons who may have the person of Atli-lyen-tlas as soon as fueling is complete."

A muted squeal from beneath the cover. A white head popped above it, crest tousled, wide-eyed. "Your honor is very kind. *Gtst* excellency will wait."

"Has—" Gods *rot* the creature. "Has *gtst* excellency any influence at this port? Any contacts to pursue? Any knowledge of stsho personnel in this area? We are in a port foreign to us in which we have neither introduction nor credentials, and a kif named Vikktakkht an Nikkatu who has led us here with dubious promises now wishes to speak with a young male crewmember regarding *gtst* excellency Atli-lyen-tlas."

A second head popped up, as disheveled. "With a *male* person? A juvenile male person? Could this possibly be the juvenile male person who assaulted our sensibilities in the corridor, the carrier of refuse, the unstable and aggressive individual? The same?"

"This Vikktakkht wishes to talk to this same individual. I disapprove. I am insulted. However I will not permit this strategem to distract me from the fulfillment of the contract. I shall go. I shall prompt this young male person in his answers to this outrageous provocation. I shall learn by that means and determine my course of action."

"Most resolute! Most deserved on his part! Let him speak to the juvenile carrier of refuse!"

Not exactly the impression she'd wanted to convey of *na* Hallan; but argument with two sheet-wrapped stsho seemed precarious. "The object, however, is the presence of Atli-lyen-tlas, safely on this deck, which I shall attempt, against all obfuscation and misdirection. I should, however, caution your excellency that every other ship in this port is kif, they are not honest trading vessels who are here, and there is the remote but not disregardable possibility of a precipitous and scarcely warned undocking and high velocity departure which would render, for instance, that most exquisite tea set a cluster of projectiles of great hazard. An alarm will sound in the event of emergency. It will be a very loud and unmistakable siren. In that eventuality, abandon all decorum, cast any loose objects into the nearest locker, preferring your own safety above all. I shall provide an abundance of unfortunately inelegant cushions, which you may pack within your bowl-chair while fastening safety belts."

"These are frightening precautions!"

"Far less so than a departure inadequately protected. If there is time, a member of my crew will assist you. But if your excellency will excuse my forwardness, which is motivated only by our deepest regard for your safety, I wish to have conveyed these cushions into this cabin immediately. I wish to take no chances."

Tlisi-tlas-tin waved an urgent hand. "At once, at once! Dlimas-lyi, assist the honorable crewmember!"

"*Most* gracious!"

"How like your thoughtful and hospitable self to take extravagant precaution!"

Interesting sight. She had never seen a stsho without a stitch of clothing. Dlimas-lyi scrambled out and hurried, bowing often. One tried not to show startlement, except to return the bow.

Every pillow on the ship, as happened. Hers. The crew's. Every pillow out of storage, including those from the dismantled passenger cabins, and mahendo'sat slept in nests of pillows, so there were no few in reserve. Plus a couple of inflatable air bags for emergency use.

"In the lift," she said, and did not say, Would your honor care to dress, we are not in that great a hurry. But she was unsure of the proprieties, and only put the door at Open-Hold.

"I remind your excellency that a face-upward reclination on any safety cushion is safest during any sustained engine use, to keep breathing passages unobstructed."

"This is a dire contemplation!"

"Think of it as a hopeful one, as in the worst and most violent eventuality your excellency and *gtst* companion will rest in a serene and safe nest."

"Your concern and foresight on behalf of your passengers is most greatly appreciated! You are white to my eyes!"

"I am deeply touched." Actually, she was. It was a far step for Tlisi-tlas-tin. "I have profound regard for your excellency's opinion."

As pillows and airbags arrived in great abundance, hasty waddling bundles of them, on two different-hued sets of legs.

* * *

The filters were all right, except one: Hallan pulled that one to wash it in the galley, which had to serve, since the downside was proscribed stsho territory. He rinsed it clean and looked around in startlement as someone strolled into the galley.

Oh, gods. Chihin. He didn't want to be here. He even considered flight. Locking himself in the crew quarters. But dignity kept him set on his job, and he only hoped she'd come after a sandwich or something and wouldn't say anything.

He kept working at the sink, drying things off. Chihin leaned past him after a bag of chips from the cabinet over his head, bodily leaning on him, resting her hand on his shoulder. And he didn't believe then it was chips she was after—but he didn't know whether it was affection, a joke at his expense, or whether she was asking him to reciprocate or what. She got the chips. She opened them and she left, and he didn't yet know what to do or what he should have done. His stomach was upset. He wanted to make sense of things and not to make matters worse, and now he didn't know at all what was going on, except just having her near him was enough to send his temperature up a point and make him short of breath, forget any clear sense, and she might have wanted him, and she might have thought he was trying to ignore her.

And if *that* was the case Chihin wasn't going to come back for another rejection, if she felt rebuffed. He could have hurt her feelings . . . if he even had a hope of understanding somebody like her. He was lost. He was just lost.

The sensors read what was going in as untainted and completely proper. And to Hilfy's small surprise, the station paid for the datadump like a civilized port, a relatively fair price, fifty-fifty with *Tiraskhti*'s competing arrival; and deducted it from the fuel bill, which likewise wasn't exorbitant for a place like Kefk, which didn't have overmuch surplus.

No trouble on the bank certificates: the kif sent a representative to the airlock to accept the certificates; and sent again at each major fraction of the load—which was more cooperation than you might get at Urtur. Tarras, delivering the certificates, was armed; the kif was clearly armed: Hilfy watched the entire exchange from the lower deck ops station on vid, with a pistol beside her hand, quite ready to shut the lock from there and trap a kif bent on mischief of any kind.

Not a hint of trouble.

And of Pyanfar's purified mail, *here*, among kif, the religious cases were completely absent, the entrepreneurs were nonexistent—there were numerous individuals offering the assassination of whatever enemies she might designate, some on speculation. There were numerous individuals listing their credentials, which might read like a police report in another society; but murder was not a prosecutable offense under kifish law. There *were* no prosecutable offenses between individuals under kifish law, only offenses against necessary collective institutions. It was, for instance, against the law for a kif or a group of kif to attack the bank and rob it; or to take independent action against a foreign government or against the kifish government, or to attack a space station in contravention of the dignity of the *mekt-hakkikt*. Pyanfar had probably dictated that one herself—since there *was* no kifish legislature, as such, merely a general consent to follow a given *hakkikt* so far as it looked advantageous, and what the *hakkikt* said *was* law so far as the *hakkikt*'s influence went. Violate it and find oneself delivered to the offended *hakkikt*, who might demonstrate his or her *sfik* above that of the offender by having the offender for dinner. Literally.

And of all the ranks aunt Pyanfar held, that she leaned the most heavily on her authority among the kif—might simply be that she had to exert it, constantly, to stay *mekt-hakkikt*, without which—all her laws were null and void; and that without her in that post, there would be no peace.

But it occasioned no few shakes of the head among hani on Anuurn, who were only disturbed that kif were constantly *about* Pyanfar Chanur. Of the realities inside kifish space, no one came here to learn.

Except Pyanfar Chanur.

Did she ever *take* any of these offers, Hilfy found herself wondering uneasily. If you were offered universal peace, and someone was in the way of that peace, grievously in the way of it, and you had this many offers, from a species that truly, earnestly didn't mind murder, either of its own kind or someone else—would one begin to weigh relative evils?

Oh, *gods,* aunt, what a daily set of choices, what a difficult No, to say time after time—or is it always No, with the peace at stake . . . when the potential violator might be kif?

What a narrow ledge to walk, aunt. Why ever did you take it?

Except no one else could have, in that day, at that time. . . .

Pyanfar, one message said, *got talk you. Got wife no sense. A.J.*

A.J? Who went by A.J? Why no header? No date. She didn't know any—

A.J? Aja Jin?

Jik?

That was a Personage among the mahendo'sat. And *Aja Jin* was a hunter ship. Wife no sense? Woman no sense? It was ambiguous in mahendi.

Jik wasn't married, last she knew. Jik . . . with more turns than a tc'a . . . was still, if he had held loyal, one of aunt Py's number one agents, and *Aja Jin* was one of those ships that didn't file its course with any trade office, or carry cargo. *Aja Jin,* like *The Pride,* just showed up here, and showed up there, and how far it could go at a jump and where it refueled was something aunt Py probably knew, but probably nobody else did.

Not even the bother to code it. And left *here,* at Kefk, across a border only fools crossed?

What in a mahen hell was this she'd let herself be maneuvered into? Aunt Py's private mailbox? A place . . . if one thought about it . . . where a ship like *Aja Jin* could kite in on the sudden, drop a message in plain mahen Trade, not even troubling to code it, beyond the necessity to know who A.J. was . . . because kif had no motive to go to anybody but another kif with the news: kif high up enough to use it were either loyal to aunt Py or outright plotting against her, but in no case would they deliver what they knew to empower any random outsider. It was just not in their interest to do so.

And make a move against the *mekt-hakkikt,* where she picked up her mail? Consider all those messages of hopeful underlings, desperate for some credit with the highest authority in kifish space.

But Vikktakkht wanted Hilfy Chanur *here?*

Necessary to tread very, very carefully. You flatter me, Vikktakkht had said when she addressed him as *hakkikt* at Kshshti—but here his message before docking had used the title: The *hakkikt* Vikktakkht an Nikkatu, no quibble about it.

The *hakkikt* said here they would find Atli-lyen-tlas, and here he would assist them, and here was where everything had to be, in what if an absolutely wild guess was right, was a place Pyanfar came, and a place presently *full* of hunter ships, and nothing else; and a place it was going to be very difficult for the *Legacy* to leave against this *hakkikt's* will.

On the one hand, it was possible a mahen lunatic with domestic problems had left Pyanfar an inane appeal for assistance.

But there were 248 messages already in Pyanfar's message stack, and more were backed up waiting for the computer's version of bomb detection. This was not a place that had low expectations of seeing Pyanfar Chanur. No few of said messages had points of origin like Mkks, and Akkti, and distant Mimakkt, all in kifish space—messages sent to Kefk.

On the one hand this could be Pyanfar's kifish base of operations.

On the other hand—it might not be. And that 'might not be' held the most dire possibilities.

The screen flashed blue: the computer spat up a message with a keyword.

The hakkikt *Vikktakkht to captain Hilfy Chanur, at dock at Kefk: Contact me.*

The message before dock was halfway cordial. This, after dock, was terse, guarded against insult, a simple and moderate demand which a mere captain would be extremely ambitious to refuse.

On kifish terms, a very clear and entirely reasonable warning: fueling was *nearly* complete. The *hakkikt* gave her a way to both comply and save her own *sfik*, having held off a superior force this long.

Definitely time to comply, if one didn't wish to challenge him outright.

Step by step down the kif agenda. And no question but that the kif wanted her, in person.

She didn't let her mind dwell on that scenario. It would come. It wasn't on her to-do list at the moment.

She swung the chair around and keyed in the com function.

The hani ship Chanur's Legacy, *at dock at Kefk, captain Hilfy Chanur, head of Chanur clan, her hand, to the* hakkikt *Vikktakkht an Nikkatu, the kif hunter* Tiraskhti, *at dock at Kefk: We are pleased to open communication.*

A moment, then:

The hakkikt *Vikktakkht to captain Hilfy Chanur, at dock at Kefk: I have the person you seek. Bring Meras.*

She did *not* like that juxtaposition. And every second of delay was a possibility of a blow-up, a loss of *sfik*, an unwanted challenge of the kif's intentions . . . the ramifications were wide and rapid.

The hani ship Chanur's Legacy, *at dock at Kefk, captain Hilfy Chanur, head of Chanur clan, her hand, to the* hakkikt *Vikktakkht an Nikkatu, the kif hunter* Tiraskhti, *at dock at Kefk: When?*

Her hand was shaking as she keyed it out. Thank the gods the kif couldn't see that. She couldn't flinch aboard *Tiraskhti.* Not if she wanted to get out alive.

The hakkikt *Vikktakkht to captain Hilfy Chanur, at dock at Kefk: An escort is on the way to your lock now.*

Gods rot the bastard! They weren't prepared for this. It was an ultimatum. They could refuse it. But you measured every such action and bet everything you had on it. She had made a play, coming in here. The hakkikt was making his throw, now, and it was a test or it was an outright kidnapping.

The hani ship Chanur's Legacy, *at dock at Kefk, captain Hilfy Chanur, head of Chanur clan, her hand, to the* hakkikt *Vikktakkht an Nikkatu, the kif hunter* Tiraskhti, *at dock at Kefk: I look forward to the meeting.*

Let *him* wonder if she was going to shoot him on sight—because *he* would have to raise the level of threat to tell her she wasn't going in there armed.

She was in formal dress now. There was the mini-pistol in her belt. There was the gun on the counter, its holster in the wall-clip, and she punched in all-ship while she was getting out of the chair. "Hallan Meras, Fala Anify, report to lower main *now,* formal dress, code red, Fala. Hallan, just wash off, clean clothes, and get yourself down here."

"I'm going," Fala said from somewhere.

"Hallan, answer the gods-be com!"

"Yes, captain! I'm on my way!"

Tarras arrived, full of protests. "The kif? You're going out there? With those two kids?"

"The Rules, Tarras. The Rules. I want the gunner, the pilot, the scan officer on the bridge. You don't deal with the kif solo, I've got to have somebody, he wants to talk through Meras: Fala's the only expendable, that's the way it is, Tarras. I'm *sorry,* cousin. It's the way it adds."

Tarras stood there in silence, hard-breathing. Then: "Tell them the gunner's unstable and gods-be upset about this."

"I'm telling them we want Atli-lyen-tlas. Or a good excuse. Keep *Chihin* on the ship. Read the Rules at her till she hears you."

"Aye," Tarras said. Thank the gods for Tarras' basic intelligence. Tarras left, grim and upset; and collided with Tiar inbound.

"Captain,—"

"Won't work this time, Tiar. Crew to stations, by the Book. *Trust* me I know what I'm doing."

"Risking your gods-be neck, captain!"

"That's fine. Neither Fala nor I navigate. Your course is Meetpoint by Lukkur or Tt'a'va'ao, if that's the only route open—if I get into trouble, run for it and let somebody know besides the kif, does this make sense to you?"

Tiar didn't like it. Not in the least, but she went with Tarras, and both of them were going to have their hands full with Chihin, bet on it. For the first time this crew was going to make the hard choice and do what they were told, by the everliving gods. And she was deeply sorry to be taking two kids into this mess, but it was exactly as she'd told them: no choice.

She heard the lift descending. That was either Tarras and Tiar on their way up—or . . .

She heard the shouting. That was Chihin. Protesting, she could figure, that she'd calc'ed all the possible courses already, and she was going. Hilfy couldn't hear the words, but she could pick the argument out of the rhythm. The voices went quiet then—muted by the doors, perhaps; the lift ascended. But someone was coming down the corridor, she heard the hurrying approach.

"Captain," Fala panted, still damp from the shower. Scared, no question of it.

"This is where we see if you can keep your head, *ker* Anify. Sorry I can't take senior crew, you're it. Remember everything—*everything* you read in the manual, and if you're scared out of your wits you don't let *them* know it. There's another gun in the locker there. Put it on."

"Aye, captain." Fala got into the locker, got the gun and holster out, and put it on. Her hands were shaking: neo nerves, the unknown, the never-experienced. That was all right. She had a few flutters herself.

"They're going to try to spook you. You put your hands on

your gun, they'll do the same, just don't for godssake escalate a gesture into a firefight, do you follow that?"

The lift had come down again. Another runner came down the corridor, heavier—out of breath when he got to the door.

"Sorry I'm—"

"You two," Hilfy said, "listen to me very soberly. I don't know what you've got going on personally, I don't care. Either you shake the stupidity out of your heads or you and I are going to blow the peace to bits, do you understand me? It's not just two young fools who're going to die if somebody doesn't get their wits together. We could be at war again, and several billion people could get killed. Is this more important than your personal business?"

"Yes, captain," Hallan said faintly.

"Yes," Fala said, ears up, scared, and not looking at *na* Hallan. "*Yes*, captain."

"That's good. That's just adequate. Can we ascend to flawless competency?" There was a beep from the board, the motion sensor on the airlock's closed hatch. The vid monitor showed two black-robed shadows coming down the access link toward the door, two doubtless armed kif. "Our escort's here. *Na* Hallan, the question, should you get the chance . . ."

"Yes, captain."

"Flatter the son. *Don't* embarrass him in front of his people. And find out what he knows about Atli-lyen-tlas."

"Is that the question, captain?"

"That's the question. What *he* knows, not where the stsho is. The second question, if we get one—there isn't one. There's nothing that isn't dangerous. Watch out for the words 'want' or 'need': a kifish *hakkikt* doesn't *need* anything; and don't push him: the odds are completely in his favor. Don't make him demonstrate it." She shepherded them out the door and settled the gun tight in its holster—no feeling in the universe like making a fast dive for cover and seeing your gun go spinning off across the floor. "Fala, you don't draw unless they do, and then don't waste shots on the hired help: shoot the highest rank target you can hit and run for the door. You *go for the door,* don't sightsee, that's all the instruction I can give you. Threat for threat, let them make the first move."

"Aye, captain."

"Gods-be right, 'Aye, captain.' *Follow orders.*"

Chapter Seventeen

The docks at Kefk had only sodium glare in the overheads, were all gray paint—kif didn't see color, at least not the way hani did; didn't see the yellow of warning signs, just the dark-light pattern; and on Kefk, it was only pattern that identified the conduits, and pattern that said walk here and not there. In all this gray and black universe, oddly tinted by the glare of apricot light, there arrived the color of hani, bronzed: Hilfy's trousers went a peculiar muted red; the spacer blues went a grayed blue; and rifle barrels and gunbelt metal on their five man escort acquired apricot highlights, while the matte graphite gray of kifish hands and kifish snouts, all that showed from beneath the robes, actually took on a livelier shade.

Do the kids credit, Hilfy thought, they didn't balk at their escort, they didn't sightsee or wrinkle their noses in disgust at the ammonia tang in the breath-frosting air; they paid attention to their surroundings, and Hilfy watched everything that passed in front of her and in the periphery of her vision, where neon signs lit a spacer's row no different than any services zone on any station trying to attract customers, except the words were kifish, and never ask what delicacies those establishments offered, and what entertainments they advertised. The neon signs were white, or the sickly color of kifish daylight; or they were neon red: *ask* what kifish vision responded to.

While all down the dockside, black-robed, weapons-bristling bystanders clustered in small groups and watched, talking behind their hands, talking with the turn of a shoulder.

Look at the fools, they might be saying.

They passed two berths where not a thing was going on; the ships might be in count, or, Hilfy thought, might be primed and ready to pull out on a second's notice; passed a third berth, where canisters were going in, but they were all the ship's-supply sort, with accesses for hoses and dispenser attachments; and just pulling up on a transport truck, cages of live animals, that squealed a thousand irate protests when a loader jolted them, and swarmed like a flow of ink up the sides of the fine mesh cage.

Akkhtish life, a kif had once said: as voracious and fast-breeding and nasty as a species had to be to have stayed alive on the kifish homeworld—the only species in the universe, in her opinion, that *deserved* the kif for predators.

"This way," the kif officer said, with a flourish of a hand from within the sleeve, and directed them to an access gate beside which a board burned with the kifish letters *Tiraskhti*.

Here we go, Hilfy thought, and climbed up the ramp in the lead, taking two kids into what could be a very, very bad situation. The kids would be the pressure point, if something went wrong. The kif understood the use of hostages, in some convolute way that had nothing to do with sentiment and maybe a lot to do with taking a valuable item and diminishing the *sfik* of the opposition by withholding it.

The airlock opened ahead, dimly lit. The ammonia stink inside was far stronger. But not improbably kif smelled hani presence just as strongly: as for the lighting, they hated the light of yellow suns, and disliked the noon even of their own. So the theorists held.

They occupied the lock, a tight, uneasy company, less the two that took up guard at the outside of the airlock; the lock cycled them through to a corridor, and more crew and personnel than a hani ship needed—met them there.

"Kkkkt," they said, that odd sound that betokened interest. Or a preface to attack—calm, she wished herself, thinking if she could get the youngsters through this corridor without incident they would be safer in wider spaces, out of the convenient, curious reach of a kifish claw. "Kkkt," ran like a wave beside their presence, as their escort shoved a way through the crowd, ahead of and beside them on their way through to the hall where a kifish dignitary entertained, and held court, and whatever other business the *hakkikt* had in mind.

That was where they came, through a door into a wide space ringed about with armed kif—she *knew* this place, or its exact likeness; and suffered a confusion of time, as if no years had intervened. There was the kifish prince, in silver-edged black; there was the same low table, with two chairs, there was the inevitable ring of witnesses about them, in light so dim a hani eye could not pick out the edges of shapes.

"You don't sit," she muttered to Fala and *na* Hallan, and walked as far as the table, seeing *here,* not the flashbacks on another ship, another place: no place to act spooked, she told herself, no place to get spooked: she had two kids to get out of here alive. The *hakkikt* had to score points, *had* to, now that she'd called his bluff all the way to this table, but he couldn't get everything without her cooperation, or he wouldn't have called her here.

She pulled a chair back, sat down across the round table from Vikktakkht, with Fala and Hallan behind her, and settled back in deliberate casualness.

Vikktakkht sat with one thin arm over the low back of his chair, his face shadowed within the silver-edged hood, except the snout—except the fine modeling of vein and muscle in what one could imagine was a very handsome, very fearsome type of his species.

"Kkkt. Captain. And Meras. Meras may sit with us."

"*Na* Hallan," she said without looking, and the boy carefully lowered his huge frame into the remaining empty chair.

"Meras," Vikktakkht said. "Ask your next question."

"Sir," Hallan said, in a quiet, respectful voice, and hesitated.

For the gods' sake, boy, Hilfy thought, *remember the question.*

"What do you know," Hallan asked, "about Atli-lyen-tlas?"

Kkkt, the murmur ran around the room. And Hallan, to his credit, didn't flinch.

"A broad question." The *hakkikt*'s arm lifted. A silver bracelet showed on a bare dark wrist, as he made a gesture about him. "I defer that answer for a moment—and offer another question."

Don't improvise, Hilfy thought. Boy. Don't try.

"May I ask a favor of you, sir?"

She hadn't expected that turn. She translated it frantically into kif, looked for ambiguities. The room murmured with startlement, seemed to hold its breath, and a few muttered, "K-k-k-kkkt," in a surly tone: *they* would not have dared that; and her heart was beating doubletime, her brain trying to figure what she could say.

But Vikktakkht made a casual motion of his hand. "Audacious. Make a request of me. If you amuse me, I may do it."

Hilfy stopped breathing, thinking, *Careful, na* Hallan. *Think*, boy.

Kif edged closer to them, listening, hissing at each other for room and silence. She felt Fala's presence closer at the back of her chair—dared not caution her, *hoped* the kid didn't shove back.

"I'd like you to understand, sir, I don't belong to Chanur. They weren't even at Meetpoint when I was arrested. They tried to get me back to my crew, that's all. So nothing I've done is their fault."

"Kkkt," broke out from a hundred throats, and died in hisses. Hilfy translated that one into kifish, running it down path after path of logic. "Offended" had too many ramifications to track.

"Kkkt," Vikktakkht said softly. "So, Meras? Is that your request? My understanding?"

While Hilfy thought: "Understand" doesn't mean "forgive." Boy, give it up. Stop there.

"If you're Pyanfar Chanur's friend, they need—they . . ."

Gods, boy, don't assign him a job in front of his followers. . . . "*Hakkikt*," she said, but Vikktakkht made a preemptive move of his hand.

"Meras?"

A silence. Then: "They think you can find the stsho," Hallan said.

"Is that your request?"

Yes! Hilfy thought. Gods, bail out, boy!

"Yes, sir."

"Isn't that two requests?"

"Then the second, sir. But I just wanted to clear that first up, in case that wasn't in your record."

"Kkkt." A motion of the hand. A servant hastened to put a cup in it. Vikktakkht didn't drink. Instead, a motion of the cup ending in their direction. "What motives, this hunger for responsibility? Is this a challenge? Is that the word?"

"No, sir. It is the word, but I'm not challenging you. At all, sir. It's my obligation to Chanur, to make clear—"

"He's saying—" Hilfy began desperately, and the preemptive hand moved sharply, then made a second gesture.

"Translate, Chanur. I recall you have some fluency."

"*Nakkot ahigekk. Sh'sstikakkt Chanur.*"

"Now he follows Chanur, you mean."

"Yes."

"And what does Chanur want?"

"*Nakkot shatik nik'ka Atli-lyen-tlas.*"

"Ah. And what opposes you? What do you suppose opposes you?"

"Paehisna-ma-to."

The long jaw lifted. The *hakkikt* stared at her down a long, dangerous nose.

"Kkkt. But the mahendo'sat *support* the *mekt-hakkikt.*"

She couldn't be wrong. She could *not* be wrong, and have followed the wrong ship. "Do they?"

"What does Hilfy Chanur think?"

"I didn't come here because I believed Ana-kehnandian."

"Kkkt. You came here because we have Atli-lyen-tlas."

"Do you?"

"Kkkt. Kkkt. The flat-toothed stsho face every breeze. They attempt to please Chanur. They launch an initiative in this direction, in that direction. *Gakkak.*"

"Herd creatures."

"Herd tactics. Exactly. They launch an initiative at Chanur's presence. They launch initiatives to mahendo'sat of rank. But the mahendo'sat are not *gakkak.* They go all directions. If you chase one, others escape, and another may join you. Thus, Paehisna-ma-to."

"Not a friend of Chanur."

"Not well-disposed to kif. Some say Hilfy Chanur is not well-disposed to kif. Some say—Hilfy Chanur would be the logical ally of Paehisna-ma-to. The logical successor to Pyanfar Chanur."

She drew in a slow, ammonia-tainted breath. "Where *is* the *mekt-hakkikt?*"

A vague move of the hand. "Where the *mekt-hakkikt* chooses. Recently at Meetpoint. As you know."

Assassins, after aunt Py? *Mahen* assassins?

"Who blew up Kshshti docks? Who fired shots at us?"

"What do you think?"

"There aren't any kifish dockworkers at Kshshti."

"As happens there are not."

"Difficult for you to get into a warehouse and steal a can."

"Not impossible."

"But why would you need to stop me? I'd agreed to go to Kefk."

"Hani have not always done as promised."

"The bomb would have heavily damaged us, without destroying the ship. And the sniper wasn't of your quality. While Kshshti wouldn't let a mahen hunter ship undock. Those ships have priority in any situation. Wouldn't you think they'd let them leave, if they let us leave?"

"But we are historic enemies."

"Kshshti put bureaucratic delays in a hunter ship's path. It more than suspected Ana-kehnandian. I haven't heard of this Paehisna-ma-to. So she's new. A rising power. Urtur—was cautious with Ana-kehnandian. Kshshti was *bravely* cautious . . . *nakkti skskiti.*"

"Kkkt." This time it was laughter, laughter that shook Vikktakkht's stillness, and rippled around the room. "*Nakkti skskiti.* That *is* Kshshti. A banner for all winds."

"I'm not. And I'm not such a fool I think kif think like hani. Or that a *hakkikt* of your stature, who wished to contact us, would make two attempts designed to scare us without killing us."

"Kkkt." A motion of Vikktakkht's hand. "You think we have no subtlety?"

"Blowing out a docking port on Kshshti?"

More laughter, that clicked and hissed all around the room.

"Salutation," Vikktakkht said, "from the *mekt-hakkikt.* Who assured me you would not be diverted by her rival."

By Paehisna-ma-to, he meant; and meant that Pyanfar leaned to the kif, to *kifish* support, which would always be loyal, while they feared the subordinates that feared *her*. . . .

She felt queasy at the stomach, having reasoned her way to that truth, having looked at it from all sides, and having decided that this *was* a place Pyanfar expected her mail delivered—however dark the paths Pyanfar traveled these days.

Maybe Paehisna-ma-to had reason, the thought came fluttering to the surface.

And drowned. Whoever had shot Chihin was not her friend. Whoever had killed innocent stsho and mahen security personnel was not her friend.

"And No'shto-shti-stlen?" she asked.

"An ally with enemies in Llyene. Hence *gtst* moved to form an alliance with the ambassador to Urtur, of a nature which you doubtless know and Ana-kehnandian does not."

"I don't know."

"You've not seen the object."

Caution held her tongue. Even with this so-named ally of Pyanfar's. "What would that tell me if I could?"

"The nature of the alliance. No'shto-shti-stlen's position within it, which of three."

"You mean sex?"

"An emblem of proposed gender."

She hoped she kept her mouth closed. Kif, fortunately, had no embarrassment in such matters.

"You have come here to present this to Atli-lyen-tlas. Is this not so?"

"Yes, *hakkikt.*"

"We have provided the ambassador such comforts as we found possible. But I think the ambassador would be far more comfortable on your ship."

"Possibly so, *hakkikt.*"

"*Sagikkt aku gtst!*"

Bring the stsho! the *hakkikt* said, and with no delay whatsoever a door opened, admitting the blinding spectrum of a paler sun. There was a moderate commotion in that quarter. Hilfy turned her head cautiously and saw, past Hallan's shoulder, kif moving within that light. A waft of perfume came out, and kif made soft sounds of disgust.

Then came the spindly outline of a stsho body, *gtst* gossamer robes backlit against the glare in her watering eyes. She was blind, as the stsho seemed to be, hesitatingly as *gtst* moved; so likewise the kif. Perhaps, she thought, it was eloquent of the condition within the Compact itself.

But the creature did not seem to get *gtst* equilibrium in the dark, and had to be guided by *gtst* kifish attendants. Something's wrong, Hilfy thought, rising from her chair. Something's vastly wrong with this stsho.

"Perhaps," Vikktakkht said, "your care will restore *gtst.* The practice of medicine is not a priority among our species. One argues for it. But medicine is still a secretive matter, practiced upon oneself. There is not, on this entire station, a medical facility, only a few supplies."

"I would first suggest," she said, she thought politely, "that *gtst* not be required to walk."

Not in time. *Gtst* collapsed. Fala made an instinctive move to assist and safeties went off guns all around the room. Fala froze. Hallan lurched for his feet.

"Hakkt!" Vikktakkht said sharply, that untranslatable word that meant something like Off guard, and safeties went back on, a more random clicking.

"And if you would tell your crew to go back on station power," Vikktakkht said, "station central control would be far more easy in its dealings."

"They're coming back," Tiar breathed, and only then realized the degree to which her nerves were wound, when she heard the advisement from *Tiraskhti* com, on aural-only.

"I'll trust it when they get into the airlock," Chihin said in her ear, on ops com; and Tarras: *"They're saying they've got* gtst *excellency!"*

"I'll believe *that* when I see it," Tiar said. And made up her mind she would start believing it when she heard from the captain's own pocket com, and when there didn't come any of the codewords for coercion that were in the Manual. She sat gnawing her mustaches to ragged ruin, and then got that thin, static-fractured advisement:

"This is Legacy One. You're going to see a transport truck pull up. Only bus this station runs. We're all right, we're coming home, we got our addressee, put on a pot of gfi, we could use it."

"That means it's really all right," Tarras said, the edge of excitement beginning to grow in her voice. And the Manual was on the bridge: they'd fed into com voice analysis every codeword that might come through. If Tarras said it was clear it was clear, and there was a next step.

"Chihin, get down to the lock, arm, don't open till they're on it, we don't trust it."

"I'm gone," Chihin said, and cleared her board to Tarras.

Everybody was all right. There was a little tremor in Tiar's hand as she reached to key aux monitoring over to her two low-level screens.

Everybody was all right. They'd gotten the stsho, *ker* Hilfy had pulled it off somehow and they could go to Meetpoint with Chanur honor intact.

Please the gods it didn't blow up in their faces.

But she didn't think she should advise *gtst* excellency yet, stsho being the easily worried creatures they were. She didn't think they should provide any good news until they knew there were no catches.

And even after the captain and the rest of them were secure in the airlock *she* wasn't going to be able to leave station. According to the Book, which had gotten them through it this far, the senior officer parked herself in the number one station, kept systems up, kept a close monitor on transmissions around them, whether or not they could decode them, the number of coded transmissions versus non-coded: and if anything surged out of recent parameters—

Then the senior officer was permitted to panic.

Gtst excellency Atli-lyen-tlas was not at all in good shape—half-dead, to Hilfy's eyes; and when the driver pulled up in front of the *Legacy*'s berth (most adamantly, she had insisted neither Hallan *nor* Fala drive) she called on *na* Hallan to vault down to the deck and stand ready to receive *gtst* excellency into his arms.

"She is a very large hani," *gtst* excellency was heard to mutter. "She will not drop us."

"She won't," Hilfy said, and *na* Hallan shut his mouth and reached up his hands. "She's a very competent person." At which *na* Hallan gave her a startled look, as if to ask did she possibly mean that.

But she had her hands full of fragile stsho at the moment, and together she and Fala lowered Atli-lyen-tlas into Hallan's arms.

"I have your honor," Hallan assured *gtst*.

Hilfy clapped Fala on the shoulder, and the two of them

jumped down. A whole squad of kif had turned up, with rifles evident, and that was worrisome, but their driver got out and waved a black-sleeved arm toward the ramp and the waiting kif.

"Essscort," the driver said. "The *hakkikt*'s. Sssafe."

It wasn't how she defined safe, but they walked and the kif didn't threaten them and didn't move, so she supposed there were no orders on the part of the *hakkikt* to try to rush the airlock. "Watch their hands," she said to Fala. "Rule of measured threat. You did just fine in there. Let's get home."

Fala didn't say anything but "Aye, captain." The kids were trying to be right. They walked past the kif, with the half-fainting stsho, and up the rampway. The access gate opened for them, which argued somebody was observing from where they'd been ordered to be, and possibly someone was waiting for them downside, which they were supposed to be. That gate shut, meaning, however fragile the tube that connected them to their ship, they were alone behind seal, and there was, one hoped, no kifish guard at their lock.

"Nobody behind us," Fala said, having actually cast a look back to see.

"Bravo, kid, you're learning." She punched in the pocket-com. "Tiar, Chihin, Tarras?"

"We're on it, captain, lock's about to open."

Upon which, it did, pale and inviting light.

Things happened, things happened on schedule and with checks, if the crew had had to do it with the manual in one hand and thumbing from page to page. She found her own anxiety like a spring slowly let go—as if somehow she didn't have to check up, she didn't have to *wonder* was anything unseen-to: things were getting checked, and when the airlock shut behind them, and the air was cycling, she could feel a queasy confidence someone was monitoring the situation outside, without her—to her giddy relief—having to think of everything at once and give the orders.

She by the gods resented it. Py scored a point, and she was

absolutely scowling when the airlock door opened and it was Chihin facing Fala and Hallan with a double armload of stsho.

"We need the gurney," she said shortly. "We need *gtst* excellency to the sickbay and we need the medical supplies, probably vitamin and mineral supplements—"

"A bath," *gtst* breathed, "oh, estimables, a bath, among first things, cleanly light, wai, the distress and the suffering I have endured—"

"*Gtst* shows improvement," Hilfy said dryly. "*Na* Hallan, never mind the gurney, just carry *gtst.*"

"Aye, captain," he said, and walked on.

"Tarras," Hilfy said, "to the dispensary."

"She's down there," Chihin said. "She's already setting up."

Good gods, initiative. Right decisions.

The *crew* knew what was going on, the *crew* all of a sudden knew it was their responsibility to move in advance of orders: it wasn't—it never had been that they didn't know what they were doing. Three of them had come in with experience.

The captain hadn't. And the old women had been right: Rhean had been right: she *hadn't* had the experience.

Mark another one for aunt Pyanfar. The crew wasn't unhappy, the *crew* suddenly had the latitude to do what it reasonably thought it ought to, the crew might be a little gods-be scared at the moment, but it was by the ever-living gods functioning ahead of the game for the first time in recent memory.

"I want a—"—thorough check against stsho parameters, she was about to say when she faced Tarras in the lab, but Tarras said to Hallan: "Put *gtst* excellency there, I've got the tests set up."

She could on the one hand feel superfluous. On the other she had enough on her hands—like getting the entire conversation down as she recalled it, like running it through the kifish translation program, looking for significances and omissions.

The captain wasn't strictly speaking a flight officer on this ship, but the captain with her head clear could make judgment calls that a protocol officer could make—and if there was a time to make them it was now.

Tell *gtst* excellency Tlisi-tlas-tin that *gtst* excellency Atli-lyen-tlas was lying disreputable in sickbay? Not yet. Not until they knew whether *gtst* excellency was going to live or die—or whether *gtst* excellency *was* still Atli-lyen-tlas.

Chapter Eighteen

There was a time one was superfluous, and Hallan had learned to know it. He hovered near the doorway while Tarras gave orders to Fala, and Fala gave him looks while she was carrying this and carrying that.

"I *do* like you," he contrived to say, when Fala's fetching and carrying paused her near him. "I really do, Fala, I just—"

Fala retrieved the kit she was after and went across the small surgery to where Tarras was ministering to *gtst* excellency with small and delicate needles, murmuring words of encouragement, assuring *gtst* that it was exactly what the computer had said to do.

Fala didn't want to talk to him. He didn't entirely blame her. He didn't feel welcome here, where people who knew what they were doing were trying to save the stsho gentleman's—or lady's—life. . . .

He found it more convenient to edge toward the door, and when no one seemed to notice that fact, to edge out it, and into the main lower corridor.

But ops was down there, and Chihin was working lowerdeck ops, and he didn't want to go down there; and did, desperately. . . .

Except it was too desperate and dangerous a situation to cause anybody more trouble than he had.

He wanted to apologize to Fala; and, really, truly, he wanted to patch it up: yes, he was attracted to Fala, at least she was pretty and she was clever and she was somebody he wanted very much to have like him, except it wasn't anything like the feeling he got when he even thought about Chihin.

Which told him it was the last place in the universe he needed to be when things were at a crisis and Chihin was supposed to be doing her job and there was a problem between them.

No business on a ship, the captain had said; and he didn't want to prove that by creating another problem for the captain. The crew lounge was where the captain had appointed him to go when she wanted him out of trouble and out of sight, and he went down the corridor as carefully as under fire, avoiding Chihin and avoiding any chance of running into the stsho, and got as far as the lift and rode it topside.

Then he could draw an easier breath. Then he could feel as if he wasn't in the way. And he soft-footed it as far as the corridor that led to the lounge.

But it equally well led to the galley and the bridge, too; and he wasn't forbidden to be there: he actually could do something useful; and Tiar was there, she'd been talking back and forth with them from some ops station and he didn't think it was downside.

Tiar was on his side, she'd always been friendly to him, she *hadn't* made his life difficult—Tiar understood what was going on.

He tended cautiously up the corridor in the direction of the bridge. The captain was in her office. The door was shut and the light was on the lock panel that meant she was there and the door wasn't locked, if you wanted to risk your neck. He didn't. He walked softly past and through the galley and onto the bridge where, sure enough, Tiar was sitting guard over the boards, with most of hers live and the screens showing the docks outside, and the station's scan-feed, and the station's docking-schema, and inputs he didn't recognize, but they were analytical, he thought, probably running system checks on the engines or something he wasn't familiar with.

He went and sat down very quietly in Fala's usual place, next on Tiar's right, the other side being the captain's place, where to save his life he wouldn't dare trespass.

She glanced at him, and looked back at the boards. So there was silence for some few moments.

"Can I help?" he asked softly, so as not to break her concentration.

"We're getting a little warm-up in a circuit. Not ops-critical, but we've put a load on us this trip. It's just symptomatic of a long run with very little sitting time."

"Dangerous?" Getting lost in hyperspace wasn't a thought he wanted even to entertain.

"No."

He was anxious, all the same. He was just generally scared, of a sudden, or it was easier to worry about a remote chance of breakdown in subspace than to worry about things that were definitely wrong, and he recognized that mental diversion for what it was. He'd nerved himself to walk in here, Tiar wanted to talk machinery, and now he'd lost his opening, which went something like . . .

"How's the stsho doing?" she asked.

"Pretty weak. Excited about being here. Glad to get into clean air. I don't blame him."

Tiar wrinkled her nose, a grimace. "It does sort of cling to you."

He hadn't washed. Nobody had had time below. And he was embarrassed. "I'm sorry. I didn't realize it was that bad."

"Not. Stay. I want to talk to you anyway."

Oh, gods. Everything was out of control.

"What did I do?" he asked.

Tiar's ears flicked, an impressive flicker of rings. "Nothing you did."

"Oh."

"What's the score with you and Fala and Chihin?"

The blood drained to his feet. His brains went with it. He

sat there a moment trying to think how not to offend anybody, or look like a thorough fool.

"Do you think Chihin likes me?"

Tiar tried very hard to keep a straight face. It wasn't quite, for a moment, and then she got it under control, quite deadpan. "I'd say it looked that way at Kshshti. Is she being a problem? Is that what's going on?"

"I—" Everybody wanted to blame Chihin. Everybody thought she was taking advantage. Which maybe ought to tell him that was the case.

Except he just didn't pick that up from her. He hadn't. He didn't, below, he had just made himself scarce, which he thought everybody appreciated, since they were busy and thinking about saving their lives, and following the captain's orders.

"You tell her back off," Tiar said. "There's no way she's going to vote for or against a berth on this ship for you on that basis. She's a bastard, but she's an honorable bastard—she just doesn't play the game like that. She's made Fala mad. But that's happened before. Mostly Fala's mad at Chihin playing games."

"You think so."

"Hey. You're not hard to look at, Fala's smitten, doesn't mean she's got proprietary rights. Tell *her* back off, if that's the way you feel. Then you can have her *and* Chihin annoyed at you for at least a week. They'll live."

It sounded like good advice. Except it sat on his heart like lead where it came to Chihin; and he wasn't used to talking back to people, not at home, not on the *Sun*. He just hadn't mastered the art of saying no.

Hadn't grown up before he'd left home. And maybe hadn't yet, he thought. In spite of banging his head on shipboard doorways, and sitting in the chair he was in with more of him than the chair was designed to hold.

He just felt awkward. At everything. And he didn't know if he could say that to Chihin. Or even Fala. In which case things could only get worse.

"You don't like that advice," Tiar said.

He didn't know what to say. He shrugged, knew he wasn't going to follow her advice, which was stupid, and maybe could lose him his place on board. But he couldn't do it.

"I'm not good at telling people no," he said.

"You want me to tell them?"

That was cowardly. And it would hurt Chihin's feelings, in a major way, he kept thinking that, even when everybody else told him Chihin was having a joke at his expense. And it would last until about the next time the two of them were in the same area of the ship.

"I like Chihin," he said. "And I don't think she's joking."

"She's *not* joking, if you mean is she serious," Tiar warned him bluntly. But Tiar wasn't stupid, and she seemed to catch on, then. "You *like* her."

He nodded.

Tiar raked a hand through her mane, sat back and stared at the boards a second as if she were dumbfounded.

"I don't think," he said, in the chance she hadn't just dismissed him, "I don't think she's acting the way everybody says she is. I just don't think that."

Tiar looked in his direction, and slowly swung her chair around. "I've known her a long time. I know her in ways Tarras and Fala don't. And if that's what you're picking up—next serious question: do you want a rescue?"

He shook his head; and Tiar looked oddly, vaguely satisfied. "You're sure."

He nodded; and Tiar frowned and seemed to have thoughts she wasn't saying.

Finally she did say: "You're gods-be young. You won't always understand her. But if you get to that side of her—good luck, you'll need it; and I'd like to see it happen. Just don't let her run over you. She needs a full stop now and again. Keeps her honest."

He sat there a moment, trying to sort through that, and deciding it meant he wasn't crazy and things were the way he thought, and things could *be* the way he hoped for—

"But Fala," he said.

"But Fala," Tiar said. "I'll talk to her."

"No!"

"She'll live. You don't dislike her."

"No. I *like* her fine, just not—"

"People have to respect that, in clans, on ships, doesn't matter: there's serious and there's not-serious, and Fala will forgive me saying she'd run the other way from a real commitment. That's what I think. I've been wrong before, but I don't think I am. If you want my further advice, I'd say Fala's more interested in feeling she's not unattractive to young men."

"Fala? She's *beautiful.*"

"Beautiful doesn't matter. She wants to be attractive. Doesn't everyone?"

"I understand."

"So you pretty well know how to handle it, don't you?"

He was just not used to things going right. Something in him was still knotted up expecting disaster, like maybe the ship would fall apart in hyperspace just when things were about to sort themselves out. The gods didn't intend he should get absolutely everything he wanted. The captain was going to throw him off the ship. Chihin was going to decide she didn't like him.

The kif were going to turn on them after all and all the ships around them were going to join in.

"I hope you're right," he said.

"Kid, you go follow your instincts—but don't present too much temptation to anybody till we get this ship out of this godsforsaken port in one piece."

"Yes, *ker* Tiar."

Besides, the stsho were down there. So he couldn't get to downside ops. He decided he should go clean up, and when he had showered, he was hungry. All of a sudden he had a ravenous appetite, when nothing had much appealed to him since before he was arrested on Meetpoint.

Even Kefk seemed wonderful to him of a sudden. He was grateful to Vikktakkht. He liked the stsho gentleman. He hoped the stsho would be all right and all of them would be happy. He liked everything and everyone around him, and he scrubbed the galley down and set up the meals for undocking, and did everything he could think of to do, the way everyone else aboard was seeing to every detail they could find. . . .

He was absolutely happy. In this port, with kif all around them, and with the ship feeling the strain of a lot of quick turnarounds. Because when Chihin came topside and off duty he could talk to her.

And beyond that prospect he couldn't get his thoughts straight at all.

Gtst was clean, at least. *Gtst* looked very feeble.

Wants to talk to you, Tarras had said, although in Hilfy's opinion Atli-lyen-tlas could do with a few hours of sleep and a minimum of excitement before they even talked about business or arranged what could become a very stressful meeting.

"Your excellency," Hilfy said. "I have the honor to introduce myself: Hilfy Chanur, captain of *Chanur's Legacy*. How may I make your excellency welcome aboard? I apologize for the utilitarian nature of this present accommodation. . . ."

"Most, most gracious." The voice was very faint. "You are more fluent than any hani I ever met."

"I was protocol officer and communications on *The Pride*. Please make requests of us for your comfort or information. I shall answer everything to your satisfaction, and not ask but one question myself, in order not to exhaust your excellency's strength at this moment. Please feel that you may be very direct and brief in your answer as we know your energy is limited. Were you fleeing us, with the kif? Please be assured we mean your excellency only help."

"Do you know of Paehisna-ma-to?"

"I have met one of her agents."

"This vile person . . ." A pause for breath. "This tasteless individual has committed violence against my staff at Urtur."

"Some of your staff left aboard a mahen ship."

"They dared not . . . dared not the darksomeness of a kifish vessel. I am greatly apprehensive for their lives and persons. The mahendo'sat are in fear of the Momentum."

Numa'sho: it was in the mahen psyche that a new force that suffered no setbacks had something—mystic about it; they were loath to fight against what had never been beaten.

"Paehisna-ma-to has met reverses. Her agents have resorted to extreme measures which may cause fear in some governments, but which have met brave resistance from the Personages of Urtur and Kshshti. And we have eluded their efforts to divert us."

"This is excellent news," *gtst* whispered. "Most excellent news, as my staff relied on these individuals regarding the selection of transportation. Please accept my profound gratitude that you followed where few hani venture. The kif made small efforts at hospitality, and they would have conveyed me on to Meetpoint, but I should have perished by then. The long, long flight . . . the food . . . I cannot describe . . ."

"We will place your excellency in tasteful surroundings and delay in this port until your excellency is able to travel."

"Has No'shto-shti-stlen sent you? Is your ship the bearer of the *oji?*"

"Yes. I hope that this is a felicitous event for your excellency. Please advise me if otherwise."

A weak hand fluttered and fell. "*I* am otherwise. I shall make all effort to accept. But I fear that I have fled too far and lost too much."

"Your excellency will recover!"

"It is indelicate to say. Forgive me. Persons of my stage in life have lost all energies in such regard. I am *gtsta.*"

Neuter?

Perhaps she let the dismay show. No'shto-shti-stlen sent a . . . whatever it was . . . and the object of *gtst* proposal was—

"*Gtsta,*" Atli-lyen-tlas said faintly. "I am incapable of accepting the inestimable distinction which *gtst* excellency of Meetpoint wished to convey. This—iiii—rarely changes."

"I should not wish to distress your excellency further. Please advise me where a hani might be ignorant, but be aware I view this as a personal matter of most extreme delicacy, and ask only for your excellency's welfare: Is there medical treatment which might avail?"

"Most excellent hani, it is age. To attempt to sustain the energies will take years from my life, yet I am motivated to do so. Paehisna-ma-to has conspired within stsho space itself to create disaffections and hesitations, which have threatened *gtst* excellency of Meetpoint, whom I most ardently have admired. I overestimated my endurance. I underestimated the persistence of the agents of Paehisna-ma-to. I can only hope to find the strength."

"Your excellency, *gtst* excellency of Meetpoint has sent a representative, one Tlisi-tlas-tin, as custodian of the Preciousness and arbiter of propriety. The Preciousness rests within *gtst* cabin and in such tasteful surroundings as we could best create."

"Take me there! I must see the Preciousness. Please assist me!"

She was apprehensive. She had visions of fragile bones breaking in the mere attempt to walk, of a stsho circulatory system failing in the effort.

But the will to live was important too. She looked at Tarras, who hovered in the neighboring surgery, ostensibly taking inventory, but watching. Tarras walked to the small screened area and Fala turned up with her.

"*Gtst* excellency wants to go to Tlisi-tlas-tin," she said. "I think it's important. Can *gtst* do it?"

"I don't know," Tarras said. "I don't know what I'm doing, but following the book. I . . . just don't know. We can see."

"Try," she said, and Tarras and Fala came in and helped *gtst* to *gtst* feet, very gently, very carefully. There was no other transport but a gurney, which would undoubtedly offend *gtst* dignity. And calling down *na* Hallan . . . *gtst* excellency Tlisi-tlas-tin would surely advise Atli-lyen-tlas that *na* Hallan was not an unusually tall crewwoman.

Which might be too much for *gtst* heart, or the system that passed for one.

* * *

The lift engaged, upward bound. And it might be the captain coming back topside, or it might be Tarras or Fala; but Hallan, polishing the chromalic of the galley to a fine gloss, paid attention, paid heart and mind and hope of finding it was Chihin.

And maybe it was the way the whole day had been going—it was. *Ker* Chihin came wandering onto the bridge by the outside corridor saying to Tiar something about a rest break, could she monitor downside ops; and Tiar saying—he eavesdropped shamelessly—that that was all right, everything was quiet, there wasn't a need for her down there, and why didn't she get a sandwich or something and take a break and then relieve her?

Ker Tiar knew he was topside, *ker* Tiar knew he was here, oh, gods, he wasn't quite ready to think and talk . . .

But Chihin walked in, did this little flick of the ears as a hello and looked into the fridge.

"Can I make you something?" Hallan asked in a small voice.

"I thought you weren't speaking."

"I don't—I didn't—I never meant you should think that."

"Oh?" Chihin said.

He was totally desperate. He said, "*Ker* Chihin, were you joking or not?"

"No," she said plainly. "Not really."

"I wasn't," he said.

Chihin's ears did a back and forth and finally didn't know where to settle.

His didn't.

"I really like you," he said desperately. "I really do."

He'd rather have faced his father with that intimacy. And that was the most dangerous hani he personally knew.

Hilfy pressed the button, signaled her presence, said, to the intercom: "*Your* excellency, I have the honor to present *gtst* excellency Atli-lyen-tlas of Urtur, would you kindly cause the door to be opened?"

There was silence.

"*Your* excellency?"

Gods *rot* the son.

She pressed the button.

On a nestful of pillows and cushions, covered with a sheet, which showed—

One preferred not to think.

"What is *this?*" asked Atli-lyen-tlas.

There was movement beneath the sheet. She had given, she was sure, adequate time for whatever was going on decently to cease.

But Dlimas-lyi's head popped up. *Gtsto* went wide-eyed; and *gtst* head popped up beside, in a blossoming eruption of pillows.

While Atli-lyen-tlas fell back into Tarras' arms, murmuring, "Oh, the beauty, wai, the elegance of this appearance. . . ."

She found no elegance. But *gtsta* breathed, "This is my offspring. This is my offspring. I have no further to see, I have no further to know. Wai, what ambition have you? Wai, the magnificence of this nest you have made!"

While Dlimas-lyi and Tlisi-tlas-tin scrambled up clutching the sheet about *gtst*selves and floundering among the pillows.

"Atli-lyen-tlas!" *gtst* said, and *gtsto* bowed profoundly, again and again. Hilfy stood ready to catch Atli-lyen-tlas should *gtsta* fall. But *gtst* excellency of Urtur seemed to draw strength from the encounter:

"Do not take distress of my presence," Atli-lyen-tlas said. "How is my offspring now known?"

"Dlimas-lyi," *gtsto* whispered, "may it add distinction to your excellency."

"I have resigned Urtur," Atli-lyen-tlas said. "And I have no more attachment to this time."

"You are *gtsta!*"

"Just so. Nor need distress my serenity with what is beyond my reach. The *oji* is not for me now. This person Dlimas-lyi is not for me. I am free."

"Your holiness," Tlisi-tlas-tin whispered. "Please utter assurances of your good favor in our condition."

"I do so. Please," Atli-lyen-tlas said, reaching a trembling hand toward Hilfy. "Please convey me to a place where I may rest. My course is clear now. I am without obligation of any tasteful sort and would not struggle to achieve more. I am completed."

Try *that* one through the translation program, Hilfy thought in dismay. There were things which one did not ask a stsho. Sex was right in the same class as Phasing. *Gtst* excellency and Dlimas-lyi stood naked as they were born and she now had a holiness of some kind on her hands, an aged stsho, resigned, retired, unmarriageable and sexless; and *therefore* not eligible to receive the Preciousness.

Gods save them.

"We will find your holiness suitable and tasteful quarters immediately adjacent. It will take a time to prepare. Is this acceptable?"

"We should be very honored," said Tlisi-tlas-tin.

"Most profoundly," said Dlimas-lyi, "we beg your holiness to do so."

A flutter of fingers. "I am beyond needs. But yes, this would be pleasant. I have no cares. Free. All free."

Whereupon *gtsta* indicated *gtsta* would walk back in the direction from which *gtsta* had come. Tarras and Fala offered tentative support; but *gtsta* said,

"I am free of needs."

Fall on his holy rump, Hilfy thought distressedly. But whatever reserve of strength Atli-lyen-tlas had found, still held. *Gtsta* fingers had been burning hot when they had touched hers. *Something* metabolic was going on, whether healthy or not—the stsho medical diagnosis program would have to tell them that one.

Gtsta walked ahead of them, wandering a little in *gtsta* steps, taking time to examine the texture of the walls of the corridor, the wall-com at the corner, *gtsta* fingered dials and button sockets *gtsta* had no claws to access, or there would have been loud-hail all over the ship, providing a most unwelcome and tasteless startlement to *gtsta*self.

Holiness seemed to have a direct and negative effect on the

brain, Hilfy decided. And on the tendency to push buttons and take walks, and the holiness' door was going to be *locked*, the minute they had *gtsta* inside.

"Guard *gtsta*," she muttered to Tarras and Fala. "Keep *gtsta* away from buttons and sharp objects."

"What do we do if *gtsta* wants something?" Tarras asked. "What's wrong with *gtsta?* What's going on?"

Tarras and Fala hadn't followed a word of it. One forgot.

"That's a holiness," she said. "Don't ask me whether *gtsta* is Phasing or what. I don't know. And I've read every gods-be book on the species."

"Nobody knows?" Fala asked.

"Nobody but the stsho," she said. "And they've refused to talk."

"I . . . you know." Hallan didn't feel he was doing well. Chihin just kept watching him, the two of them standing in the galley, Chihin leaning back against the counter, himself with nowhere reasonable to put his hands. "I just . . . well, I didn't know what you thought." He didn't want to say that Chihin's own best friends had warned him: that wasn't kind. "I just wasn't sure you were really meaning what I thought you meant, so I didn't want to talk to you until I could sort of figure out . . ."

"Same," Chihin said. "You want to go back to the quarters? Sort it out where we don't have to be proper?"

"I—" He was going to hyperventilate. He wanted to take the invitation and he was unaccountably scared to, because it would change things, and change them all of a sudden and too fast. "I—"

"Don't trust me?"

He thought about what Tiar had said. That he wouldn't always understand her. But, Do you want a rescue? Tiar had asked; and he'd said no.

"All—" he began.

"Chihin. Report downside. Pull the white paneling out of storage—move it, we're on short schedule."

Chihin scowled and said a word.

"I was going to say all right," he said desperately.

But the captain said hurry and Chihin left.

"Hallan. Report downside. We need some equipment moved. Be extremely quiet. Remember the passengers."

If he ran he might make the lift.

The hakkikt *Vikktakkht an Nikkatu to captain Hilfy Chanur, the hani merchant* Chanur's Legacy, *at dock at Kefk, by courier: Has the stsho survived in any useful way? Ships arriving from Meetpoint say that the stsho of Llyene are creating sedition and division. We must soon deal blood upon the leaders of this movement. Give us an estimated time of departure.*

The hani ship Chanur's Legacy, *to the* hakkikt *Vikktakkht an Nikkatu, of* Tiraskhti, *at dock at Kefk: We are making modifications necessary for the transport of this person. We are finding more rapid recovery than we had thought. What is a holiness? We lack reference.*

The hakkikt *Vikktakkht an Nikkatu by courier to captain Hilfy Chanur, the hani merchant* Chanur's Legacy, *at dock at Kefk: A stsho incapable of the reproductive act. A holiness has no ability to make the alliance on which our mutual ally has placed all* gtst *expectation. The agents of the rival Personage will immediately take advantage and by information lately come to us, have already moved against the* mekt-hakkikt. *Advise us of your departure and we will delight to accompany you. Peace is advantageous. We will eat the hearts and eyes of the enemy.*

. . . it shall be the reasonable obligation of the party accepting the contract to ascertain whether the person stipulated to in Subsection 3 Section 1 shall exist in Subsequent or in Consequent or in Postconsequent, however this clause shall in no wise be deemed to invalidate the claim of the person stipulated

to in Subsection 3 Section 1 or 2, or in any clause thereunto appended, except if it shall be determined by the party accepting the contract to pertain to a person or Subsequent or Consequent identified and stipulated to by the provisions of Section 5 . . .

Hilfy tapped a claw on the desk, glared at the monitor, and asked the library: *Atli-lyen-tlas who is the recipient has become a holiness. What is the result to the terms of the contract?*

It took an entire cup of gfi for the computer to run that request through translations, permutations, legal definitions, Compact law, stsho custom references, and the cursed subclauses.

Then it said: *Answer to print? File? Both?*

File, she said, having learned.

The answer, when it came up, said briefly: *The person accepting the contract must designate a second recipient who exists as the nearest degree of consequence to the first named recipient; if, on the other hand, the party issuing this contract disapproves this recipient, the person accepting the contract is obligated to double indemnity and the return of the cargo.*

Hilfy stared at it and stared at it, then got up and blazed a direct path down to *gtst* excellency's white, expensive nest, signaled her presence and opened the door without waiting—there being little of Tlisi-tlas-tin or Dlimas-lyi she hadn't seen.

"Your excellency, forgive a most hasty but necessary declaration! You must become the recipient!"

A tousled crest and wide moonstone eyes appeared from beneath the sheet.

"Of course," said Tlisi-tlas-tin. "Of course. Was this not understood?"

It was white. It was clean. There was carpet over the deck tiles and they'd contrived a plastic frame and some bent struts to improvise a stsho bed; they'd *made* a mattress out of plastic sheeting Chihin said she hoped to the gods didn't give way, but it held air, and it held water, and when they'd covered it in white drapery it would at least protect the old stsho, Hallan was sure it would. He crawled backward out of the pit with utmost care not to put a claw out and create a disaster.

Chihin gave him a hand on the escape, and sprawled, sitting, with a swipe of stiffened paint on her sore arm and plaster bits in her mane. She leaned against him, he leaned, they were all over with spatters and the way she looked at him, brow to brow and a little out of focus, said she was as tired and sore as he was.

And they had one thought, both, in that moment, it didn't take that much reading—his went something like a dread and an anxiousness to find out, and a fear of getting into what took time to discover and being called up short.

She said, "There's the downside shower. We can clean up, catch a snack . . ."

She wasn't young and rushing at things. He had that figured now, it wasn't on again, off again signals, it was just a sane sense of how things worked; and he didn't know where they could go to figure out the rest of it, but he tried to slow down his breathless haste and use his wits the way Chihin did and tell himself if they got involved in *this* room and didn't report in, the captain was going to ship them to the kif. . . .

"Wonder if the mattress works," Chihin said. But he thought he could read her now, when she was serious, when she was being outrageous.

"I don't want to walk from Kefk," he said; and he must have guessed right, because she put her arms on his shoulders then and laughed and got up.

"Shower," she said, and left him with his burning haste to be a fool, a sense things could always go wrong from here, there might not be another chance . . . Chihin could come to her senses and decide something else, or they could die and chances might not come again.

"Tiar," she said, talking to the intercom. "Tiar, we're about finished. Give us a chance to get our objectionable selves out of the passenger corridor and you can ferry the old fellow in. . . ."

"Thank the gods. Captain says get up here, we're in count, we're just about to clear the umbilicals."

Chihin's ears went flat. "In *count!* Gods *rot,* what kind of schedule does the captain think we're up to? We got a dying stsho, we got us so tired we can't see straight . . . what in a mahen hell *in gods-be count. . . .*"

The thump and clang was the umbilical bundle coming clear. Chihin was upset, besides mad. She stopped arguing, cut off the com, and looked at him, and he didn't know what help to be, but that Chihin was worried, worried him about this departure they were making, the haste they were in.

"Are we running from the kif?" he asked.

"From dead stop at dock?" She put her arms around him a moment. Stupid question, he thought. Totally stupid question, but he'd thought the situation might be more complicated than that. Maybe it was and she knew and wouldn't tell him, they never told you anything . . . it's not your business, boy, we'll take care of it, don't worry yourself . . .

He was scared of jump this time. He was really scared. "There were tc'a," he said. He could only be twice the fool. "In jump. When the alarm went off. I saw them go right through the ship and nobody was moving and I hit the alarm. In my dream, I did. And it was going off when we came out. I know it's stupid," he said, when she stood back to look at him in a worried way; and it was more disturbing that she didn't laugh, didn't offer the immediately obvious: You were dreaming, stupid kid.

"Nobody was moving," she said.

"In my dream."

"Chur dreams like that."

Chur Anify. On *The Pride.* Chur the map-maker. Chur, that they said could walk through hyperspace and see what kif saw and maybe knnn and tc'a . . .

He didn't believe that. People exaggerated, especially the world-bound ones who didn't know the limitations. You didn't expect it out of Chihin, who was Chur's cousin, if you reckoned it.

"What did you do?"

"I just got up and reached over and hit the alarm. But maybe it went off itself and I just dreamed—"

Chihin was looking at him in all seriousness, maybe thinking she didn't want to be associated with somebody that crazy.

"It's my fault, about the tc'a," he said. "Maybe that was why I dreamed it."

"Kid. If you punch any more buttons on my board you by the gods be sure what you're touching."

"Most adequate," *gtsta* pronounced, walking on strange bare feet onto the carpet they hadn't used in the decoration next door. Gods-be *right*, adequate, Hilfy thought, while the seconds ticked down in the count, and bare stsho toes curled into the white pile. "Most curious, the sensation."

"We assure you *gtst* excellency and *gtst* companion are next door," Hilfy said, while Fala and Tarras hovered near to prevent falls. "I must caution your holiness to watch your st—"

—on the rim, she had been about to say, but *gtsta* put a bare foot on the edge of the improvised bowl-chair, and Tarras made a futile grab as *gtsta* slid down the plastic foot-pad, plump! to what was surely multiple fractures.

Gtsta sprawled and bounced, a tangle of legs and gossamer. *Gtsta* trilled some note that did not seem of pain and, flailing *gtsta* arms, made another bounce that made the whole mattress quiver.

And a third, while three very time-pressed hani hovered at the edge and tried to assess the damage.

Another bounce, and a quivering like jelly. Is *gtsta* able to get up? Hilfy wondered. But *gtsta* seemed not to be distressed. Crackpot idea, she thought, a bagful of water. But if it didn't pop and drown the old son during acceleration, *gtsta* had a chance. A water-filled bowl-chair . . . and all the essential nutrients they'd been able to pump into *gtsta* fragile veins.

"Pull the nets over," she said. *Gtsta* had already had the medication, Tarras had seen to that, and it seemed to be taking effect. *Gtsta* lay flat on the ripples and rebounds, waving a languid arm, *gtsta* mouth pursed and *gtsta* eyes half-open, while Tarras and Fala hauled the safety netting over the pit and made it fast with cord.

"Blessing," *gtsta* holiness said. "Well wishes. I see the tides of the many suns. I see the oneness of them. I shall tell you their names. . . ."

The tranquilizer definitely was taking hold. And she for one had rather rely on the navigational computer.

Chihin was saying Meras might be a sleepwalker, that the kid was spooked and seeing tc'a, and that *that* had been the alarm during system drop. They had a clearance from the kif for undock and a schedule they'd agreed to in a star system the kif were clearly touchy about protecting; and, gods save them, they had a Preciousness and a handful of stsho to get to Meetpoint alive to back up No'shto-shti-stlen against the allies of Paehisna-ma-to,—*if* the old son could live through the experience.

They had a contract to declare filled; and get out of there alive and solvent—because they'd been out nearly a year as stationers counted time, and Tahaisimandi Ana-kehnandian had routed himself straight to Meetpoint out of Kshshti, three months ago—as Meetpoint counted time.

"*Gtsta* has *gtsta* nutrient packs, *gtsta* is comfortable . . ." Hilfy began; and *gtsta* murmured, "The oneness of it all. The ineffable contentment, after the darkness of my voyage. The light, go to the friendly light, for the sake of the peace. . . ."

Pretty gods-be out, Hilfy thought, and squatted down and looked through the net to be certain *gtsta* nutrients pack was still wrapped about *gtsta* frail arm. For the sick and the frail one didn't depend on the strength to hunt for it: it would feed continually, or as continually as anything happened in hyperspace.

Ask the kid, Chihin said, and was spooked, herself. They had one in the family. And she'd watched Chur go thin and otherly and sometimes as sensible as *gtsta,* when she was tracking something. What do you see? was the logical question.

And gods save them, she recalled with a chill down her back, Chur had talked about the light and the tides. . . .

They were underway, launched, outbound, so fast there was no time to wipe the dust off; and Chihin sat by him at her post, grinned at him, with a twitch of a white-smudged ear.

"I probably ought to tell the captain," Hallan said, not happily.

"I did," Chihin said. "It's all right. It's all right. . . ."

"That's *Tiraskhti,*" Fala said. "They're away."

"Salutations to the *hakkikt,*" the captain said. "Send it."

Fala did that. He heard the lisped kifish. "The *hakkikt* says," Fala reported back, " '*hold your exact course.*' '*Ssakkukkta sa khutturkht.*' —Is that right?"

"That son's going to jump with us, I knew it. Tell him we copy. Gods-rotted payback for our dock at Kefk."

Surely not for that, Hallan thought. It was dangerous. Even kif cared about their own lives.

"Tarras, Tarras, do you copy?" That was Tiar talking to Tarras, who was down below doing something the captain had sent her after. "You're clear to move."

"*Aye,*" the answer came back, and in a moment more the lift worked and opened; and Tarras came stringing hand-line, clipping it into recessed rings along the way. So they could move if they had to, Hallan thought, without *g* or against acceleration. It wasn't something the *Sun* had ever done. It was a scary contemplation. And when Tarras got into her station, the captain ordered the arms board brought up to ready.

"*Na* Hallan?" the captain said, startling him, and he was ready for the usual Be careful and keep your hands off things.

"*Na* Hallan, config to scan, Chihin, take a stand-down and trank out, I want you on-line when we come out."

"Aye, captain," Chihin said, and Hallan punched the requisite buttons to bring the aux board over to scan, his hands wanting to shake quite embarrassingly.

"Good night," Chihin said to him. "Good luck."

Panic quickened his breathing. No, not panic, healthy respect for his responsibility. Just a monitor-the-dots problem. But Chihin wasn't going to be there if anything went wrong this side.

"I'm here," Tarras said at his other elbow. "Take it easy, do your job, kid. You shouldn't get any input the computer doesn't recognize."

But in another minute or so a dot leaped on to his screen, at Kefk Station rim. His heart jumped. Chihin swore—but she'd just taken the drug. "That's number 10 berth," he read off his screen, trying to stay calm. "*Mu—Muk-jukt,* captain."

"Friendly to the *hakkikt* or what?" Fala wondered aloud.

"Ask the *hakkikt,*" the captain said; and Fala did; and said, "He says, quote, he knows. . . ."

Meanwhile another kif left the station. He reported it and he didn't push buttons.

"Gods-be kif show-outs," the captain muttered at one point. "They've got to see, they've got to be there, they'll cut Vikktakkht's throat if this goes wrong. His and ours."

You mean they're not taking orders? Hallan wondered to himself. It wasn't any hani way of doing things.

"Up *v,*" the captain said. "Let's just put a little more push on it. They've got the pillows, below." They hadn't taken on cargo. They hadn't had the time. Or they hadn't trusted it.

They were just going, and Chihin murmured, drowsily, "Wake me if you see any pretty lights, kid. Otherwise, see you otherside."

Another one and another one. Fala said, "*Na* Hallan, I forgive you."

"What did I do?" he asked, surprised out of his concentration, and between reports. Lines were converging. They were going, gods, they were going . . .

"Stand by," Tiar said sharply. "This isn't the standard drop, cousins. Let's not miss a stitch. . . ."

. . . "Well, well," aunt Pyanfar said, arms folded, feet set, the very image of herself, "you've committed yourself to the kif, have you?"

Hilfy was not surprised at the appearance. She was surprised at herself, that questions leaped into her head, Have I done the right thing? Am I a total fool, aunt Py? . . . not angry, not resentful, not any of those things, just wishing she *could* ask across space and warped time . . . ask the real Pyanfar, not the one that came and went in her mind . . .

Like what was going on at Kefk, that kif kept Pyanfar's doings behind a screen, a whole unguessed power that wasn't just *The Pride*, wasn't just one ship and a well-reputed hani who mediated the Compact's trade and treaty disputes . . .

Like: aunt Pyanfar, what have you gotten yourself into? Who *are* you, since you threw me out, downworld?

The *mekt-hakkikt*, indeed, the leader the kif could never find to unite them; the Personage of the mahendo'sat, with whatever religious mandate that conveyed—until some rival like Paehisna-ma-to came along; the President of the Amphictiony of Anuurn, no gray-nosed, doddering grandmother to quibble about two thousand year old privilege or ceremonial inheritance; that was not what was based at Kefk.

They were committed. They were beyond recall but not beyond disaster.

"Good luck," Tully said, remote from her. And she had too much on her mind, too much on her hands, to play those games of make-believe. He'd been right to walk away. He wasn't the property of some teen-aged child: it wasn't Tully's obligation to set her life in order, or to provide her some strange halfway creature to be, instead of hani: Take care of Chanur, Pyanfar had said, shoving her out of their midst, and wrapping time and black space about herself.

Who *are* you, aunt Pyanfar?

And what are you doing, in deep space, where the methane-breathers go?

Humans live in that direction. They don't come to trade. They might have; but they insisted we take sides in their war—thank you, we have enough trouble, aunt Pyanfar had said, and drawn a firm line, verbally at least.

But perhaps it was more substantial than one guessed; and vaster and more needful—

—of force? Of hunter ships at Kefk? Of spies and assassinations of hapless stsho and bombs on Kshshti dock?

. . . "Coming down," she heard Tiar say.

So they were there. Over the edge. In it up to their ears.

The song wavered, there and not there and there again. It seemed he'd heard it for a very long time; and he'd been anxious entering jump, but it was only the dream of a guilty conscience . . .

He only heard them now. And it wasn't a threatening song, just very different.

He tried to watch the screens, but they were garble. The ship was riding the fabric of space-time, skittering along the interface, to fall into the next dimple, that only a stellar mass could make, and he could see that interface going on and on and skirling anti-mass along the disturbance they were.

Maybe it was only, after all, a dream. . . .

"Going down," he heard Tiar say . . .

He tried to capture it. The moment of dropping out of the interface. But a vast disturbance sheeted down around them, and he heard tc'a voices, or what passed for it . . .

. . . Heard a machine-voice saying: "Proximity alert, proximity alert."

"Around us!" he tried to say, his eyes full of vision and dark, but Chihin said calmly, "Got it, got it, aux; Tiar, the system buoy's gone nuts and we got a heavy surplus on hunter ships out here. . . ."

"I saw ships," he said, "ten, twenty—off in the dark—"

"Dark of where?" the captain snapped. "This side, that side, where?"

"Otherside," he said, but he knew he was wrong, the ships were here, around them, arriving one after the other.

Chapter Nineteen

Twenty sleek kifish hunters, suddenly another one dropping in—and never, under these circumstances, believe all that the system buoy schema showed you, Hilfy thought, seeing what unfurled itself on her flanks. It wasn't a position she'd ever hoped or wanted to be in—center position in a fleet of kif, aimed at Meetpoint . . . a Meetpoint the station buoy showed busy with shipping: hani ships, stsho ships, mahen traders, kif, and tc'a and chi, as ordinary as she'd ever seen it, and deader emissions-wise than she'd ever heard it.

"Fala," she said, "all channels input. Stats. Percent. Who's who. It's too quiet for what they're showing."

"Aye," Fala said. Stats be feathered, the number of contacts flickering through com told her it was way down. And not due to the kifish presence: they were an hour out from station, light. The station had an hour yet to wait before Meetpoint learned they were here, and what was here with them and what maneuvers they were performing. An hour before station could react. But not before something might react that was lying silent and closer.

"Arms live," she said to Tarras, heard the acknowledgment, saw another set of lights come on her own board. They were now breaking the law. Several laws. Lane violations, safety violations, the disarmament treaty, the Station Immunity Act . . .

"Captain," *na* Hallan said faintly. "When you've a moment."

"Query, aux one?"

"I've got something. I recorded it—I think I did . . ."

Frightened neo. He didn't know how to give a report or switch images. Tiar had her hands full. "Fala," she said, "advise station we're inbound for dock and take the feed from Hallan."

It popped over from Fala's number one: matrix-com, raw transcript.

Chanur	*advise*	*Paehisna-ma-to*	*mistake*	*No'shto-shti-stlen*
Hilfy	*you*	*kill*	*violent*	*right*
all	*wrong*	*not-law*	*bring*	*choice*
stations	*death*	*ambassador*	*now*	*change*
listen	*kif*	*stsho*	*on*	*Meetpoint*
kif	*now*	*is*	*all*	*governor*
tc'a	*know*	*guilty*	*party*	. . .

Chanur advises Paehisna-ma-to ((she is) mistaken (about?)) (of the error of?) No'shto-shti-stlen. Hilfy, killing a violent (person) will be right. All unlawful wrong (deeds) bring choice/change. Stations (because of) death of the ambassador now are changing. Listen, kif, to the stsho on Meetpoint. Kif, now the governor is falling. The tc'a know the guilty party (incomplete statement.)

Killing a violent person will be right? Aunt Pyanfar?

"What is it?" Tiar asked. "What's she talking about?"

"Gods-be thing's in kifish records too. They sleepwalk, most of them. —Give me the *hakkikt!*"

"Aye," Fala said, and the click and hiss of kifish communications came through strongly in her earpiece.

"Nakgoth na sti!" she said. "Hilfy Chanur nak, nakgoth na sti, hakkikt-tak skkhta."

"The tc'a are most difficult to persuade to lie," the voice came back, cultured and fluent. *"In fact, they can't."*

"Hakkikt, with profoundest regard to your wisdom, this isn't Pyanfar. This isn't right!"

"Right?" Vikktakkht asked. *"What is 'right?' Tell us 'right,' Chanur captain. We are Pyanfar's allies. Has there been cause for her to change sides in this?"*

Kif would. On a puff of contrary wind. Intellectually Vikktakkht knew that hani were otherwise. In his gut, in a chancy situation, he might not. "Give me a moment," she said, looked desperately at the screen, and made a reach and unbelted, dizzy as she was. She snagged the nutrient pack beside her chair, bit a hole in it and got a swallow down as she was getting up.

"Captain?" Fala said. "We've got a station message."

"You can't have a station message. We're time-lagged." Another swallow.

"It says—"

"It's a gods-be lie-in-wait. Transmitted to our call number from the buoy. They know who we are. They've prepped the buoy with a false system schema. What do they say?"

"It's—" Fala half turned, as she hand-over-handed her way to Fala's station, where the translator main keys were. "They're saying . . . in the name of the stsho government . . ."

. . . and the han *and the hani you are required to dock immediately and open to inspection. You are in violation of Compact Treaty and will be subject to severe criminal penalties if you do not obey instructions. We will accept a single ship in approach with weapons deactivated.*

The ship Chanur's Legacy *is cleared for lane 1280. Acknowledge.*

"We're getting the system detail," Tiar said. "What now, captain?"

"We're getting their word what's in this system, that's what we're getting. Chihin, look alive, Hallan, we're on live-scan only, don't believe a thing station images tell you. Fala, give me the raw data on the tc'a."

"It matches—"

"I don't care what it matches, I want to see it, now!"

The kid was rattled. She shouldn't have yelled. Fala made a false start on the order and a second one and got it.

Chanur	*998*	*Paehisna-ma-to*	*86-786*	*No'shto-shti-stlen*
586	*8*	*798-897-22*	*46*	*567*
6	*57*	*868-897-22*	*1872*	*98*
9-9	*786*	*7*	*6-75*	*299-786t*
96	*76*	*10-69*	*7657*	*40y8*
786	*8=999*	*8/659*	*6-976*	*6-7/0*
5/8	*98*	*768-./768/865*	*6868/5*	*. . .*

"It's not tc'a."

"How isn't it tc'a?" Fala protested, and Hilfy reached past her, punched up the rough again.

"It's not tc'a, I've just seen too many of them. You don't get that many unknowns in the transcript. It's driving the translator crazy. —Tiar, course change to that lane and transmit compliance."

"Captain," Tarras said, and Chihin nearly on top of that.

"I know. Did I say we were going? —Where did this gods-be thing come from? *Na* Hallan? Did you capture this transmission?"

"I—heard them. I think it's what I heard. They were with us . . . I could hear them. But I couldn't see them, captain."

"Couldn't see them. 'Couldn't *see* them' doesn't explain this output. Something odd's going on with it. You can't get a capture this clear out of hyperspace."

"Mechanical?" Fala asked. "Could it be a patch-together? Something the buoy's sending us?"

The kid was using her head again. Somebody using some complicated equipment might have assembled it out of other tc'a transmissions, and rigged the buoy to send it to their specific ship ID when they dropped in. But she wasn't that sure it was an answer. The *Legacy* made a gentle burn and she caught at the chair back and the hand-line. "Look sharp, all stations. Don't gawk. They've given us a lane down which they'll be lying in wait, friends, let's not get caught by it. Tarras, missile up."

"Aye," came the flat acknowledgment.

"Fala, vertical sort. Read it down."

<table>
<tr><td>Chanur</td><td>Hilfy</td><td>all</td><td>stations</td><td>listen</td><td>kif</td><td>tc'a</td></tr>
<tr><td>Advise</td><td>you</td><td>wrong</td><td>death</td><td>kif</td><td>now</td><td>know</td></tr>
<tr><td>Paehisna-ma-to</td><td>kill</td><td>not-law</td><td>ambassador</td><td>stsho</td><td>is</td><td>guilty</td></tr>
<tr><td>mistake</td><td>violent</td><td>bring</td><td>now</td><td>on</td><td>all</td><td>party</td></tr>
<tr><td>No'shto-shti-stlen</td><td>right</td><td>choice</td><td>change</td><td>Meet-point</td><td>governor.</td><td></td></tr>
</table>

Chanur to all stations; listen to the kif and the tc'a. (I?) advise you of the wrongful death (because) kif now know Paehisna-ma-to is guilty of murder of the stsho ambassador. Mistake now will bring violence on all parties. No'shto-shti-stlen makes the right choice to change the governor (on) Meetpoint . . .

"Third sort. Diagonal on the left."

Gods-rotted matrix brains.

"Aye, captain."

No'shto-shti-stlen: mistake right. Paehisna-ma-to violent choice. Advise killing brings change. Chanur you not-law now Meetpoint. All death ambassador on governor. Stations kif stsho all ? listen now is party. . . .

"Garbage. It's not tc'a. *Hani* translator, idiomatic, vertical pass."

"Captain." That from Hallan, quietly.

"Chain of command. Chain of command, Meras."

Chanur to all stations: listen to the kif and the tc'a. They will advise you the death was murder. The kif now have proof that Paehisna-ma-to is guilty of the murder of the stsho ambassadorial personnel. A false move now will loose violent behaviors on all fronts. No'shto-shti-stlen made the right choice when he decided to bring in a new governor.

"It *is* aunt Py. Gods rot her, why in a mahen hell did she set up a hash like that? Broadcast *that* translation to the kif. Broadcast it system-wide. And watch it! That's not going to make certain individuals happy—" Meanwhile they were inbound on 1280 with an ambush of some kind set for them, no question. And *na* Hallan was sitting there with something bursting to say, for which she had no present time. "Fala, get me the *hakkikt* again. And find out if our passengers are in one piece."

She oozed back to her chair, fell into it as the earpiece sputtered kifish.

"Nak."

"Chanur nak. Pakkaktu hastakkht. 1280 lakau."

A soft kifish laughter. "Tc'a? Mau lkkto mekt-hakkikta."

Put nothing past her.

She broke off transmission for a second. "Fala, are the stsho alive down there?"

"Not happy," Fala said. "Alive. Scared. The two in cabin 2. I'm trying to raise the holiness. I'm getting sounds, I can't swear to else."

She switched *Tiraskhti*-com in. "We're going in there," she said in the Trade. "I'm calling station, advising them we're going in alone. They don't frighten us." They did, but you didn't explain that to a kifish ally. You didn't stand back here and trade ultimatums with hair-triggered kif and mahendo'sat and hope to avoid escalations.

Though wherever the trap was, their scan hadn't bounced off anything out there. And the kif hadn't seen anything they were telling about.

"Captain," Chihin said, "*na* Hallan thinks there're more ships out there."

"Where? Vector, Hallan."

"Up," came the faint answer. "They were *there*, captain."

"Tc'a?"

"I heard them. I could hear them over the com. I heard *something.*"

Gods-be spookiness. Chur was spook enough. When you had a neo wandering around in jump, the gods knew what you got. More ships? Messages at the buoy?

The buoy was the intersection, the place where ships dropped toward the local sun. The buoy recorded presences, and hadn't recorded anything but them and the kif.

Nothing, at least, that that buoy was programmed to confess to the *Legacy* and its kifish companions.

But would aunt Py set up a message that ambiguous?

"More of her gods-be mail," she muttered. "Filtered through a tc'a brain. They've dived down like a fish breaching. They're *up* there."

"*Hovering* in hyperspace?" Tiar said.

"You can't do that," Hilfy said. "You can't change vector in hyperspace, either."

But knnn did it.

"I'd hate to pay their fuel load," Tarras said.

Tc'a did take on fuel, in realspace. Tc'a did pay bills, like the rest of them. There were surely constraints of physics on what they did in hyperspace. But one had to remember that ships didn't entirely *enter* hyperspace, didn't leave the interface, please the gods they didn't . . .

"Message to station," Hilfy said, "we have tc'a ships in the vicinity. A navigational caution is in order."

Let the mahendo'sat hunter ships lurking out there worry about that one. Tc'a didn't obey lane restrictions. Not on Kshshti docks. Not in the regulated space around a station.

And the gods knew, you didn't shoot at one. Never shoot at anything, aunt Py had used to say, that you can't talk to.

"Let's get us a little more *v*, Tiar, full 1 *g* sustained."

Sustained 1 *g* push, and one hoped the stsho aboard had taken advice and remained in their beds. Things tended to go rapidly to the aft bulkhead under these circumstances.

"Kkkt," came over her earpiece. *"This amuses. We are going with you, Chanur."*

You didn't tell a kifish *hakkikt* mind his own business, either. Thank the gods it was only *Tiraskhti* that moved. And she'd never thought she'd live to say it, but that sleek hunter moving with them was a welcome sight.

And all those kif out there . . . if anything happened to the *hakkikt,* there would be a twenty-way sort-out after the leadership of that fleet. Station surely knew that. Station surely knew that it would be very dangerous to deprive the kif of a leader, if it didn't want a firefight in its territory.

But one had to ask oneself why station was staying silent—besides the fact it didn't yet know, and wouldn't, for some few minutes, that they had a kif inbound.

She punched the intercom. "How are you both faring, excellency?"

"Wai," came the breathless answer. *"Wai, the dreadfulness of ships! We are most uncomfortable! I fear for the holiness! I fear for the Preciousness! I fear for our lives!"*

"We're going to cease acceleration, your excellency, in just a few moments.—Tiar, establish with *Tiraskhti* helm, we don't want to surprise them, just stay in link with their pilot.—Fala, I'll take your board, get downside, see if *gtsta* needs attention. —Go inertial, Tiar, at your discretion."

"Stand by."

The weight that had been pushing them slantwise into their cushions became ordinary, regular orientation revised up and down. "I'm going," Fala said; and Hilfy keyed over to basic com functions on her own board. "Station, this is *Chanur's Legacy,* inbound on your instructions. Inform *gtst* excellency No'shto-shti-stlen that we return delighted with our success in *gtst* instructions."

That was stshoshi. *That* for the representatives of the *han,* who would not bother to learn the language of their trading partners.

But after the due round-trip time-lapse, mahendi came back:

"You stay lane, Chanur ship. Same ask kif ship Tiraskhti. *Stay lane. Legal matter here. No gun."*

A crackle of kifish followed, with no time-lag: *Tiraskhti. "In the name of the* mekt-hakkikt, *we will follow the treaty and we will enforce the treaty.* Parau'a mekt-hakkikta rassurrn na uunfaura, uunfaura sassurrn ma . . ."

Hani, by the gods.

And from below-decks: *"Captain,* gtsta *is saying something about tc'a and the sun and* ker *Pyanfar. Something like the stars speaking with one voice . . ."* She could hear the babble from elsewhere, something about star-drives and resonances and talking with the fields . . . *"Otherwise* gtsta *looks all right. Should I release the netting?"*

"No!" She amended that more quietly. "Tell *gtsta* where we are, tell *gtsta* the situation, tell *gtsta* it's a safety measure, and get your agile young bones up here as fast as you can."

There still wasn't a guarantee there wouldn't be shooting; but the opposition would have to be crazier than the holiness. The opposition had Meetpoint. The opposition had the Treaty and the Compact itself to hold hostage—because if the opposition didn't start shooting, the opposition held Meetpoint, and Momentum continued on the side of Paehisna-ma-to; while if *they* started shooting, the *mekt-hakkikt's* own side would have broken the Treaty. And it all came unraveled from there—even if they had the force to take Meetpoint without damage, which, with a mahen fleet hidden out there—they didn't have.

Not a nice situation, she said to herself. Not at all a nice situation, Hilfy Chanur. *Why* did you take the gods-be contract?

"Berth 22, Legacy," station deigned to say.

"Are we going to take their computer input?" Tiar asked.

"No," Hilfy said. "What's one more law? You and Chihin, just figure us in. We'll take their 22. They'll probably have guards. Lots of guards."

"Kif?" Tarras wondered.

"I'll bet you they aren't. I'll bet there was a reason old

No'shto-shti-stlen had *gtst*self nose-deep in kif. And I'll bet there were casualties. On the other hand—"

"On the other hand."

"On the other hand, stsho aren't prone to commit themselves until it's absolutely safe. So cancel the last bet. There may not have been. There may not have been a shot fired here. It's not the *han's* style. Or Llyene's. Leave that to Paehisna-ma-to. Well, well—"

She was playing with the optics. Scan wasn't showing the ambush, which in Meetpoint's sparse system didn't leave many points of cover—like keeping the station between them and the opposition, hence the lane assignment; like keeping some of them lying off in the system fringes, like between their ships and system exit, to nadir of the star.

But ships in dock caught the wan sunlight quite nicely, besides all those working-lamps and warning-lights that kept outside tenders and pushers from going splat! into a station structural part or a ship at dock. Optics was a major function on her board; and she had already been watching and capturing images.

"Ah. There's *Ha'domaren*. . . . Not out there where he could get hurt, not our Haisi."

"Gods rot him," said Tiar.

"Couple of kif we don't know. Tc'a ship shows up as a seen-before, at Urtur."

"My heart won't take the surprise," Tiar said.

"Oh, here's one. *Ehrran's Honor*."

"Ehrran!"

"We do have a *han* presence here, friends. Can we assume it's that faction which hates us with a passion? We have Paehisna-ma-to's pet hunter captain. We have assorted mahendo'sat, we have—*Padur's Victory*."

"Blast them if they're in on this!"

"Could be coincidence. They were coming this way, for probably honest reasons. But I'd *sure* like to know who was at Hoas while we were at Urtur."

"What about the *Sun?*" Hallan asked.

"I wish I could tell you not." But there it was, in evidence between two other hani ships, *Nai's Splendor*, and *Doran's Golden Hope. Sahern's Sun Ascendant,* plain to see. "*Lslil-lyest,* a good clutch of stsho ships, none of which I know, none of which library knows, which indicates they're not traders, they're from deep inside stsho space . . . do I guess, the capital at Llyene, if they've set No'shto-shti-stlen aside?"

"Politics," Tiar said. "Gods, there's something three days dead here."

"We could get out of here," Chihin said. "We could tell the kif we've had our closer look, goodbye, good luck."

"They'll outlaw us. They'll have their evidence, a cargo not delivered, right on the books. Chanur will lose this ship, Chanur will lose Momentum with the mahendo'sat."

"Better free-running than clipped at dock."

"It's one thing to say, cousin."

"We're not giving up!"

"Oh, no, no, no, Chihin."

"What are we going to do?" Tiar asked.

"I don't exactly know. Neither do they. They can try their writs and their papers. Those don't make many holes in the hull. And they'll talk to us. Talk is what they're here for. They're here to prove a case against us."

"It's a trap," Hallan said. "If the *Sun*'s with them, it's a trap—they're going to file some complaint, captain."

"Good lad, good thinking. Gods-be right they are."

"I don't want to get you in trouble."

She had to laugh. Probably to Hallan Meras it wasn't funny.

"They're not getting him back," Chihin said.

"Just run the calc," she said. "First thing is not to hit the station. Then we'll worry about Sahern clan. They're a minor problem."

"It's not a minor problem," Chihin said.

"Say he's not going to Sahern. It's one thing for *me* to throw him off. No gods-be Sahern is taking him. Two plus two, cousin, let me handle the legal work, you have your hands full and I don't want to make a mistake here. Fala, you want to make another run belowdecks?"

"Aye, captain, I will."

"I'd say we have another half hour. Get down there, there's some shifting about I want done. You *may* have to do takehold down there. Have something in mind."

"Aye, captain."

Nervy kid. It was a dangerous thing, moving about in approach. Things could happen. But the stray cargo pusher that happened into the *Legacy*'s path was going to be out of luck.

"Captain," Tarras said, "I'm still holding that missile live."

"That's where you're to hold it."

"Just confirming," Tarras said. "Thank you."

Calc was shaping up. Fala called up for instructions. Station called to protest they were out of calibration, check their computers.

"Oh, we're not using your feed," Hilfy delighted to say. "Since you can't prove you're authorized. We'll just guess our way in."

"*You damn fool!*" Meetpoint Control screamed.

"How are we doing, Tiar?"

"Oh, maybe five, ten percent one way or the other. Who knows?"

"*You lose your license!*"

"Hope we're good, Meetpoint. Or give us No'shto-shti-stlen."

"Not can do! Not can do! Brake!"

"*Have Paehisna-ma-to's adherents so little nerve?*" Vikktakkht cut in over com. "*We, on the other hand, are braking. And our weapons remain live.*"

Credit to the *hakkikt,* not one word about the missile they had armed, which with his systems he most probably knew about.

"Thank you, *hakkikt.*"

"*You stop, you stop, I call superior!*"

"Like give us access to No'shto-shti-stlen?"

"*You stop, I try!*"

"Are we calc'ed, Tiar?"

"We're steady on."

"Sorry, Meetpoint. Not in the mood now. Maybe we'll take that missile off-line. Maybe not."

"You bluff!"

"Oh, yes, sometimes. Not all the time." She shut off that com-link. "Shut it down, Tarras."

"Gray hairs," Chihin muttered, "forty of 'em."

"Just put us in soft," she said.

Hallan's mouth was moving. Reading numbers or committing himself to the gods, Hilfy thought. And punched in the take-hold.

"You damn fool break five hundred law!"

"He's hysterical," Hilfy said, accidentally into a live mike. "Take care of that, Tiar." And cut the contact. "Your excellency, I report a safe dock. You may move about now. Felicitations on your excellency's return to Meetpoint. We are now attempting to make contact with *gtst* excellency the governor, but mahendo'sat have occupied station offices. . . ."

"Wai!"

"We believe by the number of stsho ships here at dock who are not traders that some treachery is contemplated. There are han officials who have historical antipathy toward Chanur; there are mahendo'sat including Ana-kehnandian; but the ship of his excellency the *hakkikt* Vikktakkht is holding position off the station with the threat of weapons and of the Treaty and of the displeasure of the *mekt-hakkikt.* As to *gtst* excellency No'shto-shti-stlen, these outrageous persons are withholding contact with *gtst* excellency. We are in fear for *gtst* safety at this moment, or wonder if your excellency might have a word with these individuals."

"I shall execrate them."

"Please prepare to do so. I am putting your intercom in direct radio contact with Meetpoint communications. For obvious reasons we are not accepting the umbilicals, most particularly the com lines."

"We are prepared."

"You are in contact," she said, and pushed the button and eavesdropped, chin on fist.

"Outrageous and shameless behavior," was the opener, at a pitch that made the indicators spike. While on a wavelength belonging to hani official business: "Chanur's Legacy, *put me in contact with Hilfy Chanur."*

"You are there," Hilfy answered. "Good day. Is this Ehrran clan?"

"Insolence will not improve your case with the han! *You are personally and as a crew charged with piracy, kidnapping, rape, and murder; you are as a head of clan charged with treason, sedition, violation of Treaty law, . . ."*

"Speeding. You forgot speeding and irregular docking procedure, Ehrran. This is a political show and we both know it. Gods, is there a dirty business this side of Ajir you don't have your hand in?"

"I demand to speak to Hallan Meras. On behalf of Meras clan and Sahern."

That was bound to come. Hallan threw her a desperate look, Chihin looked like thunder.

Hilfy punched the transmit again. "Demand what you like, Ehrran. Chanur doesn't permit it."

Captain, Hallan was saying soundlessly. She shook her head.

"Do I have that for the record, Chanur?"

"Absolutely you do, Errhan."

"Captain," Hallan said distressedly.

"You're married. Shut up."

"I'm—"—married, the jaw said.

"As of about half an hour ago. Signed by a stsho official, a stsho holiness, an impartial witness and me as captain of this ship. Congratulations and don't disgrace us."

"Who—?" Hallan shut up again. The Eyes of the *Han* was reading more charges on com.

"Better be me," Chihin said darkly.

"First listed," Hilfy said. "Excuse us we didn't ask preferences. You were calculating approach and I thought they'd pull this."

"But," Hallan said. Before Chihin shut him up. Ehrran was repeating some question. She just transmitted the document in facsimile. And the one charging Sahern with desertion, abandonment, public insult, public indecency, malicious suit, and nine infractions of the common law of Compact space.

"And I'm adding conspiracy and defamation under the law of the Amphictiony; and conspiracy to commit breach of the Peace under Treaty law, Ehrran, against the captain and crew of *Sahern's Star Ascendant.* If she wants to go to court, by the gods, I have names and dates logged."

Strange the silence that followed that. The contact broke off. Somebody was consulting somebody.

She punched in on the conversation on the other channel. Indicators were still hitting high levels.

Let it run, she thought, and shoved back to give her legs a stretch. "I think we'll stand down a while. Put us on alarm, Chihin. Put the recording on. Go clean up . . . do whatever takes your fancy. Good luck, *na* Hallan, congratulations, welcome to the clan, we'll give you the formal party when we get out of this."

There was a general clearing out. She didn't ask to where. She sat down again, and started reviewing the messages that they weren't admitting receiving.

Not everyone had left. She saw the shadow in a dead monitor, looked back at Tiar over her shoulder.

"Need any help?"

"Might."

"The *han*'s not through yet."

"The *han*'s not through yet and Paehisna-ma-to hasn't even started."

"The bribes have to be flying. Paehisna-ma-to to the stsho, to the kif off-station, the kif on-station . . ."

"The *hakkikt* has been loyal to aunt Py for a long time."

"Some of them could be getting restive. Including the *hakkikt.*"

"I have thought of that."

"They say you can buy anything at Meetpoint."

"Except certain things. I'd say maybe the Preciousness isn't on the open market. Maybe a holiness isn't. The stsho are fragile people. They'd never take a chance that wasn't forced on them. They're hanging back now, I'm betting on it, trying to see where advantage lies."

"Politicians."

"Not all bad, politicians. The stsho are good at it. They'd have been a mouthful for somebody long since if they weren't. And if they weren't a prime source of goods; and if they hadn't ties with the methane folk."

"The tc'a business? That was extremely odd."

"It was very extremely odd. Py sent that in symbol-set. The tc'a that received it didn't read it in the ordinary way. It thought the sentences were separate-brain paths. It interpreted them that way and just nearly got us all in trouble."

"You think she's near here?"

She considered that answer a long moment. Then: "No. I don't. I think she knows what's going on but she can't get here in time."

"You can't transmit in hyperspace!"

"You can't change vector and you can't transmit. Correction. *We* can't."

Tiar made a rumbling in her throat and shook her head. "If you could do that—"

"—to blazes with the futures market, the whole way we trade? Yes to that, too. Aunt took a big chance getting that message here. Possibly Vikktakkht knows. Possibly it surprised him. Possibly he won't rush to the nearest gathering of kif and tell what he just heard. I have the feeling it scared hell out of him."

"Keep the fear in him?"

"Certainly it shook him. Certainly it made him think. Certainly we've got one ally out there that's got something new to think about. That's why I'm inclined to make a bet that we've got a little leeway with Vikktakkht. And I may do something I wouldn't dare, if *gtst* excellency can't find *gtst* excellency very soon now."

"What's that?"

"Surrender our stsho passengers."

"They are reprehensible individuals!" *gtst* excellency cried, waving *gtst* arms. "They are covered in shame and perfidy!"

"Your excellency could not then discover the whereabouts of No'shto-shti-stlen? Or is it tasteful for me to ask—"

"Your honor has every attribute of taste! Your honor is the only whiteness in a thousand worlds, wai! the treachery, wai! the reckless and shameless behavior of individuals who were born with better advantage!"

"What is the condition of No'shto-shti-stlen?"

"Dire. *Gtst* bravely holds *gtst* post. But *gtst* confides to me that *gtst* despairs. The influence of Paehisna-ma-to has reached even to Llyene, and the capital has lost confidence in *gtst* excellency, the capital has sent out other persons to displace *gtst* that may be more pleasing to Paehisna-ma-to."

"And not pleasing to the *mekt-hakkikt?*"

"One can hardly please both, as *gtst* excellency foresaw. I must take the Preciousness, I must advance onto the station, I must show these emissaries that I am disdainful of them and their gross displays of foreign force, these—"

Gtst ran out of breath and subsided onto the pillows, while Dlimas-lyi tried with gentle touches to calm *gtst.*

"I shall go with *gtst,*" Dlimas-lyi looked up to say. "I shall not permit *gtst* alone to venture among strangers."

"*Your* excellency," Hilfy said in all honesty, "your tastefulness and good qualities make me admire you exceedingly. You are the most excellent of stsho."

"You are likewise the most excellent of hani," Tlisi-tlas-tin declared, reaching up a thin, white hand. "I value your estimation."

Was it possible a hani could grow fond of *gtst* excellency? She thought so, quite profoundly fond of the fellow *and gtst* nestmate.

She knelt down, to bring herself eye to eye with *gtst* excellency, who gazed at her with no lowering of lashes or nodding away.

"Your excellency, may I ask the most extreme trust? The most reckless trust? And perhaps something of great delicacy?"

"Ask."

"May I—em—transport the Preciousness elsewhere for perhaps an hour or two? May I do things in your name which I may try to perform tastefully, but which, if I fail, will attach only to me and my ignorance? In no wise would I risk your excellencies' honor or your reputations."

Eyes lowered, hands fluttered. "You ask a most dire favor!"

"I am—aware of the nature of the Preciousness, and I will treat the Preciousness as if it were my own honor in question."

It seemed *gtst* excellency might faint or Phase, so great was *gtst* agitation. Then *gtst* seized her hand with all *gtst* slight strength.

"*Gtsta* might handle the Preciousness! In this fashion would our honor be kept!"

"Most resourceful of stsho!" she said, and leaped up in a thoroughly tasteless haste, on her way to the door before she remembered a courteous bow.

"Wai, go!" *gtst* excellency cried, waving *gtst* gossamer sleeve. "Go, at all necessary speed, dear hani, and work necessary disarrangements upon our enemies!"

Chapter Twenty

For a while there was just no thinking, even about hazards around them. It helped that Chihin was crazy; or as crazy as he was, with everything that had happened, and it helped that the other four of his wives *didn't* insist on conjugal privileges. . . .

But for a while one's brain just shorted out, and then wouldn't work, and when common sense finally came back, the two of them seemed to find it together.

"I think—" Hallan tried to say.

"Yeah," Chihin breathed.

"I think maybe we better get back. . . ."

"I think so too," Chihin said, and started getting up, so he did. He thought, We could be killed. We could all be arrested. What kind of fools are we, acting like this?

But Chihin looked at him and he straightway lost his good sense again, until she made a face and swore and shoved him out the door, where the air was colder and clearer and the ship-sounds in the corridor reminded anybody with a brain at all that there were urgent operations going on.

They went to the bridge but only Tiar was there. Tiar twitched an ear back to take in their presence, Chihin flung herself into station and punched buttons—he settled into his chair more carefully, and didn't.

"What's up?" Chihin asked.

"Captain's downside, talking to the mahendo'sat."

"What, talking to the mahendo'sat? What have we got to say to the mahendo'sat? Blow their—"

"That's what they're doing," Tiar said. "Fala's got ops lowerdeck, Tarras is with the captain, and, well, we know where you two were."

"Don't give me that! What in a mahen hell's going on?"

"Main ops channel," Tiar said.

"Well, well, now we got make deal." Haisi stood, arms folded, on the dockside, at the bottom of the *Legacy*'s ramp, and blew smoke into the frosty air. "You give *oji*, we give you clear undock, go home, safe, no trouble . . . small difficulty with kif, same we fix."

"Fix like you fixed things at Kshshti."

"Not us, hani, you got bad information. You got real close experience with kif. You forget?"

"No. But it doesn't matter to the bottom line."

"What matter?" Another puff of smoke, green and blue against the neon of some shop along the Rows. "What make matter? You in one damn bad mess, hani. You look bad, Pyanfar Chanur look bad. You got find way out . . . because if that kif out there attack this station, who bring same here? If you start shoot, who got trouble? You got."

"You say. Looks to me like we're both here."

"Wrong." With hand on large expanse of dark-furred chest. "We here with invi-tation stsho government. We got word maybe kif problem, stsho from Llyene ask us come in here, toss out kif guard on account of no good deal No'shto-shti-stlen make with marry Atli-lyen-tlas. Atli-lyen-tlas got too many 'sociations with kif. Llyene government have got embarrass' by No'shto-shti-stlen, official come here, examine record, got prepare replace *gtst*, maybe severe repri-mand. Meanwhile here come kif. Damn right here come kif. Want old job back. Want commit little piracy, a? You been number one suckered, hani."

She laid her ears back. "If you're so friendly with the stsho, how come you had to come ask *me* about the *oji*. How come that? A?"

"You know stsho. Three sex. *Gtst* do politic, *gtste* and *gtsto* very private, do sex, no public. No'shto-shti-stlen and Atli-lyen-tlas both *gtst*. So somebody got to step down from politic. Stsho at Llyene don't like Atli-lyen-tlas, long time want *gtst* come back stsho space, long time No'shto-shti-stlen protect same, now want marry *gtst*. So what sex No'shto-shti-stlen be? *Gtst* propose same in the *oji*. Maybe if No'shto-shti-stlen stay *gtst*, stsho at Llyene not upset enough come here make new government. But stupid hani won't answer question, so they come. They say you give them the *oji*, all fine."

"So where are they?"

"They watch. I promise same. Not worry."

"Where's No'shto-shti-stlen?"

"With stsho. We not touch. I tell you, you give *oji*, everybody go away happy. 'Cept maybe kif. You no worry. We fix kif."

"Vikktakkht's a friend of my aunt."

A laugh. A long draw at the smoke-stick and a slow exhale. "Vikktakkht kif. Nobody friend. Don't got word, 'friend.' Just 'advantage.' Just stab in you back when you no more scare him. Why he not come in station, a? He wait. Let stupid hani fight the mahe. Tell you what. You give *oji*, stsho at Llyene happy, we happy, no problem."

"I don't *give* anything, mahe. I'm not a charity. I got it, I keep it. Maybe I take it to my aunt."

"Make big mess. Meanwhile you got go out there tell kif sorry you make mistake. You look real bad, hani. You look like dessert. Maybe like hos-tage, a? Kif go make deal Pyanfar, hey, you want? You pay. You got experience that game."

Trying to shake her nerve, he was. She wrinkled her nose, not a friendly gesture. Or a patient one. "Maybe I get along with them just fine."

"Then you two time fool. You got chance win big here. Pyanfar got lot commitment No'shto-shti-stlen. *You* make new deal, be friend new gov'ment, all fine, easy new gov'ment be friend Pyanfar. You big important. Lot good deal for you."

She stared at him, thought about the directions power would run in the Compact, asked herself what was in it for Paehisna-ma-to, and came up with: "doublecross." Not quite a coup for Paehisna-ma-to, but no prosecution for the explosion at Kshshti, they'd blame that one on the kif; no absolute gain of power but no stop to the Momentum of Paehisna-ma-to either. Net gain, no loss, No'shto-shti-stlen out of the way, net gain there, too, putting Meetpoint in the hands of someone more attuned to other voices.

Gods, she did hate politics. And hated worse being suckered.

But if Haisi tossed off a kifish strike force of twenty hunter ships as a "we fix," Haisi had a lot of firepower out there hidden in the system—

"So?" Haisi asked her. "You want be logical? No good, the *oji,* got no value 'cept to stsho. Chanur don't want lose face. We don't want lose face. 'Specially Vikktakkht don't want lose face: what you got do is make him look good, make him go 'way."

So maybe there *wasn't* such a large mahen force. And Haisi was one good negotiator.

"You want me to tell him to go away, huh? You worried?"

A quick frown. Haisi snatched the smoke-stick from his mouth to jab it in her direction. "You want peace? You not want? That are whole question. You not just stupid hani captain, you *Chanur.* You got youself in politic, all right, you play smart. You only damn one can get that kif go 'way now. You only one can save Vikktakkht *sfik* so he don't get throat cut by own follower. Kif damn fragile, all time damn fragile. You got save him, or we got fight. I *rather* not fight. I rather not have this kif sit point gun at Meetpoint. Lot nervous people here."

Maybe Haisi was saying the same about himself—he was in a bind, a serious one. He wanted a way out.

So she'd done him damage. She had that.

"I have to give him something," she said. "I have to bring him in on the negotiations. I have to be there. This has to save face for everybody. You understand me?"

Haisi looked relieved. "Number one fine. You got million credit deal. You walk away clear. What more want?"

"No, no, no, it doesn't work that way. We've got to talk to the stsho. We've got to have a slice of this, so does Vikktakkht."

"What you want? You dumb hani captain, no make gov'ment."

"I'm Chanur, mahe. You've been using that, that's the game you've been playing, and I demand to have something out of this that's going to satisfy that kif out there, that's going to satisfy our honor, and not have any trouble with our papers, our cargoes, or the Personage's affairs. I have an obligation to her friends. I have a contractual obligation to No'shto-shti-stlen. That's *gtst* property. I can't just hand it over. I've got, for that matter, an obligation to that kif out there, who's played tolerably fair with me. So you've got what you want here, you haven't got what I have, you're not secure until you've got it, and you'd better damn well settle with our honor, and our claims, and our—pardon me—finance, because anything else is going to be expensive to the stsho and to this station, which *isn't* going to make the stsho damn happy with you, a?"

"So what you got have?"

"In trade? First off, not to have that stsho contract hanging over my head. I've got to have trade agreements with the new government, including trade agreements for Vikktakkht's interests. I've got to have Chanur's friends out of here: we're not leaving any hostages in anybody's hands."

"What friend you talk about?"

"No'shto-shti-stlen."

"No, no, no good deal."

"What no good deal? What threat is *gtst* to anybody if he's not the governor?"

A few rapid puffs of smoke. The whole dockside was unnaturally silent. "You give *oji*, I present deal to stsho."

"No. You give me No'shto-shti-stlen, or no *oji.*"

"You no damn position to bluff, hani. You want see Chanur take bad damage, you go ahead. Meetpoint dock get blow to hell, all you fault, you bring kif in. Look damn bad. We throw out kif guard for stsho, you bring back, blow up dock. . . ."

"I could *destroy* the *oji.* So nobody gets it."

Brows went up. "Not good. Holy antiquity. Belong big stsho fam'ly."

"So somebody gets badly upset if anything happens to this *oji*, huh?"

"Stop play game! We talk about you trade agreement. We get damn kif leave this system!"

"Agreements with the kif too."

"We talk."

"You want him out of here, right you talk. You talk damn serious. No doublecross."

"First give *oji.*"

"First give No'shto-shti-stlen."

"Simul-taneous."

"All right. You bring No'shto-shti-stlen, I bring the *oji.*"

"Maybe so you got Atli-lyen-tlas. Maybe you think pull trick. I tell you, we see stsho, that stsho dead before foot touch this deck. Same hani."

Now the masks were off. *Now* they knew the players. She stared at the mahe as eye to eye a hani could, at a species head and shoulders taller. "I've said what we have to have. Simultaneous transfer. Then we start talking—and talking seriously, mahe, no damn tricks on your side either."

"You got pocket com? You crew follow all this?"

What's he up to? she wondered; and said aloud: "They're listening, damned right."

"Same mine. Same stsho. We stand here, you crew bring *oji*, stsho bring No'shto-shti-stlen. All fine."

"Fine." She folded her arms. "Tiar?"

"*Aye, captain,*" the answer came back.

"When I see No'shto-shti-stlen on the dock, I'll advise you. Nothing leaves the ship before then."

"Aye, captain."

"Advise the *hakkikt* we're in negotiation and we'll keep him posted."

"I'll do that, captain."

She gave a wave of the hand. "Your turn."

A casual puff of smoke. Haisi rattled off a string of mahendi language she didn't follow that well. But it contained words like No'shto-shti-stlen, *gtst*, and stsho.

There was argument.

Haisi said, "Stsho want know no guns."

"No guns." She switched to stshoshi, figuring on Haisi's bug to pick it up. "I wish to establish friendly relations with the most distinguished representatives from Llyene. I should in no wise wish to perform a tasteless act of violence or to endanger them in any way."

Haisi didn't understand all of that, either. It was not altogether Trade-tongue.

Haisi looked just a little uneasy. So the stsho weren't prisoners. And, being stsho, they were probably treating No'shto-shti-stlen tolerably well, so long as events were uncertain, so long as there was the remotest chance of anything going contrary to their plans.

Probably too, No'shto-shti-stlen, the canny old fellow, had held out hope, so long as he had a throw of the dice left. Haisi had said *gtst*, and maybe it was the standard, safe term, and maybe it was something else. Some stsho might have Phased under such stress. But she fully expected to see *gtst* in possession of *gtst* name, *gtst* dignity, and *gtst* claim to the *oji*.

And the stsho would not be safe from *gtst* until they had the *oji*, that seemed likely from the persistence with which Haisi wanted to lay hands on it.

When *that* went into hostile hands, this emblem of whatever gender it was, evidently No'shto-shti-stlen posed no threat. And she *wished* she knew she was doing the right thing.

But time passed, and passed, here in the dockside cold with, she was sure, a good many eyes on every breath they took. Haisi smoked one smoke-stick down to a stub, extinguished it with a pinch and put it in the pouch of his kilt, from which he took out another and lit it with a good deal of fuss.

"That *can't* be good for you," she said, and Haisi let out the breath he had been drawing in while lighting it, put the lighter away and laughed.

"Not good," he said. "Keep want quit. How you? Got no bad habit?"

"Husbands," she said. "Just got my second."

Another laugh. "You marry! Heard same. Maybe you cheat on husband, we get together next port. Big party."

"With *you?* No thanks. I have *some* taste."

Haisi grinned wide. "I bet you good."

"Number one right I'm good. Ask me again sometime, oh, three, four years. I might be in the mood for a pirate."

"Honest citizen. I tell you, Hilfy Chanur, you got learn tell difference, quit lie down with kif."

She'd heard about every nasty comment on that topic there was. She put on a perfect smile. "What *is* the difference? Hah?"

"Cute hani. Pretty nose. Pretty eyes."

"You are a bastard, Haisi. A charming bastard. But you are a bastard." There had been movement just then, across the dock, on the merchant strip, a pale-robed shadow, and another, now. "Looks like stsho."

Haisi didn't turn his head to look. He angled his whole body, to watch her and Tarras up by the gate; and to see what was happening.

"They bring No'shto-shti-stlen. Where *oji?*"

"So how do we do this? Meet halfway?"

Haisi stretched out his arm to the left. "Halfway there, you bring *oji.*" And to the right: "Same halfway there, No'shto-shti-stlen. We take, you take, all fine."

"Fair," she decided, and touched the pocket com. "Tiar, they're coming. Did you follow that? We're to bring the *oji* out and put it down on the dock at about the same pace they bring No'shto-shti-stlen to a similar place some little removed. You can bring it as far as the gate, now."

Haisi was talking to his own crew, and then, apparently to the stsho, saying much the same thing.

There was the chance of a switch. But it was not a time to argue. It was highly unlikely one stsho would place *gtst*self in jeopardy by posing as another and it was unlikely the stsho with *gtst* would risk their lives by bringing a substitute. And if she slowed down the proceedings Haisi would do exactly the same, at which point everything could come unraveled. People could get shot. Including No'shto-shti-stlen.

Which was still a possibility, once Haisi had the *oji*, which was one reason Tarras was up there, in a high position relative to the dockside.

One thing she would bet on: no one in the *han* could read stsho signatures. *She* couldn't, with any certainty. It was within the realm of possibility they would have shown the marriage document to stsho, to *Haisi*'s stsho, for verification . . . so it was within possibility that the Llyene stsho knew that Atli-lyen-tlas was a holiness: signatures did indicate Mode, Phase, and Gender, among other Life Events of significance. It was within possibility that the Llyene stsho recognized the identities of Tlisi-tlas-tin and Dlimas-lyi, *and* their relationship. And the negotiations had still gone as they had gone, which didn't prove one way or the other that the stsho had told everything they knew to Ana-kehnandian . . . but by all she knew of stsho, Tahaisimandi Ana-kehnandian was in their estimation not to be confided in. Nor wholly in power over the situation: therefore not to be confided in. Perfectly logical stsho reasoning, who held self-preservation and tasteful behavior paramount.

She knew just enough to know how much she didn't know. But there was no choice, absolutely no choice. She'd done the best trading she could with the goods she had. She thought she'd come away as best she could—but she never thought that Ana-kehnandian was going to play fair.

Not by the gods likely, Haisi.

Haisi gave her a nod and walked off to stand at the appointed spot to receive the *oji*, where others of his crew showed up, armed . . . of course: *they* replaced the kif as station police.

She walked off toward the stsho, to receive No'shto-shti-stlen. And she said, into com, which doubtless was being monitored on *Ha'domaren,* by electronics the mahendo'sat had had time to install around the dock, "Is it in position?"

"*Aye, captain,*" Tiar said.

"Everything's on schedule. Bring it on out, down to the dock. They start walking, we start walking, that's the way it works. I'm going out onto the dock to wait for No'shto-shti-stlen. When you carry it out, go toward Ana-kehnandian and his crew at the same rate you see No'shto-shti-stlen going toward me. When *gtst* reaches me, you set down the case and go back to the lock."

"*Got that,*" Tiar said. The instructions were for Fala. But Tiar understood. "*She's coming out now. You'd better see them moving, captain.*"

She didn't turn to see. She had her attention divided between the stsho, who did begin tentatively to move, and Haisi and his lot, and the possibility of snipers somewhere about the dock—which was a fearful lot of real estate to monitor. At a certain point one just hoped to the gods.

"They're moving," she said.

Stsho were not going to dash into possible danger. It was a nervous, sometimes halting advance. She could see Fala now, doing almost pace for pace the same thing as the stsho, with the black case within her arms. And she could pick out the one she thought must be No'shto-shti-stlen, among the gleaming gossamer of the others, a figure no less richly dressed, no less adorned and painted, but less interested in the surroundings than looking toward her, only toward her, as if she were the destination of hope.

Closer and closer.

"Your excellency?" she asked. "No'shto-shti-stlen?"

There were bows, a deep one from the one stsho, nervous ones from the others.

"Wai, most gracious hani," said the one, in stshoshi, which the others might not know she understood. It was the only proof she could look to have . . . *gtst* looked right. *Gtst* sounded right.

"Please accompany me with all tasteful speed," she said, and added, for the others, "Please abandon this exposed place. There is danger."

No'shto-shti-stlen was willing. She struck out for the *Legacy*'s dock at a fair pace, the others were dithering, and of a sudden *all* the stsho were bolting with her.

Herd-mind, Vikktakkht had said, My gods! She didn't know what to do but run, all the stsho were running, and Fala sprinted for the ramp, but no shots came. Hilfy stopped there, a momentary pause, in the middle of a lot of stsho who were probably wishing they had bolted the completely opposite direction. "Get *gtst* into the ship!" she ordered Fala. "Your excellency, go with her!"

As she saw Haisi with the box on the decking, yonder, saw the stsho with her begin to go uncertainly in that direction. But Haisi was bound to check out the goods—to be sure of them.

Haisi opened the box. A silver spheroid rolled out—a small one. And if their wiring worked right—

Haisi dived for the cover of a station girder, right behind his men. The stsho shrieked with one voice and retreated the only direction they could, toward the *Legacy*. A moment later the silver ball exploded with a fearsome shock, a ball of upward-wafting fire, and a huge cloud of smoke.

Stsho yelped into silence, Haisi was sprawled flat not quite into cover, and just then apparently realizing the explosion behind him had not done major damage.

Thank the gods of space.

Haisi was getting up, beginning to figure it, and glared at her. She laughed and laughed harder, in spite of the fact snipers were possible. The smoke was beginning to clear and a shape to appear out of it, a pale, twisted structure tall as he was, twice as wide, lacy, white, with subtle ochers.

"Exploding rocks," she said, and shouted it, she couldn't resist it. "*Exploding rocks, Haisi, you son of an earless mother!*"

She herded the stsho for the *Legacy*'s rampway, just a little out of the way of snipers, or a direct shot from Haisi, who was just standing there, probably with his brain rattled from the shockwave, and maybe adding up the fact that that *hadn't* been the *oji,* which was still on the *Legacy,* and that she had, presumably, No'shto-shti-stlen, and that, thanks to stsho instincts, she had the Llyene officials uncertainly sheltering in the shadow of the *Legacy*'s access.

And she had a lot of kif allies out there.

"Pray go inside," she said to the stsho, "where your excellencies will find more safety. This mahe is of uncertain mood and possibly tastelessly violent behavior."

"What *is* this object?" a stsho asked.

She hadn't exactly decided what to call it. But she threw it another look, standing there wreathed in the smoke of its birth, and said, considerately, "An . . . artwork, actually, most excellent, and never of any hazard to the station."

"An artwork," one said, and something she couldn't catch. "An artwork," another said, or a variant on that. There was a sound among them she'd never heard the species make, with waving of hands and bobbing of heads, and a general milling about.

Then a mass "Iiiii," of uncertainty, but not a thing more, as she and Fala together urged them into the rampway chill, away from snipers, please the gods, away from imminent attack.

"Advance to the airlock," she advised them above their murmuring and hesitations. "All will be well." She certainly hoped so.

Tarras had the gun discreetly out of view behind the gate: "Tiar," she said to the pocket com, once they were through, with Tarras still keeping a careful eye on the docks, "Tiar, shut that gate and open the airlock, we're in, we're all in, we're clear."

She was breathlessly glad when that gate slid shut: no way to lock it against somebody stationside with a key or a master control, but she heard the lock open, out of sight around the curve of the tube—safety and their own deck was that close, and if nobody started an interstellar war while they were traversing this very fragile tube she vowed she would turn religious.

Then just as the foremost of the flock of stsho rounded the curve of the tube toward the airlock, they stopped dead in their tracks and exclaimed in startlement, refusing to budge as the back ranks crowded up against them.

A totally naked stsho was walking down the tube, bearing the Preciousness in *gtsta* hands, as inane and as happy an expression on *gtsta* face as she had ever seen on a stsho.

"No'shto-shti-stlen!" *gtsta* exclaimed delightedly. "Blessed be the receiver of the gift, blessed be the bearer of young, blessed be you, O most excellent of excellences!"

No'shto-shti-stlen—it was *gtst*—came and took the Preciousness in *gtst* arms, and bowed and bowed—there being nothing the captain, walled away from the proceedings by a phalanx of murmuring and bobbing stsho, could do to object to the situation.

Gtsta then walked, naked as the day *gtsta* was born, through the yielding wall of stsho, and past them . . . since the stsho did not stop *gtsta*, it hardly seemed safe for a hani captain to do so: she held Fala with a press of her hand, as *gtsta* walked blithely past them and on down the yellow-ribbed shadow of the rampway.

"Better open the outer gate again," Hilfy said to Tiar. "*Gtsta* wants to go out there, and we've got no right to argue."

"But—" cried No'shto-shti-stlen, standing the other side of the parted stsho, "but, Holiness, who have I married?"

Gtsta swung about, walking backwards, and waved *gtsta* spindly arms. "Tlisi-tlas-tin and Dlimas-lyi, my Dlima-lyen-lyi, my egg, my loveliest, most favored, most blessed—"

Gtsta was out of sight, then, warbling something to *gtsta*self, and the stsho around them were apparently congratulating No'shto-shti-stlen, No'shto-shti-stlen bowing and bowing, and holding the Preciousness.

It was time to get the whole party out of this tube, Hilfy said to herself, to get them somewhere safe, like the passenger quarters, if that was tasteful . . . at this point a hani was definitely out of her social depth and proceeding on guess and luck.

She worked her way through the crowd with a great deal of bowing and apologies for tasteless dutiful necessities, . . . "Including your excellencies' personal safety. Please urge everyone toward the ship, please make some decorous haste. There are infelicitous persons outside and the gate is open." Tarras and Fala, thank the gods, had taken up guard at the rear and one of them had disappeared, probably to see if *gtsta* was clear of the gate.

Evidently *gtsta* was. She heard it shut.

"We're sealed," Tiar said, breathing a sigh, and looked around to her crewmates. Who were congratulating each other, and probably not listening.

She gave her attention back to the dockside camera hook-up, which *was* operating, of a sudden, stsho officials having seemingly decided that it should. There was not a notable lot going on, except a completely naked stsho who was walking around and around the object that, reacting with the station's oxygen, had expanded into a pillar of lace.

Gtsta seemed delighted with it. *Gtsta* ran fingers over it, *gtsta* examined it high and low and from every angle. Eventually another couple of stsho showed up, fully dressed, bowing repeatedly, and likewise admiring the accident.

Not a sign of Haisi and his crew. Not a transmission out of *Ha'domaren*, which was at dock, tightly sealed.

Of a sudden, though, they were getting real station information, real system information. She contacted her opposite number aboard *Tiraskhti*, and found herself in direct communication with Vikktakkht.

"Things are quiet right now," she said, "*hakkikt*. We have the *oji*, we have No'shto-shti-stlen, the Llyene stsho are apparently aboard, and I haven't heard from my captain yet, but I think they're making some sort of contact with the stsho we have aboard."

"We have station output. Is this truthful?"

"I think it is, *hakkikt.* I've no way to be sure that's the case, we're not in direct communication with station authorities."

"Most probably you have them aboard."

"Yes, *hakkikt.*"

"Kkkt. Amusing. I wonder if Ana-kehnandian has a notion of calling in his forces . . . or what those ships out there will do as soon as the wavefront reaches them. I will offer him safe passage—for the next several hours. Advise your captain to abide by this."

"Yes, *hakkikt*, I will tell her." Arrogant son. But thank the gods they were talking about safe retreats now. In her guess, *Ha'domaren* was trying to figure out what to do, and what it had left, and whether a fight to the death right now was in Paehisna-ma-to's interest.

Or if there was a way to recover the initiative.

Not that this hani could see. Not from the moment that son had realized he'd let No'shto-shti-stlen and the Preciousness get together.

She eavesdropped on the passenger cabin. There was a great deal of stsho ooohing and warbling going on. There were numerous people in there.

"What are they up to?" Chihin asked.

"Weddings breaking out all over," Tiar said, not without a thought that, by the gods, the *han* had not a word to say: and Meras clan, remote and rural, and probably old-fashioned, was going to find itself in alliance with powerful, now solvent Chanur—

Counting a can full of what was beginning to draw a curious crowd out there; and a franchise.

Sahern was not going to say a word else on the Meras affair, by the gods not, unless they wanted an active feud with Chanur, which didn't look like a smart bet for anyone at the moment.

So a few more years for the enemies to regroup. But it didn't mean Chanur would be sitting still.

She didn't let her guard down, didn't stop paying attention to the screens. Chihin and Hallan took over watching station scan, and eventually reported outward movement out of the mahen ships that were now clearly identified on scan.

"Leaving him, they are." That was worth a call belowdecks. "Captain."

"Problem?"

"Mahendo'sat appear to be leaving system, not real organized. *Gtsta* holiness has drawn a crowd out there around the rock. No apparent trouble on the docks. I think the *hakkikt's* going to stay where he is until he's sure what *Ha'domaren's* doing, but he's offered Haisi a safe passage, I'm supposed to tell you that."

"Haisi take it?"

"He hasn't budged. Hasn't made a move. —No, wait." There was a change on the station schema. "Son's just appeared as in count for departure. He's going."

"Ha!" the captain said. *"We got him."*

Chapter Twenty-one

It surfaced like a diver in an upside-down ocean, breached near the system buoy, and dived again—up—into the interface and perhaps deeper. It was there long enough to have gathered a system map: the buoy output one; and to sing a message of its own, in its harmonic voices. This one was simple.

tc'a	stsho	kif	mahendo'sat	hani
hani	hani	hani	hani	hani
peace	peace	peace	peace	peace
Chanur	Chanur	Chanur	Chanur	Chanur
Meras	Meras	Meras	Meras	Chanur
peace	peace	peace	peace	peace

"Well, look at that," Tiar said.

"How did it know my name?" Hallan asked.

"Famous, I suppose," Chihin muttered. "The kif certainly know you. They set you up. And I'm beginning to wonder about the tc'a."

"I wonder where that son's headed."

"Same place *The Pride* is," Chihin said.

"Or maybe they don't have to," Tiar said. "I'd about bet you cousin Pyanfar *knows* what's just happened. I'll bet you that son just transmitted."

Chihin shook her head. "If we start talking through the tc'a, gods save us. It's no way to run a trading business."

"Back to trade and thank the gods," Tiar said. "Enough of politics. We got the wedding party off our deck, the Preciousness and all, we got Tlisi-tlas-tin for governor, No'shto-shtistlen's a happy bride, and we've got a can of exploding rocks to sell."

"Another Kita run, to nail down that franchise," Chihin muttered. "The stsho love the idea. I've a notion we can sell it to the mahendo'sat—"

"Kif might have an interest. To each their own uses."

Tiraskhti was in. The rest of the kif still hovered, firmly under the *hakkikt's* command, one could trust, since the effort was a success. High-level stsho turned out to welcome the *hakkikt,* to bid him to the intimate offices, along with Chanur. This was, perhaps, an unusual reception, kif and hani at once. Possibly it was unprecedented.

Or perhaps not.

"Honor to you," Hilfy said, with her escort, Tarras and Fala; and Vikktakkht with his dark-robed crew, meeting at the lift.

"Death to our enemies," Vikktakkht said courteously, and as the car arrived: "We will *share.*"

Faktkht. Share-prey, it meant: but Vikktakkht put *sotk* with it, meaning territory. Unprecedented idea in kifish, so far as she knew.

And it solved the question of precedences, with a kif who outranked a mere captain. Polite.

"You first," Hilfy said. Which required trust, of a species that didn't like to be followed.

"Kkkkt," the guards said, uneasy. So they sorted it out, with a kifish thumb on the hold button: Vikktakkht, then her, then his guard, then hers.

They stood on opposite sides of the car. There were probably weapons under the kifish robes. There were, inside their own dress-uniform belts.

The car rose.

"Profitable," Vikktakkht said, "this *peace,* this *sharing.* We will eat the hearts of those that oppose it. Ana-kehnandian will not go to his Personage with this failure. He must find a new service. I am considering taking him up myself."

"He made mistakes," Hilfy said. Kif hardly tolerated such. She was amazed that Vikktakkht was secure enough to propose such a thing. Most would not. Most would not dare.

"He was badly instructed," Vikktakkht said. "And he knows Paehisna-ma-to and her agents. Not a bad acquisition. Perhaps he will take instruction. Perhaps not. If not, his loss. I will have the information, honor to the *mekt-hakkikt.* He has not many ports of refuge. I will make him an offer."

"Generous of you."

"Extremely. And he will know it. Our guards return to duty here—our agreements are bettered. Paehisna-ma-to is now an uncertain influence at best. The Momentum is reversed. He would have no future in her service."

The car stopped, and opened its doors onto the white, nacre curtained formal hall of the governor's offices. And kifish guards were in evidence, bowing and showing all respect—to the *hakkikt,* if not to a hani captain.

Vikktakkht brushed them aside with a sweep of his sleeve. "Our escort will stay *here,*" he said in the Trade. "The guards will stay *here.*"

A bow from the guards, profound and quick. So much for the stsho's hired security. "Wait here," Hilfy said, wondering what the kif was up to, and somewhat glad of the pistol in her belt—wondering if there might be some kifish purpose against the governor, and if they might not, after all, have a piece of treachery on their hands.

But she played the game. She walked beside him, innocent as a stroll in the country, past the arches, the freeform white statues, the blowing drapery.

"We know each other," Vikktakkht remarked as they

walked side by side; and, before she could leap to the unpleasant and hostile conclusion, of her own captivity, and her kifish guards: "We were crew on the same ship."

My *gods,* Hilfy thought. The kifish slave. Skkukuk. From aboard *The Pride.*

But this wasn't at all the place to recall that name.

"Why didn't you simply say—" She started to ask. "No. Of course not. Stupid question."

"Indeed," Vikktakkht said. "It would have given Paehisna-ma-to her best opening. Had I claimed that, you would have doubted me instantly. You would have rushed to ally with Anakehnandian."

A member of *The Pride*'s crew. Amazing.

"Not rushed," she said, and still wondered if this kif was loyal to Pyanfar. He *seemed* to have acted in Pyanfar's interest. "But I would have doubted your intentions."

"Kkkkt. As you do now?"

Never mince words with a *hakkikt.* "I respect your evident power."

"Admirable discretion. But if I aspired to be *mekt-hakkikt* the peace would end. And I find it, as I say, profitable. I am *hakkikt hakkiktun.* In the name of the *mekt-hakkikt* I stand first among kif. There is nothing more a kif can gain."

"Indeed," she said conservatively. "As in Chanur. I prefer where I am."

They strolled through the last arch, into the presence of bowing stsho.

"Kkkt. Profitable. Profitable to both, Chanur."